MW00586751

THE RIVER MEN

A JOEY FINCH NOVEL

PETER J. WOODS

STINGRAY
PRESS

This is a STINGRAY PRESS book

First published in Australia in 2023 by STINGRAY PRESS
Copyright © STINGRAY PRESS 2021-2023
Cover designed by MiblArt
Edited by Creating Perfection

The moral right of Peter J. Woods to be identified as the author of this work has been
asserted by him in accordance with the Copyright Act 1968.
All the characters in this book are fictitious, and any resemblance to actual persons living
or dead is purely coincidental.

All rights reserved. No part of this publication may be reproduced, stored in a retrieval
system or transmitted in any form or by any means, without prior permission in writing of
the publisher, nor to be otherwise circulated in any form of binding or cover other than
that in which it is published without similar condition, including this condition, being
imposed on the subsequent purchaser.

CONTENTS

1

A HEAVY BEATING at my bedroom door shocked me awake.

"Get up!" someone shouted from the other side.

I grumbled a wordless reply and rolled over. Two more thumps, then the door burst inwards, spraying wood chips across the carpet as the latch bolt tore through the door frame.

"Bloody hell, Bree!"

"Put some pants on, Joey," she said. "Someone's trying to get in downstairs."

"What? Who?"

"Hurry up!" She disappeared with a swish of black hair. Seconds later, I heard her hammering on Oscar's door.

Heavy rain pelted my small bedroom window, while strong winds rattled it in its frame. In the daytime, it offered a view of the tightly packed neighbouring rooftops, but at that moment, there was nothing to see but an empty blackness.

I ran a hand across my face and dragged myself out of bed. Throwing on a T-shirt and shorts, I plodded across the room, almost tripping over a pile of books I'd been meaning to read on various arcane topics and obscure Greek mythology. Oscar's bedroom door swung open as I passed by on the stairs. He'd somehow managed to make his dishevelled, blonde-tipped hair look intentionally tousled. All he needed was a sweater thrown over his shoulders and a fifty-foot yacht, and you could stick him on a poster for Ralph Lauren.

"What's going on?" he asked, putting on his black-framed glasses.

"No idea," I said. "Be ready for anything."

Oscar nodded, and I felt shifting pressures in the air as he drew in magic. I did the same, sucking in magical energy from the world around me, holding it in my chest to be twisted into any number of spells. We went downstairs together and found Bree standing by the front door, engaged in a friendly chat with the idiot who was trying to break into the home of two wizards and a *demonbound*.

"We're not letting you in, dude," Bree yelled.

"Please, they'll kill me!" came the muffled reply. I could barely hear the voice over the storm raging outside, but could just make out the person's outline through the door's mottled windows.

I yawned as I approached. "Who is it?"

"Some guy. Says he needs our protection."

"Joey Finch lives here, yes?" the man called out. He might have had a Latin American accent, but it was too subtle to be sure.

"Who the hell are you?" I said, raising my voice so he could hear.

"Frederico de Silva. I'm with the Encantados."

I turned to Bree and Oscar, who both shrugged. The three of us had been cannonballed into the deep end of Sydney's mystical underbelly only six months earlier and had since encountered all kinds of magical creatures and supernatural beings, but this was a new one.

"We've gotta let him in," I said.

"Joey," Oscar said, pushing his glasses to the bridge of his nose. "Are you sure that's the smartest thing to do?"

"It most definitely isn't. But we can't leave him out there. We can handle him if he's up to something. And we've always got Bree as back-up." I turned to her. "Feel like punching things?"

Bree cracked her knuckles. "Most days."

Oscar rolled his eyes, but I saw the grin he was trying to hide. "Fine," he said as a yellow glow emanated from within his fists. "I'm ready."

As I reached for the door, I felt a shifting of magic. The man outside gave a pained scream that was quickly cut short as something slammed against the door.

"Oscar!" I called out and pulled the door open.

Oscar strode forward, flames of orange fury shooting from his fingertips and into the swirling, storm-ridden darkness. Bree and I sprang into action, snatching the wounded man from the threshold and hauling him inside. Oscar stood guard, casting more deadly spells into the night as we tended to the injured stranger.

The man was in a daze, his eyes wandering aimlessly. And despite being soaked through, the rain hadn't washed away all the blood covering his shirt and hands.

"Joey!" Oscar cried out as something dragged him off the doorstep and out to the street.

Shit.

I jumped up and chased Oscar out into the rain, conjuring an orb of bright blue flames as I ran – a *boule de feu et de lumière*, according to our instructor, which literally translates to *ball of fire and light*. You can't fault wizards on their practicality. Oscar and I had shortened it to *lumière*, much to our teacher's chagrin. The spell was essentially a fist-sized fireball, with the luminance given a boost and the heat dialled right down. Still, I wouldn't recommend touching it, no matter how much your housemates dare you.

I tossed the *lumière* into the air where it hovered high above the ground, bathing the street in front of our house in a soft, ethereal blue light. Thick droplets of rain sizzled into vapour as they struck the conjuration.

Two figures stood in the middle of the road, unworried by the howling wind and pelting rain. I say figures because I couldn't think of any other way to describe them. Roughly human-shaped, they seemed to consist only of dark water wreathed in swirling white foam, as if their bodies were made of endlessly breaking waves.

Water elementals.

Yes, I know water isn't an element. These things were probably named when the Earth was still the centre of the universe, and the moon was made of cheese.

One of these creatures was the owner of the watery arm that engulfed Oscar's legs, dragging him across the footpath towards them. The other elemental charged, not so much running as gliding across the road at me. I pumped more magic into my *lumière*, giving the conjuration more heat and more mass. Yes, I can create mass out of pure energy. It's magic.

With a thought, I sent the *lumière* rocketing at the elemental. It slapped into the thing's arm with an anticlimactic *plop* but did so with enough force to sever the limb. The water around Oscar's legs fell away with the rain. Everything plunged into semi-darkness again, the sparse streetlights too far apart and too obscured by trees to do their job properly.

Then the other elemental tackled me. Or, to put it more accurately, it swallowed me, enveloping me entirely within its liquid body. It felt as if I'd been sucked into an undercurrent. I kicked and thrashed about, but found myself unable to escape. Salt water worked its way into my mouth and nose, and I quickly lost any sense of which way was up.

I might very well have drowned, had a firm hand not clamped around my arm and dragged me free of the walking wave. I fell hard onto the concrete, sputtering up a lungful of what may have been either water or part of the actual creature. Gross.

I looked up to see Bree throw a couple of wild punches that could have knocked out a heavyweight boxer, but simply passed right through the watery creature. Hey, I would have tried the same thing if I couldn't do magic.

"Bree, move!" I yelled and cast a spell that I liked to call the *wall of surprise* – a wall of invisible energy that bulldozed forward, knocking down everything in its path. And if you didn't see me cast it, there was a good chance of catching you off guard. There was likely a proper name for that particular bit of magic, but it would have been in French or Latin or Cantonese or something. Magic was hard enough without having to learn a dozen languages too.

Bree dived to the side as the spell smacked into the liquid creature, which exploded like a water balloon lobbed at a window. My stomach lurched. Sure, it had attacked us, but I didn't fancy killing just for the hell of it.

My fears were eased, and quickly replaced by alarm, as the dark puddles glided into each other and began to re-mould themselves back into a roughly humanoid shape, not unlike the bad guy from *Terminator 2*, which couldn't have been a good sign.

"Joey?" Bree said.

"Back in the house!" I shouted.

"They're made of water. They can just slip under the door!"

4

"Do it!" I yelled back. "Unless you've got a better idea. Oscar!"

Oscar had his liquid opponent contained in a translucent bubble that shimmered with yellow energy every time the creature threw itself at it. My friend was so focused on maintaining his spell, he didn't see the man approaching him.

2

"BEHIND YOU!" I yelled.

Too late.

The man seized Oscar, sweeping his legs from under him and forcing him to his knees. From his belt, the man produced a curved blade that he promptly positioned at my friend's neck. Oscar's spell disappeared, freeing the water elemental.

"Not another step," the man growled.

I froze, glaring at him. He was around Oscar's height, but with shoulders twice as wide, and a jawline chiselled from granite. He had a closely trimmed beard and thick brown hair bunched up in a messy ponytail. His black, high-collared jacket was slick with rain and he wore no shoes.

I looked down at my own bare feet and shivered as the initial spike of adrenalin started to fade, exposing me to the chill of the elements. I supposed I'd just taken the equivalent of a midnight dip in the ocean.

"Let him go," I demanded, gritting my teeth so they didn't chatter.

The water elemental I'd splattered had re-formed and glided over to its watery mate behind the man with the sword, waiting for their next command.

"The Encantado sheltering in your house..." the man said, his voice deep and rough. "Give him to us."

"I'm not doing anything until you release my friend," I replied, my mind scrambling for ideas to get that sword away from Oscar's neck. I could have used my psychomantic abilities to attack the man's consciousness with my thoughts. But I hadn't yet figured out a way to do that without leaving myself vulnerable to the demons that wanted to get inside my brain.

"This doesn't concern you, boy," a woman said, slinking out of the darkness. She was dressed in much the same way as the man – dark, high-collared jacket, black pants, no shoes – with a similarly curved sword hanging at her hip.

I glared at her. "When you hold a sword to my friend's throat, it sure as hell concerns me."

"My name is Rhoswyn," the woman said with composed civility. "This is Hamish. We only wish to take the Encantado. He is a criminal."

She stepped forward. Her dark red hair glistened in the rain, thick strands clinging to either side of her face. I noted the disfigurement on her ears where the tips had been clipped.

"You're elves?" Oscar said, looking at the woman sideways without turning his head. Hamish looked down at Oscar, the large man's blade pressing a little harder against my friend's neck.

I knew some elves. I wouldn't call them friends. More like non-hostile associates. I'd never explicitly asked about the rationale behind cutting off the pointy parts of their ears. But the reason was obvious. To blend in. To avoid drawing attention. To make it that little bit more difficult for anyone wishing to find them and do them harm. Their persistent lack of footwear was a bit of a giveaway, though.

"We're selkies," Rhoswyn said. "Although we count the elves as cousins."

Selkies. My mind raced. Miss Blackthorne may have mentioned them once or twice. Ocean-dwellers. I had the vague sense they were a big deal.

"What's the man's crime?" I asked, hoping for something minor, like graffitiing or peeing in public.

"Murder," answered the selkie woman.

Of course it was.

"He is to stand trial and be held accountable for his actions," Rhoswyn said, lifting her chin a fraction. "If you are concerned that he will not be given a fair trial, then fear not. Our laws are just and implemented without bias."

Said every tyrant ever.

7

"Let's pump the brakes," I said. "I can't just hand him over. Not without talking to the guy first."

"You would risk your friend's life for a murderer?"

"Do you... do you know who we are?"

Rhoswyn's gaze tightened. "Should I?"

"Damn right, you should!" Bree called out. Her narrow-eyed gaze levelled at Hamish who still had his sword pressed against Oscar's neck. The selkie stared back, eyes flat. Bree stood shorter than me by a couple of inches and didn't cut the most intimidating figure, but the demon living inside her imbued my friend with a supernatural strength that made her more dangerous than most.

I gestured for Bree to restrain herself, which was a bit like telling water not to be wet.

"We work with Mary Blackthorne," I said, turning back to Rhoswyn. For people of the Old World, the name tended to elicit fear or resentment. Often both.

The woman reacted with neither.

"The Custodian of Sydney?" she asked.

"That's right," Bree replied, probably a bit more enthusiastic now that there were people she could actually punch.

"Then it is your duty to help us bring the Encantado to justice."

"We'll be the judge of that," I said.

The woman frowned. "Fine," she said, brushing the stray strands of hair behind her disfigured ears, somehow making the delicate action look threatening. "So be it."

I felt the shifting of magic and raised a shield instinctively. Rhoswyn raised her hand. "Get him," she snarled.

The two water elementals glided forward and slammed against my invisible shield with the roar of crashing waves. But rather than persist in breaking through, they passed over and around my defensive spell, and continued towards the door.

"Bree!" I yelled, turning back. "Get out of the way!"

It came as no surprise that she didn't listen and remained standing defiantly in the path of the two elementals as they bore down on her. Bree was strong, much stronger than anyone would guess, but that means nothing if you can't even get a hold of what you're fighting.

A blinding flash filled my vision, accompanied by a crackling explosion. I would have assumed it was lightning if my magical senses

8

weren't going haywire. I heard an agonised scream, and I rushed over to Bree.

"I'm fine," she said, blinking hard. "Can't see a fucking thing, though."

I turned back to the street where the woman lay on the wet asphalt curled in pain. There was no sign of her watery henchman, and the wet ground made it impossible to see where they'd gone.

Oscar used the momentary distraction to conjure a glowing yellow band that clamped around the selkie man's wrist. A spell he dubbed the *golden bracelet*. I had made several unsuccessful attempts to mimic the spell on unsuspecting house plants before Bree put the kibosh on it, tired of watching me destroy our indoor greenery.

With a subtle hand gesture, Oscar raised the *bracelet*, yanking Hamish's sword arm safely away from his neck. I saw my opening and cast a straight-forward, no-nonsense kinetic spell that punched the selkie in the chest and knocked him back. He lost his grip on Oscar, who clambered to my side.

"You okay, mate?" I asked.

"Yeah," he said, breathless. "Nice work with the lightning."

"I think that was the house."

"Right," he said. "Are you over this as much as I am?"

"What, you're not having fun?"

He raised an eyebrow, to which I replied with a crooked smile. He shook his head, and turned back to face the selkies, the corner of his mouth bent up almost imperceptibly.

Rhoswyn pushed herself to her feet and observed us as the two water elementals formed up next to her, rising from the wet road like liquid ghosts. Oscar and I gathered energy again. Bree approached and stood by my side.

After a few long moments, the selkie woman waved her hand and her henchmen dissolved, washing away with the rainwater.

Her broad-shouldered friend stepped up to her. "Rhoswyn?"

"We're leaving."

"But—"

"Hamish," she warned.

The man hesitated, then grunted an acceptance and sheathed his sword.

The red-haired woman turned back to us. "The Encantado has

committed a grievous offence against the selkie people. A trial will be organised. If he is not turned over to us by then, there will be a response from the selkies."

"What kind of response?" Oscar asked.

"The kind that precipitates war."

Once again, I found myself dealing with things well and truly above my pay grade. Actually, the pay for an apprentice wizard was so abysmally low, fetching the morning coffees was probably above my pay grade.

"I'm sure we can talk this out," I said.

"No. Our laws are clear." Then, with her expression softening ever so slightly, she said, "Please do what is right."

She and her burly associate left as abruptly as they'd appeared, walking into the night. Bree and Oscar went inside, while I waited until the selkies were out of view down the street before going back in the house.

I closed the door behind me and placed a hand on the frame, feeling the buzz of energy die down to its resting state. None of us, not even Miss Blackthorne, knew precisely what the protection wards did, nor who put them there. A remnant from the city's chaotic early days, our teacher had suggested. The wards seemed to behave inconsistently, like many things related to magic, but I knew there must be some underlying logic to them, some structure that we just hadn't figured out yet.

I found Frederico in the kitchen. Slouched at the table, dripping water and blood onto the tiles.

"Please tell me you didn't actually murder anyone," I said.

He looked up at me, eyes full of rage. "I strangled that selkie bastard to death in his own home," the man replied. "And he deserved it."

3

WE MADE FREDERICO SOME TEA – Earl Grey – which he sucked down quickly, cupping both hands around the mug. I fetched us towels to dry off, which the man declined.

"Take it," I said, holding it out for him. "You're dripping all over the place."

"I forget you people are picky about having water inside," he said, taking the towel. He removed his shirt and began drying himself. The guy looked only a few years older than us, with light brown skin and a slim build with knots of lean muscle, undoubtedly noted by both my housemates. Oscar and I took the other two seats at the table, while Bree propped herself up on the kitchen bench directly behind the stranger, watching the back of his head with coiled tension.

I spread my hands on the table, palms down. "Okay, Freddy," I said. "First things first. What the hell is an Encantado?"

He draped the towel around his shoulders and tilted his head. "You're the Custodian, aren't you?" he asked. "Shouldn't you know this? Being the protector of the city and all."

"Who told you that?"

"A friend."

"I'm not the Custodian," I said. "I'm her apprentice. We all are." I didn't bother explaining that Bree wasn't technically an apprentice. She wasn't even non-technically an apprentice.

Frederico eyed us cynically and scratched at his short, scraggly beard. "Fair enough. Encantados are... well, you people normally refer to us as river men."

"What, you've got no women?" Bree said.

The Encantado shrugged. "Men, people, folk. I don't care what you call us."

I crossed my arms and fixed him with my best attempt at a hard stare. "Are you... human?" It felt like a stupid question, but I learned the hard way that if it looks like a duck and quacks like a duck, it could still be any number of creatures that would rip off your face and eat it.

"Human? God, no," he said, making a face. "We're shifters. I couldn't imagine being stuck on land my whole life. Concrete and roads and cars all day? No thanks."

"We get by," Bree said.

"So, river men..." I started, but cut myself off at a look from Bree. "River folk," I corrected. "You're shifters?"

"That's right," he said proudly. "Our True Forms are far less cumbersome than what you see now and allow us to move through water faster than any fish or mammal. Means we don't have to spend too much time topside."

"You don't drink blood, or devour souls, or anything like that?" I asked, covering my bases.

"No."

The tension that had been building in my muscles eased. My first foray into this magic business had involved getting pummelled by a shape-shifting bear-warrior with serious mental stability issues. I only survived because it kind of had the hots for me.

"Who did you kill?" Oscar said, leaning back in his chair, arms crossed, looking very much like he wanted this entire business over and done with.

The Encantado stared at Oscar. "A murderer," he answered with insolent defiance, as if daring us to challenge his actions.

I did my best not to roll my eyes. "Name?"

"Ellister Kelden. The Selkie Ambassador."

I pinched the bridge of my nose and checked the clock on the wall. Three o'clock. I had class in six hours. "And why did you do that?"

"He killed my friend Lin."

I narrowed my gaze. "That name is familiar."

"She is... was... one of the river men... River folk," Frederico said.

"Her people, the Baiji, have only been here a few years, but they were family, all the same. According to our ways, my retribution was justified and fair."

Old school sensibilities were a defining trait of the Old World. With so many distinct peoples coming to Sydney for refuge from the demons, monsters, and witch hunters that plague the rest of the world, it's inevitable that friction will arise where customs and traditions and music tastes don't jell. Sometimes, that friction leads to arguments, which occasionally leads to homicide. And worse. It's the Custodian's job – our teacher's job, and therefore ours – to keep everyone in check. Often it felt like herding very angry, very powerful cats.

"And you're sure it was the selkies who killed your friend?"

"Of course, I'm sure. It was a selkie sword that killed her."

"Why Lin?" I asked, ignoring the frustration in his voice. "What reason would they have had to kill her?"

Frederico shrugged, shuffling impatiently in his chair. "You can never tell with the selkies."

"Guess," said Bree.

Frederico glanced over his shoulder at Bree, then spun back around. "They're a weird lot. Isolate themselves from the rest world, even from the Old World. They don't care much for outsiders, not even us river folk. There's always been an unspoken agreement whenever we find ourselves sharing white water. They stick to the seas and coasts, we live in the rivers. Lin was new to the city. Maybe she wandered into their catchment by accident. Or maybe she caught them crossing into ours. Does it really matter?"

"Seems excessive any way you cut it," I said. "Killing someone for trespassing?"

Frederico narrowed his eyes. "The selkies entered our river, our home, and murdered one of us. So, I did the same to them."

"Forget the selkies for a moment," I said. "Why shouldn't we take you to the police?"

Frederico jumped to his feet, knocking over his chair. If he planned on picking a fight, he picked the wrong house. Oscar reacted faster than me, conjuring a *golden bracelet* around the man's neck and forcing him against the wall. Frederico's head hit the exposed brickwork with a solid thud.

Oscar's eyes widened. "Sorry!"

"Don't apologise," I said and conjured a blue flame in my hand. This one burned hot and bright, and I pushed enough magic into it to make the ragged scars along my left arm pulse with a soft pink light. It was bloody painful pushing so much energy through my arm, like someone pressing red hot wire against my skin. But I was trying to make a point.

Frederico looked at my glowing scars, then glared at me, the veins on his neck starting to bulge.

Bree jumped off the bench and approached. "We put our arses on the line for you, dolphin boy," Bree said. "Don't be a dick."

His eyes darted between us before he gave the barest nod.

"Let him go, Oscar," I said, gritting my teeth against the pain in my arm.

"You sure?"

"Yeah." I met the Encantado's stare. "He'll behave."

The gold band around Frederico's neck dissolved, leaving a dark red mark on his skin. I let my fiery conjuration exhaust itself and my glowing scars faded, leaving behind a dull throb that I knew would remain for several minutes.

"Don't take me to the human authorities," Frederico said, rubbing his neck.

Bree frowned. "Why shouldn't we?"

"There would be... opposition from my people. From our perspective, justice has been served. They wouldn't appreciate me being locked away for upholding our laws. Especially my father."

"Is he important?" Oscar said.

"He's the Chief of the Encantados in Sydney."

"Which makes you... a prince?"

"I hold no title. I'm just his son." Frederico touched his head and winced, pulling his hand away with blood on his fingertips.

This was all getting too much for my sleep-deprived brain. At that moment, a strapping young man wearing nothing but a pair of boxer shorts came down the stairs.

"You coming back to bed, Oscar?" George said with a yawn.

"One minute," Oscar replied.

The cheeky bugger. I didn't know he had a guest. Oscar's half-naked friend nodded and went back up the stairs, seemingly oblivious to recent events. Just as well, too. I would imagine discovering the existence of magic and shapeshifters at three in the morning could be disorienting.

"Alright, Freddy," I said. "Which river do you live in?"

"The Parramatta," he said. "And we live *along* the river, not in it. Boats and houses, like you guys."

I gave a mental sigh. "Got a way to get back there?"

"I might need help with that, too."

We used Bree's Uber account, since Freddy didn't have his phone with him, and unlike Oscar and me, Bree got paid a wage that didn't technically classify as slavery. The driver showed up five minutes later and parked in front of the house.

I told Frederico he'd be hearing from us soon, which brought a resentful stare from the Encantado.

"What?" I said. "You thought you could admit to killing a dude and waltz out the door, no repercussions? That's not how this works."

He breathed out a long sigh. "Fair enough, wizard. I suppose you're the sheriff in these parts, aren't you?"

He handed back the towel and walked out to the Uber, seemingly unbothered by the rain.

Oscar closed the door and turned to me. "When are we telling Miss Blackthorne?"

I checked the clock again. "I'll drop by her place in the morning. I need more sleep."

Oscar nodded, took off his glasses, and rubbed his eyes. "I'm going back to bed," he said and moved to the stairs.

"Get 'em, tiger," Bree called after him.

Oscar looked back to see Bree and me with stupid grins on our faces. "I'm going to *sleep*, guys."

"Sure," I said with an exaggerated wink. "Try not to 'sleep' too loudly. Some of us have uni in the morning."

He rolled his eyes and disappeared into his room, leaving the children to chuckle amongst themselves. I went up to my room on the top floor and lay on my bed without getting under the covers. Rain still hammered against my window. Lightning flashed outside, followed seconds later by a crack of thunder.

Sleep came slowly, thanks to the faint vestiges of adrenaline still in my system and the thoughts swirling in my head. Somehow, I had to prevent a war between people who, an hour ago, I hadn't even known existed. In my mind, the answer was straight-forward. Sit the selkies down with the river folk and hash things out before their tit-for-tat spiralled out of control. Simple enough plan. I just needed everyone to remain calm, patient, and rational.

Yeah, right.

4

BREE and I dropped by Miss Blackthorne's place before class the next day, while Oscar went out for breakfast with George. The rain had stopped, but clouds still hung around, threatening to drop buckets the moment you walked outside. I decided to tempt fate and threw on a T-shirt and jeans. Bree wore a thick weatherproof jacket over a black shirt and denim shorts.

Miss Blackthorne lived near the university in a large, converted substation building, on a street cloaked in the constant shadow of thick eucalyptus trees. The building used to belong to the railways, then the University of Sydney. Sometime in the twentieth century, it had come under the ownership of the Master Wizard, but you'd have trouble finding any transaction history on the property. My teacher simply became the owner of a prime bit of real estate in the heart of Sydney one day. As if by magic.

The Old Substation Building doesn't appear on any maps, and if Miss Blackthorne isn't home, you can't even see the damn thing. Also, the only way to get in without the protective wards kicking you in the balls was to have a key or have the wards re-shaped to recognise you.

Bree and I pushed open the tall metal doors and entered the cavernous living space. In its original function as a railway substation, the building housed huge electrical transformers to distribute high-voltage electricity throughout the rail network. The insides had since been given a hardcore makeover to make the place more homely, with the exception of the basement, which was used for regularly torturing young wizards under the guise of training them.

Miss Blackthorne stood in front of the eighty-two-inch TV watching the news. Admittedly, not a very mystical way to keep abreast of the goings-on within your domain, but hey, if it ain't broke.

The Master Wizard wore a faded Pink Floyd shirt and had a thin purple scarf draped around her neck. Her grey hair was short and serious, much like the rest of her, and she leaned on a walking cane, having never properly recovered from a scuffle with demonic thralls earlier in the year.

"Where is Mr Lee?" she asked without turning from the screen.

"Oscar's out at breakfast," I said, dropping my backpack on the floor and moving over to the spacious stainless-steel kitchen. I placed two mugs under a big silver machine and punched a few buttons, eliciting an angry growl. Seconds later, it started spitting out rich, black coffee. Now that's *real* magic.

"I have some new books for you and Oscar," she said.

"I'm still working through the last pile."

Miss Blackthorne liked to give Oscar and me books on folklore and the occult as well as regular vanilla history. The authors had obviously never set out to write page-turners, so getting through them was a slog, especially the ones that needed to be run through Google Translate first.

I nodded to the TV. "What's new?"

"Bushfires in California again," she said, eyes fixed on the screen with unusual intensity. "Also, the city of Sofia has fallen to the Venerati Sanctus."

"Sofia, Bulgaria? How do you know?"

"People have been rioting for the past month. Protesting the imprisonment of an outspoken human rights activist. The riots stopped last night, just as the fray seemed to be reaching its peak. No government can work that fast."

"So..."

"So, the Venerati have wormed their way into the Bulgarian government. Once the witch hunters get a foothold in local politics, they're almost impossible to displace. Now they'll get on with the extermination of the country's Old World citizens."

"Have they got a Haven nearby they can go to? Sydney's a bit far."

"They will flee to Istanbul," Miss Blackthorne said. "A powerful shaman protects the city. They should be safe there." She turned to me. "Regarding local developments, the plague in Byron Bay seems to be taking hold."

I finished making the coffees, stirred a good amount of chocolate powder into one, and handed the other to Bree.

She sipped it, gave a satisfied nod, and turned to Miss Blackthorne. "Remind me, what's the deal with the plague?"

"I don't know yet," the Master Wizard replied. "So far it looks like the effects are restlessness and insomnia. They last two to three weeks before disappearing. The medical diagnosis is it's a form of mass psychosis, but there's nothing connecting the infected. The Byron Coven believes it may be demonic."

I looked at the screen and saw a hospital room of people staring at me with pale faces and lifeless eyes.

"Will it spread?" I asked. Byron Bay isn't close. It's an eight-hour drive from Sydney if you don't stop for pee breaks, but that hasn't stopped the spread of infectious diseases in the past.

"The Byron witches are keeping an eye on it. But I don't like not knowing where it came from." Miss Blackthorne turned to us. "I assume you didn't come just to watch the news and drink my coffee."

"We had some visitors last night."

The Master Wizard frowned. "Who?"

I told her what happened with Frederico and the people chasing him.

"Damn," she said. "The selkies are serious business. You are lucky the house's wards kept the elementals out. I suggest you stay inside the next time someone comes around."

"About that... Any idea yet on how the wards got there?"

"I'm working on it still. I apologise. The wards are firmly embedded in the structure of the house and seem oddly resistant to my attempts to remove or augment them."

"One of the selkies was a wizard," I said. "She controlled the elementals and could do magic."

"You don't *do* magic," Miss Blackthorne said for the millionth time. "You wield it. The woman is likely a mage, a practitioner with little ability to manipulate anything outside her chosen discipline. The selkie ambassador would have had at least one working out of the embassy, along with several warriors."

"How scared of them should we be?" I asked. "We know that the elves can be dangerous when they feel like it."

"Perhaps 'scared' is the wrong word. I would suggest caution around them. Where elves have several discrete kingdoms peppered throughout the world, the selkies have but one nation. A single domain that spans the globe and all its oceans. Their power is almost immeasurable, and they do not fear governments or the Venerati. Or wizards, for that matter." She looked at me. "There is history between the river men and the selkies."

"Folk," Bree chipped in.

"River folk..." Miss Blackthorne said, apparently liking the sound of it.

I sipped my coffee. "Let me guess. They used to have epic wars in ancient times."

"More like forty years ago. They have a long history of slavery and mass murder."

"The selkies or River folk?"

"Both," Miss Blackthorne said. "If they kick things off again, it would be a disaster for the city. We need to determine exactly what has happened and de-escalate."

"I'm not reading anyone's mind," I said, knowing that Astaroth, the Archdemon of Envy, and one of the six Dukes of Hell, was just waiting for me to open my mind so he could crawl inside my skull.

"That's not what I was thinking," the Master Wizard said. "What are you two doing now?"

"Class," Bree said. "Fluid Dynamics. But we can skip it." She didn't even try to hide her enthusiasm.

"No," Miss Blackthorne said. "Go to class. I'll pay the Encantados a visit. I want to talk to the Chief myself." She finished her tea and shuffled to the kitchen, placing her empty mug in the sink. Her limp seemed to be getting more exaggerated with each passing month.

"You sure you can handle them on your own?" I asked.

"It will just be a conversation," she assured me. "They are mostly harmless. Another reason not to provoke the selkies any further. River folk aren't built for war. Maybe the Mokoi can defend themselves, but the rest, definitely not." Seeing our blank stares, she said, "There are three groups of river folk in the city. The Mokoi, who lived here before the Europeans came. The Encantados, who immigrated to Australia in the sixties from the Amazon. And the Baiji, whom I have not had many dealings with. They arrived recently, only three or four years ago, seeking refuge from the growing Venerati presence in mainland China."

"And they all live in the Parramatta River?" Bree asked.

"Along the river. They eat and sleep in houses just as we do. But don't mistake them for one of us. They are creatures of the river and have no loyalty to anyone but themselves. And, while harmless individually, they often have strong bonds with their local river gods."

"Gods?" I said. "Gods exist?"

"Of course," replied the Master Wizard. "The Realms Above are teeming with celestial beings. You shouldn't be so surprised. You've seen demons. Why, your friend is a *demonbound* and houses one within her head. Is it so hard to believe there'd be beings at the other end of the spiritual spectrum?"

"I never really thought about it," I said. "Although it does make me feel better knowing we've got some big hitters on our side."

Miss Blackthorne fixed me with a flat stare. "Gods and demons are on nobody's side but their own. It's best you remember that."

* * *

WE MET up with Oscar at lunch, since he didn't grace us with his presence at either of our morning classes. The clouds still hadn't cleared, so we went to the cafeteria on the ground floor of the Wentworth Building just as a group of students were leaving a table. We descended upon it like seagulls.

"How's Georgie Boy?" Bree asked. "Couldn't help but notice your pretty face missing from lectures this morning."

Oscar brushed his blonde-tipped hair behind his reddening ears. "Yeah, we went back home for a bit."

Bree smirked and shovelled a mouthful of re-heated spaghetti into her face.

"He didn't see anything last night, right?" I said.

Oscar shook his head. "Still doesn't know anything. Beats me how I've kept it all secret."

"Well, he's not the brightest crayon in the box, is he?" Bree said.

Oscar grimaced. He'd met Georgie Boy a couple of months back, in a club on Oxford Street. The strapping young man had proven himself to be friendly, charismatic, but had a rather simple view of the world and repeatedly updated Bree and me on his aspirations to break into the social media modelling scene.

I shrugged. "It's like what Miss Blackthorne always says. People either ignore the weird shit around them or come up with whatever logic they can to explain it."

"To be honest, I think he just doesn't notice," Oscar admitted. "He's not very... perceptive."

"Any word from your dad?" Bree said, pasta sauce lining the edges of her lips.

Oscar's expression darkened. "He texted me a few days ago. Still working in Hong Kong. Probably won't make it back until Christmas."

"How long's it been now? Six months?"

"Eight," he said.

None of us had relatives living in Sydney, so we'd become each other's de facto family. My phone buzzed with a text message.

"Miss Blackthorne," I said. "Looks like she wants us to meet the Encantados. They live in Putney... wherever the hell that is." None of us were Sydney natives.

Oscar whipped out his phone and tapped open a map. "It's along the river. We can catch a ferry there."

I thumbed a message back, telling the Master Wizard we'd leave after class. There may be a supernatural conflict brewing, but that wouldn't put a stop to assignments and exams.

I unwrapped my peanut butter sandwich and regarded it with open disdain. I'd been eating the same lunch every day for the past month. I didn't have any particular fondness for peanut butter, but my bank account liked the price and my stomach needed something.

I frowned, took a bite, and forced it down.

* * *

WE CAUGHT the train to Circular Quay, the main ferry hub for the city. Hordes of tourists milled about, never venturing too far from the cafés in case the weather turned and they needed to make a hasty retreat.

Ultra-modern sculptures and temporary art installations had been set up as part of the annual Vivid Festival, an outdoor event put on by the city to celebrate light, music, and cashed-up tourists. At night, flashing artworks and projected imagery illuminated the Circular Quay promenade from the Harbour Bridge to the Opera House. In the sullen grey light of day, however, it all looked a bit depressing.

"One second," I said, seeing someone I recognised.

A street magician was setting up for the night, crouched over his canvas shopping bag, extracting all the cheap props you'd expect. Playing cards, metal rings, plastic cups. To his credit, he could do real magic. Even if it was geared towards swindling overseas visitors out of their Aussie dollars.

"G'day, Jeremy," I said.

He looked up and his eyes bulged. He licked his lips as his head swivelled back and forth. "Blackthorne with you?"

"No," I said. "Just us."

Jeremy narrowed his eyes, then looked past me to Bree and Oscar. He stopped unpacking the props and stood straight. The magician wasn't tall. But neither was I. He glared down at me, probably hoping to be intimidating, but I'd seen him do magic for the tourists, and hadn't been impressed.

"What do you want, then?" he said. "I'm square with the wizard."

Miss Blackthorne and the criminal-turned-street magician had an ongoing arrangement. In exchange for the Master Wizard turning a blind eye to some of Jeremy's shadier dealings, he would provide her with tasty titbits on the goings-on of the city. The man didn't see everything, but he saw a lot.

"How'd you like to be owed another favour?"

"From you?"

"From us," I said, gesturing at my friends, "and Miss Blackthorne, of course. We're a package deal."

He scratched at his unkempt beard. He had a spot of grey hair to the left of his chin. "Go on, then."

"I want you to keep an eye out for selkies."

"Why?"

"None of your business."

He shrugged. "I've seen a few of those bloody sea elves skulking

23

around the wharves the last couple of days. Can't miss 'em with their bare feet and chopped ears. The swords are a dead giveaway, too."

"What were they doing here?"

"Visiting the museum, buying didgeri-fucking-doos. How the hell would I know?"

"We'll need more if you want to earn that favour," I said.

Jeremy took off his black magician's hat and ran fingers through his greasy brown hair. "Like what?"

"Tell us if you see any more selkies around here. Especially if you see them acting... suspicious."

"They always look suspicious."

"Hostile, then."

"Expecting trouble?" he asked, one eyebrow raised.

"Most of the time."

I gave him my number, because despite both of us being capable of manipulating the mystical forces of the universe, texting was still the easiest way to keep in touch.

"I hate that guy," Bree said as we walked towards the ferries. "I feel like scrubbing myself off in the shower every time we talk to him."

"The more eyes, the better," I said. "Circular Quay is the busiest ferry port in the city, so he has a good vantage point. And he's connected."

Miss Blackthorne seemed hellbent on the idea that I take over as Custodian, should she become unavailable. Read, killed. She'd been pushing me to develop working relationships with all manner of the city's Old World, whether they be hostile or slightly less hostile. I humoured her because I didn't fancy the idea of Sydney's protection falling to witches or vampires.

"Next ferry is in ten minutes," Oscar said.

We tapped our Opal Cards and waited on a bench, watching the ferries come and go. The lights of Luna Park's carousels and fun rides shone brighter across the water as the sky darkened. A shiny red jet boat skimmed across the water, showing tourists the entirety of the harbour in twenty minutes, and giving them an adrenaline rush in the process. People ambled along the promenade with expensive cameras hanging from their necks, waiting for the Vivid lights to be switched on, since the cloud cover had robbed them of the photogenic golden hour that comes with a setting sun.

The ferry that pulled up was a single-level catamaran, whose job was to haul passengers up and down the Parramatta River all day, every day. A couple of the ferry hands cast sidelong glances our way as we stepped across the access ramp, neither of them staring for more than a second or two. I dismissed it and we parked ourselves by the window.

The ferry pulled away from the wharf and puttered out into the harbour. We had just passed beneath the Harbour Bridge when a tall, dark-skinned man sat on the seat opposite us, a big grin taking up most of his face.

He looked like he'd just been for a swim. Water dripped down his face, and his long curly hair was saturated, as were his clothes. It took a few seconds to realise the man wore the same grey polo top and black shorts as the ferry workers.

"Joey Finch," he said, never losing his smile.

"Who the hell are you?" Bree demanded.

"Name's Mick."

"You're an Encantado," Oscar said.

"Almost," he said as he leaned back and rested his hands behind his head. The movement lifted his shirt, giving us a glimpse of an impressive beer gut. "I'm a Mokoi. Got too many brain cells to be an Encantado. But we're all people of the river. I hope you don't mind me joining you. My mates noticed you getting on board."

I looked over to the crew, who were busy moving back and forth doing whatever it was ferry hands do on boats.

"I've never seen them before."

"Your reputation precedes you," Mick said, pointing to my left arm. "They saw a kid with an arm covered in badass scars and guessed it was the skinny wizard."

"That's not what people call me, is it?"

He pointed at Oscar. "And the tall one... you must be Oscar Lee." He faltered when he turned to Bree. "And..."

"Bree," she said. "So, can you turn into a dolphin, too?"

Mick laughed. "Not quite a dolphin," he said with a smile so infectious I had to grin back. "We can shift enough to not have to worry about drowning. That's about it."

"So, you're not the fastest thing in water?" I said.

"Not even close. Who told you that?"

"Do you know Frederico de Silva?"

"Ah," he said, nodding slowly. "It does sound like something he'd say. Rather passionate young fella. Prone to exaggeration. He may be quick, but there are much faster things out there." He slapped his belly. "Not me, though. Haven't got the aerodynamics for it."

"Hydrodynamics," Oscar corrected.

Mick tilted his head. "Well, air or water, no one's ever accused me of being fast."

One of the ferry hands near the front of the boat watched the conversation out of the corner of his eye.

I turned back to Mick. "The Mokoi run the ferries?"

"Some of us do. We all try to get jobs on the water. Bayside park rangers, tugboat captains. That kind of thing." He gestured widely at the surrounding view. "But ferries are where it's really at."

Yachts sailed by at leisurely speeds. Joggers and dog-walkers moved along tree-lined walkways that skirted the harbour shoreline, dotted by lampposts. Not a bad gig if you can get it.

"What do you want?" I asked.

He leaned forward, resting elbows on knees. "I heard you lot are helping us out with the selkies."

"I wouldn't put it that way."

"You can't let them take Frederico. He's one of us. Not a Mokoi, but still one of us."

"He killed a guy."

Mick lost his smile. "He doled out justice. Two very different things."

"There are still many unknowns," Oscar said. "We are yet to determine why the selkies killed the Baiji girl. Perhaps if we can determine what started this, we can find a peaceful way to resolve it. And there is always the possibility that the selkies are innocent."

Bless his pure heart. It was almost as if he hadn't spent the last six months dealing with witches, vampires, and demons.

"The selkies are far from innocent," Mick said. "Very few in the Old World are."

Oscar shifted in his seat. "I mean—"

"Yeah, yeah," Mick said with a sad smile. "I know what you mean. You're saying someone else could have killed Lin. But who else would want to? It's not like she had enemies. She was just a kid."

"We don't know yet," I said. "We need to talk with the selkies, hear their side."

Mick snorted. "Good luck with that. Those selkies have poles so far up their own arses it's a wonder they can still walk. I get the feeling they'll want their own retribution, regardless of who kicked off this shitshow."

Bree folded her arms across her chest. "You don't seem too worried."

"Why would I be? They're creatures of the ocean." Mick leaned back again and put his hands behind his head. "They might have fancy magic and old-school weapons, but if they come into our river, they'll have to deal with our god."

5

THE FERRY PULLED into Kissing Point Wharf at Putney, and I told Bree and Oscar not to get any ideas. Bree hit me on the arm.

Water lapped calmly against the shore and, after acting the tease all day, the clouds started spitting rain. Since he already had the shirt on, Mick helped the crew in securing the vessel and doing other boat-related activities that were beyond me.

He caught us again before we stepped onto the wharf.

"We're having a party tomorrow night," he said. "A corroboree to welcome some new arrivals. You guys should come. There'll be food, drinking, dancing. Girls" – he glanced over to Bree and Oscar – "and boys."

"Sure," I said. We might learn something. At the very least, we'd be meeting the people we were supposed to be protecting.

The directions Miss Blackthorne provided led us down a sandy path between the water's edge and houses that the Brady Bunch would have had trouble filling. Each property had its own ramp leading from the house down to the water, and a nice shiny boat ready to be rolled into the water for a day of sipping chardonnay on the harbour.

We came to an apartment complex that must have been built well before people with money started flooding into this part of the city. A rather standard three-storey apartment building stood next to the water, which had been copy-and-pasted into a row of brick buildings connected by a single concrete driveway. The driveway ran all the way from the road to the water, where a collection of rusted dinghies bobbed, tethered to wooden posts covered in barnacles.

Curious young faces peered down at us from apartment windows above as we started moving up the driveway. I smiled and waved but got no reaction.

"All Encantados, you think?" Oscar asked, looking up at the buildings.

"I wouldn't be surprised," I said. "Miss Blackthorne said they're from the Amazon River. Who knows how many Encantados there are out there?"

Bree looked back at the Parramatta River behind us. "Bit of a downsize."

"Only by a few thousand miles," I replied. "Give or take."

The Parramatta River twists itself right through the guts of Sydney, splitting the city in two. It only stretches about fifteen miles from the Harbour to Parramatta out in Sydney's west, but has dozens of feeder streams, rivers, and bays branching off either side. Still, any way you cut it, it's no Amazon.

"Yo! Wizard!" a voice called from somewhere above.

I looked up to see Frederico's head poking out of a window from one of the apartment buildings.

"Come on up. Level 3."

A cinder block covered in spiderwebs held the front door open. Security obviously wasn't high on their list of priorities. I was sure that would change shortly. Music drifted to us from the surrounding apartments, something with guitars and a Latin beat that made you want to shimmy until you remembered you can't dance.

The building had no lift, so we took the stairs. I still felt strong after reaching the third floor. That may not sound like much, but a year ago, the effort would have left me breathless. Ever since I'd gotten a handle on my psychomantic abilities, the nightly visits from energy-sucking wraiths had stopped, and I'd been getting stronger every day. I wouldn't be running a marathon anytime soon, but I could get through the day, no worries.

"Down here, guys," Frederico de Silva said from a doorway at the far end of the corridor. We passed several open doors, where I caught glimpses of families watching TV, cooking dinner. Just getting on with their lives. We passed a woman who stood at the entrance to her apartment, clutching a baby to her breast, watching us with a dispassionate gaze. Alright, I thought, not too hostile so far.

Frederico held the door open for us, then led us into his apartment. It had brown shag carpet and wood laminate furniture. One of the bulbs on the ceiling wasn't working and black mould covered a small pocket in the corner.

Miss Blackthorne stood with four people in quiet conversation. Two men and two women. They all looked around middle age, but that didn't mean much when dealing with the Old World. The men were shirtless and, like Frederico, had the kind of lean muscle you get from constant activity rather than hours pushing iron. The women were similarly fit and wore loose blouses that flowed behind them when they moved.

"These are the Encantado Elders," Frederico said. He moved over to one of the men and placed his hand on the man's shoulder. "And this is my father, Luiz de Silva. He's the Chief."

"Please," the man said with a smile, "*Elders* makes us sound so... old. Call me Luiz." The caramel-skinned man clasped a hand around mine, his grip strong and his palm calloused. No stranger to physical labour. "Welcome, welcome. You saved my boy. Those selkies would have strung him up like a criminal if they got their hands on him. Let me introduce to you to Marcia, Clara, and Erasmo, my family and close advisors."

The two he introduced as Erasmo and Marcia glistened in the yellow light of the apartment, probably just having had a dip in the river.

Frederico turned to Bree, Oscar, and me. "Beer?"

We all accepted. I'm pretty sure there's a law against uni students declining free beer. Frederico patted his dad on the shoulder, then disappeared into the kitchen, re-emerging with bottles, including one for himself. We twisted off the caps and drank.

Miss Blackthorne hobbled to a chair by the small window and fell into it with a grunt, resting both hands on her cane. "We have been discussing the situation at length."

Luiz tucked his thumbs into the waist of his shorts and puffed out his chest a little. "But we all agree that the repercussions have been delivered. The books are balanced."

"No," Miss Blackthorne said, flashing him an annoyed glare. "We have established that *you* believe the score is even. I am yet to talk with the selkies. Evidently, they have a very different view."

The woman named Clara snorted. "What will that achieve? They sit in their silver cities, tucked safely beneath the ocean, where witch hunters and soul eaters can't reach them. The river men are peasants to them. Slaves. They killed that Baiji girl like she was nothing, because that's what they think of us."

"River folk," Bree said.

Clara's mouth hung open for several seconds. "Excuse me?"

"River folk," Bree repeated. "Look, sister, it's for your benefit as much as mine. Fight the patriarchy and all that."

Miss Blackthorne cut in before the Encantado Elder could reply. "The selkies are not immune to troubles. Regardless of how they perceive the river folk, their attention is now on you. An Encantado killed Ambassador Ellister Kelden. You know that such an action cannot go without consequences."

Oscar pushed his glasses to the bridge of his nose. "Shouldn't we be finding out whether the selkies actually killed Lin? I mean, if it wasn't them, then Frederico had no justification for killing their ambassador."

The mood in the room did a one-eighty. Bree took a swig from her bottle, but her eyes tracked the Encantados.

Clara took a step towards Oscar. "You think my nephew is lying?"

"Not at all," he said. "I just... uh..."

"It's alright, Tia Clara," Frederico said, putting himself between us and the angry aunt. He turned to Oscar and spoke in an even tone. "I've already told you it was a selkie blade that killed Lin."

"How do you know?" I asked.

"Her sister, Aubrey, told me. I was close with both of them, showed them around the city when the Baiji arrived. Practically lived at their house for the first few months while they settled in. I trust her."

I believed Frederico's faith in his friend, but I wanted to meet the girl myself before deciding whether she could be trusted. That's Miss Blackthorne's influence rubbing off on me.

"Okay. Assuming it was the selkies—"

"It was," Frederico said, crossing his arms.

"Right. What about their motivation?"

"Motivation? They're murderers and slavers. They think they're

31

better than everyone else because they've got their government, their underwater cities, their magic."

I worked hard not to let my irritation colour my words. "Freddy," I said calmly, "you mentioned Lin might have trespassed into selkie waters."

"I also said they could have crossed into ours. The Baiji are like us, they stay away from the open waters. Our god can only protect us while we stay in the river. To leave would be foolish."

"I will talk to the selkies," Miss Blackthorne cut in. "We will not act without first understanding what has led to this point."

"You're wasting your time," Frederico said with a shake of his head.

Luiz de Silva moved over to Frederico and placed a reassuring hand on the young man's shoulder. "Easy, son," the Chief said. "Let the Custodian do her job." He turned back to Miss Blackthorne. "The selkies will talk to you?"

"Of course, they will," Miss Blackthorne said, standing up with a series of grunts. She looked at Luiz de Silva and gave him the cold stare she normally reserves for monsters, demons, and particularly slow apprentices. "In the meantime, don't do anything to provoke them."

Luiz tilted his head. Frederico remained quiet and took another pull from his beer.

The music had quietened down when we left the apartment and more people stood at their doors, watching us as we passed in the corridor. Some smoked cigarettes, despite it being very illegal inside a building like this. They didn't come across as threatening but weren't about to blow us kisses either. I didn't blame them.

People like the Encantados – the Baiji, the selkies, vampires, even witches and wizards – they don't come to Sydney for the good weather and the chance of snagging a Hemsworth brother. They're running from the rest of the world. Out there, they fight to survive against monsters and witch hunters. And something called soul eaters, apparently. They come to feel safe — relatively safe – and to get on with living.

We walked to Miss Blackthorne's car parked on the street, a boxy white Toyota Land Cruiser, manufactured at a time when maximal space efficiency was prioritised over aesthetics or streamlined air flow. We got in quickly, the weather having worsened considerably. Miss

Blackthorne switched on the ignition and the Land Cruiser's V8 engine roared to life, settling into a low rumble.

"So, we're just letting the guy get away with murder?" Bree asked as we pulled away from the kerb.

"It's a dangerous precedent," Oscar said. "If people in the Old World start carrying out revenge killings... it could spiral out of control."

"We're picking our battles," I said.

Miss Blackthorne nodded. "That's right. What would happen if Frederico was sent to prison? The river folk run the waterways that flow through the city. They run the ferries, influence the port authorities, and manage parklands along the bays. We must handle this situation delicately. With thoughtful conversation and diplomacy."

Bree smirked. "Sure you still want Joey involved, then?"

"Shut up," I shot back.

"I will need to think on the best way to approach this," Miss Blackthorne said. "In the meantime, do you have time for practice tonight?"

"Of course," I lied.

I actually had a crapload of uni work to get through, but whenever I skipped a magic lesson, regardless of the reason, the next session was always double the length and four times the pain.

"Well," Bree said, "if you guys are going to be playing hocus pocus, can you drop me home first? I've got a shift tonight."

"How's the new boss?" I asked.

Bree shook her head. "The idiot has no idea how to run a pub."

6

WE DROPPED Bree at the house and drove on, but instead of heading back to the Old Substation Building, Miss Blackthorne took us north.

"I thought we were going to practice," I said.

"You are woefully unprepared to deal with selkie water mages and their hydromancy. I need to prepare the two of you in the event you face them again."

Miss Blackthorne flicked a switch to increase the speed of the windscreen wipers as the rain picked up. Any remaining hope I had of getting home warm and dry was being washed away with the street litter.

We crossed the Harbour Bridge and hit Mosman fifteen minutes later. Huge century-old houses lined streets that curved and twisted with the contours of the topography. I had never ventured into this area before, but I knew it was popular for CEOs and financial types. A lot of old money. We popped out on the other side of the suburb onto the tip of a peninsula, rounded a hairpin, and drove down a dark road lined on either side by thick trees. No streetlights illuminated the way, and we didn't pass any other cars. It felt like we were driving down a cramped tunnel, and it was easy to forget we were still in the middle of the city.

As a general rule, it's better to hide magic as much as possible, so if we were going to be slinging spells outside, Miss Blackthorne had to take us somewhere secluded. Apart from the standard bogeymen, there are people out there, regular people, who live for the express purpose of eradicating everything supernatural from the face of the earth. That includes river folk, witches, elves – anyone with even a sniff of magic about them. From my understanding, wizards have a fairly prominent spot on that list.

Go ahead and google 'real magic'. You'll find countless homemade videos of people creating fire with their mind, making things float, turning invisible. Most will be using clever camera angles or CGI or whatnot, but a small percentage of those people are the real McCoy. Do a little digging and you'd quickly discover most, if not all, of these people have mysteriously disappeared or died in horrible accidents.

That's the work of the witch hunters. They call themselves the Venerati Sanctus; I assume, because they think going by a Latin name gives them more enigmatic appeal. I'm inclined to agree, if I'm being honest. They are cunning, ruthless, and effective. Apparently. I'd never met one and would like to keep it that way. I'm sure the Venerati could find us, if they really set out to do so, but there was no need to draw their attention if we could help it. Which was why we rarely did magic out in the open.

Miss Blackthorne stopped the Land Cruiser at a seemingly random spot by the side of the road, nothing but trees and shadows on either side. She grabbed her walking cane and stepped out into the rain. Oscar had thought well ahead and had a waterproof jacket on. If I had known we'd be spending time in the rain, I wouldn't have just worn a T-shirt and jeans.

"This way," said the Master Wizard, moving down a narrow dirt trail that snaked through the trees. We followed, conjuring *lumières* so we didn't twist our ankles on the winding roots that crossed the path. I kept my spell close to provide some warmth.

The trail led us on a gradual downward slope until the ground fell away and we stood over a small beach, enclosed on both sides by rocky cliffs. We faced east, overlooking Sydney Harbour. Across the water we could see the North and South Heads, and the ocean beyond, currently too dark to see where the sky met the sea. Selkie territory.

We descended a wooden staircase, and I quickly realised why Miss Blackthorne selected this location to practise water magic. At the bottom of the steps, we passed a large wooden sign that said, *Obelisk Beach – Nudity Permitted.*

I cast another look at the encircling cliffs and thick tree coverage.

The secluded beach would have been the perfect spot to get your junk out in the daytime. Or to practise magic out in the open at night.

Miss Blackthorne started removing her shoes.

"Wait," I said, "we're not going to—"

"Take your shoes off, you two," she said as she rolled up the hems of her jeans so they sat halfway up her calf. "Then step into the water."

"Right," I said, relieved we wouldn't be stripping down to our birthday suits.

My shirt was almost soaked through already from the rain, and I shot an envious glance at Oscar's waterproof jacket. I rolled up my jeans and kicked off my shoes, feeling the soft, cool sand against my feet. I stepped into the gentle water up to my ankles. It was painfully icy, having just reached the tail end of winter, and I had a terrible feeling I would end the night very cold, very tired, and very wet.

Miss Blackthorne tossed her *lumière* into the air, where it split into ten other balls of light, forming a circle high above us that lit up the beach like a film set. I could potentially replicate the spell, although it wouldn't leave much brain capacity to do anything else. Miss Blackthorne propped her cane against the craggy rocks and limped to the water's edge.

"Joseph, focus on how I shift the water." She started moving her arms back and forth like a hula girl, and the calm water around her began to stir. "You don't want to push or pull it. It's more of a tethering exercise. You want to embed your magic within the water, coax it into becoming an extension of your *will*."

Between Oscar and me, he was undeniably the stronger magic wielder, but I had natural sensitivities to magic that bore their own advantages. The mind-reading thing may have been put on the back burner for now, but my more passive abilities – my 'gut feelings' and my knack for sensing the invisible shifting of magic around me – let me do things Oscar couldn't.

As Miss Blackthorne manipulated the water, I felt the stirring of magic as if it were an invisible pressure against my consciousness, a cool breeze against my skin. The Master Wizard had trained us in several forms of offensive and defensive spells, but what she was doing with the water felt like neither. It was as if she was developing a partnership with the magic in the water, bonding with it. I felt a lull as the pressure withdrew, like waves getting sucked back into the ocean, and I instinctively felt what was coming.

A mini tidal wave rolled forward and rushed towards Oscar and me. It splashed against the translucent barrier I'd hastily conjured, churning around me for several seconds before spreading upwards to completely encase my spherical shield in swirling white-water. Just as I was feeling pleased with myself, I felt another shift of magical pressure and an invisible fist punched through my shield, striking me in the stomach. After training with Miss Blackthorne for six months, I should have expected that.

My shield dissipated as I stumbled backwards, and the water fell upon me like someone dumping an entire swimming pool on my head. I looked over at Oscar. He'd been washed back about twenty feet, and looked as soaked to the bone as I was. Well, that didn't take long.

"You should have sensed the kinetic spell," Miss Blackthorne said.

"Yeah, I know," I grumbled.

Oscar came to my side, pushed his wet hair back, and adjusted his glasses.

I scowled at Miss Blackthorne. "I thought we'd be learning water magic."

"Just because the selkies have an inclination towards one discipline, it doesn't mean they aren't proficient in other means of wielding magic."

"On a scale of one to you, how good are they at other magic?"

"Most spend a majority of their lives underwater," Miss Blackthorne said. "So, their repertoire primarily consists of techniques for manipulating water and currents. In general, most selkie mages cannot wield as wide a variety of magic as a wizard, but it is important to—"

"To be ready for anything," I said. "Got it."

She rolled up her sleeves. "Let's go again."

I felt magic being twisted by Miss Blackthorne and conjured a shield, stupidly expecting the same spell. As a reward for my presumption, the water around my ankles reached up like liquid tentacles and yanked my legs out from under me, dragging me away from the beach and out into deeper water. I lost sight of Miss Blackthorne and Oscar as the watery limbs pulled me beneath the surface. I panicked and threw the first offensive spell that came to mind, which happened to be a fireball. I was in no danger of being mistaken for the next Stephen Hawking.

The watery tentacles pulled me deeper, where light was a memory and directions were meaningless. This was the way Miss Blackthorne ran her lessons. Push us to the brink, to our absolute limits, and force us to adapt. I used to think it was reckless. It took me a while to realise she knew exactly how far she could push us, exactly how far she could tighten the cords before they snapped. She knew I could get out of this. She expected me to.

I tried to blast the tentacles off my legs by casting a *sneezer*. That's the name I'd given to quick, punchy spells made of bundled kinetic energy. It felt like I'd just whacked my own shin with a rubber mallet and I fought the urge to scream. The tentacles held. I needed to get them off. Needed to get air.

I focused on Miss Blackthorne's spell, the pattern of the shifting magic, the energy flowing through the water to give it purpose and shape. I tried to duplicate it, letting the magic in my chest flow out of my body and into the dark water around me, creating malleable strands of energy, like giant worms made from water. I gave the water purpose, willing it to peel off the tendrils as though I were using my own hands. The grip on my legs loosened, and I re-doubled my efforts. One by one, Miss Blackthorne's tentacles fell away.

First problem, solved.

My lungs burned, and I had to battle my body's reflex to take a breath underwater. Doesn't make sense, I know, but you try drowning and see what goes through your head.

I used the water to feel the way to the surface, quickly discovering I was upside down and the surface was somewhere ten feet past my toes. I spun around and swam, clawing at the water with frantic desperation.

I burst through the surface and spluttered for air, each breath deep and glorious. I suddenly whirled on the spot, preparing for a follow-up sucker punch from the Master Wizard. She stood at the shore with her hands clasped in front of her, seemingly content at almost drowning me. I treaded water for a few moments to get my breath back, then did a slow breaststroke towards the beach until my feet found sand.

Oscar had taken a different approach in countering Miss Black-thorne's spell. My friend didn't have the magical sensitivity to intuit spells as they were being cast and reverse engineer them like I did. So, he used what he already knew and dialled it up to eleven.

He stood inside a translucent yellow bubble that bobbed on top of the water, like a floating hamster ball. It also kept the rain off his head. I recognised it as a defensive shield spell wrapped around him entirely. The effort and magical energy required to maintain the spell must have been enormous if the strain on his face was anything to go by.

He let it disintegrate and dropped into the water.

"Very good," Miss Blackthorne said. "Both of you."

Oscar and I looked at each other. While not as rare as her fabled smiles, compliments were few and far between.

"You both adjusted to the situation well." She looked at me. "I noticed you performed a touch of hydromancy."

"Maybe," I said. "I just copied you and turned the magic into some watery worm things."

She nodded, satisfied. "I only have a passing knowledge of hydromancy. Selkie mages are instructed from childhood in how to extend their senses into water and can manipulate it with far greater power and dexterity. It is how the mage directed the actions of the water elementals you saw."

"That could be a problem," Oscar said. "Humans are two-thirds water."

"Water mages cannot manipulate the water in another person's body. Our anima protects us, in the same way it prevents practitioners from reaching into someone's chest and exploding their heart with a magical fist."

She was talking about auras, which are kind of an inbuilt defence against mystical intrusion that everyone has, and definitely not related to chakras or Bikram yoga.

"Let's try it again," I said. "I want to get a handle on these *water worms*."

"That is not the name for that spell."

I shrugged. "Well, it's one I can remember."

The Master Wizard sighed, perhaps accepting that there were some things she'd never be able to teach me. She then swayed her arms and the water around her started churning. "Prepare yourselves."

* * *

39

A COUPLE of brutal hours later, we put our shoes back on and went up the wooden stairs. My shoes were wet from the rain and now they were filled with sand, too. If she'd given us a heads up, I would have brought my flip-flops, which may not have given off the vibe of *All-Powerful Sorcerer*, but they would have been far more comfortable for wet feet.

When we got to the Land Cruiser, Miss Blackthorne pulled out a couple of beach towels from the back and threw them to Oscar and me. I only just noticed that our teacher was almost completely dry, despite the constant rain. In the dim light of her *lumière*, I could barely make out a transparent conjuration floating above her head, like a pane of glass set at an angle. The rain bounced off and slid away without reaching her. I wondered if I'd have the ability to multitask one day.

As well as being tired, cold, and wet, I was also starving, so we visited a Hungry Jack's drive-through and picked up burgers and a couple tons of chicken nuggets.

"Oscar," Miss Blackthorne said as she drove, "I would like you to talk to the Mokoi. See what they know about what has transpired. There's a lot more going on here than a simple revenge killing."

She liked to send us on these kinds of errands. I could never tell when it was to test our abilities, or when she genuinely needed the help. Or maybe she just got a kick out of sending us into danger. I guess that's all part of being a wizard's apprentice. She'd promised to tell us when we were going to face danger, which was good in theory, except that in this line of work you never knew when the universe was going to toss a curveball at you. Take the surprise visit from the Brazilian dolphin-man as Exhibit A.

"The Mokoi are throwing a party tomorrow night," Oscar said. "To welcome some new arrivals. We've already been invited. It will be a good opportunity to talk to them."

"Do that," Miss Blackthorne said. "And take Bree with you. Careful around the Mokoi Elders, though. They have no love for wizards. Joseph, I would like you to talk to the Baiji. While you are there, it would also be pertinent to examine where the murder occurred. You have friends who can help with this kind of thing."

Oh, I knew who she meant.

"And I believe you are already familiar with the girl who was killed," Miss Blackthorne said. "You met her earlier this year."

40

"Lin? When?"

"Back in March."

That's where I'd recognised the name. Lin was one of the dozen or so captives we'd rescued from a literal mad scientist who was hell-bent on summoning the archdemon Astaroth.

"First, though," Miss Blackthorne continued, "I want you to speak to the Queen of the Elves and request that she calls me. I need to discuss the situation with her."

"No problem," I said, knowing there was still no love lost between Miss Blackthorne and the elves.

The Master Wizard had never really explained why the elves had given her the cold shoulder. And she wasn't the kind of person to divulge the hot goss over a couple of mojitos. Although, ever since that issue with the demonic thralls six months earlier, her relationship with the elves had thawed. It wasn't quite at the point of games nights and Christmas cards yet, but it was getting there.

I dipped a nugget into the Sweet n' Sour sauce and popped it into my mouth. "Want me to give Queen Alehtta a heads up that we might help with the selkies?"

"No," Miss Blackthorne said. "I will discuss those details with her myself." I shot her a quizzical look, so she added, "my aim is to meet with the selkies, however they are a people constrained by their own bureaucracy. It comes as a result of having such a vast population that spans the entire globe. It could potentially take months to organise an audience with them, especially since they now lack an ambassador to the city. But the elves have an existing relationship with the selkies. Perhaps if Queen Alehtta arranges and facilitates the meeting, we could speed up proceedings."

"I don't understand why the elves still don't trust us," Oscar said. "We saved Alehtta. That should count for something." He dug into his burger, a Big Jack, not to be confused with the near identical burger from Macca's.

"It does," Miss Blackthorne said. "It went a long way. But the problems between me and the elves run deeper." She kept her eyes forward as she spoke. "I worked closely with Alehtta's parents, the previous king and queen, during the War."

"You mean the Magic War that happened at the same time as World War Two?" I asked.

41

Miss Blackthorne had been pretty light on the details whenever I'd asked about it. From what I could gather, the Magic War was a war fought in the shadows, during which the Venerati Sanctus launched their largest and most coordinated attack in history against the Old World. Killed a whole lot of people, overran countries. Even wiped out entire races. It was only due to the efforts of people like Miss Blackthorne, that the utter annihilation of the Old World had been prevented. Or at least postponed. She'd told us very little about it, but to be fair, she wasn't prone to storytelling at the best of times. I popped another chicken nugget in my mouth. God, they're good.

"The Magic War," Miss Blackthorne said, shaking her head. "I never liked the name. It really should be called the War Against Magic. And it lasted well beyond World War Two. Depending on who you ask, the fighting continued right up until the mid-eighties. For some, the war never ended."

"Like Bulgaria," I said.

Oscar frowned, so I had to explain that the country – the entire bloody country – was lost to the Venerati Sanctus.

"I fought side by side with the Elf King and Queen," Miss Blackthorne continued. "With a number of others, we formed the Vanguard, a small group dedicated to take the fight to the Venerati. And just like any other war, there were casualties. Alehtta's parents among them."

"That doesn't explain why the elves hate you so much," I said.

I sensed... something from Miss Blackthorne. Something dark and grim. A weight she bore alone.

She sighed. "There were a lot of hard choices made in the War. But choices are still choices, and mine resulted in the deaths of the Elf King and Queen."

7

I TEXTED Alehtta first thing in the morning. Well, maybe not the first thing. I woke up, had breakfast, went to class, then remembered halfway through my second lecture that I was meant to contact her. It's a busy life trying to get an engineering degree while also preventing the supernatural world from imploding.

I sent the Elf Queen a message asking if she could give Miss Blackthorne a call. Alehtta texted back minutes later, telling me to meet her at lunch to discuss my request and provided an address. She wasn't the type to play political games, at least not with me, so I guessed there was something she needed to show me, or a favour she wanted to ask. I nudged Bree with my elbow to show her the text just as two pale-skinned individuals strode into the lecture theatre.

The familiar duo wore the same high-collared black jackets and baggy trousers that billowed like parachute pants. The curved swords on their hips rested safely in glossy black scabbards, where I hoped they remained. Thankfully, they'd benched the water elementals.

"Joey Finch," Rhoswyn called out, the selkie mage's voice carrying loud and clear thanks to the room's excellent acoustics. Hamish stood beside her, the broad-shouldered selkie's hand resting on the pommel of his sword.

The students turned in their seats to face me. I'm not too worried about being the centre of attention. When you've stared down blood-thirsty vampires and literal demons, a room full of pimply university students is nothing. I considered making a break for the emergency exit, but decided I would gain more by seeing what these guys wanted. Besides, what were the chances they'd attack us in broad daylight?

"I'm... I'm sorry?" stammered the lecturer. He was a wiry man, who, if he didn't teach statistics, probably would have made a decent living punching out complex analyses for some data science company. The appearance of two black-clad individuals armed with pointy weapons seemed too much for the bespectacled professor to handle. "What are you... ah... can I help you?"

The red-headed mage looked up at the students as a quiet murmur spread throughout the room. "Joseph Finch," she repeated. "We request an audience with you."

"Um... yes... of course," the professor said, then looked up at the class. "Joseph? Are you here?"

"Not real subtle, are they?" Bree whispered.

"It's better than dropping by our place in the middle of the night," Oscar said. "As long as those swords don't come out."

I packed up my things. "You guys coming?"

They nodded and followed me down the stairs to the front. "Sorry," I said loudly to the professor. "Emergency meeting... with the Medieval Pirate Club."

Rhoswyn and Hamish narrowed their eyes, then followed us out of the room. Before the mage could speak, I raised a hand.

"Not here," I said. "Follow me."

I led everyone to the outdoor café in front of Fisher Library. We beat the lunchtime rush, so were able to snag one of the circular metal tables. A giant yellow umbrella stuck out through the centre of the table to protect us from the rain that looked about to fall any second. Hamish McMuscles remained on his feet, staying close enough to join in the conversation or poke us with his sword, if he so desired.

Bree and Oscar asked for coffees. I ordered a hot chocolate, because I'm a grown-ass man who isn't trying to impress anyone. I asked the selkies if they wanted anything.

Rhoswyn responded with a glare.

"And just some water for the table, thanks," I said to the server.

The guy had a paperclip slotted through his right earlobe and half his head was shaved. The other half was hidden behind long pink hair. He looked at Hamish. "I can pull up more chairs if you like."

"He's fine," I said.

After the server had gone, I turned my attention to Rhoswyn. In the light of day, I could see that she and her buddy had paler skin than the elves, making her wavy red hair even more vivid by contrast. She regarded me with unblinking eyes that looked too big for her face and appeared to have a sheen, as if she was about to shed a tear, but I doubted that was the reason. I wondered if the selkies had gills somewhere under all that get up.

Placing both hands on the table, I stared at Hamish before fixing Rhoswyn in my gaze. "What do you want?"

"I have told you what we want."

"Sorry to disappoint, but Freddy's not here." I looked over at Hamish. "You know, you guys should be careful. There really is a Medieval Society on campus. They might want to recruit you."

"I fear you are not treating the situation with the gravity it deserves," Rhoswyn said.

"Not true. I just don't think much of anyone who comes to my house in the middle of the night and threatens war."

"We don't want a war," said the selkie mage.

"Then don't start one. Problem solved."

She pursed her lips. "I understand your dilemma as protectors of the city. But the path of action should be obvious to you. The easiest and quickest way to resolve this is to hand over the Encantado."

"Easiest for you," Bree snorted. "Freddy's dolphin buddies will throw a hissy fit if you get your hands on him."

"There must be another way to resolve this," Oscar said.

"There's not," said the selkie mage. "The man murdered our ambassador. Our leaders want his head on a stick."

"What happened to getting a fair trial?" I said.

"He will still get a trial. But the longer it takes to bring him to us, the worse it looks for him. And the river men."

"Oh, we're calling them river folk now," I said.

Rhoswyn arched an eyebrow, then shrugged.

The server came back with table water, and I poured out two glasses for the selkies.

"The ambassador will not only be missed by us," Rhoswyn continued. "His diplomatic skills have saved you land dwellers from having to worry about children going missing at the beach, or fishing boats

45

getting sunk out at sea. Many things lurk in The Deep that we hold at bay."

The server came back, balancing a tray in one hand. He cast a sidelong glance at Oscar a couple of times as he placed our drinks on the table. My friend either ignored the looks or was oblivious. I sipped the hot chocolate and revelled in the warmth and familiar deliciousness of it, taking the opportunity to put my thoughts together.

"Miss Blackthorne is going to meet with you guys," I said. "She's going to try to smooth this whole thing over before you put Freddy on trial."

"That is unlikely. You can't simply call a meeting like you're organising a Sunday lunch. Our leadership will first need to send a new ambassador. Then, once a relationship has been established and trust has been built, the leaders will discuss whether they should meet with the Custodian."

Miss Blackthorne really dropped the ball on that one. She should have been maintaining a relationship with these people. Then again, who knew how many different races, clans, and families she had to liaise with?

"Sounds like the process will take time," Oscar said.

"Three months at least, would be my estimation," said the selkie mage.

I spread my hands on the table. "Miss Blackthorne's planning on getting the elves to chaperone."

Rhoswyn considered that. "Perhaps that could work. We have an existing relationship with the elves."

"So, you'll leave Frederico alone?" Bree said.

Rhoswyn picked up the glass in front of her and brought it to her eye. She then grabbed two sachets of salt, ripped them open, and poured them in. With a slight gesture of her hand, the water stirred itself into a mini whirlpool and she took a sip.

"If the Encantado does not present himself at the trial," she said, "his crime will no longer be viewed as a murder. It will be classed as a declaration of war. Our War Mages are already making preparations for such a circumstance. Once the banners have been raised and my people march into your city, hundreds will die. Thousands. River folk and selkies alike. Not to mention the mundane citizens ignorant of our existence. War spares no one." Her gaze drifted over the swarm of students passing by, then snapped back to me, her eyes burning with quiet determination. "I will do everything in my power to prevent that from happening."

I couldn't decide whether this woman was on our side, then reminded myself of what Miss Blackthorne said. Everyone has their own agenda, their own interests. Unfortunately for me, the Custodian's interests looked like a Venn diagram that had swallowed up all the other Venn diagrams.

I returned the selkie's gaze and held it. I wouldn't put it past her and McMuscles to whisk the Encantado away in the dead of night.

"If Frederico mysteriously disappears," I said, "it'll be the river folk who declares war."

The selkie mage gave a thin-lipped smile. "They would be forced to leave the safety of their river, go where their god can't protect them."

I rubbed my chin. "They're a tight bunch, the river folk. I reckon they'd chase you halfway across the ocean to save one of their own, or to seek vengeance, with or without a god watching their backs."

"Should that occur," Rhoswyn said, "then at least the fighting would take place away from the city. The only deaths would be river folk and selkies. Isn't it the Custodian's job to minimise collateral?"

"We're trying to prevent a war."

"So am I," she said. "The question is, what price are you willing to pay for it?" She placed her hand on the pummel of her sword as she stood up. "The trial has been organised. Four days from now when the sun is at its highest."

"Tuesday, lunchtime," I said. "Got it."

The selkie mage fixed the three of us with a stare. "Few who have lived through war wish to live through it again. Please, do what is right for the people you protect."

Oscar, Bree, and I stuck around after the selkies left, and the lunch crowd filled the seats around us.

Bree shook her head. "I can't believe they rocked up in the middle of a lecture."

"I can," I replied. "This was a courtesy call. Rhoswyn was giving us a final chance to hand over Freddy, or she'd nab the guy herself."

Bree frowned. "It sounds like there's going to be a war whether Frederico turns up to the trial or not."

"There'll be fewer people at risk if the fighting takes place out at sea," Oscar suggested quietly.

I turned to him. "You're saying we should hand Freddy over to the selkies? That's a death sentence. And the river folk would declare war."

Oscar pushed up his glasses and shuffled in his seat. "Joey, we're meant to protect this city. That's our job. Preventing a war may be too big a goal for us to hope for, maybe even too much for Miss Blackthorne. But we can influence where the fighting takes place. Delivering Frederico to the selkies may save lives in the city."

"No," I said, shaking my head. "That's not good enough. Freddy is an arrogant prick, but we can't leave his fate up to the selkies. I know we're talking one life against... I don't know... thousands, maybe. But I can't just deliver a guy to his death."

"Is that really our call?" Bree asked.

"I'm making it our call."

8

THE ADDRESS ALEHTTA had provided was somewhere in Waterloo, which was just far enough from the university to justify taking the bus. Bree and I went, while Oscar stayed behind to attend the afternoon classes. One of us had to stick around and write up the lecture notes, since the three of us were still, technically, full-time students.

We had dedicated many late nights to discussing whether we should ditch the degree and take our newfound abilities to the casino or practice magicking money out of ATMs. More often than not, these discussions were fuelled by generous quantities of alcohol, and we always circled back to the same reasons for not abusing our abilities. Firstly, Miss Blackthorne terrified us. None of us wanted to get on the Master Wizard's bad side. Secondly, we begrudgingly had to consider all the fluffy stuff, like morals, integrity and not giving the Venerati Sanctus cause to put the city under their microscope. It's funny, because I'm pretty sure our government wouldn't be too concerned about us ripping off banks, as long as we kept the Old World in check and the existence of magic on the down low.

Bree and I hopped off the bus, and I almost stepped on a used syringe. Maybe flip-flops weren't the best choice of footwear.

"Fucking hell," Bree said. She'd worn sneakers and used her toe to nudge the syringe into the gutter.

Watching our step, we walked towards a loose collection of apartment buildings that must have been delivered straight from the Soviet Union, and truly pushed the limits of *function over form*. Two narrow

49

towers stood amongst four dreary buildings that looked like grey slices of toast hoisted upright. Laundry hung over the railings of cramped balconies or drooped from makeshift washing lines. Only the colourful graffiti on the walls served to break up the drab monotony.

At the entrance to one of the towers stood a tall woman wearing a thick brown shawl over her head, trendy black jeans, and a dark green flannel shirt that looked big enough to have come from the men's rack. Unlike other elves, she wore heavy black boots. Not a bad idea, given the area we found ourselves in. She held a bow casually in one hand, like it was the morning's newspaper.

"Riss!" Bree said, leaping forward to give the elf ranger a hug.

"Hello, Bree," Riss replied, returning the embrace and looking down at my friend with fondness. "Are you well?"

"I'm good," Bree said. "Where've you been? What's happening? Seeing anyone?"

"I have been away. Elf business. I have not developed any romantic attachments since our last encounter."

Bree pouted.

I didn't know the elf as well as my friend did, but Bree trusted her, so I did too. Riss was a ranger and belonged to a group of elves separate from any of the elf kingdoms around the world. They served no king or queen and were a people unto themselves. Riss helped Alehtta and Sir Brandr with odd jobs here and there, the details of which I knew nothing about.

"Riss," I said to the ranger with a sharp nod.

"It is good to see you, Joey," she replied.

I grasped the hand she extended. "Boots were a smart choice," I said. "You'd want to watch your step around here."

"Yes," she said, surveying the area with displeasure. "I am not fond of cities in general, but this neighbourhood is particularly disagreeable."

I was very conscious of people watching from balconies and park benches. I supposed some of those people could have been elves, too. They had the drifter wardrobe and lack of footwear that elves – most elves – seem to favour. It was hard to be sure without getting up close to see the disfigurement of their ears or the quiet defiance in their eyes.

"What kind of elf business?" Bree asked.

"It is not my place to say," the elf replied. "Let us visit Queen Alehtta. I believe she has something to request of you."

Riss used a fob to buzz us into the tower and led us inside, where the smell of dank mould and stale piss assaulted our nostrils. We bustled through quickly into the lift – a stainless-steel box with a broken light and graffiti on the walls. It smelled like piss, as well. Riss hit the button for the tenth floor.

"I thought Alehtta lived with the homeless," I said. "Outdoors."

"Most of the time," Riss said. "She's here visiting a friend."

The lift pinged, and the doors opened. The elf ranger led us to an apartment and knocked on the door, which was opened by a coffee-skinned elf I didn't recognise who gestured for us to enter. We stepped into an old living room that reminded me of the Encantados' home with the added smell of cigarettes, thanks to Sir Brandr, who sat in an armchair by the window puffing away.

His lightly tanned skin contrasted sharply with his white hair, which he held back in a tight ponytail. The man's mismatched wardrobe, however, blended perfectly with the room's jumble of furniture. Like most elves, with the exception of Riss, Brandr's clothes were indistinguishable from those of a wandering tramp or a street corner beggar. He wore a loose-fitting white shirt tucked into baggy black trousers. No shoes. His one saving grace: a form-fitting purple vest, made of a supple velvet material, and a fashion statement in its own right.

The elf who let us in moved to the corner and stood alongside another elf I hadn't seen before.

"Didn't know this was going to be a party," I said.

Brandr frowned at the two elves. "They are assisting me with the queen's protection until I am able to fulfil my duties."

The elf knight had suffered near-fatal injuries when he'd put himself between a rampaging bear-warrior and the Elf Queen. It was a miracle he'd survived. Brandr put his cigarette to his lips, took a long drag, and blew smoke in the vague direction of the window.

He nodded to the ranger. "Riss. Always a pleasure."

"Sir Brandr," Riss replied with a tip of her head. She removed her shawl, letting her chestnut hair flow to her shoulders. Another thing setting Riss apart from the rest of the elves was her ears. They stuck out a good six inches or so and were decorated with half a dozen earrings. "How are the wounds?"

"Frustrating," Brandr replied, his mouth twisting into a grimace. "Any news?"

"Another dead end."

Brandr sighed. "Then we will keep trying. We must."

"Trying what?" Bree said.

Alehtta, Queen of the Elves, emerged from an adjoining room. A couple of inches shorter than me, she had flawless caramel skin and blonde hair fair enough to be white. Despite wearing ripped leggings and an over-sized Reebok T-shirt, she had an unmistakable air of royalty about her.

"Joey, Bree," she said with a warm smile. "I'm glad you could come. Oscar is not with you?"

"He's busy, Your Majesty," I said, using her proper honorific. Brandr gets a bit upset otherwise. "But he sends his regards."

The queen looked at Riss, then Brandr, who shook his head. Alehtta's forehead creased before she turned back to Bree and me. "I would like to show you something," she said, and went back into the room she had just exited.

Bree and I followed.

The vertical blinds had been drawn, leaving the room in a sombre dimness. A man lay on a bed. I could see disfigured ears amongst his thin grey hair, making him the oldest-looking elf I'd laid my eyes on. He seemed asleep at first glance but moved when we approached.

"Rest, Tomandas," Alehtta said, placing a hand on his arm. "I am still here."

The old man became still, and I heard soft, steady breathing.

"What's wrong with him?" I asked.

"He's dying," Alehtta said. "Old age."

"Christ," Bree said. "How old does an elf have to be to die of old age?"

"We do not die of old age," Alehtta said. "Disease and mortal wounds can kill us. Starvation, too. Otherwise, we should live forever. Tomandas came to us a month ago from the British Isles. Even he cannot recall how many years he has lived, but he mentioned fighting the Romans at some point in his past." The Elf Queen picked up a pair of worn trousers from the floor, folded them neatly, and placed them in a drawer. "He came here wishing for a peaceful place to die." She gestured at the room. "This is unfortunately the best we could offer."

"Is this why you brought me here?" I asked. "I really wish I could help, but healing magic is well beyond my abilities. Maybe Miss Blackthorne knows someone."

"It is too late to help Tomandas," Alehtta said. "He will die in a matter of weeks. Do not be alarmed, he has accepted his fate. But I hope to prevent further meaningless deaths."

"Hey," Bree said. "Just because someone carks it, it doesn't mean it was meaningless."

"Of course not," Alehtta said. "I apologise. I simply mean, his death was avoidable."

"How?" I said.

Alehtta sat on the edge of the bed and looked down at the dying elf. "Our ancestral homes were built around Wells of Power. Sources of great energy and life, where the very air was thick with magic. When my mother and father led our people across the oceans, they saved a great number of elves, but in doing so, severed our connection to that ancient power. Without that magic sustaining us, we are a lost people. Refugees adrift on a sea of uncertainty, with nothing but our shared struggle to hold onto. It is my responsibility to find us a new home."

I frowned. "And you want me to help?"

"You have a great sensitivity to magic, Joey," Alehtta said. "Far beyond what any elf can do. Greater even than your Master Wizard."

"That's our Joey," Bree said. "He's as sensitive as they come."

"Not helping, Bree," I said. She responded with an insolent smile.

"I have sent Riss," the Elf Queen continued, "among others, to search out Wells of Power. Unfortunately, there has been limited success. We need someone who can identify and track the trails of magic. We need a wizard."

I ran a hand through my hair and let out a breath. "I wouldn't know where to start."

Alehtta waved her hand in a dismissive gesture. "We will talk about that later. Will you aid us in our search?"

"Sure," I said, not certain what I was getting myself into.

Alehtta nodded, and her shoulders relaxed slightly. "You are a boon to this city and to the Master Wizard."

"I don't know about that."

"Yes, you do," the Elf Queen replied. "And your teacher needs you more than she will ever admit."

I bit my lip. "Alehtta, we're friends, right?"

The Elf Queen replied only with a curious smirk.

"Miss Blackthorne... she told us how she's responsible for what happened to your parents. Whatever she did... I'm sorry."

A sad smile touched Alehtta's lips. "I have no doubt Mary would claim responsibility for the deaths of our king and queen. But to say such a thing would be an oversimplification, and a disservice to the heroic acts Mary accomplished. The responsibility of my parents' death falls solely on the heads of the Venerati Sanctus, who captured and tortured them. Unfortunately, many elves do not see it that way and blame Mary for not rescuing my mother and father when the opportunity arose."

Alehtta looked down at the old elf on the bed, touched his arm gently, then looked at us and gestured at the door. We went back to the living room. Brandr hadn't moved from his seat and had lit up a fresh cigarette.

"Those things will kill you, you know," I said.

He narrowed his eyes and took a long drag, then reached across to the open window and tapped the cigarette on the ledge, letting the ashes fall outside and blow away in the breeze. His face twisted in pain at the movement.

Riss leaned against the kitchen bench, arms crossed, looking out the window. The other two elves hadn't moved from their posts in the corner of the room, looking as if someone had thrown a Vinnie's clothing bin at a couple of mannequins. Alehtta closed the bedroom door quietly as she came out.

"Now," she said, "you mentioned Miss Blackthorne wanted to speak to me. What about?"

"The selkie ambassador was murdered," I said.

Brandr sat up in his chair, winced, then relaxed again. Alehtta cast him a look, as if to chide him for moving.

"Which ambassador?" she asked, turning back to us.

Damn my goldfish attention span. "Uh..."

"Ellister Kelden," Bree chipped in. "Honestly, Joey. If your head wasn't screwed on..."

I described the situation between the selkies and the river folk,

54

trying to be quick because the cigarette smoke in the apartment was starting to tickle my throat.

"This is not good," she said. "I know Ambassador Kelden. He's a shrewd man. *Was* a shrewd man, I should say. A diplomat and master strategist. I cannot imagine he killed the Baiji girl, at least not by his own hand."

"Could have been one of his mages," Sir Brandr said, "or one of the warriors who works out of the embassy. If the selkies are behind this, Kelden would have known about it or arranged it himself. Wouldn't be the first time the selkies have killed their enemies in such a manner."

Alehtta nodded slowly and turned to Bree and me. "The selkies have little love for anyone outside their own people. In ages past, land dwellers, including the river folk, would capture selkie women, prized for their fair skin, and take them as their wives, forcing them to bear their children."

I frowned. "The Encantados never mentioned that."

A sad smile crossed Alehtta's lips. "Why would they? It goes against their perception of the selkies as a race of conquerors and murderers. It is also possible the river folk have simply forgotten – a result of their much shorter lifespans. What happened during a selkie's childhood may be ancient history to most other people."

Bree crossed her arms and leaned against the wall. "Sounds like they're as bad as each other. I've got half a mind to stand back and just let them at each other's throats."

I levelled a look at my friend. "Except that there are five million innocent people in this city who'd get caught in the crossfire."

Alehtta moved to a wooden chair next to Brandr that creaked when she sat her delicate frame upon it. "Ironically, Ambassador Kelden would have been one of the few people who could defuse this situation. The selkie bureaucrats hung on every word he said." The queen turned her gaze to the window where rain had started to patter against the sill. "Makes me wonder if there isn't some further intent behind these events."

"So, you'll help Miss Blackthorne meet with the selkies?"

"I will."

"Should I get Miss Blackthorne to give you a call?"

"I would prefer to contact her myself. Although, you will have to give me her phone number."

* * *

"So that's where you've been," Bree said to Riss as we stepped into the lift and hit the button for the Ground Floor. "Looking to relocate."

The elf ranger nodded. "Not too far, though. Queen Alehtta still wishes the elves to live close to the city. It is safer than most places."

"I take it you haven't found any of these Wells of Power, then?" I said.

"Actually, I have found several. But nothing with enough power to sustain a new home. Perhaps, with your aid, we will have more success."

We reached the Ground Floor and exited the building to a dreary sky and a light sprinkle. The elf ranger gave Bree a quick embrace, nodded to me, and left at a trot, bow still in hand.

The rain picked up while I waited with Bree at the bus stop. She was going to meet up with Oscar at the university, then they'd head to the Mokoi party together.

"Be careful tonight, Joey," she said, when her bus pulled up.

"Yeah, you too. And remember why you're there."

"Boys and beers," she said with a nod.

"Bree, you need to—"

"I need to talk to the Mokoi Elders," she said, rolling her eyes, "and see if they know why the selkies killed Lin. I know what I'm doing."

"And don't start any fights."

Bree grinned. "I don't start fights, Joey. I end them."

"Hey, remember that time you tried to punch water?"

"Ha, fuck you," she said as she boarded the bus and flipped me her middle finger, all the while never losing her grin.

I didn't like splitting up the team, but we each had our roles to play. Tonight, theirs was to attend a party hosted by the river folk. Mine was to interrogate the family of a dead girl and poke through her stuff.

Yay.

I walked the fifteen minutes to Redfern Police Station. It should have taken ten, but I was forced to walk slowly because my flip-flops kept trying to aquaplane on the wet footpath. I met Constable Kyra Devapriya in the lift lobby. She'd already changed out of her police blues and wore jeans and a black pleather jacket. She saw me approach, put her phone away, and hit the button for the lifts.

"Constable," I said.

"Finch," she replied. "I wish I could say it's nice to see you, but every time we meet someone winds up dead or the closest thing to it."

"Hertz isn't coming?"

"The detective sergeant has a family. So, unlike me, he can't drop everything to come and put out whatever fires you start."

We stepped into the lift, where Devapriya swiped her ID card and pressed the button for the lower basement level.

"Thanks for coming tonight," I said. "I could really use your help."

The lift opened to an underground carpark and Devapriya led me between rows of police vehicles and private cars.

"Remind me exactly what I'm helping you with," she said.

I gave her the highlights, then added, "I figured you're the best person to interview Lin's family, being a future detective and all."

She pressed her lips together. "My application for detective is still frozen, thanks to you. That debacle with the mad scientist set me back. Internal reviews and psychological assessments. It'll be another six months before I'm even allowed to take the exams."

"Sorry about that."

We got to her car, a beat-up silver Corolla. I threw my backpack in the back seat and jumped in the front. Devapriya slumped in the driver's seat, sighed, and rested her forehead on the steering wheel.

"Fucking River People and sea elves," she said under her breath.

"At least it's not demons this time," I said.

9

WE'D TIMED the drive perfectly to be right amongst the traffic as the wage slaves of Sydney headed home after work. We moved slowly but steadily. The Corolla's windscreen wipers worked desperately against the rain, swishing back and forth with such ferocity I thought they'd fly off any second.

"You understand we can't hand this Frederico guy over to the selkies," Devapriya said. She had to raise her voice over the din of rain hammering on the roof. The constable shook her head. "Revenge killing. There's one authority in this city, despite what you and your magic buddies may think."

"I know that," I said, choosing not to mention that most of the Old World didn't know or care for the laws of humans. Just another thing for the Custodian to worry about. "What do you think we should do?"

She pressed her lips together and kept her eyes on the road, deviating around a car going too slow for her. "I'll make a call after we talk to these Baiji people. The whole situation stinks. It's all opinions and hearsay so far. We need to verify accounts and get a clear picture of what's happened, so we don't act half-cocked. In the meantime, we just have to make sure no one kills anyone else."

I nodded; happy she hadn't mentioned arresting anyone yet. That would truly mess things up.

We passed over the Gladesville Bridge, where traffic moved a bit more smoothly. I watched the boats passing beneath us, shrinking as we moved along. The bridge was a monster of a thing that spanned over the Parramatta River, connecting the Inner West to the northern parts of Sydney. I was just thinking about how bloody long the bridge was when something in the side mirror caught my eye.

"Hey, Devapriya. Does that car look a bit close to you?"

She lifted her chin and looked in the rear-view mirror as a car rammed into us from behind.

"Fuck!" Devapriya said, pulling hard on the steering wheel to stop the Corolla from fishtailing.

The car hit us again, knocking us sideways into a black Mercedes, which earned us some angry beeping.

"Hold on!" the constable yelled. She slammed down on the accelerator, and we lurched forward, losing a side mirror as we scraped along the Mercedes. Devapriya navigated the small Corolla between vehicles, leaving millimetres of air between us and them.

"Who the fuck is that?" she yelled, eyes focused on avoiding the cars in front of her.

I glanced back. A sky-blue Audi skipped over the concrete median strip into the oncoming lanes. There were fewer vehicles headed in that direction, but more than enough to cause a serious accident. Cars swerved into each other to avoid a head-on collision. The Audi caught up to us in seconds.

"Incoming!" I yelled.

The Audi jerked, skipped back over the median strip, and slammed into our side, forcing the Corolla against the concrete traffic barrier that separated us from a narrow footpath and a five-storey-fall into the Parramatta River.

"Come on, come on! Move!" Devapriya said through gritted teeth. I didn't know if she was shouting at the surrounding traffic or her own car.

The Audi peeled away to avoid running up the back of a bus, then came back and slammed into our side. The Corolla's front left wheel caught on the concrete barrier and the whole left side of the car popped into the air before coming back down heavily onto four wheels.

"Christ!" Devapriya said.

"He's trying to kill us!" I yelled. "Shoot him!"

"I don't have my pistol!" she screamed back. "You shoot him."

Right.

"Lean back!" I yelled and cast a *sneezer*.

The snappy packet of kinetic energy burst through the window by Devapriya's face.

"Fuck!" the constable yelled.

She elbowed away the remnants of broken glass, and I threw another *sneezer* at the Audi that shattered its heavily tinted passenger window. I caught a glimpse of the man behind the steering wheel. A white mask concealed the lower half of his face, and ragged black hair covered the rest of it.

I formed another spell in my chest. A ball of energy that would blow out all the Audi's windows from the inside and push enough air into the guy's ear canals to leave him disoriented, hopefully long enough for Devapriya to do her cop thing.

I never got the chance.

The man flicked his wrist and the road in front of us exploded with a flash of red light. The Corolla's front wheels hit a bit of upturned asphalt at the same time as the Audi hit us from the side.

"Shit shit shit!" Devapriya yelled.

The nose of the Corolla jumped up on the concrete barrier, followed by the rest of the car. We spun ninety degrees and slid along the barrier, balancing like a seesaw. Something hit the car again and spun us around. We kept spinning until we slipped over the other side of the barrier and the back of the Corolla ploughed into the handrails.

The car balanced momentarily on the edge of the bridge.

"Don't move," Devapriya said.

It turned out to not be important whether I moved or not. I felt a shifting of pressure in the air as magic was manipulated. Then the car was struck by a spell that hit us with the strength of a charging rhinoceros, and our car slid backwards off the bridge.

10

—————

INSTINCTS TOOK OVER. I conjured a shield and wrapped it around us as we fell. We had passed the midpoint of the bridge, so the fall wasn't as high as it could have been. Still, whether we plunged a hundred feet or ten, the water hit us hard.

My seat broke on impact, folding backwards flat as a bed. The car bobbed back to the surface momentarily, before water started rushing in through the driver's window and we began to sink.

"Devapriya," I croaked. She looked unconscious. "Constable!" I shook her arm and got no response.

The water was up to my chest already, the weight of the engine dragging the nose of the car down quickly.

"Kyra!" I yelled.

She awoke with a start, looked at the water, then stared at me, eyes wide.

"Deep breath!" I said.

We both took in a lungful of air as the car filled with water and sunk below the surface. In seconds, we were working in the dark. I struggled with the door but couldn't push it open. I attempted to perform some hydromancy but couldn't remember how. I couldn't remember any spells. My lungs burned and all I could think about was getting fresh air.

The water pressure increased as we sank deeper into the river's murky blackness. I tried pushing the door open again. When it didn't budge, I started pounding on the window. This is what the experts call 'freaking out'.

A hand seized my arm in the darkness, and I realised Devapriya was still with me, reigniting hope that we could survive this and giving me something to focus on. I calmed myself, clearing my mind long enough to create a *lumière* that lit up the inside of the car in a blue glow.

It wasn't Devapriya holding onto me.

The creature gripping my arm had a face borne of nightmares. White, flat, and almost devoid of features, but for two small slits for a nose and two large black eyes that fixed me with an alien gaze. I lost my last bit of air as I screamed in silence.

I thrashed against the creature's grip but couldn't get out of my seat. The thing grabbed my other arm with a giant webbed hand, and I went still, my conjuration of light hovering between us. The creature released its grip on me and held up its hands, palms out, then moved one hand towards my hip. I flinched, then the seatbelt clicked open. The thing grabbed my wrist and hauled me through the driver's side window.

My new friend pulled me through the water. It felt like being towed by a speedboat. Several excruciating seconds later, we breached the surface, and I sucked in deep breaths, realising for the first time how delicious fresh air tastes. I looked up at the bridge, where several people peered over the edge to see whether we were okay. Or to hit us up for our insurance details.

I splashed around, looking for the constable. "Where's Devapriya?" I gasped. "The woman in the driver's seat."

"We've got her," the thing said. It had a perfectly normal woman's voice, which I found more disturbing than if it hadn't. "We need to get to my place. The mage is still up there."

"I can't breathe underwater," I said.

"I live in a house, you idiot," she replied. "Now hold your breath."

"Wait, I need—"

The creature dragged me under the water once again, propelling us forward with only the use of her legs. Her hand gripped my wrist like a vice, and I felt my arm trying to tear itself out of my shoulder socket. I kept my eyes firmly shut so water didn't flow into my eyes, fill my skull, and squirt out my ears.

We surfaced twice more, gaining hundreds of feet between us and the bridge each time. Eventually, we came to a stop out of sight of the bridge. However, it wasn't until my feet touched sand that I relaxed and started to feel safe. The creature hauled me onto a small beach, and I fell to my hands and knees, coughing up brackish river water. The thing grabbed my arm again and pulled me to my feet.

"We're not safe yet," she said. "Let's get in the house."

We ascended some stone steps and came to a wooden fence with a narrow gate, being held open by a diminutive young woman.

"Hurry," she beckoned.

Once we were through, she closed the gate behind us and hesitated a fraction of a second before slotting herself under my arm. The creature who'd brought me there marched up a stony path ahead of us towards a large two-storey house. I followed, helped a great deal by the woman under my arm. The yard sloped upwards towards the house, with tall square hedges along the fence line to my left and right, ensuring privacy from the neighbours.

Huge bi-fold glass doors spanned the width of the house's ground floor, the interior spacious and bright. The creature a few steps ahead of me was dressed in a T-shirt and gym shorts, and appeared as a silhouette against the bright lights, making it easy to discern powerful legs, broad shoulders. Her hands and feet looked abnormally long and wide, forcing her to take exaggerated steps as she strode forward.

Then she changed. Her shoulders narrowed, her hands and feet shrunk, and her skin lost its ghostly paleness. Dark hair sprouted from her head, somehow already slick. By the time we reached the end of the stone path, she'd transformed into a middle-aged Chinese woman.

Huh.

She pushed open the glass doors. "Inside," she ordered.

I stepped onto the tiled floor of the living room and realised I'd lost my flip-flops. No one else had shoes on, so I didn't feel too self-conscious. Devapriya sat on a beige leather couch dripping water all over the floor while an elderly man knelt before her, one hand resting below the constable's chin.

"Turn your head slowly," he said. "Do you feel any pain or discomfort?"

"I'm fine," she said, then looked up as I approached. "Finch, you okay?"

"Yeah," I said, then noticed the blood-stained towel held to her arm.

Devapriya followed my gaze. "It's fine," she said. "'Tis but a scratch."

I raised an eyebrow at the reference, struggling to imagine Devapriya watching anything that would encourage laughter. The young woman under my arm lowered me onto the couch next to Devapriya.

"Thanks," I said to her.

She nodded and left the room.

"How the hell did we survive that fall?" Devapriya said, wincing as the man pressed an ice pack to her head.

"No idea." I turned to the woman who'd just transformed before my eyes. "You're river folk."

She cocked her head to the side. "River folk," she echoed. "Yes, that sounds much better. I'm Mei Wan. We are the Baiji of the Yuan."

She closed the bi-fold doors in a hurry and started locking each section, sliding bolts into the floor and ceiling. The doors offered expansive views of the city skyline across the water, but at the moment just left me feeling vulnerable and exposed. After securing the doors, Mei moved from window to window, checking the locks. Her black hair had visible greys, but she moved with the sprightliness of someone decades younger.

"It was a stroke of luck we saw you," she said as she flitted around the room. "My daughter and I were swimming when we saw flashes on the bridge. We were just about under the car when you hit the water. Had no idea we'd be finding the skinny wizard."

"You know me?"

"The scars give you away," she said, still moving around the room. "And I saw blue energy surround the car as it fell. Broke the surface tension of the water."

So, my shield did do something.

Mei paused and turned to me. "Also, you rescued my daughter earlier in the year."

"You're Lin's mother?"

"Yes," Mei replied, her voice flat.

"I'm... I'm sorry for your loss," I said.

"Save it," the Baiji woman said, busying herself by checking the rest of the windows. "That mage is still out there somewhere."

64

"Who is it?" Devapriya said.

"A selkie mage would be my guess," Mei said. "Here to take another one of us."

The young woman returned to the room. "All doors locked. No sign of anyone at the front."

Mei nodded. "Call the others, then go upstairs and watch the street from the balcony."

"Mum, I can help—"

"Aubrey Wan!" Mei said. "Please do as I say."

The younger woman tightened her mouth, gave a final look at me, then left the room.

"Stay out of sight," Mei called after her daughter.

Mei went to the kitchen and retrieved a sword from under the sink, unsheathing the weapon from its dark wood scabbard. The straight, double-edged blade shined like new, but the cord wrapped around the grip had dirtied and frayed with use. Something in Chinese was engraved along the blade near the hilt. Mei faced the backyard, the corners of her mouth turned downwards, creating faint wrinkles.

The older man left Devapriya's side and placed a hand on Mei's shoulder. He said something in Chinese. I couldn't tell if it was Cantonese or Mandarin. Obviously.

Mei placed a hand over the man's own. "You are probably right, father. But we should be ready just in case."

I needed to call Miss Blackthorne. Reaching into my pocket, I realised my phone wasn't there. I remembered placing it in my backpack, which I'd left in the backseat of Devapriya's Corolla, which by now would be sitting at the bottom of the Parramatta River, probably next to my flip-flops.

"Hey, we need to call the Custodian," I said. "Mary Blackthorne. She can help."

Mei held her gaze on the backyard. "I think it might be too late for that."

A red haze shimmered in the darkness before the gate at the far end of the yard exploded from its hinges. A lone figure stepped through and stood on the stone path, his slick black clothes reflecting the lights of the house. The mask covering his mouth and nose appeared to be the kind normally hooked up to ventilator machines to assist patients with breathing.

"Oh, shit," Devapriya said, pulling out her phone. "I'm calling Hertz."

I drew in energy. "How long till your friends get here, Mei?"

"Too long," she replied, then said something to her father in Chinese and he scuttled out of the room. I didn't need to speak the language to know she'd told him to haul arse upstairs.

I felt the magic shift, but it wasn't me doing it. The man strode to the centre of the backyard and he started to glow. From a faint pink to a bright red. Then, a burning crimson, as if his very skin was on fire. He raised his hands as huge volumes of magical energy moved through the air.

Seconds passed, seeming to stretch out for minutes.

With a roar, the man brought down his hands, summoning a thunderous wave of dark water that surged out of the river behind him, washed over the fence, and rushed towards us.

11

———

THE WATER FLOWED either side of the man like a river passing around a boulder and charged at the house as if funnelled by invisible walls. I raised a shield, re-shaping the barrier to press against the bi-fold doors, holding them in place as water slammed against the glass.

"*Mā de!*" Mei said. "That won't last long. Get upstairs!"

I clenched my jaw. "If I go, the water breaks through."

With my defensive barrier spread so wide and thin, it lacked its usual blue shimmer and most of its strength. A glass panel shattered to my right and water started gushing through. My shield slowed the flow but couldn't stop it completely. Water spread across the tiles.

"Get out!" I said, struggling to hold back the torrent. "Devapriya! Get them out!"

On the other side of the glass, the water level rose, completely covering the doors and windows. It was like we had our own private aquarium, only the tank had sprung a leak and the great white was hungry.

Another section of glass splintered and shattered. I kept feeding my shield energy, but it was spread too wide, the water pressure was building quickly. I couldn't hold it much longer.

"We're not going anywhere," Mei said. "This is our home! I will defend it!"

Devapriya shouted something in response, but I didn't catch it due to the sizzling bolt of red energy that streaked at my head. I sensed the spell and snapped up a shield half a moment before it would have drilled into my skull. The defensive spell deflected the attack, leaving a burning hole in the fridge the width of my thumb.

With my concentration diverted, the barrier holding back the torrent of water disintegrated and a literal river burst through the glass, flooding the house in seconds. It swept Devapriya and me off our feet and washed us into the hallway. Mei braced herself against the kitchen bench and remained standing, sword held before her, ready to face the mage. She was a feisty woman, but wouldn't stand a chance on her own.

I manipulated the magic in my chest and cast a *lumière* into the water in the direction of the backyard. I gave it a few seconds before ramming a good serving of magical energy into the spell. The ball glowed bright blue, illuminating the water around it, but more importantly, showing the dark silhouette of our new friend.

I sent a stream of crackling blue energy at the shadowy figure, screaming as I forced all my remaining energy into the spell. The scars along my arm ignited with agony. My wiry frame may not be built for sport, or fighting, or anything else that requires any degree of strength or coordination, but magic is all about brains and willpower.

The spell punched through the water and looked like it struck the shadowy figure. The water went black and still, holding at chest level. The lights in the house had gone dark, probably due to a short circuit somewhere in the house's wiring. Mei seized the moment to attack and shifted into her True Form, which resembled a nightmarish dolphin. She screamed a battle cry as she charged forward, diving into the water sword first.

Constable Devapriya grabbed my arm. "Let's go, Finch!"

I pulled my arm free and stepped towards the backyard. "My spell would have barely stunned him. Mei can't take him by herself."

"We've got other people to worry about," Devapriya said, almost calmly.

I didn't like the idea of leaving anyone behind, but with the power this guy was throwing around, he would have given even Miss Blackthorne a run for her money.

There was a flash of crimson in the darkness, and I felt magic being manipulated a heartbeat before Mei exploded out of the water. She crashed into a wall and fell with a splash. Meanwhile, the windows that weren't already broken burst inwards and water yet more flooded in. Then, through the deluge and the churning black waves, I saw the man, his skin burning a furious red.

"Right," I said. "Upstairs!"

Devapriya and I helped Mei to her feet and held her between us as we waded through the chest-high water. The Baiji woman was still in her flipper form, her skin smooth and slippery. We moved slowly through the rising water, all the while expecting another bolt of sizzling red energy to hit us in the back. The stairs were only wide enough for two people to stand abreast, so I threw Mei's arm around my neck and took her weight.

"We need to move," Devapriya said from in front of me. "We'll try jumping from one of the windows up here. Hurry!"

"That man is too strong," Mei said, her voice shaky. "I couldn't even get close enough to use my *jian*."

"Just focus on getting upstairs," I said. "We'll get your father and daughter and—"

Liquid tendrils wrapped around my legs and pulled me under the surface, dragging me back downstairs. The spell felt similar to the one Miss Blackthorne used on me the night before, in the same way that a battle cruiser is similar to one of those swan-shaped paddle boats that couples rent on first dates. Still, I fought it as best I could, trying to pry away the invisible forces dragged me through the water.

I bounced around like a pinball – off the floor, the ceiling, the kitchen benches. My leg brushed against something hard on the tiles and I realised too late that it was the sword. By the time I reached for it, I had already been dragged away. I opted for a change of tack.

I gave up on fighting his hydromancy. It was far too powerful. Instead, I created another *lumière* and held it in front of me. If I was going to drown, I wanted to at least see the bastard responsible. Then the water disappeared, and I fell onto wet grass.

"You're not an elf mage, are you?" the man asked, his voice deep and coarse, and slightly muffled by the ventilator mask.

I spluttered for a few long moments and took the opportunity to suck in deep breaths. We were in a small pocket of air. Dark water raged around us harmlessly on all sides, as if we were in a submerged bubble.

I looked up at the man and recoiled.

His skin glowed, but not in the way I'd thought. Ragged scars covered every inch of exposed skin – face, neck, hands. They burned an angry crimson, bright enough to shine through his dark clothing. I had received the scars on my arms from pushing myself too hard, attempting to wield more magic than I should have. It almost killed me and was a source of constant agony. I couldn't imagine what this man had put himself through to earn his wounds.

I saw the mage's smile through the clear mask, evidently pleased at my reaction.

"Are you an elf?" the man repeated. "You don't have the ears."

"What... no. I'm a boy. Man. Human man."

"Where are your shoes?"

"Lost them," I said. "Didn't know I'd be going swimming."

The man nodded in understanding. The power emanating from the guy was staggering. It pushed against my consciousness and interfered with my ability to sense the magic around me.

"Doesn't it hurt?" I asked. "The scars?"

"Terribly."

"Who are you?"

He responded with a question of his own. "You're a wizard?"

"Apprentice."

"Ahh," he said, as if that explained everything. "You do have some command over the elements, though."

"That would be a generous way of putting it."

"It was nice meeting you," he said as he raised a glowing hand towards me. "Sorry about this, but you're being a nuisance."

This guy may have been degrees of magnitude stronger than me, but I doubted he had my psychomantic abilities. If he did, he might have sensed me manoeuvre my darkened *lumière* behind him.

I overloaded the spell, and it exploded in a brilliant flash of light with enough force to knock him off his feet, breaking the spell that held the water at bay. The bubble around us imploded and once again, I was thrown into a dark washing machine. Without the Scarred Man trying to throw me around, I could concentrate long enough to do my own bit of hydromancy.

I sucked magic in, held it momentarily, then let it flow out of me, creating *water worms* that floated unseen in the darkness. Using the *worms* as extensions of my own senses, I found what I was looking for, only for invisible hands to seize my legs once again and drag me back.

I came out of the water into another air bubble, the Scarred Man's skin a fiery red. His eyes widened, however, when he saw what was in my hands. I lashed out with Mei's sword. The tip of the blade caught him on the leg, slicing through his black trousers.

He didn't scream or howl in pain or react much in any way. He simply glared at me. Maybe they were his favourite pants. His scars glowed brighter, and I felt tremendous shifts in magical energy as he prepared to erase my existence from the face of the earth.

Hey, at least I got a hit in.

A pink shape burst through the wall of the bubble and tackled the Scarred Man into the water, followed immediately by a second figure. The bubble imploded, but rather than being thrown around in the churning currents, I felt someone grab me and drag me through the water at tremendous speed. We surfaced inside the house and I came face to face with one of the Baiji. Who regarded me with big black alien eyes.

"Where's Mei?" it said in a male voice.

"Upstairs."

The thing dragged me up the stairs, where it started calling out Mei's name.

"In here," came the reply from one of the bedrooms.

The Baiji helped me along the dark corridor. Any ambient light from outside was being blocked by the swirling water that crashed against the windows. We found Mei, her family, and Devapriya huddled by a window in what looked to be the master bedroom.

"How many did you bring, Ushi?" Mei yelled over the noise.

"Three," the man said as his body re-moulded itself into that of a lean young man wearing nothing but boxer shorts. "We came as fast as we could. Four more should be here within a couple of minutes."

"We can't fight him," I said, struggling to catch my breath. I slammed a fist into the palm of my hand emphasis. "He's too powerful. He'll tear this whole house down!"

Ever since taking up this magic business, I have noticed that the universe has an impeccable sense of comedic timing. The moment I declared our doom, the roaring waves stopped, and the water washed away from the windows. Even the clouds had cleared, allowing light from the half-moon to spill in through the windows.

I peered out the window at the backyard. Water spilled out of the house and across the lawn to the back fence, where it drained through the back gate. Seconds later, the other two Baiji appeared upstairs, having shifted back into their human forms. They must have come in a hurry because they both wore pyjamas, soaking wet.

"He's gone," said the one in the silky pink jim-jams.

"Which way?" Devapriya demanded.

"Towards the road," said the other. "We heard a car start up after the water flowed away."

"I can work with that," Devapriya said.

I still held the sword in my hand. It hummed with a strange energy, subtle but steady. I offered the weapon to Mei hilt first. "You dropped this."

Mei accepted the sword with a nod. "Let's talk."

12

TWO DOZEN BAIJI showed up at the house over the next ten minutes. Some coming by car, others from the river. They mopped, cleaned, and moved water-damaged furniture into the backyard under the direction of Aubrey, but it would be a long while before they got the dank smell of stagnant river water out of the house. Mei lent me a pair of her grandfather's shoes – an old pair of black trainers that looked like they'd done a couple laps of the country. I thought these guys were meant to swim everywhere. The shoes were a bit snug, but they fit.

One of the Baiji handed Devapriya and me fluffy white towels. We went outside and sat in metal patio seats, the least saturated pieces of furniture we could find. Once Mei saw to it that Aubrey had everything under control, and her father was resting in his bedroom upstairs, she joined us, not bothering to brush the water off the seat before sitting. The sword rested across her lap.

"Thank you for helping," she said.

"Seriously?" I replied. "We'd be at the bottom of the river if you and Aubrey hadn't pulled us out."

She waved away the comment. "You would have found a way out. I understand you defeated a demon lord earlier this year."

Devapriya arched an eyebrow at me. She knew the story. She was there.

"It was a team effort," I said.

Mei examined the constable. "Yes, I had reservations about the Custodian's partnership with the city's law enforcement." She offered

73

Devapriya a wry smile. "It seems my concerns were misplaced. Thank you for your assistance tonight, Constable."

"Likewise," Devapriya said.

I ran fingers through my damp hair, pushing it back to stop the water dripping down my face. "Can you tell us how Lin died?"

If Bree was here, she would have socked me in the arm for my abruptness. But all pretext for subtlety had sunk with Devapriya's Corolla.

Mei placed her hands in her lap and looked at the Baiji hustling back and forth. "Where do I begin…"

Devapriya wrapped the towel around her shoulders tight and leaned forward. "Why don't you start by telling us where you found her?"

Mei nodded and turned back to us. "Actually, Aubrey was the one to find her." She called out to her daughter, who came over quickly. "Dear, tell them how you found your sister."

The Baiji girl was probably around my age and a couple of inches shorter. She clenched her jaw momentarily and breathed hard through her nose.

"I heard a noise," she said, closing her eyes. "It was the middle of the night. I got out of bed to check what it was. Lin's bedroom door was open, but she wasn't in there. Then I saw a trail of blood on the floor. It led all the way down the hall, down the stairs and into the backyard. That's… that's where…" She opened her eyes. They were red and moist. She rubbed them quickly with the palms of her hands.

Mei held Aubrey's hand and squeezed gently, then turned back to us. "Lin was dead when Aubrey found her. My daughter had been stabbed several times. Stabbed in the back while she slept in her own bed." Mei spoke with rigid formality, no emotion or elaboration. She had already come to terms with losing her child. Or she had yet to face the reality of it. "She may have been trying to reach to the river. It energises us, heals us. Obviously, she didn't make it."

Devapriya focused on Aubrey and spoke with a sincere gentleness that went beyond her standard cop sensitivity training. "You didn't see anyone?"

Aubrey shook her head.

"And both of you were home at the time?"

Mei nodded. "And my father. The intruder was quiet. Well-practiced in the art of stealth."

Someone found the fuse box and flipped switches to turn the house lights back on, illuminating half of the Baiji woman's face, where I saw faint lines of worry and dark circles under her eyes.

I sat forward in my chair. "If no one saw anyone, what makes you think it was the selkies?"

"The wounds gave them away," Aubrey said. "Whoever... whoever did it... used a curved sword. A selkie sword."

"Frederico de Silva then killed the selkie ambassador as retribution," Devapriya said, looking at me for confirmation.

I nodded.

The constable sat back and frowned. To Mei, she said, "And you didn't find the weapon?"

"We did not."

"Yet you are sure it was a selkie weapon?"

"Constable," Mei said patiently. "There is no great love between the people of the sea and the river folk. I have seen enough wounds inflicted by selkie blades to recognise one when I see it."

"I won't argue with you on that," Devapriya said, crossing her arms. "Still. Pretty thin to warrant a revenge killing."

Mei's lips tightened, and she sat up straight. "We did not wish to cast blame so hastily. However, certain other river folk don't share our restraint, and bolster their confidence with the claim of superior local knowledge. Then that young Encantado went off and exacted his own vengeance. In his defence, he and my daughter were... close." She glanced at Aubrey.

"They weren't dating, Mum," her daughter said. "I told you, they were just friends."

"Were they?" Devapriya asked. "Just friends?"

Aubrey nodded. "But it didn't mean they weren't close. I've seen couples get along worse than those two." Aubrey hesitated and lowered her gaze. "It's why... it's why he got so angry. Why he killed that selkie guy."

Mei shook her head. It looked like the woman's hard exterior was close to cracking. "Such rash actions lead to more confusion. More violence. It's exactly the reason why we fled our home in the first place."

"Why the ambassador?" Devapriya said. I'd already told her why. This must have been her doing her fact checking. Or maybe she just didn't trust my advice.

"Aubrey," Mei said, turning to her daughter, "why don't you check on your grandfather? I don't want him lifting any furniture. A sprained back is all we need."

Aubrey nodded to Devapriya, gave me a small smile, and left.

Mei turned back to us. "I met Ambassador Kelden not long after we moved to the city. Clever bastard and pragmatic to a fault. Rigidly loyal to his people and their laws. If a selkie stepped out of line within two hundred miles of the city, he knew about it." She paused to collect her thoughts and when she spoke, it was with the gravitas of someone telling a grim truth. "My daughter died because the ambassador chose not to prevent it, or because he gave the order himself."

"Is there any reason why you think Lin was targeted?" Devapriya asked.

Mei narrowed her eyes. "What makes you think she was targeted?"

"I can't rule it out," said the constable. "At least, not yet."

"I can't think of any reason someone would want... want my daughter dead."

Devapriya gave Mei a few moments to gather herself before following up with another question. "The killer left the rest of you sleeping. Did they take anything? Maybe your daughter interrupted an attempted robbery?"

"We have a nice house," the Baiji woman said, "but we hardly own anything worth stealing."

"What about your sword?" I said. "It's magic?"

"It's a *jian*," the Baiji woman said, running a finger along the Chinese characters etched into the blade. "Smithed in the Ming Dynasty, funnily enough, with the intention of fighting wizards. It has minor enchantments that allow it to pierce magical constructs."

"Sounds valuable."

"But hardly rare," Mei said. "If they really wanted the *jian*, they could burgle a museum, or trawl through *eBay*."

Devapriya spread her hands. "We must also consider the possibility of mistaken identity."

"You think they were after Aubrey?" Mei said.

"I was actually thinking of you," the constable said. "You seem to hold a position of respect among the Baiji. I don't know the history of your people, but for the rest of the world, leaders and politicians have a tendency to draw these kinds of actions."

"I have had my fair share of run-ins with the selkies," Mei said, "but that is behind us. As far as I know, there have been no hostilities between the selkies and river folk since the War. There has been an uneasy peace, which we maintain by never crossing into each other's domains." She shook her head. "Why would they attack us?"

"We'll have to get back to you on that," I said. "What about the Scarred Man who attacked us tonight? He didn't look like any selkie I'd seen before."

"Just because he isn't a selkie, doesn't mean they didn't send him."

"Maybe he was the one who killed Lin," I suggested. "And maybe tonight was him attempting to come to, you know... to finish the job."

Devapriya stared daggers at me, probably wondering how to smack me on the back of the head without breaching Police Standards of Professional Conduct.

"Maybe," Mei said, and gave a thin, joyless smile. "But to me, it looked like the man was after you."

* * *

Miss Blackthorne arrived to find me dragging a mop back and forth across the floor. There was probably a spell that would make the job go quicker, but I didn't have the strength or motivation to do any magic at that point. She got me to take her to Mei.

"So, you're the Custodian," said Mei. "I was wondering when we'd meet."

Miss Blackthorne gave the Baiji woman a curt nod. "Was anyone harmed?"

"Superficial wounds only. My people are resilient."

"Describe the man who attacked you, please."

"Your apprentice got a closer look. Perhaps you should ask him."

Miss Blackthorne looked to me, and I described the Scarred Man. The spells he used, the breathing mask, the jagged lines across his face that glowed red. She frowned and got me to repeat the part about the scars.

"They were like mine," I said. "But all over his body. I'm talking from head to feet. I saw them light up under his clothes." I shook my head. "The power he gave off was mental. Even more than anything I've felt from you."

Miss Blackthorne raised an eyebrow at the comment, but let it slide.

"A selkie mage, you think?" I asked.

"I'd have to see him face to face before making a judgement. Although, I've never known a selkie to drive a car."

"Freelancer?" Devapriya said. The Old World isn't above hiring or coercing, shifty individuals to carry out dark deeds on their behalf. Human or otherwise.

"Possible. Again, we know too little."

"My people escaped persecution in China," Mei said, her voice soft and weary with fatigue. "We left the rivers our people had called home for generations to come to Sydney. This city was meant to be a Safe Haven."

"It is," Miss Blackthorne assured her. "We will get to the bottom of this. I promise."

"Thank you," Mei said. "I cannot move my people again."

Miss Blackthorne and I strode back through the house, where the Baiji worked furiously to coax out the water still covering the floor. The Master Wizard conjured a small kinetic spell as we passed that acted like a giant invisible squeegee and pushed the water across the tiles and out into the backyard. She received plenty of thanks from the Baiji but ignored them and made for the stairs. We found Constable Devapriya in Lin's bedroom, busy poking around.

"It wasn't an accident," Devapriya said. "Whoever killed Lin knew exactly what they were doing."

"How do you know?" I asked.

She gestured at the walls where thumbtacks held several photos of friends and family to a corkboard. The constable picked up a hoodie that hung off the back of a chair and threw it onto the bed. Half a wardrobe's worth of clothing covered the floor.

"Obviously the room of a teenage girl," Devapriya said. "The killer couldn't have missed all this."

"I thought girls were meant to be tidy," I said.

Devapriya made a face like I'd just asked where babies come from. She then moved over to the dressing table.

"See the drawers? All closed. Same with the drawers in the wardrobe. Spoke to Mei, and no one's gone through Lin's stuff since she was killed. People doing a smash and grab tend not to waste time closing drawers."

"Maybe they took something that was left out in the open?" I suggested.

"You're conjecturing now," Devapriya said, then lowered her voice. "We should focus on the scenario that seems most likely."

"That Lin was killed on purpose."

"Have you determined a means of entry for the killer?" Miss Blackthorne asked.

"That might be your department," replied the constable. "No signs of forced entry at the bedroom window. Or any other door or window in the house."

"So, it was magic, then," I said. "It's got to be the Scarred Man."

Devapriya tilted her head. "Or someone with a key."

"Be careful of jumping to conclusions," Miss Blackthorne said. "That's what started this whole mess."

13

WE DROVE to a large business park at the eastern end of Ryde about twenty minutes north of the Baiji house. Miss Blackthorne steered the cruiser into a parking space next to a small café, located behind a collection of cube-shaped office towers. Several outdoor tables sat on the grass, surrounded by thick gum trees and dense underbrush. If I had my geography right, the Lane Cove River ran behind those trees and fed into the Parramatta River about seven miles downstream.

The rain had stopped, leaving behind the smell of damp earth and wet leaves. A paved footpath ran across the grassed area until it hit the tree line, where it turned into a muddy path and disappeared amongst the shadows.

Devapriya hesitated.

"We'll be fine," Miss Blackthorne said as she pulled her cane out of the Land Cruiser. "I know the Mokoi best of all the river folk."

I floated a *lumière* above our heads as we walked. After five minutes of trying not to slip on the muddy ground, we came to a grass clearing at a bend in the river. I counted eighteen house boats along the water's edge, each in various states of dilapidation, with fairy lights and cheap paper lanterns strung between them. Plastic chairs had been set up haphazardly on the grass, and a large bonfire blazed in the middle of the gathering. The smell of charred meat and wood smoke drifted on the air, filling my nostrils and making my stomach grumble. A serious PA system blasted *The Best Rock Songs of The Seventies* from one of the boats, while people sang along and danced, the fire casting long shadows behind them.

"Aunty!" one of the Mokoi yelled. "Welcome to the Corroboree!" As the man approached, I recognised him as Mick from the ferry.

I leaned in close to Miss Blackthorne. "Mick's your nephew?"

"Of course not. It's simply a way to address one's elders, a sign of respect."

"Should I start calling you Aunty, then?"

She shot me a glare that could have cut through steel. "I'd rather you didn't"

With an enormous grin, Mick bent down and embraced Miss Blackthorne in a bear hug. She didn't resist but didn't hug him back, either.

"Look, everyone, Aunty Mary's here!"

Some people turned and smiled politely. Others seemed indifferent or didn't hear. A few scowled openly in her direction. It appeared that Mick's respect for the Master Wizard wasn't shared by the rest of his clan.

He looked at me, smiled wider, and held out a fist. "G'day, g'day, wizard."

"Mick," I said, returning his grin and bumping his knuckles. "My friends behaving themselves?"

"More so than the rest of us," he said with a laugh.

When I introduced Mick to Constable Devapriya, the Mokoi's eyes widened in alarm, and he shot a glance behind him where people danced and drank. He licked his lips and his jaw muscles tightened.

"Relax," Devapriya said. "I'm not here to bust anyone's balls. It's Old World business."

Mick's smile returned. "In that case, you are most welcome, Constable." He gave an exaggerated bow, making his long, dark hair fall about his face. "I apologise for my reaction. Your people and mine don't always get along."

"Maybe that's something we can work on," Devapriya said with a wry smile of her own.

"I need to see the Elders," Miss Blackthorne interrupted.

Mick's smile wavered. "This about that Encantado lad stirring shit up? Oscar and Bree have been trying to talk to the Elders all night. Obviously, no one warned them how stubborn an old Mokoi can be."

"I need to ask a favour of them."

The man smiled. "Sure you don't want to try something easier? Like curing cancer or getting the Swans to win another bloody Premiership?"

Miss Blackthorne gave him a cold stare, prompting him to raise his hands in submission.

"Okay, okay. I'll take you to them. But they barely talked to your minions. I can't promise they'll be happy to see you." He walked towards a houseboat which had two muscular Mokoi guards at the access ramp, armed with long spears.

Miss Blackthorne turned to Devapriya and me. "Find Bree and Oscar and apprise them of the situation." She cast her eyes downstream, the river barely visible beneath the overcast night sky. "We still don't know who the Scarred Man is, or his intentions."

I looked around at the Mokoi enjoying the festivities. "You think he'll come here?"

"I don't know," she said, frowning, "and that bothers me."

Mick came back and led Miss Blackthorne to the boats, while Devapriya and I headed to the throng of people by the fire.

The Mokoi river folk weren't just dolphin-esque shapeshifters. Miss Blackthorne had described them as a tribe for those who didn't have their own people. Whether they'd lost their family or had been cast out for whatever reason, the Mokoi took them in with open arms. So, even though they were a mix of mystical shapeshifters and straight up humans, they were all river folk. They were all Mokoi.

We found Bree and Oscar standing with a group of young Mokoi men and women by the fire.

"Hey, Joey!" Oscar said, grabbing me in a hug. "We missed you." His words were slurred, and his eyes seemed unable to focus properly. He let go of me, turned to Devapriya and straightened. "Good evening, Constable."

Bree watched him with a smile, then turned to me. "Fuck, dude," Bree said. "Answer your phone. You've missed half the party."

I inclined a head towards Oscar. "How much has he had?"

"The Mokoi are very generous hosts," Bree replied, turning around to raise a bottle to the small group around us. "We tried talking to the Elders, but they're crusty old bastards. Wouldn't answer any of our questions. They said we could eat and drink as much as we wanted, though, so they can't be all bad." She wrinkled her brow as her gaze flicked between Devapriya and me. "You guys look like shit. Did you go for a swim?"

I explained what happened at the bridge and the Baiji house and watched the sobriety slowly return to Oscar's eyes.

"Sorry to hear about your car," Oscar said to Devapriya. I'd already forgotten about it.

"Thanks, Oscar," she replied. "It was insured. I should be able to buy a second-hand bicycle with the payout."

"This Scarred Man," Bree said, "were his scars... like yours?"

I nodded. "He was throwing around some serious magic."

She let out a whistle and Oscar pushed his hair behind his ears.

"Sorry, what's the significance of the scars?" Devapriya said.

"If you push too much magic through your body, you can literally blow yourself up. It's how I got these." I held up my arm and showed off my own scars. "The guy who attacked us is covered in them. It means he's always pushing himself, constantly trying to expand his limits. It means he's disciplined and crazy powerful."

"And a fucking psycho," Bree chipped in. "So, did he kill the Baiji girl, or what? Must have been him, right?"

I shook my head. "Too early to tell."

Oscar adjusted his glasses. "How... how can we stop someone like that?"

"I think we best leave the Master Wizard to deal with him," I suggested.

"But what about after that?" Oscar said. "Even if Miss Blackthorne catches him, what can we do? There's no prison that could hold him. If the man is responsible for Lin's death, and if he's trying to kill Joey and Constable Devapriya, we might have to consider stopping him... you know, permanently."

I blinked. "You mean kill him?"

Bree scoffed. "Settle down, *Die Hard*."

"Think about it," Oscar said. "He attacked a police officer in full view of everyone on the bridge. If he's willing to openly attack the police, who knows how far he's willing to go? Killing him might be the only way to stop him."

I found myself quietly agreeing with Oscar's logic. And it scared the hell out of me.

"Alright, you've definitely had enough to drink," Bree said.

"No one's killing anyone," said Devapriya, with what was quickly becoming her catch phrase. She puffed up her chest, looking like she was about to give us a masterclass on due process and the separation of powers.

"Where are the newbies?" I asked, not willing to sit through a lecture outside of university hours.

Smiling with relief at the change of subject, Oscar pointed to the fire. "See all those people dancing? They came here last week. About twenty of them." He pointed to another group, huddled together on one of the boats and keeping to themselves. "They came a week before that. The Mokoi are expecting a few more before the end of the year, too. As are the Encantados and the Baiji."

"That's a lot of river folk," I said.

"We're stronger together," Mick said as he approached. "And safer. I just left your Master Wizard with the Elders." He shook his head. "I give it two minutes."

"Safer?" Oscar asked.

"Oh, the usual. Bunyips in the Daintree. Maenads trying to harvest our organs. And those Venerati bastards, of course." He spread his arms wide. "For all its shortcomings, this city is our own little oasis."

I asked why the Mokoi didn't like wizards.

Mick chuckled. "It's not a blanket rule. Most of them just aren't too keen on Mary Blackthorne. As far as I know. She is the only person to have ever been kicked out of the Mokoi."

"She was part of your tribe?"

"Once upon a time," he said. "But that was years ago. Over a century. So, don't ask me what she did to get exiled. Unfortunately, my people can hold grudges for generations. I'm probably one of the few who generally get along with her."

A commotion erupted on one of the boats. Mick checked his watch and let out a low whistle. A shouting match between several grey-haired Mokoi spilled out onto the grass. Before long, the music stopped and everyone at the gathering turned their attention towards the disruption. Miss Blackthorne appeared on the deck, leaning heavily on her cane, stoic as ever, her eyes narrow slits as she observed the Mokoi arguing amongst themselves.

"Get that damn sorcerer out of here," one of the women said.

"She can help," a man replied. He had a long white beard and a ring of hair around his scalp. "She's the Custodian."

"She's a damn murderer, is what she is," another man said. "And now she's working with the police. We're fine without her!"

"We need her!" said someone else.

It went back and forth like this for a while.

Mick grimaced. "Yeah, the Elders who grew up around here don't have much love for your Master Wizard. Not sure why. Some of the new Elders just plain don't like wizards. So, now we've got a dozen tribal leaders from all parts of the country, all wanting to run things their own way." He sighed and looked at us with a forced smile and shrugged. "Forty thousand years of being separated by desert and rain-forest. This is what you get when you jam them back together. We're all still learning how to play nice." He smirked at me. "But you guys would already know all about that."

"We've had some experience," I said. "How about you? Do you trust her?"

"Blackthorne? Yeah. I reckon she does a pretty good job at holding the city together. I feel safe. My family feels safe. That's all I care about. People forget how dangerous it is for us out there."

One of the Elders, a tall thin man with a neatly combed beard and wild grey hair held down by a brown headband, broke from the group and approached Miss Blackthorne. They exchanged a few words before the Master Wizard frowned at the man and limped off the boat. She stalked over to us, ignoring the bickering Mokoi Elders.

"So," I said. "Looks like that went well."

"Let's go. I won't get any further with them."

"I'd better go calm everyone down," Mick said, leaving at a run towards the Elders.

By the time we reached the tree line at the edge of the clearing, the music had started up again and people were back to the business of having a good time.

The constable took the front passenger seat when we got back to Miss Blackthorne's Land Cruiser and the rest of us got in the back. The SUV technically fit five people, but squashing three in the backseat was never comfortable, even for young wizards with notoriously skinny frames. I didn't much appreciate Oscar and Bree forcing me into the middle seat, either. We drove back to the Inner West in silence and dropped Devapriya off at Redfern Police Station.

"I need to log the car accident," Devapriya said. "I really should have done it an hour ago. Don't know what the hell to put in the report, though."

"I'm sorry to have put you in harm's way tonight," Miss Blackthorne said.

The constable fixed her the Master Wizard with an emotionless stare. "I'll see if anyone's reported a stolen car. The Scarred Man would have had to turn up on a traffic camera somewhere."

"You don't need to do that," Miss Blackthorne said.

"It's not a hard process, I just need to submit a request to—"

"You misunderstand me, Constable. Don't go after him, he is dangerous."

Devapriya remained silent for several seconds, her jaw muscles clenching. "I'll log my traffic incident and get an Uber home," she said eventually.

"Good idea," Miss Blackthorne said. "Thank you again for your assistance tonight."

On the way back to Newtown, Miss Blackthorne took an abrupt left turn, guiding the car through backstreets towards her place. I got a sudden sinking feeling in my stomach. Oscar asked where we were going.

"It's Thursday night," Miss Blackthorne replied. "You've got practice."

"Come on!" I said. "I was almost killed tonight. Killed! I'm bloody wrecked. Oscar's half pissed. We need to—"

She drove straight past the Old Substation Building without slowing down.

I traded a look with Oscar and frowned. "So, we're not training?"

"Of course not," Miss Blackthorne said.

"Was that your attempt at a joke?"

"I needed a little levity," the Master Wizard said, straight-faced as ever. "The next few days will be hard enough. You need some rest."

There you go, miracles can happen.

I thought it might be a good time to follow up on what Mick had told us.

"You used to be part of the Mokoi tribe," I said, earning an uncertain glance from Oscar.

"Correct," Miss Blackthorne replied.

"But they kicked you out."

"Do you have a question?"

"What happened?"

"I'm not answering that. And I'd appreciate it if you didn't bring up the subject again."

"Fine. Can you at least tell us what happened on the houseboat that got the Elders all riled up tonight?"

"Oh, that. I asked them to take me to their god."

14

THE CONJURATION of green energy dragged itself through the air towards me. I could have stepped to the side and let it pass, but that wasn't the point of the exercise. I willed a shield into existence and let the spell slap against it.

"Feed it more energy," I instructed.

"I can't!" Isabella yelled through gritted teeth. "I'm doing as much as I can."

"You can do it," I called back. "Just a bit more!"

The curly-haired woman screamed, and I felt a slight increase in the push against my defensive spell. Then the energy disappeared, followed by the spell itself. Isabella leaned forward, hands on knees, gasping for breath.

"That was good," I lied.

"You're improving," said Oscar, even less truthfully.

"Thanks guys," she said, looking up. Her face glistened with sweat. "No need to bullshit, though. I just can't push any harder."

Isabella Mendez moved over to the couch and fell into it, a hand on her forehead. "It feels like my brain's about to explode."

Since finding out she'd been getting magic lessons on the sly from Miss Blackthorne's last apprentice, the late Bruce Longley, Oscar and I had taken it upon ourselves to continue with her training. We maintained a strict regime of weekly lessons every Saturday morning. Unless we were hungover. Or she had a shift. Or we just felt like having a bit of a sleep in.

We generally practiced in our living room, which was narrow but long. Punching holes through the walls or windows wasn't of major concerns. Isabella had plateaued early on, seemingly unable to attain the levels of control or power Oscar and I reached after only a few weeks of instruction. It could have been genetics, could have been attitude. Or maybe Saturn's moons weren't in position the night she was born. The fact is, no one really knows what makes one person more adept at wielding magic than another.

"Maybe I should do the sparky spell again," Isabella said hopefully. The spell zapped your nervous system like a mild Taser and was pretty cool if you weren't on the receiving end.

"You can already do that one," I said.

She frowned.

"Look, everyone has different strengths. Different limits. You need to push yourself if you want to improve."

"And get scars like you?" she said, wincing half a moment later. "Sorry. I just wish I was as good at making spells as you guys. I can't even do that *sneezy* thing you do."

"*Sneezer.*"

"Yeah, that one. Are you sure we shouldn't tell Miss Blackthorne about me?"

"Definitely not," I said. I didn't want Isabella getting dragged into the dangerous world of monsters and demons and scarred mages with serious cases of road rage.

"It's better if you keep a safe distance from what we do," Oscar said. "Really."

"I literally almost got murdered last night," I said.

Isabella tilted her head, unsure whether I was joking.

A tall, blonde pile of muscle came in through the front door, carrying a cardboard tray with four coffees. Well, three coffees and a mochaccino.

"Timing," I said, and grabbed the drinks for Oscar and myself. "Cheers, Alex."

"No worries. Now where's my spicy Mexican?" he said with a dimpled grin. "Ah, there you are."

Isabella grabbed a coffee and planted a big, fat kiss on Alex's lips. They let the kiss linger just long enough to make me feel awkward, then separated. Alex took the last coffee from the tray and sat on the couch, while Isabella plonked down next to him, resting both legs over his lap.

Alexander Hammond captained the First-Grade university rugby team and was a former teammate of Bruce Longley. He had honest eyes, a disarming smile, and a ridiculous jawline. He and Isabella had met at Bruce's funeral earlier in the year and made their relationship official a month later. The week after that, Isabella came clean on the whole magic thing to him, despite explicit instructions to keep a lid on it.

"How's the lesson coming along?" Alex said, taking a tentative sip of his coffee.

"She's doing well," I lied again.

"I suck," Isabella said, pouting at him.

"That's fine," he said, and squeezed her calf reassuringly. "You just need practice." He looked at Oscar and me. "Right?"

I shrugged. "Maybe. We haven't been doing this for too long either, remember? We're still trying to figure out how it all works. Magic is weird."

Truth is, we could have pushed Isabella harder. Could have forced her to grow as a magic user. It's what Miss Blackthorne did to Oscar and me. What she still does. We suffer through the pain and brutality of her lessons almost every night of the week. Effective, sure. But it takes a special kind of person to inflict that kind of pain on someone with such dogged consistency.

"Just keep practicing," I suggested.

Alex nodded and gave Isabella an apologetic look, as if to say sorry on behalf of the universe.

"We should probably call it a day anyway," I said. "We've got some errands to run."

* * *

WE HIT a pawn shop on King Street that had everything from second-hand saxophones and collectible movie posters to diamond rings and old-timey cuckoo clocks. An overweight white guy with round spectacles that were too small for his head smiled at me from behind the glass counter.

"Back again?" he said, grinning with the knowledge that I usually dropped about a hundred bucks every time I walked through the door.

"Got anything new?" I asked. "Old new."

He gestured at the counter. "Take a look."

I examined the phones. They ranged from recent folding touch screens to the Nokias that cavemen would have used to send each other woolly mammoth recipes.

I hated spending money on phones. I'd gone through five that year already. A girl had broken one when she rudely interrupted our first date by trying to kidnap me and offer me up as a vessel for a demon. Isabella had zapped a couple by accident. I'd also dropped a phone onto the concrete when I tripped over an uneven bit of footpath. Then there was the one sitting at the bottom of the river.

I selected a seven-year-old refurbished Samsung, checked that it worked, then handed over a hundred and twenty hard-earned clams.

"See you next time," the guy said.

As Oscar and I headed for the door, I caught something on the edge of my senses. A vibration in the air. I stopped and looked around, seeing nothing out of the ordinary.

"Looking for something else?" the guy called out from the counter, an edge of hope in his voice.

"Just browsing," I said.

What the hell was it?

"You ok?" Oscar whispered.

"Yeah, there's something..." I moved over to the rings on display by the window, but the vibrations eased, so I stepped back. I followed the tremors to a row of plastic containers, opened one, and found a collection of mismatched earrings and cheap bracelets. This must be where the guy stored the less flashy bits of jewellery. I poked through the containers until my fingers brushed along something that buzzed against my skin. I pulled out a necklace made of brown cord with two rectangular pieces of brown cloth, one on the back, one on the front.

The man's smile faltered when I took it to the counter.

"Twenty bucks for that," he said.

I frowned. "You're kidding. It's just a bit of string."

"It's a scapular," he said. "Catholics reckon you can't go to hell if you wear one when you die. Bargain, in my opinion."

I handed over a twenty, but not without grumbling. It did sound like a good deal, but as a rule, I don't trust magical items. And I trusted the guy slinging used electronics even less.

"Finding religion?" Oscar asked when we left the shop.

I held up the scapular and inspected it. One of the cloth rectangles had an image of a monk dressed in robes, holding a shepherd's crook, the other had a woman in armour. Latin text bordered both images. Yes, I can identify Latin. But don't ask me to translate it.

"There's magic in this thing."

Oscar raised his eyebrows. "Are you sure?"

"Positive."

"Do you really want to hold it that close to your face, then?"

I've been told by several people wiser than me not to touch magical items if I don't know what they do. So, naturally, I put the scapular around my neck. I couldn't help it. I'm the guy that has to touch the pan if someone says it's hot, or to run my finger across the fence if there's a *wet paint* sign.

Oscar leaned away from me. "Anything?"

I shook my head, noticing nothing besides a tightness in my chest, as if the small reserves of energy I held there repelled the magic in the item. Like two magnets pushing apart.

"Feels a bit funny."

"Okay, come on, then. Take it off," he said, like a mother telling her child to remove a T-shirt stained with chocolate. "We need to give it to Miss Blackthorne."

"Yeah, yeah," I said, removing the scapular and putting it in my pocket. Having magical trinkets sprinkled about the city was dangerous. The right magical item in the wrong hands was a recipe for disaster.

We walked the half hour to Miss Blackthorne's place, taking advantage of a break in the rain. The smell of wet asphalt hung around, mixed with the inviting smell of fresh bread from the bakeries and cafés along the road. I asked Oscar how Georgie Boy was doing.

"He's good, I guess."

"You guess?"

"It's hard keeping such a big secret from him," Oscar said, his eyebrows pinching together. "Even for someone who misses as much as he does."

Having the ability to wield the unseen powers of the universe can be a tricky gift to hide. Especially when your housemates are equally weird.

"Have you thought about telling him?"

"All the time," Oscar said. His voice was tight, so I dropped the issue. Oscar's a big boy. He could make his own decisions.

We let ourselves in to Miss Blackthorne's place but couldn't find her in the cavernous living room or the eight rooms that branched from it, so we headed to her personal library at the back of the building. Books, ranging from century-old medicine texts to trashy horror novels, filled massive bookshelves that reached the two-storey ceiling, along with knick-knacks that could have been worthless or priceless. Light spilled in through the tall, arched windows that offered expansive views of the railway below and the rooftops of the Inner West.

We moved to the small door in the back corner of the library and descended the staircase, our footsteps echoing sharply against the bare concrete surfaces. At the first landing, we entered a corridor. The stairs kept going down to lower levels, but Miss Blackthorne warned us not to go down there or we could very well die, and I was more than happy to heed that particular bit of advice, as she was not prone to hyperbole.

We stepped into our usual training room, full of old furniture and haphazardly scattered rugs. Scorch marks and fist-sized holes decorated every surface. The room was notably absent of any Master Wizards.

"Maybe she got delayed?" Oscar suggested. "She still has to organise that meeting with the selkies."

I shook my head. "She said she was home."

Miss Blackthorne entered the room and fell heavily into one of the armchairs by the wall. She let the cane drop to the floor and sat silently for a few moments before looking our way.

"What are you two doing here?"

"You told us to come," I replied.

Miss Blackthorne frowned. "I said midday."

"It is midday," Oscar said.

"Already?"

Oscar flashed me a nervous glance.

I approached her and said, "Are you okay? You... did you even sleep last night?"

"After dropping you home, I visited the Fish Market to find out

93

about the Scarred Man. I can't very well have an unnamed mage knocking cars off bridges and assaulting my apprentices."

"The Fish Market?" I said.

"I know some water mages there. Unfortunately, nobody knew of anyone powerful enough to do what you described at the Baiji house. So, I returned here and have spent some time downstairs looking for answers."

"You still haven't told us what's down there."

"And I have no intention of doing so at the present time."

I lowered my voice a little, not to sound threatening, but just to remind her of what she promised me when I agreed to be her apprentice. "Remember, be straight with us."

"I am," she said, meeting my stare.

"Do you think the Scarred Man was working for the selkies?" Oscar asked, dispelling the unseen tension in the air.

"It's possible," Miss Blackthorne replied, "but that wouldn't explain why Joseph was attacked. And the only selkie I know who could have arranged such a mercenary was Ambassador Kelden." She paused, then said, "Perhaps he was working of his own accord..."

"Add it to the list of questions for when you meet the selkies," I said.

She tilted her head to the side. "An option. But as you have undoubtedly noticed, people of the Old World aren't always forthcoming with the truth." Present company included, I thought. "Queen Alehtta has arranged a meeting with the selkie ambassador tomorrow," Miss Blackthorne continued. "What did she request in return for her assistance?"

I shrugged. "I need to find a Well of Power so she can move her people to a new home."

She remained silent for a full minute, then sighed deeply. "That... is a formidable task."

"So, I've heard. May as well give it a crack though, right? I mean, I should just follow my magical nose until I stumble across one."

"There are no Wells of Power in this city. At least not anymore."

"Are you sure?"

"I am almost certain."

Oscar frowned. "The way Alehtta described them, I got the impression they existed for thousands of years."

"It depends," Miss Blackthorne said. "Wells of Power are tears in reality. They touch all planes of existence, from the Realms Above to the Realms Below. Think of them as highly concentrated points of The Cascade, where the magical energy permeating the universe is especially dense."

"And the magic, what... leaks out?" I asked.

"Essentially."

"If the Wells of Power are tears that extend to all realms, that means they reach all the way to hell... and the Dark Realm. Shouldn't demons be constantly pouring through?"

"Magic flows from high energy areas to low. Going against the current would be like swimming up a waterfall. Of course, that's not to say it hasn't happened."

I had the sudden urge to renege on my deal with the elves. Miss Blackthorne hoisted herself out of the chair and Oscar rushed forward to pick up her cane.

"Thank you," she said. "I will need you boys to organise an audience with the god of the Parramatta River."

"Sure, I think I've got him on speed dial."

"Don't be a smart alec," Miss Blackthorne said, leaning on her cane. "And I believe the god is, in fact, a goddess."

"Gods can be male and female?"

"And everything in between." She walked to the door while she talked. "If I am to meet with the selkies tomorrow, I need to be prepared. The goddess will know whether a selkie has been in her river. She might even know who the Scarred Man is."

The Master Wizard led us back to the concrete stairs.

"If I'm not mistaken," Oscar said, "the Mokoi already refused to take you to their goddess. What makes you think they'll listen to us?"

"You're not going to the Mokoi," she said and sighed. "I would like you to get in contact with a friend of mine. Arthur. He has lived here longer than anyone, gods and goddesses notwithstanding, and fought by my side against the Venerati Sanctus as part of the Vanguard. If there's one person besides the Mokoi who can get in contact with the river goddess, it's Arthur."

"Okay," I said. "Do you have his number?"

"He doesn't have a phone. And getting to his residence is... difficult," Miss Blackthorne said. Of course it is. We wouldn't want to make things too easy. "I am in no shape to take you. Luckily, there is another who knows how to get there."

After Miss Blackthorne told us, she turned and hobbled out of the room, then descended the stairs into the darkness of the lower levels. As Oscar and I left, I kept wondering who had killed Lin. The Scarred Man was the obvious choice, but why? And why would he use a selkie weapon to do the deed? Maybe it was a ritual, or potentially a sea elf version of a political assassination. Or perhaps the ambassador had orchestrated the murder and deserved the lethal retribution. Whoever killed Lin, and whatever their motivation, we had three days to figure it out. Three days to prevent a war.

Yet, despite the impending violence, the one thing that really stuck with me was the fact that, for the first time since I'd known her, Miss Blackthorne admitted to having a friend.

15

WITH TRAINING CANCELLED for the day, I found myself with a rare three hours of free time and because I'm a good boy, decided to get stuck into an Engineering Dynamics assignment due the following week. I pulled out the notes Oscar took for the classes I'd missed and got to work.

I stopped when my stomach rumbled and called Oscar to see if he fancied grabbing dinner at the pub. He heartily agreed with my suggestion. There are only so many bowls of rice and tuna you can eat before your stomach refuses to accept it anymore. Apparently, there's something about a risk of mercury poisoning too, which would honestly be a surprising way to go, given my extracurriculars.

It rained as we walked to Nelly's, the Irish pub on King Street where Bree slings us free drinks whenever she can get away with it. It sits in the off-kilter heart of Newtown, the bohemian centre of Sydney's Inner West, where the city's more colourful individuals like to spend their time.

The pub had been semi-demolished by a rampaging bear-warrior back in March but had since come under new management and been renovated, complete with identical dark wood furnishings and faux-Irish memorabilia. They'd even reinstated the floor to its original stickiness.

The Saturday night crowd had come out in force, and we couldn't find a free table. Even the old granny couches with the cracked leather had people perched on the armrests.

"You guys looking for a table?"

We turned to see Bree, flustered but grinning. She wore black jeans and a black polo top, with a chequered blue dishcloth slung over her shoulder.

"Yeah," I said. "Looks like we should have come earlier."

"It's been busy all day. Shitty weather always drives people to the pubs early. I'll get you a table over here."

"You don't have to, Bree," Oscar said as she led us through the crowd. "We can stand."

"Oh, hush," Bree said and approached a table of three young men, well on their way to a rough morning. They all sported carefully styled hair and button-up party shirts. "Sorry, guys," Bree said to them. "Up you get. Table's reserved."

One of the men eyed Bree and scratched at a tasteless soul patch before taking a long sip from his rum and coke. His gaze lingered on her before sliding past her to Oscar and me.

"Didn't see a sign," he said in a slow drawl.

"Doesn't matter. You're going to have to find another table or stand, sorry."

"Look, love," Soul Patch said. "We've been here for hours. We're spending the money that pays your salary. Don't you think it's fair that we should stay?" He waved a hand through the air as if to shoo us. "Just give them a different table."

Bree smiled at them sweetly. "Come on, guys. Maybe you should find somewhere else to spend the rest of the night."

"Is that an offer?" Soul Patch replied with a lopsided grin. His mates smirked at each other. "You know, I don't normally go for Lebo chicks, but—"

Bree reached across and grabbed a fistful of the man's perfect hair, yanking him out of his seat and dragging him across the table. Glasses smashed, drinks were spilled. Soul Patch brought up both hands and tried to pry away Bree's fingers. He had no chance. Not with that demon inside her. Bree brought the man's face close to hers, so they were an inch apart.

"I strongly recommend that you and your buddies find another establishment." When the man didn't reply, she pulled on his hair and jerked his head back. "What do you say?"

"Sure," the man choked out.

She let go, and he fell to his hands and knees. His mates shot out of their seats, unsure of what to do. Bree was more than happy to offer a suggestion.

"Fuck off," she said.

They almost tripped over each other as they pulled Soul Patch to his feet and stumbled towards the exit.

"You really didn't have to do that," Oscar said.

"They come in every week and drink till they pass out or start a fight. Let me clear this shit up for you." Bree disappeared behind the bar, returning with a bin and a multi-purpose cleaning spray. She cleaned up the broken pieces of glass, then wiped down the table.

"If you're here for dinner, try the nachos. We just added them to the menu."

I went to the bar and ordered drinks and food. I returned to the table to find a woman sitting opposite Oscar, dressed in a figure-hugging white dress that stopped just above the knee. Raven hair fell over pale shoulders as the woman fixed Oscar with a seductive grey-eyed stare. I placed the two pints and our food buzzer on the table and took a seat.

"I see you've made a new friend, Oscar."

"I feel... weird," he said, eyes half-closed, his voice far away. "Joey... I think she's a—"

"Vampire," I said and glared at the woman, who gave me a thin-lipped smile. "What are you doing here?"

"I just came to say hello and meet you in person," she said, her voice smooth and seductive. "The whole Family is abuzz with talk of the skinny wizards ever since the debacle with Clémence and Vikto-ria." I felt her glamour pushing against my senses. I've had literal demons try to claw their way into my mind, so this was more like a light cranial massage.

I glanced at Oscar before turning back to the woman. "Cut it out."

"Whatever do you mean?"

"Don't make me ask again," I snarled.

She gave an exaggerated sigh, and I felt the invisible press of her glamour subside. Oscar blinked hard, then removed his glasses and pinched the bridge of his nose. He'd be fine.

"Shouldn't you be off trying to seduce teenage virgins?" I said, hoping the false bravado would conceal my unease at being the subject of conversation among the vampire Family Dragos.

"I thought I was."

"Nice try, but no." I leaned in. "I could burn you to a crisp, you know. Encase you in fire so hot you'd look like an overdone chicken kebab."

She leaned back and regarded me with an amused smile. "So, do it."

Oscar put his glasses back on and stared at the woman. "Is there something we can help you with?"

"Sure. How about you two quit?"

"Excuse me?" I said.

"Give it up. Throw in the towel. You didn't impress everyone when you thwarted Astaroth's attempt to invade this world. From what I heard, it's more a case of dumb luck that we don't have a demon army rampaging through the city right now."

I rolled my eyes with as much insolence as I could muster. "And you think Family Dragos could do a better job? Blah blah, change the record. Penni is on board with Miss Blackthorne as Custodian, and so is your Father, Vasily. Get used to it."

The woman's eyes flashed red, and she sprang to her feet in one quick, fluid movement. I was about to let loose a *sneezer* – strike hard and strike fast, Miss Blackthorne says – when another vampire appeared.

"Yvette," Stefan said. "You're not causing trouble in my pub, I hope?" His voice betrayed amusement more than concern.

"Just having a friendly conversation," the vampire woman replied icily, keeping her narrowed eyes on Oscar and me as their colour returned to a lifeless grey.

Stefan grinned. "Now when have you ever engaged in a friendly conversation? I don't think Penni would appreciate you causing trouble in the Family's brand-new establishment."

Yvette scowled at him and looked around the room. "The place reeks of beer and sweat. And flesh. How do you stand it?"

"It's all about finding your centre," Stefan said pensively. "Striking that balance between hunger and abstinence. Plus, I like the hours. And trivia night is a right hoot."

"It's disgusting," Yvette said, almost spitting the words. "This isn't what we do. It's not who we are. Penni is a fool for trying to ingratiate us with the humans."

"I'm sure he'd love to hear your opinions firsthand," Stefan said cheerfully. "We all know how receptive he is to constructive criticism." I had met Penni, the acting leader of the vampires in Sydney. He seemed like the kind of person to accept criticism as readily as a stake to the heart.

Yvette scowled.

"Woolies is still open," Stefan said. "Go buy yourself a steak. I think the T-bones are on sale."

The woman glared daggers at him, to which he responded with a smile, his grey eyes shining. Without another word, Yvette left, slinking through the crowd like a snake through tall grass. Stefan chuckled and took the seat she had vacated.

"Ahh, Yvette," he said, shaking his head. "Sorry about her. Her head's stuck in the Middle Ages. Still sees you as food and not the delightful sources of mischief and mayhem that you truly are."

I shifted in my seat uncomfortably, while Stefan leaned back in the chair and ran his thumbs up and down his leather suspenders. He'd started wearing them to fit in with the theme of his new role as the resident publican of Nelly's Irish Pub. He claimed it gave him a more folksy vibe.

"Oh, Yvette's harmless," Stefan said. "Wouldn't dream of breaking Father's rules, lest he get wind of it upon his return. Did you boys get food? The nachos are fantastic."

"You can't taste them," Oscar said.

"That's true. But I hear great things. You didn't pay, did you?"

"We got a discount from the bar staff. Miss Blackthorne doesn't want us accepting handouts," Oscar said. "Says it's a path to corruption."

"Even if it's just a plate of melted cheese on Doritos," I grumbled.

"Hard to believe the old bat has grown some morality," Stefan said. "But I guess we all change, don't we?"

"We... have a favour to ask," Oscar said.

Stefan grinned, rolled up his sleeves, and rested his elbows on the table. "Brilliant. Another adventure. I'm in."

Oscar and I made a face.

"Come on, boys," the vampire said, spreading his hands. "Despite what Mary tells you, not everyone in the Old World operates on favours. We've saved each other's lives."

Stefan hovered in that grey area between acquaintance and friend. Although he had proven himself to be worthy of at least a little trust.

"We need to visit a friend of Miss Blackthorne."

"I assume you mean Arthur?" Stefan said.

"Yeah, how'd you know?"

"Jörmungandr could count the number of friends Mary has on one hand."

I stared blankly.

"He's a snake," the vampire said. "So, he doesn't have... never mind."

Bree came by carrying two plates with double the regular amount of nachos, with added chips and calamari rings dumped on the side.

"I got them to add as much extra shit as they could fit in."

I nodded and gave a thumbs up, already with a mouthful of corn chips and melted cheese.

"We're going on an adventure," Stefan said. "Care to join us?"

Bree frowned and looked at us. I was working on forcing the nachos down my throat, so Oscar filled her in.

"We're visiting a friend of Miss Blackthorne. He might be able to take us to the Goddess of the Parramatta River."

She raised an eyebrow. "I'll pass. I'm on till midnight."

"Don't worry about that," Stefan said with a wave of his hand. "As your omnipotent boss, I give you permission to come with us. The others can cover for you."

"What, and leave them short-staffed on a Saturday night? You're dreaming."

"What did I do to deserve such a devoted employee?" he said sweetly.

"Piss off, creep," Bree said, then turned to us. "Be careful, guys." She glared at Stefan once more before moving from table to table, collecting empty glasses.

"That woman is a firecracker," the vampire said. "We can go when you finish up your dinner. Make sure you go to the loo. It's a bit of a drive."

16

AFTER OUR MEALS, Stefan took us out the back to a bright red Mercedes S-Class.

"Traded in the Porsche?" I said as we got in.

He gave me a confused look. "Why would I trade it in? I love my Porsche. I thought this baby could be useful, though. It's actually got a backseat. You know, in case you fellas need to drag my corpse around again."

That had been an ugly night. Stefan had been mangled by a rather nasty demonic thrall, while Oscar and I almost had our eyes clawed out by another. It had served as a rude awakening as to just how insanely dangerous the Old World could be.

"Hey," I said as I got in the car, "aren't you already a corpse?"

Stephan laughed.

We drove north for an hour and entered Ku-ring-gai National Park, speeding along winding roads that meandered through the dense eucalyptus forest. Stefan drove with reckless abandon, his super-human senses allowing him to see bends in the road before the head-lights lit them up. I gripped the door handle and suppressed my urge to yell at the vampire to slow the hell down.

We stopped at a small car park that looked like the starting point for several hiking trails. I was glad I'd worn shoes this time.

"This way," Stefan said, getting out of the car and starting down one of the tracks.

Oscar and I followed close behind, conjuring *lumières* for ourselves.

A wooden staircase that still smelled of fresh timber led us down a slight incline before dropping us into a valley. The ground levelled out and the wooden walkway gave way to a dirt trail enshrouded by ghostly white gum trees.

After several minutes, Stefan led us away from the walking trail, taking a sharp right into thick woodland, where the smell of wet earth and rotting leaves hung heavy in the air. In the darkness, in the dead of night, I could see why we needed a tour guide. And I couldn't imagine it being much better in the day. Branches and underbrush pulled at our clothes, and I tried not to think about the creepy crawlies that had probably worked their way into my hair. We kept walking until we hit a small stream.

"Damn," Stefan said.

"Problem?" I asked, stepping up next to him.

"I forgot about the rain. I don't do running water."

"What do you mean? It's not too deep. We can just walk across."

Stefan grimaced and looked upstream then down, his sensitive eyes searching for something that obviously wasn't there. "Running water purifies," he said. "Being a creature of darkness" – he made quotation marks in the air – "my body objects to such impositions. It's a vampire thing."

"We crossed the Harbour without any trouble," Oscar said.

"We took the tunnel, which is embedded in solid sandstone thirty feet deep with metre-thick concrete walls." He put his hands on his hips. "It may be narrower further upstream, so let's head this way and find a place thin enough to cross."

"I don't think that's necessary," Oscar said. "Joey and I can get us over."

"We can?"

"Well, not over. But... we can try re-directing the flow."

I examined the stream in the pale light of our spells. It was twenty feet across and probably wouldn't even reach past our knees. But there's a reason why so many people drown in floods. Water in motion is a force not to be underestimated.

"You want us to re-direct a river?" I said.

"It's hardly a river," Oscar said. "Look, it's easy. We dig out a new trench, then you can use your water magic to change the stream's direction."

With no other ideas, I agreed to giving it a try. We used basic kinetic spells to dig the trench. I found it easiest to conjure a *sneezer* with its origin point beneath the ground, then explode it upwards, like I was breaking ground for an incredibly small mining operation. Oscar had taken a far more efficient approach and created a river of dirt and stone that twisted through the air like an earthy snake, drawing soil from the ground and displacing it just in front of Stefan. He moved dirt three times quicker than I did, and a hundred times more gracefully, all the while maintaining his *lumière* for both of us.

Ten minutes later, we had a trench ten feet wide by three feet deep that ran parallel to the stream.

I wiped the sweat from my forehead. "Tell you what. If this magic schtick doesn't work out, we can get into the backyard pool business."

"Impressive, boys," Stefan said as he stepped onto the small mountain of excavated dirt before him. "I'll just wait up here, shall I?"

I turned to the stream and flexed my hydromancy muscles, injecting my magic into the stream to control the water from within. However, every time a *water worm* took shape, it disappeared almost immediately. After three unsuccessful attempts, I gave up.

"It's not working," I said. "Any magic I infuse into the water gets washed away."

Oscar pressed his lips together in thought. "Shields?"

"That's a lot of water pressure, man."

"I believe in you, boys," Stefan called out from atop his pile of dirt.

Oscar and I conjured translucent barriers that curved away from us. Defensive spells naturally curve around you, so re-shaping them takes a bit of brain muscle. We stood side by side and let the stream slam against our shields and flow to the side.

After several minutes, we'd successfully re-directed the flow of the stream behind us and redistributed the mound of dirt to serve as a makeshift levee at the bend to maintain the new flow path.

"Forget pools," Oscar said, taking off his glasses to wipe his brow. "Do you know how much earthworks companies make?"

I didn't reply, too busy sweating and gasping for breath.

Stefan put a tentative foot on the damp ground that minutes earlier had been the stream bed. He chuckled. "I really need to spend more time with you, lads. This way."

We came to a waist-high barbed wire fence, the kind you see

around sheep paddocks. It bent and twisted around the trees, with no sign saying what was on the other side. We squeezed through and I was careful to avoid the rusted barbs, afraid that even the smallest cut would trigger Stefan's base instincts. I'd seen him go full vampire before, and that was something I didn't want to be on the receiving end of.

We moved deeper into the forest where the moonlight failed to penetrate the dense canopy and the bush became so thick, we had to hold our *lumières* right up to our faces.

I heard something among the trees to our left. The rustle of dead leaves, the snap of a dry twig. I dismissed it as a wallaby or a large lizard, until I saw something else on our right. It moved slowly, its shadowy silhouette disappearing then reappearing in the gaps between the ferns and trees.

"I think we're being followed."

Oscar adjusted his glasses and looked around. "Are we?"

"Don't mind them," Stefan said. "The forest is home to several dryads and spriggans, and they're rather protective of our friend. Don't show any signs of aggression and we'll be fine."

The canopy thinned momentarily, and in the pale moonlight, I saw the creature shadowing us. It looked almost like a lion made entirely of twisting white branches and dead wood, stalking through the forest no more than fifteen feet away. Its shoulder would have reached my chin, but despite its size, it moved through the vegetation with barely a noise. With its head lowered, it watched us with glowing green eyes.

I sensed another beast on our other side. Made of the same gnarled branches, but covered in more green foliage, this creature was smaller and resembled a large dog or a wolf. It too watched us with eyes that burned the colour of emeralds.

"What are they?" Oscar asked.

Stefan shrugged. "Woodland sprites, I suppose. They must have upped the security recently. The last time I was here, a dryad guided me right up to Arthur's house."

"Wilfully?" I said.

"I didn't threaten her, if that's what you're asking," the vampire replied. "She did it out of the goodness of her little green heart. Although, I might have helped her see the benefits of assisting me."

Meaning he used his glamour. As far as vampires go, Stefan's one of the better ones. But he's still a vampire.

He led us through the bushland and the sprites followed, paralleling our movements like a guard of honour. In my eagerness to appear non-threatening, I shoved my hands in my pockets, where my fingertips brushed against something. I pulled out the brown scapular I'd forgotten to give to Miss Blackthorne. I glanced at the creatures either side of us and decided a little more protection couldn't hurt.

As it turned out, it could. And the woodland sprites weren't what I should have been worrying about. Once the scapular was around my neck, I felt the magic within the cord necklace push against my own.

Oscar froze.

"What's wrong?" I asked.

"Stefan?" he whispered.

The vampire had stopped a few strides ahead of us, head cocked, as if listening to something the rest of us couldn't perceive.

"Oh, shit," Oscar said.

I looked at my friend. "What—"

In a flash, Stefan launched himself at us, flying through the air like a well-dressed missile. His eyes burned blood red and his jaw hung open, displaying several rows of shark-like teeth. He bounced off the shield Oscar had been clever enough to conjure and disappeared amongst the trees. I dropped my *lumière* and brought up a shield, just as Stefan attacked from the other direction. He slammed against my barrier and vanished again.

Oscar pumped up the brightness of his light spell. A shadow darted through the trees above us. I only caught glimpses as it moved limb to limb before melting back into the darkness.

"What the hell!" Oscar called out to the forest. "Stefan, stop!"

The scapular pulsed against my chest. I brought up a hand to remove it when Stefan leaped down from above. Our shields held the vampire aloft as he clawed at the translucent barriers with manic intensity, before he started bashing the translucent barriers with his head.

Vampires aren't any stronger than humans. It's their enhanced predatory senses, their agility, and their hunger-fuelled rages that makes them dangerous. Seeing Stefan up close like this was like watching a rabid animal.

A glowing ring formed around Stefan's neck and dragged him to the ground. Oscar waved his hand and pinned the vampire to a tree with the *golden bracelet*. Stefan clawed at the spell, his fingers digging into his own pale flesh, drawing dark red blood.

"Stop, Stefan!" Oscar pleaded.

I dropped my shield and tore off the scapula. The faint hum of energy faded the moment I took it off. Stefan's thrashing slowly subsided. His eyes reverted to their usual calm grey and his mouth returned to normal.

The vampire breathed heavily, head bowed. His light-brown hair hung limp in front of his face. "Sorry, boys. I... I don't know what came over me." He lifted his gaze and looked past us. "Seems like we drew a crowd."

I turned. Several pairs of green eyes glowed in the thick under-brush. I could make out some of the creatures by their silhouettes, but most stayed hidden in the shadows.

"Easy," came a soothing voice. A dark-skinned man emerged from the shadows, tall and lean, dressed simply in blue jeans and a grey sweater. "Stefan, is that you?"

"Evening, Arthur," Stefan said, still held to the tree by Oscar's spell.

"How's your Father?"

"Still a vampire." He gestured to Oscar and me. "May I introduce Oscar Lee and Joey Finch. Mary's apprentices."

Arthur gave us a warm smile. I sensed no hostility or guile from the man, but I've been wrong before.

"Welcome," he said. "Tea?"

17

WE SAT around a small table while Arthur inspected the scapular. "Why would you use a magical item without knowing its use?"

"I thought it was meant to provide protection."

"Who told you that?" Arthur said with a half-smile.

"The guy in the pawnshop," I said, fully aware of how stupid that made me sound.

"I see," he said, and lifted the necklace in the air as if judging its weight. "Doesn't feel like an artefact of protection. But I doubt the man was an expert."

"You can wield magic?" Oscar asked.

"No, no. At least, not anymore. I could construct a basic spell or two once upon a time, but that was long, long ago. And I never really had the patience or discipline to keep at it. Now I'm just a regular person who's been around long enough to have a nose for magic." He reached across the table and handed me back the scapular. "I would suggest giving it to your Master Wizard. She'll know what to do with it."

Stefan gave a thin-lipped grin, pulled out his phone and started scrolling, likely checking financial news. Most vampires in Sydney had a day job – or night job – of managing several billion dollars' worth of financial asset for clients around the world. Stefan was still adjusting to his career change, although right now he seemed to be focusing on his phone a little too intently.

The kettle started whistling.

"Ah, excuse me," Arthur said. "Won't be a sec."

The tall man strode to the other side of the room. He removed the kettle from one of those portable camping stoves that are powered by disposable gas cannisters the size of deodorant cans.

"Earl Grey alright?" he called out.

"Yep," Oscar and I replied.

"Got any blood of an unmarked virgin?" Stefan asked.

Arthur opened the fridge and pulled out a bundle of something wrapped in white butcher's paper. "How about a tenderloin? Fresh. Picked it up yesterday."

"That should suffice," Stefan said. He spoke calmly, but I sensed a strained edge to his voice. "I think I'll have my breakfast outside if no one has any objections." He took the package and left the cabin.

While Arthur busied himself with the tea, I took a moment to look around. There wasn't a whole lot to see. He lived in an old colonial cabin that must have been built in the old bushranger days, with timber floors and walls and a rusted tin roof. Two rooms – one for the bed and one for everything else. A couple of naked light bulbs hung from the crossbeams, bathing everything in a warm yellow glow. A large water tank outside provided fresh water, solar panels on the roof supplied power.

The place was noticeably bare. For a guy supposedly older than most religions, I would have expected more... souvenirs. Maybe a Roman short sword, an original da Vinci. All I could see was a stone-tipped spear in the corner of the room, next to a broom and umbrella.

Arthur placed mugs on the table. "Careful, it's hot."

"You think Stefan's okay?" I asked, leaving my tea to cool. "He seemed on edge."

"The man's got an iron will to suppress his urges. Give him a minute, he'll be fine." Arthur spoke slowly and calmly, every word considered before leaving his mouth. Essentially, the opposite of my general process.

"Nice place you've got," Oscar said. "Cosy."

Arthur gave another half-smile. "I know it doesn't have all the whizz-bang conveniences you probably have in your home. It usually takes me a while to catch up. The light bulbs are a bloody godsend, though." He took a seat and held up his tea. "Cheers."

We clinked mugs.

"Now," Arthur said. "Very important question. How are the Rabbits doing?"

I shared a confused look with Oscar.

"The South Sydney Rabbitohs!" Arthur said, leaning forward with a big grin. "Rugby's one of the few indulgences of the modern age I enjoy. Haven't been to a game in years though, and I don't much fancy watching it on the television. It's not quite the same."

"We... we don't watch much sport," Oscar said.

Arthur sat back and nodded. "I suppose an apprenticeship with Mary leaves little time for much else."

I ran my finger along the table. "You're the first person I've heard Miss Blackthorne call a friend."

He chuckled to himself. "Friend. Yes, I suppose she would call me that. I would have said we were more like family. Something happens when you fight side by side with a person long enough, when you're down and dirty in the trenches together, relying on each other to stay alive. You really get to see the true heart of a person, which normally goes one of two ways. You either develop an unbreakable bond, or you condemn the person having seen them as the monster or the coward they truly are."

"You and Miss Blackthorne fought in the War together," Oscar said.

"That's right. Has she told you about the Vanguard?"

"She's mentioned it," I said.

Arthur leaned back in his chair. "The Venerati Sanctus are slippery suckers. Not only do they have the numbers and the firepower to seriously hurt the Old World, but they also have the cunning. They infiltrate governments, religions, private organisations to amass power and spread their influence. The War was their latest push to eradicate the Old World completely. Or, at least, as much as they could.

"In response, Mary established the Vanguard to be the spearpoint in the fight against the witch hunters, to take the fight back to them rather than simply waiting for them to strike. The Elf King and Queen were part of it, as was Vasily—"

"The head of Family Dragos?" I asked, surprised.

"He's a terrifying man, but not so bad as far as vampires go. Very reasonable. There was also a Beast Master, a priest, and probably a few others she kept secret from the rest of us. We were successful for the most part, which is why Australia has so many Safe Havens for the Old World."

"Sounds like a team of superheros," I said.

Arthur's face became grim. "We were far, far from being heroes. But we did what needed to be done."

I sensed an opportunity to learn about the enigmatic Master Wizard. "The Elf King and Queen died during the War, right?"

Arthur gave the barest nod.

"We know Miss Blackthorne had something to do with it but—"

The man put up a hand. "Let me stop you there, Joey. We've all done things we're not proud of. You'll have to ask Mary herself if you want to hear her war stories." He picked up his tea and took a sip. "Now, maybe you can tell me what brings two young wizards up here disturbing my neighbours?"

"We need to see the Goddess of the Parramatta River," I said.

Arthur's face didn't betray a reaction. "Why?"

Oscar and I recounted the events of the past few days. Arthur listened intently, regarding us with deep brown eyes.

"So, Mary wants to ask Anjea if she's noticed any selkies poking about."

"Anjea?" Oscar said.

"That's her name. The Goddess of the Parramatta River. I assume Mary has tried asking the Mokoi?"

"She has," Oscar replied, "but apparently they don't like her much."

Arthur nodded, seeming to understand. He took another sip and placed his tea on the table. "I'm afraid I can't help."

"Why not?" I said.

"I don't get involved in these kinds of things," he said. "Not anymore."

Oscar frowned. "But you helped her before. You fought the Venerati, defended the city during the War."

"It was a different time," he said, almost sadly. "A different fight. What you're describing is—"

"It's still a war," I said. "The selkies are going to tear the river folk apart unless we stop them."

Arthur nodded. "The fighting won't just impact the Old World. The violence will overflow into the mundane population." He clasped his hands together and looked out the window before turning back to us. "I've fought in many wars. So many. As a soldier, as a leader. Always with the best intentions." He shook his head. "It's horrible. The whole mess of it. Waste of life and a waste of time. But war is part of us, the Old World and the New, always drawing us back into its bloody embrace. There are breaks, sure. Intermissions which last months, years, centuries. But sooner or later, everyone is back at it again."

"You can't just turn your back on everyone," Oscar pleaded.

He smiled, and I sensed a resigned sadness. "I already have," he said. "And I'm far too tired to get involved these days. I am sorry. Truly."

My mind raced for something to offer. Then I wondered what Miss Blackthorne would do. I took a sip of tea as the beginnings of an idea formed, then solidified, in my head.

"How long have you lived here?" I said. "In the National Park."

Arthur tilted his head. "Fifty years. Give or take."

"And in that time, I take it you've seen a number of changes. New hiking trails. Car parks. Litter."

His eyes narrowed. "As is to be expected."

"Since you've pretty much given up on the world, you want to stay here, right? Away from everything."

He nodded slowly and took a sip of tea. The corner of his mouth twitched behind the mug.

"Well, eventually this park will get eaten up by the city," I said, choosing my words carefully. "Or they'll slice it up with new roads and highways. Either way, the powers-that-be may oppose having someone living within protected parklands. It's only a matter of time before someone comes knocking on your door to get you to clear out. I can stop that from happening."

Arthur, smiling openly now, said, "I had no idea apprentices wielded such power to sway the whims of government policy and urban development."

"We know people in government," I said, knowing that there was a big difference between knowing a few public servants and being able to influence governmental policy. Still, I continued. "It's better having someone looking out for you than no one at all."

"And if I don't assist you?" he asked. "You will refuse to protect my home?"

I clenched my jaw and said, "That's right."

He slapped the table and laughed. There was no malice in it, just pure enjoyment. As if I'd told him the best joke he'd heard all year.

"I don't believe a word of that," he said. "Oh, don't look so surprised." He ran a hand over his short, thick hair and fixed me with a gaze brimming with mirth. "Listen, son. You're no Mary Blackthorne. Take that as you wish, but I mean it as a compliment. You'll fight for anyone who needs it, I can tell. You have that spark." He looked at Oscar. "And I'd wager you're the same. Mary doesn't always get it right with her apprentices, but I think she's hit gold with you two." He threw back the rest of his tea. "I'll help you."

"You will?" Oscar said.

"Yeah. Bugger it. Mary's been trying to drag me back into the thick of things for years. Maybe this will get her off my back for another while." He went to a chest of drawers and pulled out an old paper map, unfolded it, and placed it on the table. "Let's meet here tomorrow," he said, placing a finger on Woolwich Marina. It sat right near the intersection of the Parramatta and Lane Cove Rivers. "Do you know anyone with a boat?"

"We can get one," I said.

Arthur nodded. "It will be safest to meet Anjea at low tide when she will be at her weakest. Just in case."

"Low tide is at 3 p.m. tomorrow," Oscar said.

Arthur tilted his head and Oscar showed him his phone display.

"Amazing," Arthur said. "Three it is, then."

"We only need to ask her a few questions," I said. "It should be pretty straightforward."

Arthur gave a pained grin. "You wouldn't be saying that if you'd met a god before."

18

———

WE FINISHED our tea and went outside where we found Stefan, hands in pockets, looking up at the sky. One of the woodland sprites, the one shaped like a wolf, sat on its haunches next to him. Several pairs of green eyes watched from the darkness of the surrounding forest.

"You know," Stefan said, "there are trillions and trillions of stars in the universe. If even the smallest fraction of those contain life, then that would make space seem very crowded all of a sudden. Makes you wonder what other gods and demons are out there." The vampire snapped out of his reverie and turned to us. "I was listening. You boys did well in there."

"We were worried about you," Oscar said. "Are you okay?"

Juices from the meat dripped from Stefan's chin. He wiped away at them self-consciously with a shirt sleeve. "Sorry about stepping out. That necklace of yours really did number on me." He patted his stomach. "I should be good for the drive home."

We hiked back through the forest, the sprites trailing us all the way to the stream, which Oscar and I re-routed once again for Stefan. We found the wooden walkway and moved back along the trail up to the car park. The rain had ceased for the time being but left the air heavy with moisture. I'd built up a decent sweat by the time we got back to Stefan's Mercedes.

Once we were on the road, I asked the vampire if he wanted to visit the river goddess.

"We could do with your help," I added.

"I'll pass," Stefan said. "Not really my scene. I have no interest in meeting any god, and I'm sure the feeling is mutual. Besides, running water. Remember?"

We dropped Oscar off at Georgie Boy's place, and Stefan shot me a sly grin. "Anyone special I can leave you with?"

"Home is fine."

He dropped me off, and I went straight upstairs to my room, falling face-first onto my bed. I would have fallen asleep if my phone didn't ring.

"Hello?"

"Joseph," Miss Blackthorne said. "We will meet the selkie delegation at eleven tomorrow morning. Rooftop of the Pan Pacific Hotel in Bondi. How did you go with Arthur?"

I sat up and swung my legs over the edge of the bed. "He'll take us tomorrow afternoon. Three o'clock at Woolwich Marina. Apparently, we'll need a boat."

"I can get one," she said. A long pause hung between us before she spoke again. "How is he?"

"He's good, I guess. Healthy. Embracing rustic living. Seems happy despite not having a TV."

"Good," she said. "Very good. I will pick you up at ten tomorrow morning. Get some rest."

I hung up and texted Oscar and Bree the plan for the next day, then lay back down on the bed. My phone rang again.

"Hello?"

"What's with the attitude?" came the voice. It was Devapriya.

"Sorry," I said as I rubbed my eyes and sat up again. "Just tired."

"We found the car the Scarred Man had stolen. He dumped it a mile from Mei's house. Forensics are out there now, dusting the vehicle for prints. I'll make the request for analysis as soon as they arrive, but the lab won't get to it until the morning."

"I thought Miss Blackthorne told you not to go after him."

"She's your boss, not mine."

I was too tired to argue. "Okay. Be careful."

I hung up and remained sitting there a moment, looking out through my small bedroom window. I remained still and gathered energy, twisting the magic into a spell that could burn flesh from bone.

"I know you're there," I said in a low whisper.

"Impressive," came a reply from the shadows of my bedroom. A woman's voice, soft and sensual. Dangerous. "Better wizards than you have failed to sense my presence. I may be losing my touch."

Yvette slinked out of the darkness. The vampire wore the same heels and white dress she had on at the pub earlier in the night.

"How did you get in?"

"I don't know. To be perfectly honest, I have tried entering your home before with no luck. It seems the wards that protect this house are rather inconsistent."

"Tell me why I shouldn't blast you through my wall," I said tiredly.

"Very feisty," she replied. "Without your friends around, I would have taken you for someone who—"

I threw *sizzle cuffs* at the vampire – a spell that involves conjuring burning bands of crimson energy and using them to bind your intended target. I'd aimed for the vampire's arms and her ankles, but most of my practice with the spell had been against antique furniture. My execution lacked the speed and finesse of a Master Wizard.

Yvette leaped away as the glowing bands sailed past her and disintegrated upon contact with the wall, leaving blackened marks. She crawled upside-down across that ceiling, fingers digging into the plasterboard, jaws hanging open to display rows of razor blade teeth.

I cast a bolt of crackling green energy that caught the vampire on the thigh. She wailed and dropped to the floor, tried to jump at me but found her legs didn't work. I threw a quick *sneezer* that slapped her in the face and followed up with the *sizzle cuffs* again. One of the red bands looped around her neck, eliciting a shrill cry from the vampire.

The spell wasn't like Oscar's *golden bracelet.* I couldn't throw her around the room once I'd snagged her. I could, however, make the bands very uncomfortable for the woman.

"I'll ask once more," I said, concentrating on keeping the *cuff* around her neck. "What are you doing here?"

Yvette chose to snarl instead of providing a response, so I pumped energy into the spell. The *cuff* lit my room with a sinister red glow, and I felt the growing heat from across the room. She shrieked and fixed me with a red-eyed glare.

"I wanted to remind you that vampires are to be feared," Yvette said with a snarl. "That this arrangement you have with our Father is only temporary. We are vampires. We feed on flesh and blood. The banishment of Clémence the Betrayer has only strengthened our resolve."

"Define *we*."

She bared her teeth in what was probably meant to be a smile. "Those who wish for things to return to the old ways. There are more than you suspect. More than anyone suspects."

"Why the heads up?"

"This was merely a warning. A final chance for you to leave your chosen path."

"Ah," I said. "I didn't realise you had such altruistic motives. And I suppose the fact you'd have one less wizard to deal with is just a happy convenience."

She craned her neck from side to side. "I can see you're determined to keep working for the Custodian."

"No shit, Sherlock." I let the *cuff* disappear. The skin on her neck showed dark red and black marks. That'd be the *sizzle* part of the spell. "Get out. If any vampire rebellions start up, I know exactly who to go after."

She didn't move for a long while and I thought she might be gearing up for round two. Eventually, the red drained from Yvette's eyes and her face returned to normal. I escorted her to the front door, holding magic in my chest like a coiled spring, ready to be unleashed. She walked with the casual air of someone certain in their own safety.

Before she left, Yvette spun around. "It's a dangerous job working with the Custodian," she said with a sinister grin, her voice teasing. "Lots of people in the dark. Watching, waiting."

"Come here again and I'll kill you," I said, not sure whether I believed it.

Yvette gave a final smile and left.

I locked the door, went back up to my room, and sat on my bed. My heart raced; my hands trembled. I stayed there, sitting on the edge of my bed, waiting for the after-effects of all the adrenaline to subside. Sweat ran down my back. I don't know how long I stayed sitting there, but at some point, I heard Bree come in through the front door and enter her bedroom.

I had fought demons and beasts before. Each one was just as terrifying as the last. And now I knew our house wasn't monster-proof. Sleep came when exhaustion finally won the battle against worry.

19

I AWOKE to the smell of bacon and eggs. I stepped into a pair of jeans, threw on an old T-shirt, and went downstairs. The sun sat high in the sky, poking through gaps in the dark clouds.

"Morning," Oscar said. He slid a plate in front of me with scrambled eggs, bacon, and a couple of pieces of toast.

"Brilliant," I said. "Thanks, mate."

Oscar had a habit of cooking breakfast for the house the morning after getting laid, which may have been one of the reasons I hoped his fling with Georgie Boy would last. That, and the continued happiness of my friend, of course. But also, breakfast.

"Thought you'd be spending the morning with Georgie Boy," I said before shovelling scrambled eggs into my face.

"He dropped me off on the way to work."

"Modelling?"

"Of course not. He's started a new job at a gym."

"All part of his grand plan to be an Insta model?"

Oscar poured me a glass of orange juice and shrugged with a small shake of his head. "Apparently."

Bree poked her head out of her room. Her bedroom lies right next to the kitchen, so she gets to hear whenever anyone's banging pots and pans around. Upsides include proximity to midnight snacks and a first dibs on any meal that serves more than one person.

She sniffed the air. "Bacon?"

Oscar smiled and showed her the pan.

Bree disappeared back into her room and came out wearing a baggy old USYD T-shirt and pyjama bottoms. She sat at the table and Oscar laid a plate of bacon and eggs in front of her.

"Get inside me," Bree said as she started shovelling food into her mouth. "Still haven't told Georgie Boy about your extracurriculars?" Oscar grimaced and Bree cut in before he could reply. "No pressure, dude. Honestly, you'll tell him about magic and demons and shit when you're ready."

Oscar nodded. "Thanks, Bree."

"Heads up, though," she continued. "It's not a great feeling, knowing you've been lied to. Just keep that in mind, yeah?"

I put down my knife and fork. "Guys, there's something I need to tell you." Oscar and Bree turned to me, waiting. "Last night, I had a visit from Yvette, that vampire from the pub. She got into the house."

Oscar leaned forward. "How? I thought the wards around this place prevented enemies from getting in?"

"I thought so too. But apparently, we were wrong because she came right into my bedroom."

"Lucky you," Bree said.

Oscar frowned at her before turning back to me. "What did she want?"

"She advised we make a career change and suggested that continuing our apprenticeships could be detrimental to our health. I politely requested she leave before I torched her."

"We can handle one *rogue* vampire," Bree said.

"She alluded to there being more," I said. "Much more."

We ate the rest of our bacon and eggs in silence.

* * *

AFTER BREAKFAST, Oscar and I threw spells at each other to pass the time while we waited for Miss Blackthorne to arrive. Bree sat on the couch with her laptop.

"Boxing!" Bree said suddenly, before typing furiously, the sound of clacking keys drowned out by the whistles and pops of our magic. Her shoulders slumped. "Oh, that's some bullshit. Lady boxers are so underpaid."

"Still trying to find the best way to exploit your gifts?" I said as I magicked an empty drink bottle into the air and launched it at Oscar. He swatted it away easily.

"If by *gift* you mean the demon inside my head, then yes."

"You should play tennis," Oscar said as he threw a ball of shimmering orange light. "Those women make a killing."

"You need coordination for that," I said, blocking his spell. "Not just strength. You'd be better off with boxing."

"Maybe I could be an enforcer," Bree suggested. "You know, for a kingpin or something."

"We live in Sydney, Bree. Not Chicago in the 1920s. Maybe you should just keep your superhuman abilities to yourself. We don't want to draw attention."

"Says the guy driving cars off bridges."

"Hey, I was just the passenger."

Bree looked up from her laptop. "I can't let being a *demonbound* go to waste. Who knows how long I'll be like this?"

"What do you mean?"

"I mean, I love beating the entire rugby team in an arm wrestle, but there's got to be side effects. A demon can't just take up long-term residency in my head without consequences."

Bree was one hundred per cent right. Only she wasn't going to be the one suffering the consequences. The deal I'd made with the demon was that it would reside within Bree for seven years before taking up permanent residence in my head. Maybe not the best deal in hindsight, but I was desperate at the time. And I still had seven years of freedom. Well, six and a half now.

"You're reading too much into it," I said. "That demon wants you to stay strong and healthy just as much as you do." I lowered my voice. "He's behaving himself in there, isn't he? Not trying to fully possess you or anything?"

"Yeah, hasn't made a peep. Why?"

"Just checking."

Bree went back to tapping away at her computer.

Oscar conjured a tiny yellow bird that zigzagged through the air before darting towards me. I deflected the spell easily, but missed the *golden bracelet* he followed up with. It clamped around my ankle and pulled out my leg from under me. I hit the floor hard.

"Shit!" I said. "Good shot. I still haven't figured out how to counter that one."

"And I hope you never do," Oscar said with a grin as he helped me up.

* * *

BY THE TIME Miss Blackthorne arrived, the three of us were gathered on the couch watching a true crime show. The clouds had darkened again, so I grabbed my red waterproof jacket and Bree grabbed the house's lone umbrella – one of those giant things the corporations hand out at university careers fairs in the hopes they'll get free advertising whenever the weather turns shitty.

We piled into the Land Cruiser and headed east.

Sydney is a bastard to drive through. A combination of poor city planning, narrow roads and too many people wanting to go to too many places. It took us almost an hour to reach the Eastern Suburbs. There are people who can literally run faster than that. Not me, but there are people.

We pulled up in the car park that ran along Bondi Beach. It might have been trickier to find a spot if the clouds didn't look like they were about to piss down something severe. Miss Blackthorne paid the extortionate parking fee, and we crossed the road to the meeting place.

The Pan Pacific Hotel isn't much to look at. The white four-storey building sat above a supermarket, a handful of fashion stores, and a half dozen cafés where people were getting on with the important business of drinking coffees and having brunch.

We entered reception and bypassed a sharply dressed gentleman at the desk.

"Hello, may I help you?" the receptionist called after us, a plastic smile on his face.

"No," Miss Blackthorne replied, leaving the man to stare at us open-mouthed as we entered the lift.

We came out at the roof where restaurant staff busily worked cranks to unfurl large canvas covers. A portly man with slick hair and a tight suit bustled over.

"I apologise," he said without bothering with the fake smile. "There is currently a private function in progress." He cast a disapproving gaze over us, seeming to take particular umbrage at Miss Blackthorne's black AC/DC T-shirt and her tatty green scarf. "The restaurant will reopen to the public at midday. In the meantime, please feel free to—"

Miss Blackthorne swept an abrupt hand through the air and the man slid to the side as if he was standing on ice. There was no malice in the gesture, it's just the way the Master Wizard gets when she has her game face on.

We strode past him. Oscar spared a second to explain to the confused man that we were, in fact, part of the private function.

Only one table was occupied.

Alehtta sat at one end, wearing a black tank top beneath a faded blue tracksuit jacket. Riss stood behind her, bow in hand, shawl wrapped over her head. Beside the elf ranger stood the two body-guards, replacing Sir Brandr as the queen's escorts.

Also sitting at the table was a tall, sour-faced man who I took to be the new selkie ambassador. Rhoswyn and Hamish stood behind him, along with a bearded old selkie who had long pointed ears similar to Riss, only more swept back. He wore a dark blue robe with a notice-able bulge at his hip, which I assumed to be his own selkie blade. Or maybe the man just really loved diplomatic meetings.

The ambassador rose from his chair and approached with a stiff smile. Like the selkie mage and warrior, the ambassador favoured clothes that were sleek and black. His high-collared coat extended down to his knees, however the cut appeared to be geared more towards fashion than efficiency of movement, with a subtle pattern woven into the fabric that only showed when the light hit it a certain way. Bandages covered both his ears.

"Leave the speaking to me," Miss Blackthorne said quietly as we walked towards the man. "They're insistent upon etiquette and hierarchy."

"Custodian Blackthorne, it is a pleasure to meet you," the man said formally. "I am Ambassador Calder McBrae." He gestured at his ears. "I've been in the job less than a week, so I apologise in advance for any faux pas on my part. Please, join us." He turned and led us back to the table. The man lacked the grace of the elves and moved with heavy footsteps, as if the ground shifted beneath him. The guy wasn't just new to the job, he was new to being out of the water.

Miss Blackthorne greeted Alehtta and took a seat. The ambassador followed suit. Riss flashed us a quick smile before facing forward. She had her hands in front of her and adopted a more relaxed pose than the two elves on her flanks. Rhoswyn and Hamish observed us with neutral expressions, but the bearded old man beside them regarded us with open loathing.

The slick-haired host hurried over with a jug of iced water and quickly filled the glasses of those sitting at the table. He cast a beady-eyed glance at the attendees remaining on their feet and decided he'd be better off not overhearing whatever shady business was underway, choosing instead to disappear in a sweaty huff.

Ambassador McBrae emptied a sachet of salt into his glass and swirled it with a finger before drinking. Alehtta took a sip of her water. Miss Blackthorne didn't touch hers.

"Ambassador McBrae," Miss Blackthorne said. "Thank you for agreeing to—"

The ambassador raised a hand. "One moment, please. We have not yet introduced all our attendees. I have brought with me Rhoswyn Guilfray, our embassy's magus. She helps with—"

"Let's get on with it, shall we?" Miss Blackthorne said. "We've all got places to be."

Ambassador McBrae hesitated, looking thoroughly put out by the interruption. "Of... of course," he stammered. "Perhaps, Queen Alehtta, as the moderator of this meeting you can—"

"We all know why we're here," Miss Blackthorne said sharply, having exhausted her reserve of good manners. "We want to determine why events transpired the way they have, and by doing so, we may avoid an unnecessary war. Agreed?"

Alehtta dipped her head, while Riss did a decent job of hiding her grin.

The ambassador's mouth hung open, the man struggling to get over the shock in the breach of protocol. Rhoswyn and Hamish remained stony faced. The old man in the robes may have been scowling, but it was hard to tell with the beard.

"Your predecessor," Miss Blackthorne continued, "Ambassador Ellister Kelden was murdered in his home, the selkie embassy, approximately one week ago. Frederico de Silva of the Parramatta River Encantados freely admits to committing this crime. However, his justification is that the death is a retaliation for the murder of a Baiji woman, Lin Wan. My question is this: did Ambassador Kelden organise the killing of Lin?"

"Of course not," McBrae said hotly.

"I should warn you, Ambassador, that I have a psychomancer with me. I do not wish to have him invade your mind, but I will if I must. Care to try again?"

McBrae glanced at Oscar and me, as if figuring out which one was more dangerous. He sipped his water again before speaking.

"Ambassador Ellister Kelden was not, in any way, involved with the killing of the Baiji woman known as Lin. Nor was any selkie."

"The stab wounds to the Baiji girl were inflicted with a selkie sword."

"There are thousands of selkie weapons along this stretch of coastline. It is not beyond the realm of possibility that one ended up in hands that were not our own."

Miss Blackthorne stuck her chin out at Hamish. "You, there. Have you ever misplaced your sword?"

The broad-shouldered warrior looked to the ambassador who nodded for him to answer.

Hamish straightened. "I have never misplaced my weapon."

"What about your peers? Could they have lost their swords?"

He hesitated, then said, "That is... unlikely. Selkies deployed to ambassadorial duties are required to have their weapon within arm's reach at all times. Even when sleeping. Goes for mages, security, and ambassadors themselves."

Miss Blackthorne looked back at the ambassador. "Logic follows that a selkie attacked Lin. Or a selkie blade was provided to a third party."

McBrae narrowed his eyes. "You are implying an assassin."

Miss Blackthorn didn't respond.

The robed man behind the ambassador rested his knuckles on the table and leaned forward. "You dare accuse us of sending a hired killer? If we wished, we could destroy that girl's entire home and everyone in it!"

Ambassador McBrae turned in his seat. "Calm yourself, Glenroch. You are here as an observer. Nothing more."

Miss Blackthorne pressed her lips together. "Perhaps it was not wise to bring a War Mage to a meeting of diplomacy."

The old man squinted. "You know what I am?"

"Of course," Miss Blackthorne replied. "It's my job to know these things."

Glenroch crossed his arms and stepped back. Rhoswyn's eyes may have turned skyward for a brief second.

"Custodian," the ambassador said, interlocking his fingers in front of him. "The selkies are not in the business of hiring assassins. We have strict protocols in regard to... that kind of thing."

"Officially or unofficially?"

"Both. And even if Ambassador Kelden did organise such an... activity, he certainly wouldn't have been complacent enough to give the killer a selkie blade to accomplish the task." The ambassador paused. "I must ask, though, have you confirmed that it was indeed a selkie blade? Do you have, in your possession, the murder weapon?"

Miss Blackthorne remained silent, and Oscar shot me a worried glance.

"I didn't think so," the ambassador said, using that small fact as a foothold for his confidence. "You merely have hearsay and supposition." His expression turned serious. "Frederico de Silva, however, is irrefutably guilty of murdering Ambassador Ellister Kelden. To which you have provided nothing substantial to justify his actions."

"The Encantados will not turn him over."

"Then the Encantados will be held accountable!" War Mage Glenroch burst out.

Ambassador McBrae flashed him an annoyed glance before turning back to us. "Custodian Blackthorne, we have held a delicate armistice with the river folk for decades and wish to maintain that peace, for both our peoples' sake. But our foremost ambassador to this domain was murdered in cold blood. You must understand that my people need to see justice."

"I do," Miss Blackthorne said. "However, I must question whether war is an appropriate response."

Ambassador McBrae sipped his water. "War," he said with a sigh. "No one wants war. But those decisions are out of my hands. Kelden may have held sway with the leadership back home, but I am little more than a glorified messenger." He levelled his gaze at Miss Blackthorne. "I can freely tell you that our forces have started preparing a response in the event the Encantado is not turned over."

"Ambassador!" Glenroch said.

"Oh, it's no surprise," McBrae said. "And they should know we are taking this matter seriously... and that we will respond in kind if we need to."

"Keep in mind, Ambassador," Miss Blackthorne said, fixing him with a steely gaze. "I will not tolerate a war being brought to my city. Before your forces take on the river folk and their goddess, they will need to first get through me."

The ambassador hesitated and his jaw muscles tightened. "If that's what must be done." He shook his head, exasperated. "This can all be prevented simply by providing the Encantado to us."

"I am well aware that the trial is a façade. For all your advances in technology and magic, the selkie attitude towards justice has remained unchanged since the Middle Ages. I will not send a man to his death. Not when he may have been justified in his actions."

"Then you have decided war."

Alehtta cleared her throat, drawing the attention of Miss Blackthorne and the ambassador. "Ambassador McBrae, Custodian Blackthorne. Let's not be too quick to condemn. Enough people of the Old World are being killed without us adding to the number. There is time yet until the trial, correct?"

The ambassador nodded.

"Good," Alehtta continued. "Perhaps if the Custodian can prove Ambassador Kelden is responsible for the killing of Lin Wan – whether he wielded the blade himself, or had it arranged – then his death would be classified as a justifiable retaliation, and you could request your people to stand down."

"Of course," Ambassador McBrae said. "However, if she cannot prove it, beyond any doubt, the Encantado must be brought to us to stand trial."

"I will bring him to you myself," Miss Blackthorne said.

"Very good," said Ambassador McBrae. "Our forces are standing by. We will make no actions against the Encantados until the time of the trial. You have forty-eight hours."

* * *

"WILL YOU REALLY TAKE FREDERICO?" Oscar asked as we walked back to the car.

"If I must," Miss Blackthorne replied. "The selkies are not like the elves. They are one of the most powerful forces on the planet and leave destruction in their wake whenever they leave the oceans en masse. I do not wish to deliver Frederico to the selkies, but I will if there is no other option."

"That's cold," I said.

"It's our job to not let it get that far," she responded.

"Shouldn't we let the Encantados decide for themselves whether to hand over Frederico?" Bree said.

"There are more lives at stake than those of the river folk. Regular people will inevitably be drawn into any conflict that occurs within the city. Thousands would die."

"We should warn Katherine Powell," I said. "Aren't you meant to tell her about this kind of thing?" If she and her shady government associates hadn't already caught wind of it.

"I will involve Kat when I need to. Right now, there's no reason to bring the government into it. We need to find the killer. And do it fast."

"We don't have much to go on," I said.

"Hence our imminent conversation with the river goddess. I need to verify some information."

As we reached Miss Blackthorne's car, someone called out to us. I turned to see Alehtta and Riss approaching, the two escorts close behind.

"That could have gone better," said the Elf Queen.

"It went how I expected," Miss Blackthorne replied. "Could you perceive their intentions?"

The Elf Queen shook her head. "Their minds were closed to me. As is to be expected at a diplomatic meeting."

"How is Sir Brandr?"

"Much like you," Alehtta said. "Healing."

Miss Blackthorne tapped her own leg with the cane. "I have almost fully recovered," she lied.

The Elf Queen stepped forward and placed a light hand on Miss Blackthorne's shoulder. "I don't mean your physical wounds." Alehtta fixed our teacher with a steady gaze, her pale green irises a stark contrast to Miss Blackthorne's dark brown. "I don't blame you, you know. And Brandr... he will see reason, eventually. You had no choice."

The Master Wizard's face betrayed no emotion. "There's always a choice."

I looked at Riss, who shrugged back at me.

Alehtta turned to me. "Wells of Power. Keep your eyes open."

"Yes, ma'am."

The Elf Queen gave Miss Blackthorne a faint smile and left.

"Get in the car," Miss Blackthorne said, her voice a fraction more gruff than usual.

20

RAIN DANCED off the water by the time we reached Woolwich Marina. Arthur stood at the end of the pier, his tall form leaning against one of the thick wooden posts, seemingly unworried about the rain. A row of private yachts bobbed up and down in the unsteady water, their owners deciding to stay home and sip champagne by the fireplace. Or whatever it is rich people do when the weather is garbage.

Bree and I huddled under the giant umbrella as we walked along the pier. Miss Blackthorne used magic to slide the rain away before it reached her, which Oscar copied with less success.

"Arthur," Miss Blackthorne said, barely audible over the rain.

The man smiled. His white teeth shining bright against his dark skin. "Good to see you, kiddo." He stepped forward and embraced Miss Blackthorne in a strong hug, his long arms wrapping around her, holding her for several seconds.

They separated and held each other at arm's length.

"You sure you want to do this?" Miss Blackthorne said. "I know it is not a pleasant experience for you."

He shrugged. "It won't be the first time."

As she looked up at the man, I caught a glimpse of the young woman Miss Blackthorne must have been once upon a time. Long, long ago.

Arthur's gaze drifted to Bree, and he furrowed his brow.

"This is Bree," Miss Blackthorne said. "She's temporarily harbouring a demon."

A flash of concern passed over Arthur's face, quickly replaced by his warm smile. "Pleasure to meet you," he said, taking Bree's hand in his and kissing the back of it. Somehow accomplishing the antiquated gesture without seeming tacky.

Bree blushed a shade I hadn't seen before. "Yeah, same here."

"Here comes our ride," Miss Blackthorne said, looking out at the water.

A small houseboat, its coloured lanterns swinging gently as it pulled into the marina. Mick the Mokoi gave a friendly wave, his long curly hair blowing in the wind.

"G'day all," he said. "Mind if we don't dilly-dally? The Elders wouldn't be too pleased about me helping you lot."

"Do they realise we are trying to protect the river folk from selkie reprisals?" Miss Blackthorne said as she stepped onto the boat.

Mick shrugged. "You know how they are, Aunty. Crusty old bastards. They're convinced the selkies don't have the balls to waltz into our river."

"I just met with them," Miss Blackthorne said, "and can confirm they do indeed have the balls."

After we all hopped on, Mick steered the boat towards Cockatoo Island. It's a small island that lies right in the middle of the river, only a quarter of a mile from the shore on either side. Apparently, it was initially used as a prison back in the day to dump Irish convicts, because shipping them off to a sweltering continent on the other side of the world wasn't enough. It then became a dockyard for building warships. Now it's mostly used for picnics, music festivals, and art exhibitions that make use of the massive empty buildings.

We chugged past a glamping site that ran along the northern edge of the island for those who wanted a taste of the great outdoors, but still wanted the option of grabbing a cappuccino and chocolate croissant in the morning.

"Just pull up over there," Arthur said.

Mick steered us past the Sydney Ferries wharf and manoeuvred the houseboat up to the sandstone block sea wall on the eastern side of the island, swinging the vessel around in a sweeping arc as if he was handling a semi-trailer. The boat ride took all of five minutes.

Mick climbed over the handrail atop the seawall. "Toss up that rope would you, mate?"

I passed him the rope, then turned to Arthur. "Shouldn't we park somewhere a bit more secluded? I mean, there's a café right there."

"They won't mind," Arthur said. "This is the last place I encountered Anjea, and our best chance of her making an appearance. And it's called *mooring*."

A few bored people watched us from inside the café, their Sunday outing sidelined by the weather. I didn't see what they had to be looking sorry about. At least they were warm and dry. The rest of us climbed over the slippery railing, some of us finding it more difficult than others. And I'm not referring to the cane-wielding Miss Blackthorne.

"I'll hang back and grab a cuppa," Mick said.

"You don't want to meet Anjea?" I asked.

"Nah, not really keen on getting face time with the boss. Sure, she's the god of my people and all that, but we only live in the river by her good graces. She could wipe us out no trouble if she's having a bad day. Scares the crap out of me."

"Be ready for us," Miss Blackthorne said.

Arthur led us along a brick path that paralleled the sea wall. It took us to a flat stretch of grass where the wall's sandstone blocks were replaced by large grey boulders that sloped into the water. Through the rain, you could just about make out the Harbour Bridge a few miles downstream.

"Wouldn't it have been easier for Mick to summon her?" Bree said. "It's his goddess, after all."

"Communicating with a god or goddess is a vague affair and mostly involves enacting their will in return for rewards or power."

"Enacting their will?" Oscar asked.

"Some gods require sacrifice – crops, animals, humans – others simply wish to have prayers uttered in their name to show they've not been forgotten."

"So, how do we summon the river goddess?" I asked.

"You don't," Miss Blackthorne said. "Gods aren't like demons. You can't force them to have an audience with you. Not even minor gods like Anjea. You get their attention, and they choose whether to respond. Luckily, we have someone who's on a first name basis with her."

Arthur stepped out onto the rocks. He bent down as if searching for something and picked up a boulder the size of a watermelon, holding it in both hands. He stepped into the water, moving deeper until the gentle waves lapped against his chest.

I moved forward. "Wait! Arthur, what are you doing?"

"Knocking on the door," he replied.

"You'll drown if you carry that rock in with you," Bree said.

"That's the point," Arthur said. "Last time I saw Anjea was some years back. I was working on a ship here, a maintenance job, when I suffered a 'workplace accident'. These days, they'd probably label it as a murder. Anyway, the fellas tossed me into the river, and I stayed down there four days before Anjea pulled me up. Hopefully she recognises me a bit quicker this time. What do you say, Mary? An hour?"

"Whatever you're comfortable with."

"Let's say an hour. If I'm not back by then, pull me up yourself. Just don't leave me down there. I don't want to have to wait for the river to dry up before I come back."

"Be careful," Miss Blackthorne said.

"That would defeat the purpose," Arthur replied with a grin and disappeared under the surface.

I put my hands in the pockets of my waterproof jacket and pulled it closer against my body. Bree, Oscar, and I had huddled together under the umbrella. I eventually released a breath, not realising I'd been holding it since Arthur went under.

"How long's it been?" I asked.

"Two and a half minutes," Miss Blackthorne answered. "Don't worry, he's immortal."

"Have you met Anjea before?" Oscar asked.

"No."

"Never?" I said. "But you've been around for ages."

She raised an eyebrow at me.

"You know," I said, backpedalling furiously. "Relative to us."

"Remember that gods and goddesses are immense celestial beings occupying the Realms Above. Most of the ones you know – the Olympians, the Aesir – have an influence on our world that is often too vast for us to perceive. For them to interact with us in our realm directly would be like trying to fill a thimble with a fire hose. So, they cut off little slivers of themselves to feed their followers, who then enact their will. And thus, the circle continues. This is how most

133

priests, witches, and even some sorcerers draw their power. Sometimes without their knowledge."

"Realms Above..." Bree said. "So, they're creatures of light? Celestials?"

Miss Blackthorne frowned. "Technically, yes. They exude magical energy, much like how creatures of darkness feed upon it. But don't get too caught up on the semantics. Gods can be as fickle and malevolent as any other being. Why, you are supposedly a creature of darkness, yet I find you quite pleasant."

I bet that was a compliment Bree had never heard before.

"So how big a deal is Anjea?" I said.

"Quite powerful as far as celestial beings go. But as a god she falls into the lowest tier. After all, the Parramatta River is no Ganges or Mississippi. Like the Christian Seraphim, minor gods can take physical form, and even walk among us unnoticed. Of course, you would already know this from the books I've left you."

"Yes of course," I said. "The books."

Twenty minutes later, I felt a wall of pressure push against my senses. It rapidly gained strength, and I had to concentrate on erecting a psychic barrier to stop the invisible force from squishing my brain.

White bubbles frothed on the surface of the water, surrounded by a dim blue glow.

"Not very inconspicuous," Miss Blackthorne grumbled. She turned towards the café and waved her hands, muttering gibberish I couldn't decipher. A wash of pressure passed over the area and a translucent screen materialised between us and the café. The illusion spell scattered the light passing through it, so that anyone who happened to look our way would just see a few blurry shapes enjoying the rain.

I turned back to the water and did a double take as a towering figure emerged, easily over eight feet tall, covered head to toe in mud and silt.

In its arms, it carried Arthur.

The creature walked through the water towards us, as if the river was no deeper than a few inches. With each step, the mud slid away, eventually revealing a stunning woman with flawless dark skin, strong jawline, and glowing green eyes. She wore a shimmering emerald dress that ebbed and flowed across her body in time with the waves lapping against the shore.

She stepped across the rocks and walked straight past us, delicately placing Arthur's still form on the grass. Seconds later, his body convulsed, and he coughed up a lungful of water. Arthur sat up, rested his arms on his knees, and groaned.

"Drowning's not so bad," he croaked, "but coming back is always a bit of a bastard." He looked up at the woman and smiled. "Good to see you again, Anjea."

When the woman spoke, the sound was deep and strong, and conjured images of twisting mangroves and wet mud. "Ankotarinja," she said.

"I go by Arthur now," he replied.

The goddess lay a hand upon his face. "The years have been kind to you."

"You too," he replied. "Have you gotten taller?"

"The humans have changed their ways. The river is still not as clean as it was before the white men arrived, but it is improving." Suddenly, she stood straight and looked around. "A child of mine is here. A Mokoi."

"He's busy at the moment," Miss Blackthorne said.

The river goddess looked down at Miss Blackthorne, eyes blazing green. She stepped close to the Master Wizard, and to our teacher's credit, she didn't step back, but looked up at the goddess with a defiant gaze of her own. The power emanating from Anjea doubled, which didn't seem to affect Oscar and Bree, but I had to grit my teeth and expend more energy to keep my psychic barriers up.

"This is Mary Blackthorne," Arthur said. "Master Wizard and Custodian of this land."

"A formidable responsibility given the state of the world," Anjea said. "And who are these young ones?"

"My apprentices," Miss Blackthorne said.

The goddess inspected us closely one at a time. I tried not to flinch as she bent down to meet us at eye level.

When she got to Bree, she frowned and said, "I do not like this one."

Bree crossed her arms. "Well, you're no can of peaches yourself."

Anjea moved closer, so she was almost nose to nose with Bree. "You remind me of..."

The goddess's eyes widened, flaring with emerald fire. She stepped back and bellowed a scream that sounded like the crashing of a thousand waves. The ground trembled as glowing water rushed up from the river and crashed over us. I'd been too focused on keeping up my mental barrier to prepare a shield, and the water sent me tumbling across the grass. Anjea grew to twice her size and shot an arm forward, the goddess's limb turning into a torrent of mud and water that pummelled Bree into the ground.

Oscar ran to Bree's side and conjured a shield, but the barrage of elements cut through his defences like they were papier mâché. Miss Blackthorne strode forward, tossed aside her cane, and raised both arms towards the towering goddess. A wall of crackling red energy sprung up in front of her, taking on the full force of the torrent with a ferocious roar. The goddess attacked with greater intensity, which Miss Blackthorne matched with her own energy, her crimson barrier casting long shadows behind us.

"Anjea!" Arthur called out, stepping to Miss Blackthorne's side. "Calm down! We just want to chat." I could barely hear him over the thunderous onslaught raining down from the river goddess. "Come on, love!"

Anjea didn't acknowledge him and continued her assault on Bree and Miss Blackthorne's shield. With a flash of resignation and clenching of his jaw, Arthur stepped in front of Miss Blackthorne's shimmering barrier, disappearing amongst the goddess's deluge of power. Anjea ceased her attack immediately.

Arthur's still form lay on the ground, his body twisted at unnatural angles. Miss Blackthorne dropped her spell and hobbled over to him, bending down to hold his head in her arms.

Anjea shrunk back down to her modest eight-foot height and tilted her head. "Is he alright?"

Miss Blackthorne glared at Anjea with such open detest I think even the goddess was taken aback. "He'll live," she said. "It's what he does."

The goddess stepped around Miss Blackthorne and gazed down at Bree, who lay in the centre of a muddy crater that had been bored into the ground. Bree looked around, confused, then focused on the goddess standing over her.

"Wiljara," Anjea snarled. "I thought you had been cast into the Abyss."

"Sorry, lady," Bree said. "Demon's not available. Care to leave a message?"

Miss Blackthorne stepped between them, looking haggard after her brief duel with the goddess. "Bree is a *demonbound*. She is merely *containing* a dark spirit. Acting as a temporary prison for the creature. The demon is under her control. And *she* is under *my* protection."

"I can destroy the demon now if you wish," Anjea said with such detachment it gave me goosebumps.

"Don't touch her," Oscar said, taking a step forward.

Anjea raised her hands. "It was simply an offer of assistance. I have no stake in the matter." She stepped back, her gaze lingering on Bree for a few seconds longer.

Arthur groaned and sat up, and Anjea went over to him.

"I take it you did not hurl yourself into my river for no reason?" the goddess said.

Satisfied Bree was in no immediate danger, Oscar retrieved Miss Blackthorne's cane and handed it to the Master Wizard who accepted it wordlessly. I turned to the café, expecting to see people spilling out to investigate what all the commotion was. However, through the translucent screen, I could see no one had stepped outside. Apparently, a battle between a river goddess and a Master Wizard didn't warrant leaving the comfort of a warm café. Also, kudos to Miss Blackthorne for maintaining the screen while duking it out with a god.

"There's trouble brewing in the city," Arthur said, getting to his feet with enough sprightliness to put the Energizer Bunny to shame. He craned his neck from side to side. "You know, I think that's the quickest I've ever died."

"There is always trouble brewing here," Anjea said. "Ever since those humans arrived on their wooden ships." She cast a seething glare at me, which made me realise I was indeed the whitest-looking person of the group. I decided to busy myself with helping Bree out of the mud.

"I meant something more specific."

"The river folk, your people, are in danger," said Miss Blackthorne, her breaths heavy. "An Encantado has committed a grievous crime against the selkie people. If he is not turned over to stand trial, the selkies will strike at the Encantados, the Mokoi, and the Baiji."

"They can try," Anjea said. "This is my river, and the people who dwell within it are my children. If the selkies dare invade my domain, I will destroy them."

"They have several warriors and mages," Miss Blackthorne said.

"You think mortals pose a threat to me?"

"Not you, but certainly all the river folk." She didn't bother mentioning regular residents of Sydney who were also at risk. I had a feeling the goddess wasn't empathetic to anyone outside her sphere of responsibility. "Your people are spread miles apart all along the river. I understand you are the ultimate power in your domain, but even you cannot be everywhere at once."

"I will hold them at the harbour," the goddess said. "Prevent them from entering the river."

"All due respect," Miss Blackthorne said. "But selkies have legs."

Anjea looked across the water, as if trying to see what the selkies were doing right now. "Then we must destroy the selkies before they strike," Anjea said with a snarl.

"Unless you're willing to venture into the domain of the ocean gods, that doesn't appear to be an option," Miss Blackthorne said.

"I presume you have another idea?"

"A Baiji girl was killed a week ago," Miss Blackthorne said, and pointed west. "Upstream about two miles."

"Yes," Anjea said with a trace of sadness. "The Baiji. New to the city. A strange people. Their resilience has been tested. They grieve for their lost daughter, even now."

"If we can prove it was the selkie ambassador who killed her, or that he orchestrated the killing, then the selkies would see the ambassador's death as justice being served. We can avoid a war."

"You wish to know if any selkies have entered my waters," Anjea said.

"Have they?"

"No."

"Are you sure?" I said. "She was in her home when she was killed. Not actually in the river—"

Anjea whirled on me and my blood froze. "My domain may stop at the water's edge," she said, her voice booming. "But I see far beyond it in ways your mortal mind cannot comprehend."

I nodded and tried in vain to cast a spell to remove the foot from my mouth.

The goddess turned back to Miss Blackthorne. "The soul of a selkie has a distinct... scent, and their magic disrupts the flow of energy within my waters." She lifted her chin, stretching to her full height. "You have my word that a selkie has not been within a half mile of this river for several months."

Oscar leaned in and whispered, "How close did Lin live next to the river?"

"Less than half a mile," I replied just as quietly.

Anjea walked back to the river. Before she reached the water's edge, she turned. "You might find it interesting to know that the Baiji ventured beyond the Heads regularly, out into the ocean."

"Was it Lin?" I asked.

The goddess glared at me again, but this time she spoke with significantly less venom. "I cannot say whether it was one person or twenty, let alone give you a name. But the fact that the Baiji are willing to leave my protection and venture into the selkie domain is highly unusual, is it not?"

Miss Blackthorne tilted her head. "Many thanks, Anjea."

"It was good to see you, Arthur," said the river goddess. "I hope we meet again soon."

Arthur placed a hand over his heart. "As do I."

Mud and water covered Anjea's tall form, wrapping around her like a second skin as she moved deeper into the water. When the goddess was waist deep in the river, her body dissolved, becoming one with the water around her. The pressure pushing against my head lifted, replaced by a splitting headache as if someone had spent the last ten minutes pressing a boot to my brain.

"You okay?" Oscar asked.

"I'm fine. Looks like we wasted our time, though."

"No," Miss Blackthorne said. "But it supports a hypothesis. Let's go back to the Substation. Joseph, there is something I must show you."

We picked up Mick from the café, pulling him away from an animated conversation he was having with an elderly couple. We climbed back over the handrail and onto the boat. Miss Blackthorne needed assistance this time.

"You okay, Aunty?" Mick asked. "You're looking a bit rough."

"She went head-to-head with Anjea," I said.

Mick's eyes almost fell out of his skull. "Bloody hell! That's wild. I didn't know you had the chops to take on a god!"

"I'm fine," Miss Blackthorne said with her trademark gruffness. "I doubt she was showing us her true strength."

Mick untied the rope and tossed it into the boat, jumping in after it. "Just take a seat, Aunty," he said, pushing the sea wall to give the boat some space so he could turn around.

The weather had worsened. None of us felt like being pelted in the face with rain anymore, so we sheltered inside the makeshift cabin on the boat. Bree had also lost our umbrella, which was understandable. The cramped living space looked similar to the interior of a caravan, only wetter and more disorganised. Miss Blackthorne and Arthur exchanged words out on the deck before entering. She fell into one of the plastic chairs with a loud sigh, while Arthur leaned against the wall and watched her with a smile.

"How does it work?" I asked. "You can recover from anything?"

Arthur shrugged. "Everything so far."

"What if your head was cut off?" Bree said. "Or your body got destroyed?"

"You guys planning to kill me?" he replied with an amused smile. "The truth is, I don't know. I've recovered from burns, grown back limbs and organs. Even regrew my brain when most of it was blown out the back of my head about a hundred years ago. Pretty sure I got the Spanish Flu at some point too, but it only hung around for an hour or so. If you removed my head, my guess is I'd just sprout a new body. Or maybe I'd grow a new head..." He tilted his head to the side. "That would be something to see. Now, if you were to completely disintegrate every cell in my body... I don't know. Would my soul drag together atoms and form a new body? Or would I finally be truly dead? Your guess is as good as mine."

"What's it like?" Oscar said. "Dying."

Arthur lowered his gaze and pressed his lips together. "Peaceful, mostly. I don't feel pain, or at least I don't remember it. Like I said, it's the coming back that's the worst part. Growing new nerve endings is particularly painful."

"You never tried to walk towards the light?" I said.

"Every time. Somehow, I keep getting dragged back." He looked up, his eyes not focused on anything. "But for those moments between life and death, I swear I'm not alone. Whenever I die, there's always someone waiting for me on the other side."

The boat's engine cut out as we cruised up to the marina, the momentum of the clunky vessel carrying us forward.

"Hey, guys," Mick called out from the front of the boat, an edge of tension in his voice. "Were you expecting company?"

We looked through the window to the marina, where a lone man in a dark coat stood on the pier amongst the yachts. The wind blew wet black hair across the man's face, but there was no hiding those scars.

21

JAGGED BLACK TENDRILS of solid shadow exploded forth and tore the roof off the boat. Everyone ducked down, except for Miss Blackthorne, who stood tall and responded with a stream of burning red energy. The Scarred Man deflected it with a wave of his hand and the spell drilled into the side of a yacht, blasting a hole through its hull.

"Get us out of here!" Miss Blackthorne yelled.

Mick started up the engine and gunned it, while Miss Blackthorne, Oscar, and I conjured shields holding the Scarred Man's attacks at bay. We hadn't moved more than a boat length before one of the shadowy fingers found a gap in our defences and drilled into the back of the boat, ripping out chunks of wood and fibreglass.

"Fuck!" Mick yelled. "Engine's gone!"

"Everybody out!" Miss Blackthorne cried.

We clambered up onto the pier, Bree effectively throwing me up there herself. Oscar threw a hand forward and conjured a *golden bracelet* around the Scarred Man's neck, jerking the man's head back and staggering him. But only momentarily. The Scarred Man brought up a glowing red hand and pulled the ring from his neck, the golden band disintegrating in a spray of soft sparks. I followed up with a hasty *sneezer* that the man swatted away with a contemptuous wave of his hand.

While not getting us out of the woods, our spells had distracted him long enough for everyone to get onto the pier, except for Mick, who had vanished under the surface with the boat.

"Behind me," Miss Blackthorne said, pushing her way in front of Oscar and me.

"We need to call Anjea!" I shouted.

"She's a goddess," Miss Blackthorne yelled back, "not the police."

The Scarred Man again lashed out with black tendrils that raced towards us, slamming against our shields.

"Get off me!" Bree screamed.

One of the tendrils had come up from under the pier and wrapped itself around her waist. It would have coiled around her neck too if she didn't have the demonic strength to hold it back. I shot a lance of bright blue fire that cut through the shadowy conjuration, disintegrating it into thick smoke.

Miss Blackthorne expanded her shield, taking the brunt of the black tendrils and freeing up Oscar to go on the offensive. He conjured an eagle out of blazing gold energy, which shot into the air with a single beat of its wings before it turned abruptly and came screaming down like a heat-seeking missile, striking the Scarred Man in the chest.

"Argh!" the Scarred Man cried. He staggered back a step, and the tendrils ceased beating against Miss Blackthorne's barrier.

Oscar attempted another conjuration, but the Scarred Man performed a sharp gesture with his fingers and Oscar's spell backfired, creating a small flash that popped in the air inches from his face. My friend went down screaming, holding his head with both hands.

Bree rushed over to him. "Oscar!"

The Scarred Man raised his hands to the sky and the water around him burst upward before rolling forward like a seismic tidal wave. Yachts crashed against each other, breaking apart as the oncoming wall of water lifted them high into the air. Not to be outdone, Miss Blackthorne stepped forward and clapped her hands together, creating a shockwave that ripped through the air like a thunder crack, splitting the wave in two so it passed us on either side.

The Scarred Man screamed and slapped a hand down on the pier. The woodwork exploded around him, and with a violent gesture, he sent the debris rocketing towards us.

The air pressure from Miss Blackthorne's spell had left me momentarily disoriented, but I had enough sense to form another shield to protect Oscar, Bree, and me. One of the wooden projectiles

143

got past Miss Blackthorne and impaled Arthur in the chest, sending him tumbling into the dark water.

"Arthur!" I called out.

"Focus!" Miss Blackthorne yelled.

The Scarred Man raised his arm towards us again just as a dark form burst out of the water. Mick, having shifted into his True Form, tackled the man around the waist and pinned him to the woodwork. The Mokoi then proceeded to beat the ever-loving heck out of the man with his dark muscular arms.

There was a flash of red, and Mick went flying backwards, smoke rising from his body. The Scarred Man got to his feet, his coat hanging open, flapping in the wind. The ventilator mask hung away from his face, connected to a metal box on his chest by a thin plastic tube. The ragged scars across his face burned red as his mutilated mouth twisted into a snarl.

"You bastard!" Bree shouted, running forward.

She ran headfirst into an invisible wall conjured by Miss Blackthorne.

"No!" said the Master Wizard. "Stay back!"

The Scarred Man glared at us as he grabbed the mask and refitted it over his face. Then, without a word, he turned and left.

I faced her. "We're just letting him go?"

"Or he's letting us go," Miss Blackthorne replied, finally dropping her barrier. "I don't know about you, but I don't have much fight left in me today." Her face twisted into a grimace, and she stumbled. I caught her before she hit the pier.

"Bree!" I called out. "Get over here."

She helped me lower Miss Blackthorne to the deck. When I stepped back, my hands had blood on them.

"Shit," I said, pushing back Miss Blackthorne's coat to reveal an inch-thick wooden spike embedded in her upper chest near the shoulder. "I can't pull it out. You'll lose blood."

Miss Blackthorne took a raspy breath. "Arthur... get Arthur."

I turned to Bree. "Stay with her."

"Let me help," Oscar said, getting up. Blood ran from his nose and a blood vessel had burst in his right eye. He'd lost his glasses at some point during the scuffle.

"Check on Mick," I said, as I removed my shirt and jacket. "Make sure he's breathing." I kicked off my shoes and looked down at the dark water. "Back in a jiffy."

I dived in and let myself sink. Ten feet below the surface, immersed in the dark water and away from the rain and the wind, I closed my eyes and drew in the magic around me. I breathed it in before letting it flow out of me, creating *water worms* that drifted through the gloom, searching.

I found nothing at first, so I sent the *worms* deeper, down to where the light couldn't reach. My magic touched upon a shape on the riverbed that didn't belong. I focused on it, feeling with my magic, until the solid image of Mick's boat formed in my mind. I pushed the magic further, and sensed Arthur's lifeless body inside, tangled amongst the wreckage. I tried using the *worms* to pull him out of there, but my lungs started to burn. I dropped the spell and swam to the surface.

"Find him?" Bree called out.

"He's at the bottom!" I yelled, sucking in deep breaths. "One sec."

I ducked back under. My *water worms* got a hold of him this time. I instinctively took great care to be gentle as I manoeuvred his body out of the sunken vessel, despite knowing the man was already dead. Again.

The moment we breached the surface, Bree grabbed Arthur by his jacket and lifted him onto the pier with one hand.

"Fuck," Bree said, looking at the thick plank of wood that had embedded itself in the man's chest and made its own messy exit through his back. "Jesus."

"Bree," I said, sharply. "Can you take it out?"

"Yeah, but—"

"He'll be fine. But we need to get this thing out of him."

"Shit. Okay." Bree winced as she placed one hand on Arthur's shoulder, grabbing the wood with her other hand.

"Like a Band-Aid," I said.

She held her breath and gave one violent pull, tearing the plank out of his chest. A bit of the red stuff sprayed over us, and I idly hoped the rain would wash it off. Bree set Arthur's limp body on the pier before falling back on her haunches.

"Give him a moment," I said and moved over to Oscar, who knelt by Mick, next to the great hole in the pier created by the Scarred Man. The Mokoi was still in his True Form – featureless face, slick dark skin and a muscular frame with webbed hands and feet. His clothes were charred black, and there were patches of raw pink flesh where he'd been burned by the Scarred Man's spell.

"He's okay," Oscar said. "But he's hurt pretty bad..."

Mick opened his abnormally large eyes and pushed himself up to lean against the thick wooden post. "I'm fine," he said, and once again I was shocked at a regular human voice coming from such a creature. "Bloody hell, that hurt." Mick seemed to wince – it was hard to tell without him having a human face. "Water. I need water... from the river."

Oscar and I magicked some water out of the river and dumped it on the Mokoi.

He sighed with relief. "Yeah, that's the stuff." I didn't know what made the water different from the rain falling from the sky. Perhaps he was siphoning power from his goddess.

"We'll take you to the hospital," I said.

Mick closed his eyes and rested his head against the post. "No," he said. "Get me back to my people. We've got a few good healers who can patch me up. That guy was a nasty piece of work. Who was he?"

"Possibly the guy who killed Lin," I said. The theory was full of holes, but it made more sense than anything else at the moment. I put a hand on Oscar's shoulder. "How are you?"

He grimaced. "My head's killing me, but I'll survive. Joey, that guy... he's in another league. If he's after us..."

"We'll figure it out," I assured him. "For now, just keep dumping water on Mick. I need to check on the Master Wizard."

The Mokoi gave us a tired thumbs up.

I went back to Miss Blackthorne. Blood soaked her clothes around the wooden spike. "We're taking you to the hospital."

"Nonsense," she replied.

"Don't be stupid," Arthur said from behind me. The massive wound in his chest had already filled in, the only evidence of the injury being the gaping hole in his shirt. "You can't move your arm and that splinter may have punctured your lung. You're no good to anyone like this. Let your apprentices take care of you."

She glared at him but conceded the point.

"We'll take her to the hospital," I repeated. "Arthur, can you take Mick back to the Mokoi? They live up the Lane Cove River?"

"Of course."

"Do you have a car?"

"I do not. I caught a bus here."

Bree organised an Uber, while Arthur and I carried Mick to the road. Five minutes later, a black Honda Civic showed up. I hated to think what the extra charges would be for soaked seats and blood stains.

"Don't you worry about us," Arthur said as he got in. "Just see that Mary gets some help."

Bree ducked under Miss Blackthorne's good arm and helped her to the Land Cruiser. Our teacher had lost her cane, but she wasn't in any state to use it, anyway. Her face was pale, her breaths short and sharp.

Bree took driving duty, since Oscar was still recovering from his backfired spell, and I was unquestionably atrocious at operating a manual transmission. Miss Blackthorne reluctantly handed over the keys, and we put her in the backseat between Oscar and me, careful not to bump the spike sticking out of her chest.

She suddenly reached over and grabbed my wrist. "That man..." Her voice came out weak and raspy. "He was no selkie. No mage."

"Then what—"

"That man is a wizard."

22

We rushed Miss Blackthorne to Royal Prince Alfred's Emergency Department. A doctor inspected her quickly, before diagnosing the Master Wizard with a bad case of stake-in-the-chest and directing a couple of nurses to lay her on a wheelie bed.

"We'll remove the weapon immediately," the doctor said.

"It's not a weapon," I said. "There was an accident—"

"Right," he replied distractedly, obviously not caring about the backstory. His loss. "Well, we'll remove it now. Might take a few hours depending on the extent of damage to the lung. Longer if it nicked the brachial plexus. Give your contact details to the desk and they'll call you when we're done." He then turned and helped the two nurses wheel Miss Blackthorne out of the room through a set of double doors.

The old lady at the admittance desk waved us over. She had a grey bob and warm smile. "Just fill these out, dear," she said, handing us a couple of forms.

None of us knew Miss Blackthorne's birthday, Medicare details, or even the actual address of the Old Substation Building.

"Pretty wet out there, isn't it?" said the woman.

"What? Oh, right," I realised we had brought a decent amount of the river with us and were now depositing it all over the tiled floor. "Sorry."

"Oh, don't worry about that. Can't be helped. Our cleaners have been mopping the floors all day."

I wrote down my number on the form and handed it back. "Can you call us when she's up? I'll fill out the rest later."

"Of course," the lady said. "She's your mother, is she?"

"Not quite."

* * *

HALF AN HOUR LATER, Bree, Oscar, and I sat in our living room, not talking, not caring that we were soaking the furniture. After about fifteen minutes of silence, Oscar was the first to speak.

"Beer?"

"God, yes," said Bree.

I nodded as well.

He grabbed some cans of VB from the fridge and tossed them to Bree and me. We cracked them open and drank without speaking for another good while. Eventually, Bree was the one to voice our general sentiments of the afternoon.

"Well, that was pretty fucked," she said before taking a long pull.

"Just a little," I said. "Feeling better, Oscar?"

"Head still hurts," he replied with a wince, then held up the beer. "This helps."

Confusion passed across Bree's face. "What happened to you?"

Oscar shrugged. "I don't know. I tried to cast a spell, but it's like it... got stuck in my head."

"It backfired," I said. "At least that's what it felt like. I could feel the spell as you formed it. *Bracelets*, right? When you were about to release it, the Scarred Man cast something similar, almost an inverse of your spell. Whatever it was, it blocked your magic from leaving you."

"Like a potato in a car's exhaust pipe," Bree said, nodding.

"Sure. Dude can throw some serious magic."

Oscar tapped the top of his beer can thoughtfully. "He went toe to toe with Miss Blackthorne."

"To be fair," I said. "She'd just thrown down with a goddess, so she wasn't working with a full tank of gas."

Oscar picked up his beer and took another sip. "Still..."

Bree drank the rest of her beer in one go, wiped her mouth with the back of her hand, then went and got another from the fridge. "Who was he?" she asked. "He can't have been in the city long. We would have known about him."

"Miss Blackthorne doesn't know everything," I said. "I mean, she still doesn't even know about us training Isabella. Maybe she missed the Scarred Man too. Although my gut tells me she knows more than she's letting on. I'll have to have a word with her when she gets out of surgery."

"Can we wait that long?" Oscar asked.

I frowned. "What do you mean?"

"The Scarred Man tried to kill you at the Baiji house. Then he tried to kill all of us together. And almost succeeded. He's trying to stop us. For whatever reason, he doesn't want us to find out who killed Lin." Oscar's expression turned serious as he cast a quick glance at the window. "And now is the right time for him to strike. While we don't have Miss Blackthorne to protect us."

"We can handle ourselves," Bree said stubbornly.

"No," I said, "we can't. Oscar's right, the Scarred Man is dangerous. We need to take the threat seriously. Also, we have to consider the vampires. Yvette's out there somewhere, with God knows how many *rogue* vampires behind her."

"Yvette could have been lying about there being more like her."

"Do we really want to take that chance?"

Bree threw up her hands. "So, what, we need to find babysitters?"

"No. We need allies."

* * *

By the time Constable Kyra Devapriya and Detective Sergeant Jonathan Hertz came to the house, we had all had showered, changed into dry clothes, and finished dinner. Oscar was even sporting a fresh pair of glasses.

Hertz closed his umbrella, flapped it a few times to shake the rain off, and leaned it against the wall. The law enforcement veteran wore jeans, boots, and a thick half-zip sweater that looked too big even for his lanky frame. Devapriya had her black pleather jacket on that had flaking cracks at the shoulders. She'd forgone the bun and let her thick black hair fall to either side of her face. The constable still had the steely eyed wariness she seemed to adopt whenever she was within my vicinity.

"Your hair looks nice," Bree said. "You should wear it like that when you're in uniform."

"Uh, I can't," Devapriya said, caught off-guard by the compliment. "Regulations."

"Sorted out your car situation?" I asked.

The constable grimaced. "The insurance company loaned me a replacement vehicle until I get the payout. It'll be bugger all, so I'll have to save for a while before I can afford anything bigger than a bicycle."

Hertz ran a hand through his thin greying hair, brushing it to the side. "Something smells good."

"That's Bree's handiwork," I said. "Steak and veg. Can I get you a drink? We have beer."

"I'd prefer if we got right down to it, if you don't mind." Hertz fixed me in his blue-eyed gaze. "Sundays are normally movie nights with the family."

Oscar dragged a couple of extra chairs into the living room for Devapriya and Hertz. I had to move the clothes rack with all our soaked apparel to the kitchen to make space.

"Where's Miss Blackthorne?" asked Devapriya.

"Hospital," I replied. "We had another run-in with our scarred friend."

Devapriya's eyebrows shot up. "What happened?"

"An epic wizarding battle that ended with Miss Blackthorne getting a wooden spike through her chest."

Hertz pulled out his phone and tapped away at something.

"Jesus," was all Devapriya could manage to say.

"She's fine now," I assured the constable. "Hospital called an hour ago and said the surgery went fine. The spike missed the lung. But they're keeping her overnight."

Hertz's bushy eyebrows pressed together as he read something on his phone. "Did this 'epic wizarding battle' take place at Woolwich Marina, by any chance?"

"Uh... maybe," I said.

Hertz flipped his phone around, showing us a very recent news article covering the destruction of several yachts and a significant portion of the pier.

"It's being reported as freak weather," Hertz said dryly. "Must have been quite the fight."

"The guy's not subtle."

Hertz chewed his lip. "Dangerous and unpredictable. I don't like the idea of another magic-wielding individual out there waiting for an opportunity to hunt you down."

"I can get on board with that thinking," I said.

"Good," said the detective sergeant. "Because I'm going to need you to stay here. All of you."

"What?" Bree said. "You can't do that."

Hertz leaned forward and spoke gently. "This man has tried to kill you, Joey, twice. He's reckless... His behaviour is consistent with a psychopath, which puts not just you, but everyone around you, in danger. My instincts tell me to take you all to the station for your protection, but to be honest... I fear that would just put my colleagues at risk."

"What about the selkies?" I said. "The murder of the Baiji girl?"

Hertz raised a hand. "Constable Devapriya has fully apprised me of the situation. I am aware of the conflict arising in the city's Old World. But that is a burden for Mary Blackthorne. From what you have told me, you three cannot stand up to this Scarred Man if he chooses to come after you. And you mentioned this house has some kind of protection magic around it?"

"It's inconsistent."

"Better than nothing. And you're a far cry safer here than out there. Much like any lawful authority, the three of you have enemies, whether they be known or unknown to you. The Scarred Man, demonic thralls—"

"We took care of the thralls," I said.

"You know what I mean," Hertz said patiently. "My point is, inconsistent as its protection may be, you are safer in this house than you are out there. I'm obviously no expert on the subject, but I would have expected you to be under constant assault if this house did not offer some degree of security."

"Let's say you're right," I said. "We can't just sit around here watching Netflix while the river folk and selkies go to war."

"I understand what you're saying, and you're right. But this problem is not yours to resolve. Miss Blackthorne is responsible for the supernatural community within this city. And I'm responsible for everyone else." He looked at Devapriya. "Constable, can you stay with them for the night? I'll talk to the Superintendent, let her know you're on special duties."

Devapriya pressed her lips together, unhappy, but nodded anyway.

"I'm going to the hospital to talk to Miss Blackthorne," Hertz said. "See if we can't resolve all this with a bit of level-headedness and reason. I won't have people running around killing each other like it's the Wild West." Hertz stood up. "You can call me if—"

Someone knocked on the front door.

We looked at each other uncertainly. After all, the last person to unexpectedly knock on our door kicked off this whole debacle.

Two more knocks.

Bree rolled her eyes, got off the couch, and disappeared into the corridor. We heard the door open and close, then heard footsteps echo down the hallway. Bree appeared, followed by Riss. The elf ranger wore darker clothes than her usual earthy palate. Even the shawl covering her head and shoulders was a midnight blue. She threw back the head covering, making her pointed ears poke out from luscious brown hair.

"Riss," Hertz said with a nod. The detective sergeant had met the ranger when they'd fought side by side against a small army of demonic thralls. He eyed the weapon in her hand, a simple recurve bow made of wood and matte black carbon fibre. "Keeping out of trouble?"

"More than most," replied the elf ranger with a wry grin. Her gaze flicked over Bree, Oscar, and me. "Spending time with these three makes it near impossible."

"You're telling me," he said.

The elf turned to me. "Joey, I have identified a Well of Power. We must move quickly before it is extinguished."

I frowned. "That was quick. Haven't you been searching for years?"

"Centuries," she said. "I find them regularly, but they are often very small, too weak and unstable to be of any use, and gone within a day or two. I suspect this one is the same, but I would like you to examine it, so it may leave its magical imprint upon you."

"So, I can sniff out a bigger one?"

"Correct."

"He can't go anywhere," Hertz said. "There's a dangerous individual out there intent on harming these three."

Riss's expression clouded, and she gave the detective sergeant a look that carried centuries of battle-hardened resolve. "There are *several* individuals who wish them harm. But the young wizard has promised to lend his assistance to the elves. Joey is coming with me."

The veteran law enforcement officer seemed unfazed by the ranger's icy glare, but conceded nonetheless, holding up his hands, palms out. "They're not children. They can decide for themselves." Sensing that whatever was going to happen was out of his hands, he turned to Devapriya and said, "Stay with them. Call me if you need me."

The detective sergeant left, obviously unhappy.

"Where are we going?" Bree asked, excited for some reason. Maybe she was relieved at not being under house arrest, or perhaps the beers had just given her a good buzz.

"Not you sorry, Bree," Riss said. "I cannot let you get close to a Well of Power."

My friend pouted. "You don't trust me?"

"I trust you utterly, both as a friend and confidante. I do not trust the demon within you. Having a creature of darkness so close to a source of power that strong is... dangerous." She smirked and added, "Despite how strong-willed the human vessel is."

"I'll come," Oscar said, getting off the couch.

Riss shook her head. "I'm sorry, but the fewer people that come, the better. I wish to be quick and unseen."

Oscar gave her a level gaze. "The Scarred Man is out there looking for us. If you come across him, I'm the best chance you have of getting away." He shot me an apologetic look. "No offence, Joey."

"No, you're right," I said, then turned to Riss. "Oscar's got twice the firepower I have. He's coming with us."

Riss's gaze jumped between Oscar and me as she furrowed her brow. Eventually, she gave us a single firm nod.

Bree looked at Devapriya. "Looks like it'll be a girls' night in."

Devapriya stared at her for a long moment and sighed. "You know what? I think I'll have that beer now."

23

WE CAUGHT an empty train to St James Station and were lucky enough not to encounter any transit officers on the way. They might have raised questions about Riss's handheld accessory, since openly carrying weapons on public transport tends to make people a bit edgy.

We walked up the stairs, tapped our Opal cards at the gates, and entered a long tunnel, where we passed a man shredding on an electric guitar to a backing track being played through tinny speakers. I made a non-verbal apology for not having any spare change on me.

St James Station sits below Hyde Park in the middle of Sydney's CBD, so when we emerged, we were greeted with the roar of buses and taxis and the constant din of rain which just didn't want to quit. We stayed under cover inside the tunnel entrance as we waited for Riss's contact.

"My source should be arriving soon," she said, scrutinising every vehicle that drove past.

I cast a sidelong glance at the elf ranger and asked something I'd wanted to know since the first time I'd seen her. "What's with the boots?"

"You're probably curious about the ears, too. Yes?"

I shrugged. We all took a step back as a bus raced past, splashing a mini tsunami over the footpath.

"Queen Alehtta and her people don't wear shoes because they're accustomed to the forests of the Samelands – the northern region of what is now the Scandinavian Peninsula. Soft earth. Bubbling streams.

It helped them feel closer to their home, closer to the magic that weaved itself through their cities. However, I've always found covering one's feet beneficial when you need to traverse varying terrain."

"Alehtta's not your queen," Oscar said.

She turned to him. "Rangers are... nomadic. We move from place to place. Kingdom to kingdom. Often helping our brethren when they need it. When the elves started leaving their home and... disfiguring themselves to avoid attention, we chose instead to keep moving, never staying in one place too long. Alehtta's people live on the fringes of human society. My people live outside it."

"Are you sure you live outside of it?" I said. "Because you definitely go to better clothing stores than most elves."

The corner of Riss's mouth ticked upwards. "I will take that as a compliment." She looked down the street and lost her smile. "My contact is here."

A man hustled along the footpath towards us, his narrow figure hunched against the rain, head swivelling back and forth between the traffic and the park as if he expected something to jump out from the shadows at any second.

"Jeremy?" I said.

The magician frowned at me, then Riss. "Where's Blackthorne?"

"She was unavailable," the elf ranger replied.

Jeremy narrowed his eyes at Oscar and me and ran his fingers through his greasy brown hair, slicking it back. He wore his street magician outfit that he used when performing for tricks for tourists, but had left behind the cape and top hat. "Alright," he said, looking around again. "Let's get this over with."

He led us back into the tunnel towards the station.

"Go home, Clint," Jeremy said to the man still ripping on guitar. The busker stopped mid-strum and started packing up.

"Expecting trouble?" I asked as we walked.

"You've always got to expect trouble in this town," the magician replied.

We went back through the ticket barriers and down the stairs to the station platform, passing a cleaning lady who was busy emptying the bins. She gave us a funny look as we passed but didn't say anything.

Jeremy led us to the southern end of the platform, where the train tracks disappeared down a dimly lit tunnel. Suddenly, the squeal of metal on metal scraped at my eardrums, followed by a strong gust of wind as a train emerged from the tunnel. A half-dozen people alighted and shuffled up the stairs. By the time the train rolled out of the station, the platform was empty again except for us and the cleaner at the far end.

Jeremy looked up at the CCTV camera, cracked his knuckles, then wiggled his fingers in front of his face while muttering something under his breath. Four smoky figures appeared next to us, almost invisible at first, but increasing in opacity until they took on the exact image of a greasy magician, an elf ranger, and two skinny wizards.

"Come on," Jeremy said. "The illusion will last a while, but I can only keep us invisible for a few seconds."

I spun around. "What?"

Jeremy was gone.

So were Oscar and Riss. I looked down at my hands and could only see the grey tiles of the station platform. Bringing my hands to my face, I noticed a slight bending of the light, like *Predator*, but even more subtle. "How... how did you..."

"Hurry up!" Jeremy said. His voice came from somewhere in the tunnel.

"You're on the tracks? What if a train comes?"

"We'll be splattered across the front of it. So, you better move your arse!"

"But how can we even see? I mean, if the light is passing right through our retinas—"

"It's fucking magic, okay?" Jeremy said, his voice strained. "Now, you've got about ten seconds before there are two of you on the platform. I doubt the Master Wizard would want that recorded on camera."

I felt a hand on my shoulder. "Let's go," Riss said.

I lowered myself onto the tracks, which was surprisingly difficult now that I couldn't see where my I was placing my hands and feet.

"This way," Jeremy said.

I followed the magician's voice into the tunnel, feet crunching over the uneven ballast. Lights lined the tunnel wall thirty feet apart. I could hear everyone's footsteps, but it still felt like I was the only one there.

"You here, Oscar?" I said to the air.

"Yeah," he replied, somewhere on my right.

A few seconds later, the invisibility wore off, and I found myself thankful for being able to see our little band of tunnel explorers again. A short way into the tunnel, Jeremy ducked into a recess in the wall concealed in shadow. He stood before a large piece of plywood that acted as a door, like the ones you'd find on the perimeter of a construction site. It was secured with a hefty padlock and had a sign on it that said *DO NOT ENTER* in big red letters. The plywood had warped over time and no longer sat snugly in the portal.

Jeremy pulled a key from his pocket, unlocked the padlock, and pushed the door open. It scraped the floor and dust crept into my nose, sending me into a minor sneezing fit. When I recovered, I followed the others through the doorway, relieved to no longer be standing on the train tracks.

"Do you mind providing some light?" Riss said. "Even I cannot see in pure darkness."

Oscar conjured a bright yellow *lumière* and tossed it into the air, where it hung suspended, casting its light over the room. It was actually less a room, and more like an underground cavern. Graffiti-covered concrete walls extended upwards fifty feet before curving across the expansive space to form one giant arched ceiling. In one of the corners, milk crates and several empty beer bottles lay next to filthy mattresses and a metal drum full of burnt wood and garbage.

"I've read about this," Oscar said, looking up at the dirty ceiling. "These tunnels were excavated to be extensions to St James Station, but it never went ahead. They used them as air-raid shelters in the forties. There are some at the other end of the station, too. The Ghost Tunnels, I think they're called."

Riss walked to the metal drum and mattresses, broken glass crunching under her boots. "I believe some of Alehtta's people used to reside down here on occasion," she said, nudging an empty beer bottle with her toe.

"Why'd they leave?" I asked.

"The same reason we shouldn't fuck around," Jeremy said. "Because it's bloody dangerous, down here." He moved briskly to the far end of the room, his voice echoing back to us. "The Ghost Tunnels extend farther than any one person knows. Underground lakes, sewer systems, tunnels dug out by machine and creature alike. Explore too deep and I guarantee you'll find things a lot scarier than ghosts. Now if you don't mind." He conjured a light in his hand, a white beam focused like a torchlight, and disappeared through a narrow opening.

A train squealed on its rails and rattled through the tunnel on the other side of the plywood door. I found some comfort in the knowledge that the station, and hence other people, weren't too far away.

We followed Jeremy into a room as big and dark as the one we'd just left. The magician stood at the far end of the space, next to a door made of rusted steel bars. He unlocked it and held it open for us as we approached.

"Down the stairs," he said. "There's a corridor. After about a hundred feet, you'll find a metal grate—"

"You're coming," Riss said.

Jeremy put up his hands. "Whoa! I'm not going down there. I'm just here to point the way."

Riss took a step closer to him. She was taller by maybe an inch, but it wasn't her height that made her intimidating. "You are here to take us to the Well of Power. Do the job or you will not be paid."

The magician licked his lips, and his gaze flitted about the room. Eventually, his eyes fell to the floor, and he spat. "Fuck." He pointed at Riss. "You're going in front." The magician then whirled on me, saying, "And you're at the back."

We descended the stairs in single file – Riss, Oscar, Jeremy, then me. Oscar maintained a small *lumière*, so we didn't slip down the staircase. The temperature dropped the farther down we went, and the air got thick and heavy.

"What kinds of things are down here?" I asked.

"The kind with good hearing," Jeremy snapped.

I took the hint and shut up.

At the bottom of the stairs, we hit a narrow tunnel. Empty metal racks lined the walls, bolted into the sides at eye-level. They looked like they might have carried communication or electricity cables once upon a time, but now they held nothing but dust.

We came to a square metal grate in the floor.

"Open that up," Jeremy instructed.

I frowned at him.

"Hey," he said. "I'm showing you the way, aren't I? Never said I'd be doing any heavy lifting."

I rolled my eyes and crouched down. "Give me a hand, Riss?"

The elf slung her bow over a shoulder and got down, while Oscar watched both ends of the corridor. Or at least as far as the light would go.

"Make sure you lift with your legs," Jeremy suggested.

"Yeah, thanks," I replied.

It took us a few tries to heave the grate out of position – I'm not built for manual labour. Once free, we slid the grate to the side in explosive jerks to reveal a rather ominous hole with metal rungs in the side. Without a word, Riss jumped in and quickly began descending. I moved to follow, but Jeremy grabbed my jacket and yanked me back.

"You go last," he said.

Oscar and Jeremy went down into the hole and I followed. The vertical shaft was tight – about three feet by three feet – just enough room to move without succumbing to a claustrophobic panic.

I cast a tiny *lumière*, no bigger than a candle flame. It hovered above my head and helped me find the rungs, while also staving off the disoriented insanity you get when you spend too long in the dark. As I descended, the sounds of running water began to fill the silence, getting louder and louder, until it thundered like a raging river. I reached the bottom and almost fell into the flowing water as my foot skidded off the slippery edge. I felt a tight grip on my arm as Riss and Oscar pulled me against the wall.

We stood in some kind of major drainage tunnel. Narrow ledges lined the sides, with a twenty-foot-wide channel of water violently flowing through the middle curtesy of the recent rains. The entire tunnel curved like a giant cylinder, built of moss-covered bricks that gleamed with moisture in the light of my *lumière*.

"Watch your step," Jeremy said.

The magician led us deeper into the Ghost Tunnels, ensuring Riss stayed no more than an arm's length away. We left the drainage tunnel and crawled through the labyrinth of broken stairs, rusted ladders, and crumbling cavities. Crept through old utility passageways, some still with orange PVC ducting running along their length. We moved along drainage tunnels with water no deeper than a puddle, and others with literal rivers of dark churning water that forced us to clamber along the ledges.

As we clambered through the underground maze, a soft magical pressure began to brush against my senses. It felt nothing like the shifting of magical energies when Oscar or I cast spells. It was more... pure. Almost alive. The feeling came and went like a soft pulse, getting stronger the deeper we delved.

"It's through here," Jeremy whispered as we entered yet another drainage tunnel. We followed the flow, stepping through water just deep enough to wet my ankles and get in my shoes. The air grew damper and cooler, and the sound of rushing water grew louder.

We came to a chamber twenty feet wide and long, with grime-covered walls that rose fifty feet. A pool of fetid water covered the entire floor, fed by the tunnel we just exited, as well as a series of culverts above us that were dumping waterfalls into the large space. Directly across the chamber lay another tunnel that drained the water away. Jeremy grumbled something about not agreeing to get wet. I'd given up any hope of staying dry long ago.

The magic pushing against my senses deepened, buffeting against my consciousness like waves in a storm, pulsing every few seconds.

"Can you feel that?" I said.

Oscar shook his head.

Riss looked up at the water flowing in from the above culverts. "I cannot sense it either. The Well of Power is too small for me to perceive."

Jeremy glanced back down the way we came and rubbed the back of his neck. "Can you guys do what you need to do so we can get out of here?"

I ignored him and, with a thought, moved my *lumière* to the centre of the chamber until it was completely immersed in the waterfall pouring in. On the next pulse of magical energy, my spell lit up like a sun, flooding the room with blazing white light. Agony flashed across my scars. I averted my eyes and dropped the spell.

"What the hell was that?" said Oscar, blinking hard.

I shook my arm to loosen it up. "Hey, can you block the water for a sec?" I asked.

Oscar looked up and tilted his head. "Sure," he said and stretched both arms upwards, hands splayed out. Water slid to the side as if we stood under an invisible umbrella.

I moved towards the middle of the room. The pulses maintained their regularity, but the power in each beat increased exponentially with each step I took. My scars began to glow, as did the searing pain that shot through them. By the time I reached the centre of the chamber, I was in agony and the scars on my arm glowed so brightly I had to turn away.

Then I saw it.

A tiny sphere of... something... hung in the air at about chest height. I didn't see it exactly, not with my eyes, but I knew it was there, knew its shape and size instinctively.

The Well of Power.

It radiated energy like nothing I'd encountered. Even the awesome display from the river goddess didn't come close. Impressive for something that was no bigger than my fingertip.

As the magic washed over me, I realised that calling it a Well of Power was misleading. To me, it felt more like a doorway. A portal. A tear in reality that pierced every realm from the Realms Above to the Realms Below. And behind it lay The Cascade, the omnipresent ocean of cosmic forces that permeates everything in existence.

Naturally, I reached out to touch it.

Riss seized my wrist. "Someone approaches." Her eyes focused on the outlet tunnel. How she could hear someone's footsteps over the crashing water was a mystery to me.

"Then let's go," Jeremy said in a harsh whisper.

The elf whirled on Jeremy, her shawl fanning out behind her like a small cape. She grabbed the magician by his collar and pulled him in so they were nose to nose.

"I grow tired of your cowardice," Riss snarled, and pushed him away. She turned to Oscar and me. "If someone else knows the location of this Well of Power, then I must know who it is."

Jeremy scowled at the elf ranger and rubbed his throat. "Christ, woman. All you had to do was say so. I suggest we vacate this chamber, though. Unless you plan on shaking hands with whoever's coming."

I took one last look at the point in space that held so much power and potential, then followed the others into the tunnel we'd come through. Oscar dropped his arms, and water once again crashed to the middle of the chamber, enshrouding the Well of Power. We went about a hundred feet into the tunnel and crouched in the ankle-deep water. Jeremy spread his hands, and the air shimmered around us, becoming translucent.

"They'll see us," Oscar whispered.

"Nah," Jeremy replied. "Spell looks different to anyone looking from the outside. All they'd see is shadows." He cast his gaze behind us. "But it's dark enough in here that the chances of them actually spotting us are slim to none. Even the elf wouldn't be able to pick us out. The only thing that could give us away is Finch's heavy breathing."

"Sorry," I said.

"Quiet," snapped Riss, her voice low and tense.

Oscar extinguished his *lumière*, and we waited in the dark. A minute later, a dull, red glow emanated from the outlet tunnel on the other side of the large space. A cold spike of adrenaline shot through me as the Scarred Man stepped into the chamber.

24

―――――――

A FIST-SIZED BALL of sizzling red energy hovered in front of him, casting everything in a hellish light. He brushed his scraggly black hair out of his eyes and looked up at the water. With a wave, he diverted the falling water to the sides of the room.

He removed his coat to reveal he wore no shirt underneath, although the flickering red light showed off dark ragged scars that criss-crossed all over his body. I couldn't see a clear patch of skin more than three inches across. Then I saw the machinery.

Jeremy hissed out a breath next to my ear. Riss gave him a sharp elbow.

A series of electrical and mechanical devices hung off the Scarred Man's chest and stomach, secured to his torso with wide black straps. A plastic tube ran from one of the boxes to his ventilation mask. I couldn't see any oxygen tanks, so I assumed it was a purely mechanical device, physically pumping air in and out of the guy's lungs.

He made a small gesture with his hand and a shard of concrete broke away from the wall, sticking out at a dangerous angle. He used it to hang his coat, then turned back to the centre of the chamber.

The Scarred Man extended his arm and walked forward. The scars on his arm flared to life, throwing even more red light around the room, and a strained grunt echoed towards us. With his jaw set in grim determination, he waved his arm back and forth, the energy coursing through his scars telling him whether he was getting hot or cold. Suddenly, he reached out and grabbed the Well of Power.

The effect was immediate.

A blinding flash of scarlet light filled the chamber, followed by a howling wind and a freight train of magical pressure on my brain. I let out a small cry, surprised at the sudden pain. Luckily, the Scarred Man was too busy screaming to notice.

He fell to his knees in the water and bellowed an agonised roar. The scars covering his body glowed an intense red, too bright to look at. The pain coursing through his body would have been unbearable. When he finally stopped screaming, he stayed on his knees in tortured silence for a full minute as the light in his scars died down. With shaking hands, he pushed himself to his feet.

I put my mouth to Riss's ear. "We should—"

The elf ranger clamped a hand over my mouth and stared daggers at me, then inclined her head back towards the chamber. She held my head so tightly I could only move my eyes.

A dark figure climbed down the wall of the chamber behind the Scarred Man, moving with spider-like grace. Then another appeared. And another. Before long, the Scarred Man was surrounded by a dozen red-eyed vampires, and more kept coming, crawling from the culverts at the top of the chamber. They bared rows of shark-like teeth as they clung to the walls, using minuscule cracks and protrusions for purchase. Half of them wore suits and business dresses that wouldn't have been out of place at a certain investment company.

The Scarred Man glanced at the creatures nonplussed and casually plucked his coat from the wall as if he was about to pop down to the shops.

"You made it," he said, his voice calm and level. He put the coat on and fastened the buttons, covering the ventilation equipment.

One of the vampires spoke. "This place... we couldn't have met somewhere more convenient? We had to convince a water mage to help us traverse these damn tunnels." I recognised the voice because I had threatened its owner only the night before. Yvette crawled down the chamber wall, stepped into the water, and frowned. "These were Jimmy Choos."

"Huh," the Scarred Man said, voice piqued with minor interest. "I thought you were only scared of water running over earth."

"We're not scared," she snapped. "Streams can kill us. Natural streams especially." She gestured around her. "We can tolerate sewers... but it weakens us. And it's filthy."

"Delicate little things, aren't you?" the Scarred Man said.

Yvette scowled.

Two vampires climbed down the wall, carrying a man between them like a life-sized rag doll. He wore a hi-vis orange vest over a chequered shirt. They lowered him into the water, where he slumped against the wall, dazed but conscious. Likely under the effects of a glamour.

A fire burned in my chest. I couldn't leave this man's fate up to the vampires. Hands grabbed me, holding me back before I realised I'd started moving. I turned back to Oscar, who shook his head slowly. Even in the near complete darkness, I could see his eyes were wide with fear. Riss shook her head too, holding a finger to her lips. My brain knew I couldn't do anything for the man. But every other part of me wanted to try, anyway.

Yvette crouched and inspected the man, using a finger to lift his chin. "Don't pass out, dear," she said. "We still need you to get back." The vampire stood and faced the Scarred Man. "Blackthorne is in hospital. Her apprentices and the demon girl were sheltering in their home the last time we checked. Hiding from you, no doubt."

The Scarred Man raised an eyebrow. "And now?"

"Still at the house, most likely."

"Most likely?"

Yvette glared. "We had to leave two hours ago to retrieve the water mage from the Fish Market. Then we had to waste time finding our way through this stinking maze."

"And you left no one to watch the house?"

Yvette glared. "Of course, I did. I'm not stupid. My *rogues* may have even gone inside if they could get through those wards. But there's no signal in these cursed tunnels, so I won't know for sure until we leave."

"The children aren't a problem yet," the Scarred Man said with an indifferent wave of his hand. "They showed surprising strength, especially the tall one. But nothing I need to concern myself with right now." He lifted a hand in front of his face, inspecting it closely as he opened and closed his fist. The scars emitted a soft glow. "It would have been good to destroy Blackthorne."

Jeremy hissed a breath. I turned to see the magician was red in the face, thick veins protruding from his neck. He hadn't been expecting to hold the spell this long. Yvette spun like a whip at the sound and stared straight at us, her blood-red eyes becoming slits as she tried to pierce the darkness. I held my breath and froze, hoping everyone else was doing the same. Presumably Jeremy was doing a bang-up job because Yvette turned back to the Scarred Man.

"I am more than happy to kill Blackthorne for you," the vampire offered. "I would suggest striking at her now, while she is vulnerable. She has meddled in the affairs of vampires for far too long. She pollutes the minds of even the most ardent members of Family Dragos."

"That so?" the Scarred Man replied with disinterest. "She's not a problem, even if she gets out of the hospital. The wheels are already in motion."

The vampires climbed a little lower down the walls. The Scarred Man didn't seem to notice. Or simply didn't care.

"Don't forget your promise, wizard," Yvette snarled. "We've done what you asked. We've observed the wizards, we've watched the river men, and spied on our own kin. Now you owe us."

"Ah, yes," the man said. "Your little rebellion."

Yvette narrowed her eyes. "There's nothing *little* about it," she said with venom. "You have no idea how far this reaches."

"Oh, you'd be surprised," the Scarred Man said. "Tell me. When I gave you instructions to watch the Custodian and her apprentices, why did you feel the need to make yourself known to them?"

"They need to know their place," Yvette said with a smirk.

"It was unnecessary," the Scarred Man replied, "and, to be frank, quite stupid." He raised a hand and blasted a lance of fiery red energy at the man in the hi-vis vest. The spell drilled through his chest and blew concrete chips out of the wall behind him.

The hands holding me back gripped me tighter as the man's lifeless body slid into the water.

Yvette leaped back and snarled at the Scarred Man. "We needed him to get out, you fool!" she hissed. "Damned if I cross streams! You will have to clear the waterways for us now."

"I don't think so," he said. I couldn't see it through his mask, but the amusement in his voice made me think he had the beginnings of a smile. "You will not be leaving these tunnels."

Yvette's eyes widened, and she gave a shrill cry of pure animalistic rage. She flew at the Scarred Man, the other vampires leaping from the walls a nanosecond later. I felt a tectonic shift in magical energies as the Scarred Man slammed a glowing fist into the ground, sending a concussive blast of fiery red energy in every direction.

Violent magic roared towards us, but I'd already conjured a defensive barrier, Oscar following suit. Crimson fire slammed against our shields, and I cried out as my scars burned from the massive amounts of energy being spent to maintain my shield.

"Hold on, Joey!" Oscar yelled over the roar of the Scarred Man's spell.

The fire died away, replaced by thick steam from the vaporised stormwater. I dropped my shield and peered through the haze to the chamber, where the Scarred Man and the vampires stared right back at me.

25

"Run!" I shouted.

Riss, who had taken cover behind Oscar and me, hauled Jeremy to his feet and pushed him along the tunnel.

"Go!" she yelled.

The Scarred Man threw a nasty band of thin red energy, sharp and wide, that ploughed through the sides of the tunnel as it sped towards us and may have sliced through skin and bone too if Oscar hadn't doubled down on his shield. The spell slammed into his semitransparent barrier, creating gold ripples across its surface.

"Fuck!" Oscar screamed through gritted teeth.

Vampires swarmed over the Scarred Man, and I took the opportunity to grab Oscar and spin him around. "Let's go, potty mouth!"

We took off after Riss and Jeremy, the magician's spell illuminating the tunnel just ahead of us, while sounds of chaos and destruction came from behind. I glanced over my shoulder. The tunnel was quickly filling with vampires as they peeled away from the battle in search of less dangerous fare, their silhouettes dark against the firestorm taking place in the chamber.

I ran with a *lumière* in my fist, willing my legs to pump harder while Oscar blindly threw spells behind us. We heard the occasional hiss of pain as the odd spell hit home, but still the vampires closed in, their ragged breaths and bloodcurdling shrieks getting closer by the second. The constantly running water around our ankles did bugger all to slow them down.

Something whizzed past my ear and a vampire screamed. Further up the tunnel, Jeremy and Riss had stopped just before the tunnel bent to the right. The elf ranger stood straight, nocked another arrow, and let it fly. It sailed over my head and struck a vampire that was clawing its way along the tunnel ceiling. It fell with a scream and a splash, the other vampires screeching in wild frustration as they rushed past their fallen comrade.

"Close your eyes!" Jeremy yelled as he spread his arms wide.

I complied but didn't stop moving. I felt a soft wave of pressure followed by a warm breath of air as blinding light tried to work its way between my eyelids. Agonised wails came from behind me, but any relief I felt quickly evaporated when I tripped and went sprawling into the water. Turns out, running with your eyes closed is not a great idea.

Hands grabbed me and hauled me to my feet.

"Eyes open!" Jeremy said. "That'll only buy us a few seconds."

The four of us rounded the curve and I could already hear the vampires pick up the chase again. We leaped up stairs, down some others. Climbed ladders and squeezed through broken passageways, the vampires never far behind. We were at the mercy of Jeremy's knowledge of the underground maze. Funnily enough, the magician had no qualms about being up front this time.

"Should we hide?" Oscar panted as we ran.

"They will find us," Riss said. "Keep moving."

My legs burned, my heart thumped in my chest. I'd banged up my hands and knees pretty good from climbing rusty ladders and scrambling over bricks and concrete. Sweat poured off me, but that may have just been the drainage water. Furious shrieks echoed through the tunnels behind us, making my blood turn cold and my hair stand on end. We'd put enough distance between us and our pursuers so as not to see them whenever we looked back. But they were there.

We hit a T-junction and Jeremy faltered, falling to his knees.

"I... I can't," he said with a shake of his head, barely able to get the words out.

His eyes were half closed, and sweat streamed down his face, reflecting the light from our *lumières*. The illusion spell he had used to mask us from the Scarred Man must have really taken it out of him.

"Which way?" I demanded. "Hey! Which way?"

"Left," he whispered.

I turned to Riss and Oscar. "Get him up and go!"

They quickly moved to either side of the magician and carried him forward, turning left at the junction. I looked back and saw red eyes in the darkness.

I extinguished my *lumière* and spared a moment to draw energy and conjure a large blue sphere between my hands, the size of a basketball. I sent it rocketing down the tunnel and counted to five before giving it another jab of energy. The spell exploded amidst the vampires in a hail of white and blue fireworks, and the creatures screamed as fire burned skin and clothes. A tangle of bodies, writhing like snakes out of a twisted nightmare.

Yeah, time to leave.

I turned tail and ran, casting another *lumière* to light the way. The sound of rushing water filled the tunnel as I hurried along, the noise growing to a constant roar. I caught up to the others, and I realised we'd circled around to the brick drainage tunnel we'd started from, somehow ending up on the wrong side of the turbulent underground river that separated us from the vertical shaft and our way out.

"The vampires... won't be able to cross," Jeremy panted.

"Neither can we," I said. There's a reason so many people die in floods. It's not the depth of the water that's a killer, it's the power behind it.

"Better think fast then, wizards," Riss said. She let Oscar take the full weight of Jeremy, then unslung her bow, and in precise, fluid motions began firing arrows into the dark behind us. I couldn't see the hits, but I heard the screams.

"I'm done, dude," I said, struggling to simply maintain my *lumière*.

Oscar looked left and right before his gaze drifted up to the tunnel's curved ceiling. He dumped Jeremy onto me and extended his hands to the crown of the arching brickwork. I felt power well up inside him, which then exploded forward, hitting the tunnel ceiling with a resounding crack as chunks of brick and mortar burst from the lining.

"You'll cause a cave in!" I said.

"The load will be directed around the holes," he said. "If I knock out the bricks in a line, it should only trigger a local collapse."

"Sure," I said.

I'd been getting through my degree mostly by copying Oscar's uni work, so I could vouch for his engineering judgement. He conjured another kinetic spell that smashed more bricks free of the tunnel lining.

"They're here!" Riss yelled behind us.

Oscar raised his hands above his head and brought them down with a cry of effort. A massive chunk of bricks crashed into the water, prompting a collapse of the brickworks that fell away from the tunnel lining in a straight path perpendicular to the direction of the tunnel. The large masses of brick and mortar had fallen in a rough line, creating convenient stepping stones.

"You'll have to go yourself, mate," I screamed at Jeremy.

The magician didn't waste time, and with a surprising burst of energy, skipped across the chunks of brick to the other side of the tunnel, quickly disappearing up the ladder.

"Go, Joey!" Oscar yelled.

"No, you should—"

Oscar pushed me towards the water. Neither of us were particularly strong, but his six-foot-four against my five-seven went a long way. I lost my balance and had to jump onto the first mass of bricks to avoid going headfirst into the current. I bounded the rest of the way across, hitting the wall hard on the other side.

Riss aimed and fired with quick, flowing movements, each arrow eliciting a pained howl from the dark creatures on our tail. Her quiver was almost empty. Bloody hell, how many vampires were there?

One of the dark creatures materialised from the shadows, her shark-like teeth gnashing at the elf. She received an arrow through her skull and tumbled along the ground, only to spring to her feet moments later. Where were the crucifixes and wooden stakes when you needed them?

Oscar stepped beside the elf and conjured a wall of white fire as more vampires clawed their way forwards. Then, with a surge of energy, he sent the spell hurtling down the tunnel and I felt the dramatic change in pressure, not just from the shifting of magic, but from the physical displacement of air as well. Agonised screams echoed from the darkness.

"Come on!" I yelled, beckoning frantically for them to get a move on.

Riss shoved Oscar my way, and he leaped across the stepping

stones to my side. The elf spun and followed. As she got to the water's edge, a vampire, scrambling along the top of the tunnel, came down upon her, his jaws open wide, displaying several rows of teeth aimed at her jugular. She must have heard it, because she whirled at the last second and brought up an arm which saved her life. The vampire latched onto her upraised forearm like a rabid dog. The elf didn't make any sounds of pain, instead taking a step to widen her stance. With calm precision, she withdrew a knife from under her jacket and brought it down onto the vampire's head, and with a sudden twist, levered the creature from her arm. It fell to the ground, dead.

Riss spun towards us and jumped across the water, clearing the twenty-foot gap in two nimble bounds. Another vampire leaped after her, but Oscar shot a hand forward and caught the snarling creature around the neck with a *golden bracelet*. With his face set in a grim frown, Oscar dipped the vampire in the rushing water, eliciting a high-pitched wail that hurt my ears. The cries stopped seconds later, and he launched the vampire back against the opposite wall where it slumped to the floor, the creature's face a molten mess of grey skin that fell away like soggy newspaper, exposing bone and teeth.

The other vampires reached the edge of the water. There must have been at least a dozen of them, broken arrow shafts sticking out of their charred bodies, making them look like angry pin cushions. They saw their fallen comrades and glared at us with unblinking red eyes. I had a *sneezer* ready to slap them down if they tried to cross.

Yvette slithered to the front of the group. The battle with the Scarred Man had all but destroyed her. Her clothes had been incinerated, displaying a mottled mess of charred black skin and blistering red sores that covered her entire body. Her raven hair was gone, burnt away, and her face was unrecognisable, melted into a featureless mask. It was the eyes, full of unbridled hatred, that gave her away.

The vampires behind her seemed to wait for her signal, but she didn't cross, didn't even scream at us. She just watched.

"Let's not waste time," Riss said and swung herself up the ladder with a flourish of her shawl.

"You go," I said to Oscar, keeping an eye on the vampires across the water.

He shook his head. "You should make sure Riss and Jeremy are okay." Which was a polite way of saying he was stronger and had a better chance of holding off the vampires if they tried to cross.

I cast a quick look at the horde of creatures, lined along the wall like athletes at a starting line with Yvette at the centre, crimson eyes boring into me with fierce intensity.

"Come up right behind me, okay?"

I climbed the ladder. My legs were heavy with fatigue, and my palms throbbed with every rung I gripped. I emerged in the utility tunnel, where Riss and Jeremy grabbed me by the armpits and pulled me out of the shaft. The elf's sleeve was saturated with blood.

"You okay?" I asked.

"Vampire saliva has an anticoagulant," she said as she cut a wide strip from her shawl and wrapped it tightly around her forearm. "I need medical attention, or I will bleed out."

"You're not going to... turn, are you?"

She cocked an eyebrow. "Into a vampire? I think that requires more than a simple bite."

I looked back down the hole and saw no sign of Oscar. No sound came from below. No light. Seconds dragged by agonisingly slowly.

"Your friend is strong," Riss said quietly. "He will be fine."

An eternity later, Oscar poked his head out. I grabbed a fistful of his jacket and dragged him out of there. Riss and I hauled the metal grate back into place, then Oscar and I spent a couple of minutes using concentrated heat spells to weld the grate in place. We only did the corners, otherwise it would have taken hours.

We ran back through the utility tunnel and up the stairs to the giant caverns. I kept glancing back, expecting to see a horde of vampires crawl from the shadows. We waited at the plywood door for a train to pass before jumping onto the tracks and running back along the tunnel to the station. We climbed back onto the platform, where Jeremy's illusion spell had surprisingly held. Kind of. Our hologram twins had lost some of their opacity and now appeared as four ghostly figures with vacant expressions. The cleaner stood a couple of feet back, waving her broom through the apparitions, probably unsure whether to call the ghostbusters or a psychiatrist.

She screamed when we appeared and swung the broom towards us. Riss caught the broom in her hand, the cloth around her forearm already soaked through with blood.

The cleaner looked from us back to the ghost versions. "What... where did you..."

"Shift's over," Riss said, taking the broom from the cleaner's hands and placing her good arm around the smaller woman's shoulders.

The cleaner's eyes drifted from Riss's bleeding arm, to the bow on the elf's back, to the ears sticking out of her hair. "But..."

"Let's get you out of here," Riss said gently, steering the woman towards the stairs.

26

WE CAME out of the station to the glorious cool night air and the smell of wet concrete. Traffic sped past, headlights reflecting off the glistening asphalt. Rain fell as a barely noticeable light sprinkle that I found refreshing after crawling through the dank sewers.

"Go straight home," Riss said to the cleaner. When the small woman gave Riss a confused look, the elf smiled again. "Just tell them you didn't feel well."

The cleaner turned and walked away, completely oblivious to the creatures that lurked below her feet.

"We sealed the grate," I said. "The vampires can't follow us."

"There are dozens of doorways to The Ghost Tunnels," Jeremy said. "Bloody rabbit warren." Sweat ran down his face, and his skin was paler than usual, but at least he could walk and talk again.

In a blur of motion, Riss grabbed Jeremy's shirt and held a bloody knife to the magician's throat. "From whom did you get your information? Tonight's expedition felt suspiciously like a trap."

The magician held up his hands. "Hey, easy! They wanted to kill me too, remember? The information came from a Beast Master. I swear I had no idea anyone else knew about it!"

"And where did the Beast Master get the information?"

"Rats!" Jeremy said. "Honest! Rats. They picked up on something unusual down there and told my contact about it. Of course, he didn't know what it was, otherwise he might have asked for a bit more than he did."

The elf ranger kept the blade at the man's neck. I placed a hand on her arm. She looked at my hand, then released Jeremy with a frustrated sigh.

"Those vampires," Oscar said. "I recognised some of them from Double Point Investments. They're part of Family Dragos, meant to be following their Father's rules."

"*Rogues*," Jeremy said as he rubbed his neck. "Penni and Vasily may have a tight leash on most of their family, but at their core, vampires are fucking animals. Every single one of them wants to dig their teeth into our flesh and rip it from our bones. Anyone who thinks otherwise is an idiot. *Rogues* just happen to be the only ones who act upon their impulses."

"Penni would have noticed this many vampires going bad," I said.

Jeremy frowned. "I'd bet my left nut most of them are from completely different families, different cities. The important thing is they don't see us as anything but food." He ran a hand through his hair. "And now they know I'm not a simple street magician." He jabbed a finger at us. "Don't fucking call me for any more favours. Any of you." Looking at Riss, he said, "I want my payment by the end of next week."

He turned to leave.

"You saved us down there," I said to him. "Thank you."

Jeremy furrowed his brow, pressed his lips together and nodded once before walking back in the direction of Circular Quay.

Riss pulled a phone from her pocket because even creatures of legend aren't immune to the trappings of technology. She called her elf friends to pick her up, requesting that they hurry.

"You're pretty handy with that bow," I said.

She inclined her head in acknowledgement. "I've had ample practice."

"The Well of Power wasn't what I was expecting. It was tiny, but the power was... staggering."

"And that was a mere fraction of the power that used to bathe elf cities in years past."

"What happened to them?" I asked. "The Wells of Power? Destroying something that big would be like..."

"Like a nuclear explosion," Riss said. "Or a volcanic eruption. It is likely that some Wells of Power have been destroyed, but from what I have observed, most of them still exist. They are guarded by the

Venerati Sanctus waiting for elves to return so they can finish us off. Hence why we must find new ones."

"I felt... something behind the Well of Power," I said. "Like it was a doorway straight to The Cascade."

Riss shrugged. "You would know more about that than me." Her expression turned serious. "Do you think you will be able to aid me in locating others?"

"I'll do my best," I said honestly. I'd have to figure out the specifics later.

The elf ranger gave a sharp nod, then said, "Do you think the Scarred Man killed the Baiji girl?"

"He's the only psychopath we've seen knocking about. And he could have used magic to break into the selkie embassy and steal the Ambassador's sword."

"Why use a sword to kill Lin when he could have just used magic?" Oscar asked.

"Why kill her in the first place?" I countered. "Maybe he wanted to frame the selkies, or kick start a war. Or maybe the ambassador hired him to kill Lin and told him to use the blade to send river folk a message. We still don't know enough."

"These questions are beyond me," Riss said. "But I do know that a selkie is never separated from her weapon. It would be like me parting with my bow. Unthinkable." She looked back at the train station as if expecting the Scarred Man to appear at any moment. "That man is a formidable opponent, and you would do well to avoid crossing his path in the future."

"Maybe the vampires finished him off?" I said.

Riss cocked an eyebrow. "Do you think so?"

I didn't respond.

Her ride arrived. A twenty-year-old Ford Falcon driven by a sandy-haired elf whose belly almost touched the steering wheel. Not everyone can be Legolas.

"Joey!" Oscar said suddenly. "Bree and the constable!"

Shit. I'd been so caught up in not getting eaten, I had forgotten what Yvette had said. Vampires were watching the house.

"Get in the car," Riss said.

* * *

178

LUCKILY, the streets weren't too crowded, so we raced through the city, right on the speed limit. Bree's phone kept sending me straight to her voicemail. The vampires may have already gotten to her and Constable Devapriya for all we knew. I needed to think about something else. Worrying wouldn't get me anywhere.

"How much did you have to offer Jeremy to help us?" I asked.

"He didn't ask for money."

"That's surprising. What did he want?"

The elf shrugged. "He wants me to help him see his daughter. Apparently, your laws are unfavourable to those who have spent time in prison."

Well, there you go. Maybe the magician wasn't as obnoxiously self-centred as he appeared. Still a dick, though.

My phone buzzed.

"Bree," I said, picking up.

"What's up, man?" she yelled. "You guys are still out?"

"You're okay? Everything's good at home?"

"No, it's not okay," she said. "Our pizza hasn't arrived. They are three... no, four minutes late." Her syllables dragged like she was pulling them through mud. "Oh, we started on wine, but there's lots of beer left—"

"You haven't seen vampires or anything?"

"You mean real or TV?"

"Real."

"No vampires here. No way."

"Good. Keep an eye out, Bree. There're monsters about."

"Big boss man. Okay. Oh, pizza's here!" She hung up.

"Bree's okay," I said, relaxing a fraction. I thought on it a moment, then leaned forward in my seat. "Can we make a detour?"

* * *

IT WAS WELL past midnight when we pulled up to Nelly's on King. Before Oscar and I jumped out, Riss turned in her seat and spoke to us.

"You acted with bravery," she said. "Both of you did. I am beginning to understand what the queen sees in you. Although she will wish to remain neutral in the coming conflict."

"Yeah, I figured."

Riss gave a half smile. "The city is in good hands with you two and Bree watching over it." She looked out the window, up at the dark sky. "There is a storm coming. Don't let it catch you unawares."

We got out, and the elves sped off into the night to whatever mystical healers they had on staff. Although, I'd seen elves being admitted to regular human hospitals before, so maybe that's where they were headed.

We approached the Māori bouncer standing guard out the front of Nelly's. He had the proportions of a rhinoceros, the personality of a puppy, and a giant smile that made his eyes squint so hard they disappeared.

"Hey fellas," he said. "Closing in an hour, so you better get 'em in quick." He held the door open for us.

It was a Sunday night, so the pub was mostly empty. A couple of tables had people stubbornly trying to milk out what they could from the night. A guy and girl were making out on a leather couch in a dark corner at the back, well past the point of self-consciousness. That is, if there was any to begin with.

We went upstairs, where the atmosphere was even more subdued. Stefan stood behind the bar with his staff, waving his arms in dramatic flourishes as he told a story that had them exploding with laughter. He saw us, then excused himself and came over.

He took one look at our ragged appearance and said, "Grab a seat, lads," then went back behind the bar while Oscar and I plopped ourselves at a table. The vampire returned with three beers and sat with us.

"You fellas don't look too hot," he said with an amused grin.

"Feel worse," I said. "We shouldn't be drinking these for free."

He made an open gesture with his hands. "Looks like you've deserved it tonight. What have you been up to?"

Oscar and I tapped our glasses and drank. God, that felt good. Even the cold glass in my hand eased the stinging on my palms where they'd scraped against concrete and rusty ladders.

"We just had a little adventure in the tunnels."

Stefan lost his grin. "The Ghost Tunnels? What were you boys doing down there? It's dangerous. You've got the jorōgumo, hags, and worse."

"Repaying a favour to the elves," I said. "Don't worry about that. We need to tell you about what we saw."

Stefan frowned and took a sip of his beer.

"Can you even taste that?" I asked.

"Yes," he said. "The taste is rather ghastly. But I like going through the motions sometimes. Nostalgia."

"We encountered vampires," Oscar said.

Stefan put down his drink and his expression turned serious. His demeanour turned even more grave as we detailed our exploits in the Ghost Tunnels, and when we told him that we recognised some from Double Point Investments, Stefan held up a hand.

"My Family?" he said, his voice tight. His grey eyes were ice. "Family Dragos? You're sure?"

We nodded.

"They were being led by Yvette," I said. "Stefan, we're talking about *rogue* vampires. Vampires who are going against the laws of your Father. You need to tell Penni."

"*Rogues* have always been a problem," Stefan said. "Vampires resistant to change, unable to fight their base instincts. They decimate entire towns, cities, leaving death and destruction in their wake, isolating themselves from the Old World and drawing the attention of the witch hunters. They would never have tried this if my father was in the city. Damn, I wish he was here."

"I can empathise," Oscar said with an ironic half-smile.

Stefan downed the rest of his beer and wiped his mouth with his sleeve. "I'll see Penni at once. He may be a hard-headed bastard, but he's on the level. He takes his job as Vasily's understudy very seriously and doesn't appreciate having his authority undermined."

"What will the other vampires think?" I said.

Stefan rubbed his chin. "No one likes bashing their own people, but these are the rules laid down by our Father. Penni's judgement won't be questioned. He'll find out which members of Family Dragos are caught up in this. Then may God have mercy on them."

* * *

OSCAR and I arrived home deep in the night and were met with an utter lack of violence and chaos. We found Bree and Constable Devapriya asleep on the couch with the TV still on. Two empty wine bottles stood on the coffee table, along with several empty beer cans and a half-finished pizza.

I'm glad at least someone had fun tonight.

I turned the TV off but left everything else as it was so as not to wake them. Oscar got a spare blanket and threw it over Devapriya. I grabbed Bree's duvet from her bed and lay it over her.

"They look so peaceful," Oscar said.

"Yeah," I said. "You wouldn't pick them for two of the most dangerous people in the city."

Oscar rubbed his eyes and yawned. "To be honest. I think Bree had a claim to that title even before becoming a *demonbound*."

We chuckled quietly and moved up the stairs. Oscar turned morose. He saw my look and gave a deep sigh that was a result of more than just physical weariness.

"I killed someone tonight, Joey," he said, looking at his feet. "That vampire back in the tunnels... I stuck him under the water with every intention of hurting him as much as possible. And I would have killed every vampire that tried to cross that stream. The scary thing is, I made that decision before realising I'd made it."

"It was us or them. You did what was needed."

He looked me in the eye. "I don't want it to be that easy. Hurting people, killing things. Even if they are vampires. I don't want to end up like Miss Blackthorne."

I put a hand on his shoulder. I was a couple of steps higher, so the gesture wasn't too awkward. "Mate, you're a far cry from our teacher. But let's keep an eye on each other, yeah? Keep each other in check. It's a bloody slippery slope in this business."

He gave a small smile.

I made a fist and tapped him on the chest. "Get some sleep. Tomorrow's a big day."

27

I SLEPT THROUGH MY ALARM. I wasn't too concerned about missing classes. I'd already decided today would be busy enough without worrying about the finer points of Engineering Mechanics and Cost-Benefit Ratios.

I dressed and went downstairs to find Bree sitting in the kitchen feeling very sorry for herself. Elbows resting on the table, face buried in her hands.

"Looks like you guys had a good time last night," I said.

She gave an annoyed grunt without looking at me. I made some toast slathered with peanut butter – crunchy, of course – then placed it in front of her, along with a glass of chilled water.

"Ugh," she said. "I can't eat."

"You'll need the energy. It's getting hectic out there."

She lifted her head and gave me a bleary-eyed stare. "What do you mean?"

I gave her the highlights of what went down in the tunnels.

"Shit," she said, when I was done. Her eyes widened suddenly. "Devapriya went outside to fetch coffees. The vampires—"

"Relax. I doubt they'd still be watching us. They were only doing it because the Scarred Man said he'd help them with their rebellion. They've got no reason to watch us now. Also, the sun's up."

Bree closed her eyes. "Right, right."

I looked at the gathering clouds outside. There'd be more rain before the day was through.

"We need to see Miss Blackthorne," I said. "She'll know what to do."

Bree drank the water and took a miserable bite out of her toast. "Friggin' demon. It can give me super strength but does fuck all for hangovers." She rapped her knuckles on her own skull. "Oi, Wiljara. Pull your weight, man."

The front door opened and Devapriya entered bearing caffeinated gifts. She looked tired, but nowhere near as rough as Bree. I picked up a coffee. She'd gotten four flat whites. Not my preferred drink, but even if she'd known about my proclivity for a mochaccino, I doubt she would have changed the order. I sipped the drink and actually found the bitterness comforting.

"Just got off the phone with Hertz," the constable said, setting the rest of the coffees on the table. "Blackthorne's up." She poked her head in the living room, then looked back at us. "Where's Oscar?"

"He's still sleeping."

"Well, get him up. Blackthorne wants us to meet her at her place. She and Hertz have convinced the selkies and river folk to meet today. Blackthorne wants to nip this thing in the bud before it gets any more out of control."

I heard the door to Oscar's room open, followed by a croaky voice drifting down the stairs. "Do I smell coffee?"

* * *

WE PILED into Miss Blackthorne's Toyota Land Cruiser, which was still parked at the sharehouse, and drove to the Old Substation Building. Devapriya was in the driver's seat, since Bree probably still had enough alcohol in her system to incapacitate a buffalo. My friend wore her biggest pair of sunglasses and remained uncharacteristically quiet. I had my Speedos on under my jeans, because I anticipated there being a ninety-nine percent chance of going for a swim before the day was through.

We entered the Old Substation Building to find the Master Wizard and Detective Sergeant Jonathan Hertz huddled shoulder to shoulder in the kitchen, poring over a large hand-drawn diagram spread out over the marble bench. Miss Blackthorne seemed to be explaining something deeply complex, while Hertz gave her all his attention, nodding occasionally, his chin cradled in his hand. Miss Blackthorne looked up and beckoned us over.

"The selkies will meet the river folk today prior to the trial tomorrow," she said. "We have until four o'clock this afternoon to either prove Frederico's actions were justified or hand him over to the selkies."

"How are you feeling?" I said. "You got impaled by a stake."

She huffed a short breath out of her nose. "Hardly impaled. It was little more than a splinter." She looked sideways at Hertz, clenched her jaw, and said, "The detective sergeant will attend this afternoon's meeting in my stead."

I felt my eyebrows lift. "Is that... are you allowed? I mean he's not—"

"Not part of your Old World?" Hertz said with a wry grin. "True. But the decisions made in that meeting will affect the people I am sworn to protect. People who are oblivious, vulnerable to all of... this." He gestured vaguely at the air. "Miss Blackthorn's injuries are far more serious than she's letting on. The spike missed the bundle of nerves in the shoulder, but still did some serious tissue damage." He cast her an annoyed glance that held a tinge of admiration. "She's been running me through the major players on both sides."

"All four sides," Miss Blackthorne said. "Remember, the Encantados, the Mokoi and the Baiji are three distinct peoples."

"Right," he said, observing the diagram, which looked like a pretty basic organisational chart. I noted Frederico's father, Luiz de Silva, sitting at the top of the list of Encantados, above Frederico's aunts and uncles.

"Cast of thousands," I said.

"Only one delegate from each of the river folk will be there," Hertz said. "Any more than that and it'll be too hard to control. Each can bring up to two attendants."

"Selkies look outnumbered," Oscar said, grabbing an apple from the large fruit bowl on the bench.

"Don't worry about the selkies," said Hertz. "The onus will be on the Encantados to placate the ambassador. Do you mind coming with me, Oscar? As mediator, I don't believe I'm required to have an entourage, but my words may carry more weight amongst your peers with your presence."

"What about the rest of us?" I said.

"You'll be working on our Plan B," answered Miss Blackthorne.

"Which is?"

"To find incontrovertible evidence of who killed Lin."

"Isn't that what we've been trying to do for the past three days?"

Miss Blackthorne came around the kitchen bench. She had a new walking cane made of dark brown wood. She leaned on it more heavily than normal and held her right arm stiff against her body. Her jaw clenched with each step.

"I'm working under the assumption you haven't been idle while I've been in the hospital." She raised her eyebrows expectantly.

"Oh, right," I said, and explained what happened in the Ghost Tunnels.

Miss Blackthorne's expression darkened. "Damn. I'll need to inform the fisherman that they lost one of their mages."

Hertz's frown became a carbon copy of Miss Blackthorne's. "I was under the impression that the vampires in this city were under specific orders to not attack humans."

"They are," Miss Blackthorne replied. "But just like the mundane world, now and then rules get broken." She lapsed into a long silence before saying, "Jonathan, Oscar, you should go set things up with the Mokoi. They've agreed to play the role of hosts, being the closest thing to a neutral party in all of this."

Technically, Detective Sergeant Hertz was also a neutral party, but I doubted anyone would wish to hold the afternoon's soiree at the local cop shop.

Constable Devapriya crossed her arms. "We're just going to forget about the *rogue* vampires? Never mind their attempt to kill these two." She gestured at Oscar and me. "Vampires unimpeded by oversight can't be good for the residents of the city."

"That's a problem for tonight," Miss Blackthorne said. "For now, we must focus on having a smooth meeting. It is our last chance to prevent a war."

Hertz rolled up the diagram and tapped it on his head in a lazy salute. "Get some rest, Mary. We'll take care of this. Come on, Oscar."

Once they were gone, Miss Blackthorne turned to Devapriya. "Constable, perhaps you can make Bree a coffee. She looks like she could do with a pick-me-up."

"I've had a coffee, I'm fine," Bree said, slumping onto one of the high stools in the kitchen and resting her head on the bench.

Miss Blackthorne's eyes narrowed meaningfully. "I insist."

Devapriya pressed her lips together. "Coffee beans?"

"Pantry. Top left."

Devapriya made herself busy with the coffees while Bree remained dead to the world.

"Follow me please, Joseph," Miss Blackthorne said, then turned and left the kitchen.

I followed the Master Wizard into the library. She moved slowly, the cane hitting the hardwood floors with a loud crack at each step. Agony emanated from her like a beacon, and I suspected her wounds were even more severe than what Detective Sergeant Hertz had said. Yet the pain only served to add fuel to Miss Blackthorne's fiery determination, tempering her resolve at the cost of a weakened body.

We entered the narrow stairway at the back of the library, and as we descended, I sensed a growing tension within my teacher. Like she'd been holding in a breath for too long.

"Giving me a private lesson?"

"Of sorts," she replied.

We came to the corridor that led to the Training Room, but Miss Blackthorne kept going downstairs. My mouth went dry.

"Whoa," I said, slowing my pace. "We're going downstairs?"

"Obviously."

"You said never to go down there. I remember it specifically because you said we could wind up dead."

"That hasn't changed," she said, continuing down the stairs without stopping.

An icy knot formed in my stomach as I followed. We passed a stub tunnel that branched off the staircase to a door made of heavy wood and rusted steel brackets.

"This room is where I keep certain objects for safekeeping," Miss Blackthorne said.

"Oh, wait a sec," I said. "I've been meaning to give you this." I pulled out the brown cloth scapular that I'd been holding onto for the past couple of days.

Miss Blackthorne examined it closely, without taking it from my hands. "What is it?"

"It's a scapular. A necklace Catholics use to—"

"I mean, what does it do?"

"I don't know, but it made Stefan freak out and try to eat us."

Miss Blackthorne pressed her lips together, then snatched the scapular from my hand. "Wait here." She entered the room, and I caught a glimpse of a full-on suit of armour and a coffin propped up against the wall before she came back out.

"What else you got in there?" I asked.

"Items too dangerous to be out in the wild. Do you remember the uncoupled air elemental you encountered earlier this year?"

"The one missing its twin?"

"Correct. I kept that down here too." She brushed a hand along the door in the direction of the grain and I felt magic locking the door in place. "The scapular will remain here until I can fully understand its properties."

"Is this what you wanted to show me?"

"No," she said and continued down the stairs.

I followed.

The temperature noticeably dropped, and the concrete walls gave way to giant blocks of stone carved from dark granite, like we were in some kind of medieval stairwell. There were no lights down here, so we conjured *lumières*, the smooth stone reflecting the flickering light. We kept going down, far below the library, far below the level of the train tracks outside.

"What we do isn't easy," Miss Blackthorne said abruptly, "but we save lives. We're responsible, not only for the five million people living in this city, but for the people living across the country. And everyone else in this realm. The world is getting darker by the day and we are the ones who must face these threats."

"Sure," I said slowly. I'd heard this sales pitch before.

Miss Blackthorne hobbled slowly down the last few steps, where there was nothing but a blank wall. She bowed her head and sighed.

"It's no coincidence that wizards make the strongest Custodians, and why people turn to us in times of crisis. We have the knowledge and experience to evaluate and overcome any situation. But more than that, it's our will. The same will that forges us into formidable wielders of the forces of the universe gives us the fortitude to make choices other people can't. Or won't."

"What are you driving at?"

She let her *lumière* burn out, leaving my small conjuration as our only source of light, so that when she turned to me, half her face lay in shadow.

"You can judge me," she said, "but understand that this is necessary. And you'll need to come to terms with it."

She placed a hand on the wall and I felt the shifting of magical pressure. A second later, glowing white lines etched themselves into the stone, creating the image of an arched doorway. Text ran across the edges. Two dozen languages, maybe more, in bright lettering – Ancient Egyptian hieroglyphics, Old English, Norse runes, and something that was either a string of random consonants or Welsh.

"Don't show fear," said the Master Wizard, and pushed the glowing section of stone wall. It swung inwards with a deep rumble, and I followed her inside.

28

I BLINKED HARD against the harsh white light, taking several seconds to adjust to the brightness. We stood atop a marble staircase that led down to a warehouse-like room, where the light didn't come from the ceiling, but from the floor – the actual polished stone surface itself. Square marble blocks shone brightly like a dancefloor from the seventies, but without all the happy colours.

Nine giant black cubes lay before us, arranged three by three, each one twenty feet in width and height. And when I say *black*, I mean black. They didn't shine or reflect any of the light emanating from the floor. They just sucked it all in without giving any back. My eyes couldn't find a point to focus on, as if I was looking at nine black holes. There was also some kind of thick cabling wrapped around the base of each cube.

Magic filled the room, thick and swampy. As if I could reach out and scoop a handful of the stuff from the air. I took a few seconds to recover from the excess energy before I found my voice.

"What are they?"

"Cages," Miss Blackthorne said as she moved down the stairs and walked among the cubes. "Holding things too dangerous to be allowed to roam free."

"Things? Like what?"

She stopped at the cube in the back left corner of the room, and looked up at it, both hands resting on her cane, a sheen of sweat on her brow. Miss Blackthorne may have been over a hundred years old, but she was miles fitter than me, and I'd witnessed her accomplish far more physically demanding tasks than descending a staircase. Her injuries were taking their toll.

"Remember the demon issue we had earlier this year?" she asked.

"If you mean the Duke of Hell and his demonic army who almost killed Oscar, Bree and me, then yes. I remember the demon issue."

Her mouth made a thin line as she shot me a level glare. She looked back at the cube. "When they took Bruce Longley, I spent several long nights searching for him. In the course of my search, I stumbled upon something I did not expect." She paused for dramatic effect. "The Venerati Sanctus."

"The witch hunters? But I thought you drove them out of the city at the end of the War, back in the eighties."

"So did I," she said. "It seems I missed one."

Miss Blackthorne waved a hand through the air and the black cube in front of us became transparent, almost as if it was made of glass, but with a sparkly shimmer that showed letters and symbols across the surface.

Inside the cube was what appeared to be a small studio apartment, furnished with a bed, table and a large bookcase. A small section in the corner was closed off by a curtain, which I assumed was the toilet.

On the bed, with his feet stretched out in front of him, sat a middle-aged man, currently engrossed in a paperback. Small and thin, he wore dark trousers and a button-up shirt that may have once been white, but had faded to a pale brown-yellow from dirt and sweat. The man's thick horn-rimmed glasses accentuated his alert brown eyes as they skimmed across the pages. He had a full head of hair with thick dark grey curls, and a closely trimmed beard shot through with white. He smiled contentedly as he flicked to the next page of his book. A romance novel, judging by the half-naked hunk of meat on the cover. Maybe from Miss Blackthorne's 'previously read' list. I knew for a fact there was a surprisingly large portion of shelf space dedicated to romance novels in her personal library.

The man was doing a particularly good job of ignoring us.

"He can't see or hear us," Miss Blackthorne said. "Not unless I want him to. These cages are some of the most secure structures you will see. Don't touch the cables. They're siphoning power from the railway electricity grid. They power the wards that prevent anything from leaving these cages."

"You can do that?" I said.

"It's not a simple process," she said. "All energy carries magic with it, but working with this much power is dangerous." She looked at the man. "Matthias Voigt. He is, or was, the commander of the Venerati's Sydney chapter. I found him above a shop in Chatswood, in an old apartment they used as a base back before the War. As far as I've gathered, he was trying to re-establish a Venerati presence in the city."

I let out a breath. "You've kept him here the whole time? Since March?"

"That's correct," she said, watching the man.

"But that's... six months! You can't do that. You can't just make people your bloody prisoners!"

She turned to me. "No? What would you have me do? Hand him to the authorities? I may as well set him free right now. Or perhaps I should kill him while I have the opportunity? The world would undoubtedly be much safer for it."

"No, of course not. I just—"

"I've tried, Joseph," Miss Blackthorne said. "With dozens of people and creatures like him. Tried to reason with them, rehabilitate them, help them see the wrong in what they're doing." She gave a deep sigh and her shoulders dropped a little. "This is the least heinous way to deal with them. I remove them from the world, so that they can no longer influence it, no longer harm anyone. They are provided food and water and even entertainment. Believe me when I say it's far better treatment than you'd receive if the roles were reversed."

I watched the man. He had deep, dark circles under his eyes. He looked frail, tired. Harmless. But, in this business, judging someone by their looks is a good way to be rudely surprised.

"Don't let your emotions rule you, Joseph. His organisation is responsible for thousands of deaths throughout history. Millions."

"Why are you showing him to me?"

"You wanted me to be honest with you." She gestured at the small man. "This is me being honest."

I looked at the other cubes, wishing I could have remained ignorant of this place. Too late. It was done.

"It's not easy," Miss Blackthorne said, "being Custodian. But I believe you have the strength to bear the weight of these decisions. Otherwise, I would be searching for another apprentice to take over."

I glanced at the other back cubes in the room. What else was she holding here? Who else had she claimed as a prisoner? Maybe at some point in the future I could turn things around, come up with a way to deal with the bad guys that didn't involve stuffing them in cages. For now, I had little choice but to defer to the Master Wizard's judgement.

I clenched my jaw and hissed out a breath. "I get it. I don't like it, but I get it."

Miss Blackthorne gave a sharp nod. "Good, because there is something I must ask of you."

I frowned.

"I'd like you to enter his mind," she said.

"No," I said, giving the response by pure reflex. I took another moment to consider her request, consider what could be gained against what it would cost, and said, "Not a chance in Hell."

"Joseph—"

"I can't!" I said. "You know that there's a demon out there, a bloody Duke of Hell, I might add, who wants to turn me into its thrall. Waiting for me to open my mind so it can crawl into my brain and take over. No, thank you!"

"I have tried to extract information from the man myself," Miss Blackthorne said with a grimace. "The Venerati are well-trained. Against all forms of interrogation."

I looked at the man again, noticing the dark bruises around his collarbone, the raw skin at his wrists.

"What have you done to him?"

Miss Blackthorne turned to me. "Nothing he couldn't handle. Unfortunately, it wasn't enough. Which is why we need to make use of your psychomantic abilities." She sighed. "Joseph, there are several lives at stake here. Not just the selkies and the river folk. Their war would spread beyond the rivers and the sea, swallowing entire neighbourhoods, suburbs. Hundreds, if not thousands, will die as collateral."

I ran a hand across my face. "Fine. What am I looking for? I don't want to have my mind open any longer than I have to."

Miss Blackthorne's posture remained tense when she spoke. "You will have more luck without assistance from me. If you go in with preconceived notions, he may use that to deflect or re-direct you. It's better you go in unprepared."

"Of course it is."

She turned to the cube and waved her hand again. The text and symbols shimmering across the surface disappeared, while the transparent structure of the cage remained.

Matthias Voigt looked up from his book and gave us a warm, grandfatherly smile. He placed a bookmark in the pages, closed it and set the paperback aside, then approached us. He tilted his chin down and regarded me over the top of his glasses.

"Mary, Mary," he said. "Do I have the pleasure of meeting your new apprentice? I take it you never found the one who went missing." His voice was smooth, educated, with sharp syllables and well-rounded vowels. "Or perhaps you found him too late?" He clasped his hands behind his back. "Making this a bit of a habit, aren't we?"

Miss Blackthorne turned to me. "Stay in there only as long as you need to."

I nodded.

Voigt's eyes sparkled, and he brushed a fingertip across his lips. "Oh my. A psychomancer? What are you doing working with *her*?"

I ignored him and closed my eyes, clearing my thoughts as best I could. I conjured a mental barrier around my consciousness by imagining a steel bank vault and focusing on its strength, its sturdiness. One of the problems with reading minds is it's a two-way street. More of a mind meld, really, experiencing each other's thoughts, feelings, memories.

The other big drawback, of course, is the fact it leaves you exposed to creatures crawling into your head not just from our own world, but from the realms beyond. I'd need to be quick.

I closed my eyes a little tighter and opened my mind.

29

I SLAMMED face first into a psychic wall.

I'd expected resistance from the old witch hunter, but I was terribly out of practice, so it hurt. It made sense that the Venerati Sanctus would train their members in psychic defence techniques. Handy when facing vampire glamours, succubi charms and pestering wizard apprentices.

I used the abundant magic surrounding me to push through. Matthias Voigt's mental barriers were strong, well-constructed, and should have been difficult to penetrate, but once I focused my will and surged forward, I felt his defences weaken. I wasn't all that surprised given the state of the man. Exhaustion, hunger and sleep-deprivation can erode your willpower and disrupt your concentration.

I burst through his mental barrier and our minds connected. I kept a small part of my brain focused on maintaining my own defences while I used the rest of my mental bandwidth to explore the inside of his skull.

If my brain could blush, it would have gone the colour of a tomato. Images of naked men and women filled my mind, no doubt fuelled by the man's unlimited supply of romance novels. Hundreds of bodies, twisting and moaning in a sweaty heap, their movements rhythmic and sensual. Very distracting and not a bad second line of defence.

I re-focused and delved deeper.

Recent memories of physical agony surfaced as Miss Blackthorne's face flashed before me. An exchange of words, vague and jumbled, came through, but I could make no sense of them. I went deeper.

So much hunger, so much pain.

I remembered sitting in a café, watching the elves outside. Observing the way they moved, mentally separating the fighters from the followers.

I remembered monitoring the Baiji as they established themselves in a new city. Vulnerable and few, but quick to adapt. A preference for peace over violence.

I remembered my apartment, and a figure dressed in black, his mechanical ventilator clicking and wheezing. The two of us in conversation. I recalled the man's scars and wondered if they still hurt. I asked if he was strong enough to take on Blackthorne. The Scarred Man replied that he will be.

Then darkness flooded my mind. A vast expanse of nothingness that overwhelmed my senses, psychomantic and otherwise. The witch hunter's mind snapped closed and retreated, severing our connection. Energy left me. Sucked out of me like I was floating in the vacuum of space. I didn't have the strength to close my mind.

A voice rung out through that never-ending blackness. A voice that filled me with dread, turned the blood in my veins to ice, made a hundred thousand insects crawl under my skin. It was the voice of Astaroth, the Archdemon of Envy, and the Duke of Hell.

"Joseph," he said. "Been a while."

Malevolent claws raked at the steel vault containing my thoughts. I drew in energy, but it was taken away before I could do anything with it. I felt myself falling, slipping into non-existence. Two giant eyes opened in the dark expanse above me, ten miles across and white as dried bones.

"You are stronger than before," Astaroth said. "Good. Very good. And what's this..." The demon paused. "Oh, that is very interesting."

I couldn't move, frozen in fear. I clung onto consciousness and used every shred of strength I had to reinforce the barrier around my mind.

"I have not seen anyone wield power in this manner for a hundred years. I wonder what it is that makes you so special..."

The eyes expanded until they filled my vision. I was losing it. The vault was weakening. I focused once more, using every damn ounce of concentration and willpower I had. I drank in the energy around me.

Sucked it in as hard and as fast as I could, and with a final surge of effort, I poured every bit of magic into slamming my mind shut.

"Damn," came Astaroth's voice. "Another time then…"

Darkness gave way to blinding light as I opened my eyes. I was still on my feet, surprisingly. Miss Blackthorne supported me with one hand, while managing to stabilise herself with her cane. My throat hurt and I realised I'd been screaming.

"You're okay, Joseph." Miss Blackthorne said in a calm but stern tone. "You're okay. Breathe. Just breathe. You're safe."

"I… I saw him," I stammered. "He… he spoke to me."

"Okay, okay."

Matthias Voigt watched us with amusement on his face.

"Dangerous skill, psychomancy," he said. "For everyone involved." He scratched at his beard. "I was never good at those mental exercises. I suppose that's the problem with purging the world of wizards. Not too many to practise with. But we would do well to have someone like you on our team, Joseph."

I looked at him breathlessly.

"The Scarred Man," I said as my senses returned to normal and my eyes adjusted. "He works for you. He's a witch hunter."

The man clasped his hands behind his back. "Cat's out of the bag, then. But I presume Mary here already suspected as much. Didn't you?"

Miss Blackthorne turned to me and spoke with urgency in her voice. "Was it the same Scarred Man we faced earlier?"

"I think so. Why? You think there are more like him?"

The man chuckled. "You haven't told him? That's hardly fair. But that's how you operate, isn't it? I suppose it makes it easier to get blind trust when you keep everyone in the dark."

Miss Blackthorne glared daggers at the man. Power gathered around her, and she waved her hand and muttered a word under her breath. The barrier between us and Matthias Voigt became a touch less transparent, and the protective wards shimmered along its surface. The man could no longer see us, but that didn't stop him from staring in our direction, unsettlingly cool and relaxed. He remained there for a full minute before returning to his bed, where he reopened his book and got back to reading.

I turned to Miss Blackthorne, my heart still racing. "How is the

197

Scarred Man a witch hunter? The Venerati are meant to kill magic wielders, not employ them."

"The Venerati aren't stupid. Ghouls and monsters they can deal with, even witches and shamans to an extent. Most of the time, they use magic-negating weaponry against practitioners of magic, but in most cases the best way to deal with a wizard is with another wizard. I believe this is the situation we currently face."

"But why would a wizard join them? It doesn't make sense."

Miss Blackthorne grimaced. "Most don't have the choice. The Venerati Sanctus actively search out magic wielders and coerce them into service through blackmail, ransom or thorough indoctrination. Children, in particular, are favoured. Brainwashed from a young age to both hate and fear the world of the supernatural. They are taught that the Old World is a scourge that must be eliminated, and grow up with the sole purpose of destroying us."

"That's messed up."

"Indeed."

"How do they find these kids? I mean, you found me and Oscar with a magical maths test."

"It depends," the Master Wizard replied. "Sometimes a child may show an early aptitude at channelling magic. Maybe they miraculously survived a car crash or have shown an extraordinary connection to wild animals. Perhaps they've accomplished an otherwise impossible feat, such as surviving weeks lost in the bush, or have shown exceptional academic ability. The Venerati Sanctus pays attention to these stories and investigates. If they deem there is a possibility of the child being proficient in wielding magic, they are stolen away for training and indoctrination."

Goosebumps prickled along my skin.

Miss Blackthorne's face twisted into a scowl. "They push these children. Push them well beyond their limits. Constantly, relentlessly. The children are forced to channel more and more power until the magic literally tears through the child's body."

I subconsciously ran a hand along ragged the scars on my left arm. A constant reminder to be wary of channelling more magic than I can handle.

"Once the child heals," Miss Blackthorne continued, "they do it all over again. And again, and again. Very few children survive their time with the Venerati. Those who do survive become formidable magic wielders, albeit with serious imbalances in their minds."

I clenched my jaw at the nausea growing in my stomach. I knew the Venerati Sanctus were a bunch of despicable bastards, but this was something else. This was evil. Proper evil.

"Maybe now you are starting to understand the kind of monsters we face," Miss Blackthorne continued. "I am receiving an increasing number of reports of these Scarred Ones turning up around the world. I fear the internet has only made it easier for the witch hunters to identify magic users."

I considered the Scarred Man. Each scar indicated where magic had literally exploded out of his body, ripping skin and muscle and bone as he overexerted himself. He had torn his own body apart over and over. For years. Christ. How long had he suffered at the hands of the Venerati? No one could come out of that a stable individual.

Remembering what Matthias Voigt had said, I turned back to Miss Blackthorne. "Voigt said you're hiding something. Is that true or was he just messing with my head?"

Miss Blackthorne fixed me with a level gaze before she looked away and sighed. "My apprentice, the one before Bruce Longley, was one of those children taken by the Venerati Sanctus and raised to be a Scarred One. Her name was Helena Rake, and she was but a girl when I rescued her from their clutches. At great cost."

The mental cogs turned slowly in my head and something clicked into place. "This happened in the War, didn't it? The Magic War. Arthur told us about how you'd formed the Vanguard to fight the Venerati Sanctus, but wouldn't go into details. Something happened when you rescued Helena, didn't it? Something that resulted in the deaths of the Elf King and Queen."

Miss Blackthorne's face betrayed no emotion besides the slight clenching of her jaw. "Simply put, there was no time to save the child as well as Alehtta's parents. I needed to choose. They would have understood."

I didn't know whether Miss Blackthorne was talking to me or herself. It now made sense why so many elves had such loathing for Miss Blackthorne, especially Sir Brandr. She had sacrificed the lives of their beloved monarchs for the sake of one girl.

"What happened to her?" I asked, in a voice barely above a whisper.

"There was nowhere I could hide Helena where she would be safe, so I took her on as my apprentice. The girl showed great promise and could have grown to be a great practitioner. But Helena fell to the witch hunters in the end, like so many wizards before her. The Venerati Sanctus is not something one simply walks away from."

I sensed there was more than Miss Blackthorne was letting on, but story time would have to wait.

"We need to move," I said. "There's only one Scarred Man out there at the moment. Maybe we can stop whatever he's trying to do." I recalled Voigt's memories of the elves, the Baiji. Everything started coming together. "The war between the selkies and the river folk... it's gotta be Voigt and the Scarred Man, right? The Scarred Man somehow got his hands on a selkie sword and used it to make it look like the selkies murdered Lin. Now, the Venerati are trying to kick off a war to get the selkies and the river folk to kill each other."

Miss Blackthorne nodded, and there might have been a hint of approval in the gesture. "That seems to be the most obvious answer. If the river folk and the selkies go to war, the toll on the selkies would be small, but the impact on the river folk would be catastrophic. And that's not to mention the thousands of Sydney residents who'd get caught in the crossfire. As usual, the witch hunters operate with little regard for the damage and death inflicted upon everyone else."

"We need to catch up with Hertz and get to that meeting," I said. "Tell everyone it's the Venerati behind all of this."

"I said that was the most obvious answer, Joseph. It may not be the correct one. Let's examine the facts. The Scarred Man is working for the Venerati Sanctus, but we are not yet certain whether he was involved with Lin's death."

"He had to be! You were with me and Devapriya at the Baiji house. You saw Lin's room. The killer would have needed magic to break in."

"Unless they had a key. Or if it was a family member. Truth is, we still don't know who killed Lin Wan. We don't even have the murder weapon. If we are going to start casting blame, we'd better be damn sure about who we're pointing fingers at. That's why our Plan B is to identify Lin's murderer. If we can prove with utter certainty that it was the Scarred Man, then that will change the dynamics of the discussions between the river folk and the selkies."

"And what if we find out it was Ambassador Kelden who killed Lin after all?"

"It would mean Frederico had reason for exacting revenge on the ambassador, and may give cause for the selkies to look more leniently upon his crime. But we'd need hard evidence to prove it."

"Okay, so we find out who killed Lin. If it was the Scarred Man, then they'll need to discuss the larger problem of the Venerati Sanctus. If it was selkies, then Frederico was justified in killing the ambassador. Easy."

Miss Blackthorne shook her head. "Not so easy. It remains a fact that Frederico de Silva killed Ambassador Kelden. The selkies may still require restitution, regardless of the young Encantado's motivations or the machinations of the Venerati Sanctus. Murdering an ambassador is no small thing. That is why we have Plan C."

"Which is?"

"We hand Frederico over to the selkies. Forcefully."

"Plan C sucks. I won't do it."

"If diplomacy fails, Joseph, it may be the only way to prevent the needless deaths of thousands. Men, women, and children. Keep in mind that Frederico is not innocent in all this. He killed a man."

I pinched the bridge of my nose. "I doubt his dad would allow his son to be taken away to almost certain death. In fact, it's more likely he'd rally all the Encantados to prevent that from happening."

"Then you must talk Frederico into turning himself in. Or find a way to deliver him to the selkies yourself."

My head hurt. I didn't like my chances of convincing Frederico to hand himself over. It was more likely I'd have to drag the guy kicking and screaming from his home and deliver him to the selkies myself. If it saved the lives of thousands, it would be worth it. Wouldn't it?

This must have been one of those hard choices Miss Blackthorne was talking about. It got me thinking about the lengths people would go to prevent a war. A thought suddenly hit me like a slap to the face.

"Oh, shit! Rhoswyn!"

"The selkie mage?"

"She said she would do anything to stop the selkies going to war, and I don't think she was exaggerating. We need to get to the Encantados!"

Miss Blackthorne gave a sharp nod and waved a hand at the giant cube. Matthias Voight disappeared behind the impenetrable wall of black. I ran to the stairs, but when I looked back, Miss Blackthorne had only taken a few steps, apparently out of breath.

"Go," she said with a pained grimace. "I'll only slow you down."

I was about to object, but she rapped her cane sharply against the floor.

"Go!"

Damn.

I ran up the stairs, taking them three at a time. There's no signal in the Substation's basement levels, so I didn't receive the text from Jeremy until I popped out in the library.

People moving through the Tank Stream. Information comes from that Beast Master I told you about. He gets his info from rats, so make of that what you will. Thought you should know.
J.

The Tank Stream is an underground waterway that runs right through the guts of the city. Long before it was covered over by progress and urbanisation, it served as a major source of fresh water for both the Aboriginal people and the Europeans. It's the main reason why Sydney is where it is.

Could the selkies be using the Tank Stream to sneak through the city? From memory, it ran to the Harbour, not the ocean, but it still would have been connected to the maze of sewer systems and passageways that made up the Ghost Tunnels. So anything was possible. I had to get to Freddy pronto.

I checked the timestamp on the text message. It had been sent fifteen minutes ago. We might already be too late.

I hesitated.

Why was I rushing to save someone I might be handing over to the selkies, anyway? The outcome would be the same. Thousands saved at the cost of one man's life. And therein lay the answer.

I knew I couldn't let Frederico be murdered in cold blood. Not if there was a chance that this could be resolved without anyone dying. I had faith in the ability of Detective Sergeant Hertz to get the selkies and river folk talking to each other. Maybe he'd even get them to get let bygones be bygones and move forward as one big, fishy family. Failing that, Plan B was still on the cards: find out who killed Lin. I would consider delivering Frederico to the selkies only if Plans A and B failed.

I sent Jeremy a quick thank you and threw in a winky face because I thought it might annoy him. Bree and Constable Devapriya were lounging on the big couch in Miss Blackthorne's living room sipping on coffees. The worry must have shown on my face because they both sat up straight the moment I walked in.

"We need to go," I said. "Now."

30

I KNEW something was wrong long before we reached the Encantado apartments. A column of dark smoke rose into the air and we could hear the fire alarms from a block away. Devapriya parked Miss Black-thorne's Toyota Land Cruiser on the street and the three of us rushed towards the apartments. The spectacle had drawn a few curious people from the surrounding homes, some still dressed in their pyjamas and dressing gowns, clutching large mugs of steaming coffee.

I didn't see any of the Encantados on the street, but realised they would have evacuated to the river. Duh.

"Stay back!" Devapriya called out to the spectators as we hurried past.

"We should call the fire brigade!" I yelled over the alarms.

"They'll be on their way already."

Smoke billowed from the windows of Frederico's apartment build-ing. None of the other buildings seemed to be on fire, yet people were still streaming out and heading to the water. We got to the entrance as a woman exited in a rush, a small child held at her breast.

I stopped her. "Where are the de Silvas?"

She seemed about to tell me to bugger off when she saw my arm. "You're one of the skinny wizards."

I repeated my question.

"I heard the chief is meeting with the selkies today."

"What about Frederico?"

"Luiz's boy? I don't know. Please, I must get to the river."

I let her pass, and we ran up the stairs, alarms pummelling our ears. We reached the third floor where smoke had collected and thickened along the corridor ceiling.

Bree coughed and lifted her shirt over her mouth and nose. "Joey, can you open some windows?"

"No," Devapriya said. "That could create a back draft. We don't want to feed the fire more oxygen. Let's find Frederico and get out."

At that moment, two bodies crashed through an apartment door into the hallway. They wrestled on the floor, both covered in bloody cuts, their clothes torn. Hamish wrapped a thick arm around Frederico's neck and the Encantado's face went red.

I cast a *sneezer* that created eddies in the smoke as it sped down the corridor and knocked the two fighters back. Bree ran forward just as a mini tsunami burst out of the apartment and slammed her sideways, leaving a Bree-sized crater in the drywall.

She fell to the carpeted floor. "Ow."

The water gathered itself into the humanoid form of a water elemental as Rhoswyn stepped out of the apartment. The selkie mage looked at Bree, then at me. "Stay out of this, wizard. It's not your fight."

"We need to talk!"

The selkie mage apparently did not share my desire for conversation and shot a ray of sapphire energy from the palm of her hand. I caught it on my shield as Devapriya sheltered behind me.

Bree scowled at the mage and jumped to her feet, only for another water elemental to exit the apartment and tackle her into the wall again. The two watery creatures merged and immersed my friend in a block of roiling water as high and wide as the corridor, creating a liquid wall that separated us from Frederico and Hamish.

"I will not let there be a war!" Rhoswyn yelled over the alarms, then spun on her heel and stepped through the wall of water.

The smoke in the corridor was thickening, stinging my eyes and scratching at my throat. I dropped my shield and ran to Bree, her blurry form thrashing against the currents of her prison as it twisted her around wildly.

Devapriya moved to grab her.

"No!" I said, seizing her wrist. "The water will suck you in."

"Do something, then!"

Seeing few options, I drew in energy and formed it in my chest. I whispered a quiet apology to Bree, then willed forth a kinetic blast that tore through the wall of water and hurled Bree through the other side.

The water split into two separate elementals and both came at me.

Bugger it.

"Stay close!" I called out to Devapriya and ran forward. With the constable at my side, we charged the water elementals. I waited until the last possible second before conjuring a *wall of surprise* that did indeed catch them unawares, and splattered them against the walls and ceiling before they could overwhelm us. That would buy us a few seconds.

Rhoswyn stood over Bree, pinning my friend to the floor with an unseen force. Behind them, Hamish had Frederico on the ropes, the burlier selkie using his pure mass to out-wrestle the Encantado.

Rhoswyn must have been employing all her mental capacity to hold Bree down, because she withdrew her sword and levelled it at me, which is a bit like bringing a knife to a magical gunfight.

"Don't," said the selkie mage.

I cast a *sizzle cuff* that wrapped around Rhoswyn's waist and pinned her arms to her sides at the elbow. Devapriya leaped over Bree and did some cop ju-jitsu to tear Hamish off Frederico and get the selkie warrior face down on the floor, his arm jammed up behind his back, face contorted in pain.

Frederico de Silva stood up, looked at his assailants being restrained, and decided to make a break for it. Bree was up and on him in a flash. She grabbed his arm and swung him into the wall. He thrashed against her grip, but she kept him there with insolent ease.

I checked on the water elementals behind me. They were already reforming into something that could pummel me. Alarms still blared, and the thickening smoke made it increasingly hard to breathe.

I turned to Rhoswyn. "Call them off!"

The selkie mage glared back as the glowing red bands tightened around her, burning her clothes.

"I just need to talk to you!"

Still no response. I glanced back at the water elementals closing in.

"I know who killed the Baiji girl!"

Rhoswyn frowned and the water elementals ceased their approach. "Explain yourself, wizard."

"Happy to, but can we do it outside?"

The selkie mage glanced at her warrior partner, whose face was still being forced into the carpet by an irascible Constable Devapriya.

Rhoswyn turned back to me. "As you wish."

* * *

We stood out on the road by the Land Cruiser in order to keep some distance between Frederico and the river. If he reached the water, he'd disappear, along with any chance of preventing a war. The fire engines arrived. Men in tan-coloured coveralls with hi-vis strips piled out and immediately got busy unreeling firehoses and questioning bystanders to check whether anyone was still inside. Devapriya went over to see if she could assist.

"You could have used the water elementals to put the fires out," I said to Rhoswyn.

The red-haired mage crossed her arms. "They are living creatures, not tools. I can request their assistance, but it is always up to them whether they accede to my requests. I would never request that they hurt themselves by dousing the fire."

"The fire that you started," Frederico said, glowering at the selkie. "You could have killed someone."

"There was to be only one death today," she replied icily. "Our offer still stands. You can come with us peacefully."

"Un-fucking-likely," Frederico replied.

Rhoswyn shook her head. "You'll bring a war on your own people."

The Encantado clenched his fists and stepped forward. "I don't care how many damn warriors you've got. Our goddess will tear you apart!"

Bree put herself between them and placed a firm hand on Frederico's chest. "Put your dicks away guys."

"Tell that to the ocean freaks."

Rhoswyn tilted her head. "Freaks?"

"You guys have no idea who you killed, do you? Lin was one of the smartest, kindest people in this godforsaken city." Frederico's voice wavered as he spoke. "Tell me, did you do the deed yourself? Was it your blade that ran through her back?"

I spoke up before Rhoswyn could reply. "The selkies didn't kill Lin."

"What?" Frederico turned his furious gaze on me. "What do you mean?"

"Firstly, we spoke to your river goddess," I said, which made Frederico's eyes widened a fraction. "Anjea said no selkies have been in the river for months."

"That doesn't prove anything," he replied, with a little less bluster. "They could have used the sewers. Or paid someone to do it."

I shook my head. "It's the Venerati Sanctus."

Frederico stopped pushing against Bree's hand. "I thought Blackthorne drove them out of the city."

"She did. They're back, and trying to get the party started again by kicking off a war between the river folk and the selkies. We've squared off against one of them, a powerful wizard covered in scars."

Frederico crossed his arms again. "The Venerati Sanctus kills wizards. They don't hire them."

"Trust me on this. He's Venerati. And he's been pretty bloody persistent about stopping us from resolving this thing between you guys."

"This is indeed troubling news," Rhoswyn said. "However, it does imply the selkies did nothing to warrant the murder of our ambassador. Perhaps this new information will convince the Encantados to comply with our request."

Frederico set his jaw. "And hand myself over? Not a chance." He looked at me. "This is all hypothetical. I need proof."

"Sure," Bree said. "We'll just pop down to the Scarred Man's secret hideout and deliver him to you. Express post. We'll even put a little bow on him."

The Encantado scowled. "It was a selkie sword that killed Lin."

"But what if someone stole the sword?"

Rhoswyn absently placed a hand on the pummel of her own weapon. "Impossible. Our weapons do not leave our side while we are landbound. They would have had to steal it from the home of a selkie, which are inaccessible to all but our own."

"Exactly," I said. "Freddy, when you... uh... killed the ambassador, did he have his sword on him?"

"He didn't," Frederico said. "It was over before he knew I was there."

Hamish shifted on his feet and for a second I thought the selkie warrior might try to deck the Encantado. Thankfully, he didn't, contenting himself with breathing heavily through his nose.

"The Embassy is the only selkie building not in the ocean, right?" I asked.

Rhoswyn nodded. "The only one in this city. That is correct."

"Well, I'm guessing the ambassador didn't hang around his living room with his sword on his hip all day."

"True. He only wore it as a matter of ceremony upon leaving the Embassy. Otherwise, the sword was kept secured in his study. Ambassador McBrae hasn't moved his effects into the embassy yet, so Kelden's sword should still be there."

Bree spoke up. "So, we go to the ambassador's house, and if the sword's missing, dolphin boy turns himself in."

"No," Frederico said quickly. "A missing sword would only prove it was stolen. Another selkie could have taken it for all we know. Or he could have given it to someone to carry out the murder." We all glared at him and he backed down. "But... a missing sword would raise questions," he admitted. "Even I know the selkies don't misplace their blades."

That was about as much cooperation as we were going to get from the Encantado. It would have to do.

I arched an eyebrow at Rhoswyn.

"It will not be easy," she said. "The Embassy is considered selkie territory and now has additional security thanks to the murder of Ambassador Kelden. If we are caught, you will be deemed trespassers and will be dealt with as such. And even if I get you in, there is no guarantee I can open the chest where the ambassador kept his valuables."

"Leave that to me," I said. "I know a guy."

31

I HATE DRIVING. The constant fight against angry traffic, the suicidal cyclists you are legally obliged to avoid. Driving Miss Blackthorne's monolithic Toyota Land Cruiser through Sydney's narrow inner-city streets was an exercise in patience. Add the rain and my jerky attempts at working the manual transmission, and it was paramount to torture. For everyone in the car.

It didn't help that Frederico de Silva and Rhoswyn were my only passengers. The Encantado and selkie, who minutes earlier had been willing to tear out each other's throats, now sat inches apart in the backseat. I put on the radio to drown out the silence.

We needed to keep numbers down, so Bree and Devapriya caught an Uber to the Mokoi houseboats, where Hertz would be facilitating discussions between the river folk and the selkies. The constable had also clearly stated her preference to not be involved with any breaking and entering shenanigans, especially if it involved foreign embassies.

I didn't know where Hamish went. He simply said he'd meet us there and left on foot. I didn't dwell on that too long; I was too focused on wondering how I would rope in the next member of our little gang.

I pulled up at Circular Quay in a spot reserved for buses, because good luck getting a parking spot around there. People sheltering from the rain at the bus stop watched us with curiosity.

I turned in my seat. "I'll be back in just a sec. You two play nice."

They both crossed their arms and looked out their respective windows. I didn't care, as long as they weren't killing each other.

I found Jeremy in the same spot as before, doing a cheap trick for a modest crowd of onlookers. His current performance involved dramatically waving his hands above and below a levitating white handkerchief.

I pushed through the thin crowd, extended my hand and set the handkerchief alight with crimson fire. Jeremy's beady little eyes widened, then upon seeing me, narrowed into angry slits. The crowd loved it though and burst into applause.

I smiled at the audience and created a ball of light that I threw into the air where it exploded in a shower of red and yellow fireworks. More cheers. I bowed and plucked Jeremy's black magician's hat from his head and threw it at my feet.

"Please give kindly," I said. "The poor man is still paying off his student debt to Hogwarts."

Jeremy grabbed my arm. "What the fuck are you doing?" he said in a harsh whisper. His curly hair seemed extra greasy today and lay flat against his head. He'd skipped shaving that morning and, apparently, brushing his teeth.

"I need you," I said.

"I don't care."

"The Venerati Sanctus are back in town. That wizard with all the scars? He's a witch hunter. And he's doing everything he can to make sure the selkies and river folk go to war."

"Not. My. Problem." He shoved me away, then set about thanking the visitors and collecting his earnings. I doubted he'd be cutting me in for my assistance.

"I can help you see your daughter."

He whirled on me and would have taken a swing if not for the crowd. "Don't you dare talk about her."

"I've got friends in the police. They can help. You were in prison, right? A show of support from two well-respected cops will go a long way. You wouldn't have to sneak around with Riss, or whatever your plan was."

"You're as bad as Blackthorne," he said. The comment cut a lot deeper than it should have. He poured the coins from his hat into a steel box, then folded all the notes and put them in his inner jacket pocket.

"You need a moment to pack up?" I asked.

"Nah, the bloody unicycle juggler will take my spot. Pretentious prick." He placed his hat on the table and ran nail-bitten fingers through his hair. "Let's just get this over with."

"Sure, you don't want to wear the hat?"

"Piss off."

* * *

I DROVE, while Rhoswyn provided directions to the selkie Embassy, which turned out to be a three-storey house in the ritzy cliff-side suburb of Dover Heights, lying between Bondi and the South Head. The Land Cruiser stood out amongst the Bentleys and Jags, so I parked us around the corner.

"Not really subtle, using the front door," Frederico said.

"We have had people watching the cliffs ever since your last visit," Rhoswyn said. "We go in through the front."

"Jeremy?" I said.

"I can put a veil over us, but..." He squinted at the overcast sky and scratched at his stubble. "Middle of the day. I don't know, it's risky. The guards would see the distortion of light."

"I can distract them," Rhoswyn said.

I turned back to the magician. "Anything else we can do to help?"

"Can you make it rain? Or blind the guards?"

"No."

"Then you can't help."

"We'll need to mask our footsteps, too," I said.

"That is unnecessary," Rhoswyn said. "Our sense of hearing is heavily impaired when we are out of the water."

I traded a look with Jeremy, who shrugged.

"I don't know how you tolerate communicating on land," Rhoswyn continued. "Sounds travelling through air are so harsh and you practically need to stand shoulder to shoulder. It's no wonder you invented mobile telephones."

"Let's go," I said. "In and out. No violence." I added the last part because I saw Frederico stretching his arms as if preparing for a fight. I turned to Jeremy. "Lead the way."

The magician grabbed my wrist, and I held Frederico's. A wisp of power passed over us and we disappeared, becoming nothing more than a shimmer in the air. I could easily make out Jeremy's outline, and a bolt of worry ran through me at the thought of getting caught. The spell had been much more effective in the darkness of the Ghost Tunnels. I pushed my worries aside and focused on the task at hand. Get inside, find the sword.

"Follow me," Rhoswyn said. "And wait for my signal before entering." She turned and strode towards the massive three-storey house.

"Don't let go of each other," Jeremy said as we started following. "And keep your mouth shut." I heard the strain in his voice already.

Hedges six feet high surrounded the property, a tall wrought-iron gate the only apparent entry point. Rhoswyn stopped at the gate and called to someone out of view.

"Toroway, open the gate."

"Magus Guilfray. The ambassador has left—"

"Time is pressing."

"Of course."

The gate slid open, and the selkie mage stepped inside while the rest of us waited behind the hedges. I heard Jeremy's laboured breathing in front of me. Whatever Rhoswyn was planning, it needed to happen fast.

A colossal explosion rocked the ground, followed by the sizzling cracks of a lightning storm. I guess that was the signal.

Jeremy led us around the hedge and I had to fight the impulse to raise a shield. Sparks and exploding waves of energy filled the air, while Rhoswyn stood in the yard throwing brilliant blue spells at the house. They struck an invisible barrier a couple of feet from the building, spitting out a cacophony of strobing fireworks and explosions and creating violent blue ripples along the ward's surface.

We moved down the driveway, our approach concealed by the chaos of light and sound around us. The selkie guard watched the light show, his mouth hanging open. He yelled at Rhoswyn as we passed within only a few feet of where they stood.

"What is the meaning of this, Magus?"

"This won't do at all," Rhoswyn replied, shaking her head with disapproval. "The wards will need to be reconstructed."

"But... you just put them in two days ago."

"I am aware of that," she snapped.

A male selkie came rushing out of the house to see what all the commotion was about, only to be left bemused at seeing the selkie mage hurling spell after spell at the embassy. He'd also conveniently left the front door open.

Rhoswyn glanced our way and said loudly, "The wards will have to go for now. I will weave new ones tomorrow." She waved her hands, and I felt the wards disappear.

Jeremy, Frederico and I ducked inside just as the noise outside came to an abrupt end. We were halfway across the huge foyer when Jeremy's spell dropped.

"Jeremy?" I whispered.

"Why... why the fuck did I let you drag me into this?" he said between deep breaths, before turning to Frederico. "And how the hell did you manage to get past those wards on your own?"

Frederico shrugged. "They weren't here last time."

I also suspected the Scarred Man of providing covert assistance to the unwitting Encantado by disabling the embassy's protections, allowing Frederico to sneak in undetected.

I cast a quick glance around the room. Counting the two selkie guards out front and the two with Ambassador McBrae at the meeting, the house should have been empty, according to Rhoswyn. There'd be one more on the stairs leading down the cliff face to the water, but Rhoswyn said he wouldn't abandon his post. Nevertheless, I had no desire to hang around any longer than we needed to.

"Where's the study?" I asked Frederico.

The Encantado led us up the stairs and down a corridor lined with paintings and giant vases that looked to be made of some kind of greenish rock. I fought the urge to run, tiptoeing briskly instead. No need to test the selkies' hearing. We entered the study, which resembled a small apartment in itself, with a plush couch, over-stuffed book-shelves and great big windows that looked out to the ocean. A couple of small marble statuettes stood on pedestals by the wall, setting the room apart from your run-of-the-mill home office.

Behind the big oak desk lay an honest-to-God pirate chest made of dark stained wood, complete with a huge, rusted iron latch.

"Jeremy, see if you can get us into this."

"What do you take me for?" he said with fake indignation.

"A swindler and a thief. Can you open it?"

He bent down and examined the chest, first placing his hand on the lock, then resting his cheek on the lid. He ran a hand along its edges, leaving a faint trail of swirling aquamarine light. "It's what the selkie chick said. There's a spell keeping the lid shut and a physical lock for good measure." He pulled out a set of small, narrow tools. "The protective spell is fine, but the lock is garbage. All old and rusted. It might break my picks. And we can't just break the lock off, it could set off an alarm."

"Get started on the protective spell," I said. "I'll see if I can find a key." I turned to Frederico, who stood at the window looking out to the horizon. "Freddy, keep watch."

"Amazing isn't it," he said. "So much space out there." He turned to me. "You know, not even us river men know all the creatures that lurk in the deep. We've never felt comfortable with the ocean. Maybe it's because we didn't want to encroach on selkie territory. Or maybe we're just a big bunch of wusses."

"Freddy, the door?"

"Sure." He cast a glance at Jeremy, then strode over to the door, swinging it almost all the way closed, leaving only an inch gap to monitor the hallway.

I started rummaging through the desk drawers and got a strong sense of déjà vu from all those years of searching through my dad's stuff to find out what he'd gotten me for Christmas. My dad was a lot better at hiding things than the ambassador because I found the chest key in the third drawer I tried. A big iron thing. It was the exact kind of key you'd expect to open a pirate's chest.

"Key," I said and tossed it to Jeremy. It hit the carpet next to him, so focused was he on unweaving whatever magical wards protected the late ambassador's valuables.

I was about to close the drawer when something caught my eye. I pulled out a worn leather-bound notebook, opened it, and started flicking through the pages. I felt my eyes widen as I read.

Holy shit.

32

"COMPANY," Frederico said, taking a step back.

Rhoswyn came through quickly and closed the door behind her. "Did you find the sword?"

"Almost there..." Jeremy said. "Bingo."

I felt a small movement of magical energies as the magician finished unravelling the wards. He picked up the key from the floor, unlocked the chest with a satisfying clunk, and lifted the lid.

Jeremy looked back at us. "No sword."

Rhoswyn pressed her lips together. "That's where Ambassador Kelden kept his weapon. If it's not there, it's been stolen. Perhaps your Venerati wizard has been here." She moved across the room, put her boot on the chest and slammed it closed.

"Hey!" Jeremy whispered, pulled his fingers back before they got crushed.

"Everything else in this chest is not your concern."

Frederico crossed his arms and licked his lips. "Like we said earlier, the ambassador could have given his sword to someone and instructed them to kill Lin. Maybe it was that scarred guy you mentioned. I'm still convinced that the most logical explanation is that Ambassador Kelden, for whatever reason, had Lin killed."

"Maybe this will change your mind," I said, holding up the notebook. "The ambassador's diary. Rhoswyn, have a look. Some of it's written in... what's that, Celtic? Gaelic?"

Rhoswyn snatched the diary from my hands. "Yes. East Gaelic." Her eyes widened as she kept reading.

"What?" Jeremy said.

"A lot of it is written in English," I said. "From what I read, it looked like Ambassador Kelden had been meeting with Lin regularly."

"Are you saying they were lovers?" Frederico asked. "You think this was some kind of heart-broken revenge."

"No," I said, trying to keep my voice calm. "Not at all. The ambassador had been meeting with Lin in a strictly platonic sense. Once a month, sometimes twice a month, for the past two years. They've been working out agreements."

The Encantado frowned. "Agreements?"

"Territory," Rhoswyn said, flicking through the pages. "Land rights. Easements. They were working out a way to share the coastline around Sydney. Here, take a look. This part's in English."

Frederico flicked through the diary. His eyebrows inched together and his face turned whiter with each page. "Lin was killed..."

"Because she was working out a way to live with the selkies," I said. "She was working *with* the ambassador to figure out a way for the selkies and the river folk to share the same space peacefully, without you lot ripping each other apart. With so many river folk around the world seeking refuge, Lin knew it was only a matter of time before Sydney became overcrowded. She was doing what she could to help the city live up to its name as a Safe Haven for the Old World. For her people. For *your* people."

The Encantado shook his head slowly and looked at me with red-rimmed eyes. "She was a good woman. And a close friend. And had the brains and stubbornness to see her mad plan through." He turned to Rhoswyn. "I... I was wrong. Your ambassador didn't kill her."

Rhoswyn inclined her head towards him.

"It must have been the Scarred Man," I said. "He must have broken in, stolen the sword and killed Lin. He wants a war." I held up the diary. "We're going to the meeting and showing this to everyone. Maybe if we explain the Venerati situation, everyone will calm down a bit and use their heads. Lin and Ambassador Kelden set the groundwork for some actual bloody peace between the selkies and the river folk, and I want to get the ball rolling again. Which means you two" – I pointed at the selkie and the Encantado – "need to sort out your differences."

A high-pitched whine started coming from the sea chest. It started small but quickly swelled to an ear-piercing shriek. There was no way the other selkies in the house couldn't hear it.

"Shit!" Jeremy said, looking up at us. "It was booby-trapped. I missed it."

The chest started glowing. Shards of pink and gold light poked through the thin gap under the lid, and a strange energy thrummed against my senses as the wailing grew until it sounded as if someone were taking a power drill straight to my ear canal.

"What's happening?"

"Don't know," Jeremy said, backing away from the chest. "But we should—"

The chest exploded. I knew it was coming. Or at least, I knew something was coming. I felt the magic within the room vibrate on a feedback loop and sensed the point at which it would reach critical mass a fraction of a second before it got there. I ducked in front of Jeremy and encased the chest in a dome of shimmering blue energy. The chest exploded with a muffled *whumpf* and I felt the floor shake through the soles of my shoes.

A mini tornado of pink and gold energy thrashed against my containment spell. The outward pressure quickly became too much to contain. I could have held it longer, but only if I wanted to score myself some cool new scars and earn a few days' rest in a hospital bed. No, thank you.

"Get back!" I yelled as something within me buckled and the blast ripped through the blue dome. The effect of a failed spell differs from person to person, from spell to spell, with the only similarity being that it frigging sucks. This felt like someone had just punched me in the heart. I'm not being figurative either. It was as if someone had thrown a full-blown haymaker at the centre of my chest.

As my spell failed, I managed to shape the last vestige of my energy to direct the blast away from us. The explosion shot across the room and blew out the massive windows, sending the two marble statuettes tumbling into the ocean. Probably only a minor inconvenience for the selkies.

I fell and Frederico caught me by the arm.

"We need to go!" I said.

"No shit," Jeremy replied.

We moved back down the hallway, no longer concerned about making noise. A selkie guard appeared at the end of the hall, the one Rhoswyn had called Toroway.

His hand went to the sword on his hip and he furrowed his brow. "Rhoswyn?"

It was all he could get out before Hamish appeared behind him and wrapped a thick arm around the man's neck. Toroway struggled against the chokehold, but Hamish was simply too strong. The guard quickly lost consciousness and the larger selkie lowered him to the floor. Hamish dripped with water, his long brown hair saturated and splayed over his shoulder. He must have come up the stairs on the cliff face.

I turned to Jeremy. "Can you make us invisible?"

He shook his head. "I'm stuffed. I'd need at least another hour to do that."

"Shit."

"In there," Rhoswyn said, pushing us into the closest room, a bedroom, as it turned out. Hamish dumped the unconscious guard on the bed.

"The other guards are coming," Rhoswyn said in a hurried whisper. "Wait until they pass, then go."

"We'll wait for you," I said.

"No! You need to get to the meeting. Show them the diary and tell them about the involvement of the Venerati Sanctus. My people may be unyielding in their protocols, but this should be enough to buy more time for further conversations to happen. Or at the very least, it should buy our Encantado friend here a lighter sentence." She looked at Frederico and stuck out her hand. "I understand your motivations. Even if I don't agree with your methods. The death of Lin was a great loss to both our peoples."

Frederico gave a sharp nod and clasped the mage's hand in a firm shake.

We heard footsteps thump past us down the hallway, and Rhoswyn quickly exited the room, shouting once more about the woeful inadequacies of the house's protections. When we judged that she'd herded them all into the study, we hurried downstairs.

I fully expected to receive an arrow in the back, or an expertly thrown sword, as we ran across the yard. But nothing came. We scrambled over the wrought-iron gate at the end of the driveway and ducked out of sight behind the hedges, where I immediately fell to the ground, breathing hard. Jeremy collapsed onto the grass next to me and lay on his back, breathing just as heavily as me.

"You guys need to exercise more," said Frederico with a derisive shake of his head. The Encantado couldn't comprehend the physical and mental strain that comes with wielding the unseen powers of the universe. But he was also right. I was unfit as buggery.

I pushed myself to my feet with a grunt. "Let's get out of here before they start looking around." Jeremy didn't move, so I tapped his foot with my own. "Coming?"

"No."

"What do you mean?"

He sat up on the grass and tilted his head as he looked up at me. "I mean fuck you and fuck Mary Blackthorne. I'm not getting dragged into any more of your shit."

I wanted to remind him that he wasn't doing this for free, to reassure him that I'd talk to Devapriya and Hertz to see what they could do for him to see his daughter. But sometimes less is more.

"Be careful," I said.

"Whatever," he replied. Then, with a grunt twice as loud as mine, he got up, buried his hands in his pockets and walked away, shooting a quick glance at the house as he passed the driveway.

"He's an odd man," Frederico said, watching the slightly stooped figure of the magician shuffle down the street.

I fished the car keys out of my pocket. "Shall we go prevent a war?"

33

WE MANAGED to hit the middle of the city right as peak hour started. At the rate we were moving, it'd be touch-and-go as to whether we'd make the meeting on time. It may have been quicker to walk the fifteen bloody miles to the Mokoi houseboats. I changed lanes to slip in front of a bus and settled in behind a black Audi.

"Where do you think the sword is now?" I asked Frederico, breaking the silence between us.

"Could be anywhere. The bottom of the river, the ocean. But it's more than likely sitting in a landfill somewhere collecting rust. Doesn't really matter. With the missing sword and the diary you found... it pretty much confirms that Ambassador Kelden had nothing to do with Lin's death."

"What will you do?" I asked.

"Find the man who killed her."

"Leave that to me and Miss Blackthorne. I mean, what will you do about the selkies?"

Frederico shrugged his well-muscled shoulders. "Dunno." He looked out the window. "I fucked up and made a proper mess of things, didn't I? I suppose I should hand myself over to the selkies."

"That would make things easier."

"You know what they'll do to me?"

"No," I replied, steering the Land Cruiser into a gap in the next lane. Someone honked their horn at me, but I'm pretty sure I had the right of way.

"Me neither," Frederico said. "Although, historically, the selkies don't value the lives of river folk very highly." He sighed. I didn't need to open my mind to sense his regret. He'd been wrong to go after Ambassador Kelden. He killed an innocent man, and he knew it.

"What about your father?"

"What about him?"

"He won't want you to go."

"Well, it's not his choice," Frederico said with a note of defiance. "My father's a stubborn bastard, but he'll have to see things my way. It's for the good of our people. And the selkies. It's what Lin would have wanted."

I called Miss Blackthorne as I drove, using the loudspeaker because the last thing we needed was to get pulled over for a traffic violation. I filled her in on what we had discovered.

"Breaking into the embassy was a very stupid thing to do, Joseph," she said. "And you are lucky you were not captured. You would have been out of my reach if they had taken you away." It honestly felt like I was copping a dressing down from my mother. I didn't have to look at Frederico to know that, despite the incredibly tense situation, he found humour in my embarrassment.

"Uh, you're on speakerphone," I said.

"Yes, I know that," came the terse reply. "Frederico. I do not know what will transpire at the meeting. Detective Sergeant Hertz will do his best to direct proceedings towards peaceful resolutions for all parties, but the fact remains you murdered the selkie ambassador. You must be willing to give yourself over to the selkies."

"I know," he said through gritted teeth. No one likes being told what to do, especially if they'd already made the choice to do it.

"Good. There's more at stake than just your life. You don't want a war with the selkies. Their numbers are almost limitless and their resources, seemingly infinite. Fighting would destabilise the precarious balance in the city, leaving it ripe for the Venerati Sanctus to swoop in."

"I know what's at stake."

"Very well. Joseph, call me if you think the meeting is headed south and I'll do what I can to intervene."

She hung up.

"Good chat," I said to no one.

"Bit bossy, isn't she?" Frederico said.

"That was her being warm and fuzzy."

* * *

I parked the car and walked with Frederico through the trees to the same grassy clearing where the Mokoi had held their corroboree. The difference in mood to the last time couldn't have been starker. Gone were the fairy lights, the bonfire, and the joyous dancers. A morose silence hung in the air, like when you visit an empty pub or arrive at a party after everyone's gone home. The grey clouds had darkened, and the rain had picked up. Thunder rumbled in the distance.

All the houseboats were gone except for one. It was a beast of a thing, about a hundred feet long, and looked like someone had plonked a two-storey cabin on a floating barge. A couple of Mokoi guards stood on either side of the ramp leading to the boat, armed with spears made of gnarled wooden shafts and steel heads.

The meeting was already underway, but hopefully no one had pissed anyone else off too much.

"Frederico de Silva," one of the guards said as we approached. He was tall and thin with wild black hair that reached his shoulders. He leaned on his spear with apparent nonchalance but scrutinised us with alert dark eyes. "You're late."

"I need to get inside."

"It's nasty in there, brother. You fucked things up good and proper."

"I know." Frederico glanced at me before looking back at the guard. "That's why I plan to fix it right now."

"Good man," said the guard with a nod. "Careful of those selkies. They're a real piece of work."

We stepped onto the boat, the old woodwork creaking beneath our feet, and entered the cabin. We had to duck to walk through the doorway. And by *we*, I mean Frederico.

About a dozen people were in the room. The three river folk representatives sat at a large oval table across from Ambassador Calder McBrae, with Detective Sergeant Hertz at the head of the table. Attendants and escorts stood behind their respective dignitaries, all keeping a close eye on one another. Several small circular lights in the ceiling washed everything in a dim yellow glow. The air had a damp, musty quality, the undersized windows not doing too much for air flow.

"It's our bloody river!" Luiz de Silva yelled, seemingly oblivious to our entrance. "You have no right to exercise your laws outside your own territory!"

"Mr de Silva," Ambassador McBrae said from across the table. "We have already established that Frederico, your son, has committed the grievous crime of murder inside the selkie Embassy, which, as you know, is selkie territory, and as such, is under the jurisdiction of our laws and customs." He spoke just as loudly as the Encantado, but without the emotion, his point carrying more weight because of it.

Hertz sat at the far end of the table, his bony fingers interlocked and resting on the table in front of him as he watched the argument intently, clear blue eyes flicking back and forth under bushy grey eyebrows. He'd combed his hair and wore a police-issue navy-blue suit with epaulettes on the shoulders indicating his rank. Bree, Oscar, and Constable Devapriya stood behind him, none of them looking particularly comfortable with the situation unfolding.

Next to Hertz sat Mei Wan, with Aubrey behind her. Aubrey flashed me an uncertain smile before returning her attention to the selkies.

The Encantado Chief puffed out his chest as he squared himself up for another tirade. "My son only killed your ambassador because of the crime committed in *our* territory." Luiz jabbed a pudgy finger at the selkie ambassador. "A murder committed by the selkies!"

"You have repeatedly stated this, yet brought no evidence to support your accusations," Ambassador McBrae replied calmly. The two selkies behind him continually scanned the room, their hands resting on the pommels of their swords.

"It was a selkie sword that killed the Baiji girl," said the Mokoi representative. "Everyone knows your lot can't be parted from your weapon." I placed him as one of the Elders who kicked Miss Blackthorne out of the party the other night. I didn't recognise the two Mokoi with him. Like the guards outside, they held spears and kept their unwavering gaze on the selkies.

"So, you claim," the ambassador said with cool composure. "Who's to say these aren't lies to justify the murder of an innocent selkie? For all we know, it was one of the river folk who killed her."

Luiz de Silva came out of his seat and launched a verbal assault on McBrae. The two selkies behind the ambassador gripped the hilts of their swords, bringing them an inch out of their sheaths. The ambassador himself remained sitting.

"You dare blame us?" Luiz spat. "We all know selkies have a history of murdering river folk in their homes!"

"And the river folk used to steal our women and take them as slaves," the ambassador replied coldly.

I looked at Mei, who hadn't spoken yet. Her eyes were closed, her head bowed, resting on the palm of her hand as if she had an oncoming migraine. The way this conversation was playing out, I couldn't blame her.

"Sit down," Hertz growled in a voice that cut through the racket. "Now."

I'd never heard the detective sergeant raise his voice before. It gave me a snapshot of what he must have been like in his younger days as a beat cop, knocking heads together and kicking drunks out of pubs.

The Encantado Chief hesitated, looked to the Mokoi Elder and returned to his seat, licking his lips as if preparing to launch another attack on the ambassador.

"Mr de Silva," Hertz said, his hands still clasped on the table. "You're talking in hypotheticals, and your attitude is counter-productive to this meeting. We're not trying to prove the guilt or innocence of your son. We are simply discussing whether your son must stand trial by the selkies."

"He must," the ambassador said.

"You'd have to kill me before taking my son away!" Luiz said.

Hertz raised his hands to get everyone to shut up. "We will decide after reviewing all the information available." The detective sergeant spread his hands on the table and looked at each representative in turn. "Come on, people. No one wants fighting to break out in this city." He gestured to Frederico and me. "Perhaps the late arrivals can enlighten us on the events preceding the death of Ambassador Kelden."

All eyes in the room turned to me. They probably stared at Frederico too, but it sure as hell didn't feel like it. I lifted my chin and stepped forward, holding up the leather notebook.

"This diary belonged to Ambassador Kelden."

McBrae's eyes narrowed. "How did you get that?"

"Rhoswyn helped," I said, which was technically the truth. "In the diary, Ambassador Kelden has detailed his meetings with Lin. They'd been meeting every month for the past two years."

Mei lifted her head and sat straight. "Why?"

"Peace," I said. "They were working out a way for all of you to live together. The selkies, the Mokoi, Encantados and Baiji. With the number of river folk increasing every year, Lin knew space would quickly run out. So, she was trying to get the selkies to share some of their coastline."

Ambassador McBrae narrowed his eyes. "This is news to me."

"Me too," Frederico said. "Lin never told me, and I was one of her closest friends."

"Someone found out about these meetings," I continued. "About what Lin and the ambassador were trying to achieve. This someone didn't like the idea of the river folk getting cosy with the selkies. So, they killed Lin and cast the blame on the selkies to kick off a war."

Mei frowned. "Who did this?"

From the look she gave me, I could tell she already knew the answer.

"The Venerati Sanctus."

Everyone at the table shifted uncomfortably, and quiet murmurs filled the room.

"We left China because of the witch hunters," the Baiji woman said quietly. "They were spread wide, and their influence over the government continues to grow. Sydney was meant to be a Haven for us. A place to start a new life."

"I know. But that's why we've got to work together to get through this. All of us."

"Ridiculous," Luiz said with a huff. "The Venerati haven't been in the city for decades!" He spoke as loudly as before, but with a slight waver in his voice.

"Well, they're making a comeback."

"You can believe him, father," Frederico said. "It... makes sense if you think about it."

Ambassador McBrae stroked his chin. "The Venerati Sanctus obviously do not pose as much of a threat to the selkies as the rest of you. But if they have been manipulating these events, then perhaps I can lobby my superiors for a more lenient sentence. We would still need to take Frederico de Silva into custody."

Luiz slammed his fist on the table. "No, dammit! He's not going with you!"

The ambassador clasped his hands together and spoke slowly, as if explaining the finer points of politics to a child. "Misunderstanding or not, the fact remains that Frederico de Silva murdered the selkie ambassador on selkie territory. Need I remind you that selkie forces are currently standing by and our War Mages have spent the better part of a week preparing themselves should war be declared?"

The Encantado Chief seethed. He looked to Mei, then to Hertz for support, but got none. The Mokoi Elder had a strange look in his eye. Almost as if he didn't care one way or the other. Luiz de Silva stood up with such force it knocked his chair backwards, but Frederico spoke before the older Encantado could get a word in.

"I'll go," Frederico said and looked over at Ambassador McBrae, who stared back coolly.

"No, son!" Luiz said. "I won't stand by while—"

"Shut it, dad!" Frederico yelled, stepping towards his father. "For once in your life, this isn't about you." He turned back to the selkie ambassador. "I'll go with you. I acted rashly and on bad information," he cast an accusing glance back at his father, who stood there open-mouthed. "I can't take back my actions, but I can at least stop this stupid war from starting."

The ambassador inclined his head. "Thank you. Our leadership is not unreasonable. I'm sure once I talk to them—"

"We're not done here," came a gravelly voice from behind me.

I pivoted on the spot and found myself face to face with the Scarred Man.

34

———————

OSCAR REACTED FIRST. A sizzling lance of golden fire streamed across the room only for the Scarred Man to wave his hand and deflect the spell as if he were swatting away flies. The burning streak of energy tore a hole through the wall.

I tried to throw a *sneezer*, but the Scarred Man shot his hand forward and an invisible force picked me up and hurled me across the room. I slid along the table and fell off the end, landing at Hertz's feet.

The detective sergeant helped me up. "Who the hell is that?"

"The guy who put Miss Blackthorne in the hospital."

"Damn."

Bree stepped forward, but I grabbed her wrist. She threw me an impatient glance, and I responded with a shake of my head. We couldn't take him on. Not in this small space.

"Who are you?" Ambassador McBrae demanded, flanked by his selkie escorts on either side, their curved swords held in front of the ambassador defensively. Even with the ventilation mask covering half his face, I could see the Scarred Man's smile.

Mei rose slowly, her stare drilling into the newcomer. "This is the man who attacked my home," she said, her voice quivering with rage. "This is the man who killed my daughter."

The Scarred Man looked around the room before settling his gaze on Mei. "Oh, that wasn't me. I simply acquired the sword for the dirty deed. But the true killer is certainly here and probably feeling rather silly right about now. Isn't that right, Luiz?"

Everyone turned their gaze to the Encantado except for me. I kept my eyes on the Scarred Man, ready to defend myself and my friends. Through the ragged black hair that fell about his face, I saw the glint in his eye. He had the look of a man full of confidence, a man who had won.

Eventually, I turned to Luiz de Silva, who had gone pale and looked desperately at everyone around the room. He backed away from the table.

Frederico took a step towards him. "You? You killed Lin?" His voice was quiet, but his hands had closed into fists that trembled at his sides.

"Listen to me, son... it's not what you think!"

"Explain it, then," Mei said, and unsheathed her *jian*. She raised the sword and positioned her body square to the Encantado Chief, feet wide, ready to strike.

Luiz pointed at the ambassador. "It's them! There is no bargaining with the selkies! They are cunning and treacherous as snakes!"

In a flash, Mei's sword came to Luiz's throat and pressed against his skin. The movement served as a starting gun and in the space of a heartbeat, everyone with a weapon had it in their hands and did their best to look menacing.

Unfortunately, NSW police officers don't carry guns, Tasers, or even extendable batons when they're off duty. So, there'd be no hidden six-shooters drawn from waistbands, no SIG P-whatevers being pulled from ankle holsters. Even so, Hertz stepped away from the table and spread his arms wide to shield Devapriya, Oscar, and Bree. Or to hold them back.

I noted that the Scarred Man hadn't moved. With hands clasped in front of him, he watched the proceedings like a spectator at a particularly boring boxing match. It wasn't lost on me that he had positioned himself firmly in the doorway. No one was getting out of this room unless it was through him.

"You killed my daughter and risked war, all because of your goddamn prejudices?" Mei said, pressing the *jian*'s blade against the Encantado Chief's neck firmly, but not hard enough to draw blood. "We had peace, you damn fool!"

"There will never be peace," Luiz said, eyes burning with defiance. "Not truly. Not while we have selkies breathing down our necks."

The Mokoi Elder, the only person still sitting, pushed himself to his feet with visible effort and very gently placed a hand on Mei's arm. She shrugged him off.

"Luiz is not the enemy, Mei," the Mokoi said, sadness in his voice.

Mei looked from the old Mokoi back to Luiz de Silva with red-rimmed eyes. "Both of you are in on this? But... why?"

"The selkies are the ones we must fight," the Mokoi said, not meeting Mei's stare. "For too long, have we tolerated the presence of our former slave masters. Making deals with them is the last thing we should be doing."

"Listen to him, Mei," Luiz said. "This is our chance to drive the selkies from the city. We can finally be rid of them! We can finally have peace!"

Frederico crossed the room, grabbed his father's shirt, and slammed him against the wall. "We already had peace, you stubborn idiot! And Lin would have turned that peace into an alliance." Tears fell freely down his face.

"I couldn't let her do that," Luiz said quietly. "We don't share waters with selkies, and they certainly aren't our allies."

"You killed Lin... you used my key to get into her house, didn't you? You went into her room and stabbed her while she slept."

I recalled Frederico mentioning that he had lived with the Baiji when they'd first arrived in the city. If he still had a key to their place, all Luiz had to do was find it, and he could have literally walked in through Mei Wan's front door. No magic involved whatsoever.

Frederico's voice trembled. "And then you blamed the selkies because you knew I'd go after them. You knew I'd want revenge for her death."

Luiz lowered his gaze. "There has always been fighting between our people, but rarely have we had the advantage. Killing the ambassador was the only way we could draw the selkies away from the ocean and into our domain, into our river where we have numbers and our goddess."

"Is that how I killed him so easily?" Frederico snarled. "You had this Venerati bastard disable the wards protecting the Embassy?"

"I didn't know he was Venerati," the Encantado Chief said with what sounded like genuine remorse. If not for his actions then at least for being fooled. "Son, I am sorry your friend had to be killed. I'm sorry you killed the selkie ambassador. But it's for the good of our people. Trust me. You'll see."

"You killed my best friend and used me as your political tool." Frederico shoved his father away. "I hate you."

Luiz looked at his son, his own eyes brimming with moisture. "If that's the cost of expelling the selkies and keeping our people safe, then I'm willing to pay it."

Ambassador McBrae cleared his throat. "I can't tell you how to govern your people, but I would hardly think instigating a war with one of the most powerful governments in the world could help. We are far more powerful than anyone here realises. But there is an obvious solution to prevent my people from seeking retribution." He straightened and lifted his chin a fraction. "Frederico de Silva, you are charged with the murder of Ambassador Ellister Kelden on selkie territory. Will you come peacefully so that you may stand trial for your crimes against the selkie people?"

The Encantado cast a final hate-filled glare at his father. "I will."

Ambassador McBrae visibly relaxed. His shoulders fell as the tension within him eased. In the corner of my eye, I noticed the Mokoi Elder give the barest nod to the Scarred Man, who grinned back at him. Then I felt magic shift.

"No!" I yelled.

Darkness gathered around the Scarred Man as he thrust a hand forward, casting forth shadowy tendrils that shot across the room. I cast a hasty shield to protect myself and my friends, but we weren't his target. One of the selkie guards was quick enough to summon a wall of pale blue energy, but the conjurations tore through his defensive spell as if it were tissue paper, impaling Ambassador McBrae and the selkie guard with a dozen shadowy spears. The dark tendrils burst through their backs with a spray of red and punched several holes in the side of the boat, before disintegrating in a cloud of black smoke.

The guard and the ambassador fell to the floor, dead.

Hertz charged forward, his tall, slender frame hunched under the low ceiling but moving with more speed and grace than you'd expect from a guy his age. He posed no threat to the dark-haired wizard who, with a flick of his hand, threw the detective sergeant back across the room. Oscar and Devapriya caught him, falling to the floor in a heap.

The Scarred Man turned to the remaining selkie guard, who held his sword in front of him, waving it from side to side. His eyes flicked between the Scarred Man and everyone else in the room.

"Go," the Scarred Man said to him. "Tell your people there will be no peace between the river men and the selkies."

The guard hesitated, which brought a wicked smile from the Scarred Man.

"Don't worry," he said, stepping out of the doorway. "The guards outside won't stop you."

The selkie looked down at the bodies of the ambassador and his fallen comrade, then moved cautiously to the door. Once he was safely out of the room, he bolted.

"You're not really with the Venerati Sanctus, are you?" Luiz said, his voice small.

"What does it matter?" replied the Scarred Man. "Everything is in motion as you wanted."

"And you will help us fight them?"

"I'll be around."

"What's your name?" Hertz said, back on his feet.

The Scarred Man tilted his head. "I cannot remember the name my mother gave me. But I go by the name Castille now."

"Well, Castille, you're under arrest."

The Scarred Man, Castille, raised an eyebrow.

Luiz turned to Hertz. "Detective, please do not provoke him. We need him to—"

A sword burst through the Encantado Chief's chest. His eyes bulged as he looked down at the blade of Mei's *jian*, glistening red with his blood. Luiz de Silva fell to his knees and slumped to the floor.

"I needed him!" Castille yelled as he cast a stream of fiery black energy at the Baiji matriarch. Mei moved with liquid grace, but the spell still managed to clip her shoulder and she went down with a pained scream. At the same time, Oscar sent a torrent of burning yellow energy across the room. Castille raised a hand and caught it on a shield, splaying out Oscar's spell and filling the room with blinding golden light.

I ran forward, yanking the *jian* out of Luiz's body as I passed. It thrummed in my hand as I charged at the Scarred Man. The blinding light faded and Castille's face took on an expression of mild surprise at the sight of me wielding Mei's bloody weapon. I thrust the sword forward. The thrums along the *jian*'s grip turned into violent vibrations that shook my whole arm as the blade pierced the Scarred Man's shield.

He yelled in shock and stepped back, but I kept pushing until the tip dug into his thick black coat. My momentum carried us out the door, where we fell sprawling onto the slippery deck. The rain came down hard, soaking me in seconds.

Castille and I got to our feet at the same time. I looked to the right and saw the bodies of the two Mokoi guards lying on the grass at the end of the ramp, blood seeping through ragged puncture wounds.

The Scarred Man looked down contemptuously at the sword sticking out of his chest. He grabbed the handle and let it drop to his feet, the tip biting into the wooden deck with a dull thud. He opened his coat and one of the metal boxes connected to his ventilator fell apart, although he'd suffered no apparent injuries.

Damn.

"You don't need to do this," I said. "People like us need to stick together."

"People like us?" Castille sneered. "You're worse than the rest of them. Vampires, elves, selkies. What's next? Demons and banshees? The Fae? You protect the Old World like they're defenceless children, when they've been our oppressors since the Stone Age. We're nothing more than food to them. Their slaves, their playthings." He looked down at the machinery on his chest, tapped it, and when it didn't respond, ripped it off and tossed it in the river along with the plastic ventilation mask. He fixed his gaze back on me, his mouth twisted in a disfigured scowl. "It wasn't until the Venerati Sanctus was formed that we could fight back!"

"The Venerati kill innocent people, too."

"Only when it's needed. Or unavoidable. Or if they get in the way."

"They kill wizards."

He spread his arms wide. "They haven't killed me."

I heard someone step onto the deck and turned to see Bree and Oscar a few steps behind me.

I turned back to Castille. "They won't destroy themselves. The river folk and the selkies know it was you behind it. They'll see reason."

He laughed with harsh, ragged breaths. "Reason? Please." He smiled, spreading the scars that decorated his lips. "It's a funny thing. I was just following the directions of the river men. They're the ones who wanted to pick a fight with one of the strongest people on the planet. Maybe it's just the natural order of things for the Old World to destroy themselves. God knows it'd bring some damn order to the world for a change."

"If you were hoping for the river folk to be wiped out, then you're shit out of luck. They've got a goddess to defend them." I heard more people stepping out onto the deck behind me.

The Scarred Man gave a lopsided grin. "Oh, I'm counting on it. Hopefully, the selkies bring something equally impressive to the fight. It must be a sight to see them go to war."

"Leave," Oscar said, stepping up next to me. "Don't think that we can't take you."

I felt the coalescence of magical energy around my friend; the pressure pushing against my senses. I drew in magic too.

Castille cast his gaze to the growing crowd behind us, then looked back at Oscar and me. "I see lots of potential in you two. With the right training, you might even become as powerful as me."

A spear sailed between Oscar and me, hitting an invisible barrier inches from Castille's face. Aubrey charged forward. To do what, I don't know. Bree caught her before she got very far and held her back.

"No!" Bree said. "You can't help."

Castille ran a hand across his face, dragging the wet hair from his eyes and exposing the criss-cross of pink scars.

"Try not to get involved in all this, wizard. It isn't your fight."

"I won't stop protecting this city."

"Protecting the city? The Old World brings nothing but pain and ruin, and you will be left standing in the rubble. Why, the city has already started to come apart. Can't you feel it?"

"Feel this," I said.

Oscar and I released synchronised blasts of energy that drowned out the rain with a sweltering roar and hit Castille's defensive spell with an almighty crash. I swear we don't practice specifically to cast spells in tandem, but train with the same person every single day and you're going to start working on the same wavelength.

I poured more energy into the spell and felt Castille's barrier giving way. My heart quickened. We could beat him right here. Then I realised his shield was only receding so he could fuel something else. He fixed his dark eyes on me.

"Shields!" I yelled.

The Scarred Man slammed his hands onto the wooden deck, generating a sphere of crimson energy that exploded outwards. My shield must have held because I wasn't instantly incinerated. I crashed back into something hard.

The scars on my arm glowed from the effort of maintaining my defensive spell. It should have hurt. It should have been agony. But any pain I felt was being conveniently tucked away by my subconscious. Only when I tried to take a breath did I realise I was under water.

Where was Oscar? Bree?

Lights danced beyond the surface of the water. I tried to swim towards it, but something big and heavy and made of wood pushed against me, dragging me down into the blackness of the river. I tried forming a spell but couldn't get my thoughts to line up.

In a panic, my brain seemed to think it was about the right time to try breathing again, and I was rewarded with a mouthful of murky water. A few seconds later, I tried again, only to swallow more water as the darkness of the river surrounded me.

35

My whole body spasmed as I coughed uncontrollably, trying to expel the water from my lungs. Coughing gave way to vomiting and violent convulsions that lasted what could have been ten minutes, but were probably less than one. I was cold, wet and tired. At least I'd worn my Speedos under my jeans.

I lay back on the grass as rain pattered against my face, and looked up at the figures around me, silhouetted by the light of Oscar's amber *lumière*.

Devapriya knelt beside me, her hair plastered to her face.

"Did... did you just give me mouth to mouth?" My voice came out harsh and scratchy.

Devapriya rolled her eyes and pushed herself to her feet. Bree offered me a hand. I grabbed it and let her drag me up. I got light-headed and felt my knees buckle, but Bree kept me upright.

"Easy, Joey," said Detective Sergeant Hertz. "You were only down there for a minute, but you took in a lot of water. There could still be some in your lungs. You need to get checked by a doctor immediately."

I looked around. The boat was gone, resting on the riverbed save for a few bits of debris that bobbed to the surface and floated away with the current. The ambassador's body, and the body of his escort, were likely still down there, or perhaps the river was already pushing them out to the ocean.

The Encantados and Mokoi were gone, including Frederico and

everyone who had just been straight up murdered in front of me. How many was that? Five, including the Mokoi guards?

"Where is everyone?"

"Preparing for war," Mei said. Blood had seeped into the sleeve of her white blouse from where Castille had clipped her with a spell. "The Encantados and the Mokoi are attempting to enlist the aid of the river goddess. They plan to offer up the bodies of Luiz de Silva and the Mokoi guards as sacrifices to convince the goddess to unleash her wrath on the selkies."

"But they're already dead," Oscar said. "Will that work?"

"I don't know. I'm not all that familiar with the local deities, but bringing a river goddess to the fight will get messy fast."

"Frederico went with them," Aubrey said, her clothes soaked through. "He wanted to stay with you but ended up deciding his efforts were better spent talking reason with his family."

"You pulled me out of the river?" I asked.

Aubrey smiled. "Bree helped."

"You got caught under a chunk of the boat," Bree said. "Not a big piece, either. You probably could have pushed it off if you exercised for once in your life."

"It's on my list," I said. "Have we called Miss Blackthorne?"

"Joey," Hertz said. "We need to get you looked at."

I shook my head, more to clear it than anything else. "There's no time. The war has started. The selkies have been preparing for this moment for a week. Maybe longer. They'll strike tonight."

"Where?" Bree said.

I thought about it. They could hit the river folk in their homes, attack while they were clustered together. Easy targets. But would the selkies attack families?

"I need to speak to Rhoswyn."

"How do we get a hold of her?" Oscar said. "Selkies aren't great with technology last time I checked. Should we talk to the elves?"

"I doubt they'd be much help right now. If anything, they'd be hunkered down waiting until all this blows over. We'll have to go to the Embassy. I just hope they don't realise it was me who blew up half their building."

"You did what?" Devapriya said.

I waved the question away. "It was an accident."

"You accidentally blew up a building?"

"It was barely more than a room, really."

"Joey," Hertz said, his voice gaining an edge of urgency. "I know you want to help, but I won't have you dropping dead because we were too careless to have you examined properly. The after-effects of nearly drowning are just as dangerous as actually drowning. We're talking pulmonary damage, brain damage, cardiac arrest."

"I know!" I said sharply. "I understand the risks. But we can't afford to waste time right now." He frowned and was about to argue the point again, so I cut him off. "Look, I'll go see a doctor as soon as this is over. Promise."

The detective sergeant thought about that for a while. "As soon as it's over," he said and turned to Devapriya. "Let's go back to the station. We need to raise the Alert Level. Also, a change of clothes wouldn't hurt."

Devapriya's eyebrows almost flew off her forehead. "Seriously? You want to play the terrorism card?"

"We've got no choice. There's going to be a fight which may involve a literal goddess, and we have no idea where it will be. Raising the Alert Level will put every officer in the entire city on standby." He looked at me. "I would suggest your teacher requests support from her government contacts. We will likely need their assistance tonight, if only for the cover-up after the fact."

Devapriya put a hand on my shoulder. "You sure you're okay? We don't need heroics. You're no good to anyone dead."

"I'm fine."

She gave my shoulder a brief squeeze in an uncharacteristic show of affection. She must have really been worried.

"I know it's pointless to say don't do anything stupid," Devapriya said. "Just tell us if you find anything. We need to know where the selkies will strike."

Devapriya and Hertz left at a jog back to Hertz's car.

I turned to Mei and Aubrey. "We could do with a hand."

Mei shook her head. "I'm sorry. I will be instructing the Baiji to retreat to their houses. We cannot rely on our Encantado and Mokoi cousins to protect us. I don't even think I can call them cousins when this is over. Too much blood has been spilled." She looked at the spot where Devapriya and Hertz had just disappeared into the trees. "And I am hesitant to entrust our well-being to the government. Not after what we went through in our home country." She lifted her head and regarded me with a tired gaze. It took me a moment to realise that with Miss Blackthorne out of the picture Mei was relying on me to fix this mess.

I offered to give them a lift to their house, but Mei said she'd be better off swimming. Something about the waters soothing the pain.

Oscar, Bree, and I jumped back into the Land Cruiser. Bree drove while I called Alehtta, just in case she felt like sending us some elf reinforcements. It went straight to voicemail, so I hung up and called Miss Blackthorne on speaker phone.

"I expected you to call sooner," she said.

"We had a surprise visitor at the meeting," I said, and explained what happened.

"You need to see a doctor."

"I will. After."

She paused, then said, "Is everyone else okay? Bree? Oscar?"

"We're dandy," Bree called out.

"Heading home now to change," I said.

"Where is Frederico?" Miss Blackthorne said.

"He went with the Encantados and the Mokoi to call the river goddess," I said. "Using his dead papa and the Mokoi guards as sacrifices. Will that even work?"

"I doubt it," Miss Blackthorne replied. "A dead body is hardly regarded as a sacrifice. You need intent as the deed is being done. Regardless of whether Anjea grants them an audience, she will defend the river. In a sense, she *is* the river. The Sydney waterline will not be a safe place tonight. We need to find Frederico." She gave a weary sigh. "What the hell was Luiz thinking? And the Mokoi Elders should know better."

"They're scared," I said. "Scared of what the world is turning into. Scared of the selkies wanting to exert control over them again. They were desperate to protect their people."

"Kicking off a war is a bloody stupid way to go about it, I reckon," Bree said from the driver's seat.

"No arguments from me, sister," I said. "Miss Blackthorne, where will the selkies attack? The Baiji are hunkering down in their homes, and the Encantados are probably scattered up and down the river by now. I have no idea where the Mokoi went, probably further upstream. The selkies could strike anywhere."

"No," replied the Master Wizard. "The selkies have regulations about this kind of thing. Policies that dictate how they must act. Their first target would be military installations."

"Do the river folk have any military installations?"

"Not in Sydney," Miss Blackthorne said.

"They'll hit the transport hubs then," Oscar said. I looked at him and he nodded vigorously. "Standard rules of war. No hospitals or non-combatants. At least not initially. They'll aim for buildings and fortifications used for military purposes, then move to other infrastructure seeking to cause maximum disruption. Like transport hubs."

"Transport hubs... holy shit. You're thinking Circular Quay."

Oscar nodded. "The largest ferry terminal in Sydney. And given its location and the surrounding landmarks... it'd make a statement don't you think?"

"I got a text from Jeremy earlier today. He said there were people moving through the Tank Stream. It flows into Sydney Harbour, doesn't it?"

"Indeed it does," Miss Blackthorne said. "Right near Circular Quay."

"Jesus," Bree said. "The Vivid Festival! There'll be thousands of people hanging around there. *Tens* of thousands."

Even with the rain, the turnout would be massive.

Oscar adjusted his glasses. "Rules of war generally include stipulations against attacking civilians."

"Sure," I said. "But who do selkies define as *civilians?*"

Bree kept her eyes on the road, but I saw the muscles in her jaw clench. We all knew what the Old World thought of regular people. At best, they saw them as equals. At worst – pests, slaves, cattle.

"Devapriya and Hertz are flagging the attack with the other cops," Bree said. "They'll probably send in the bloody army or something."

"Not the army," Miss Blackthorne said. "The government has counter-terrorist special forces units located within the city. They'll be at Circular Quay within minutes of being mobilised."

I desperately wanted to ask how she knew that, but we didn't have time for stories.

"I don't care how special these forces are," I said. "The selkies have been planning something big. They've got water mages and elementals. I don't think a few bullets will stop them. We need to get that area evacuated. I think it's time to bring in Katherine Powell."

"I haven't been sitting on my hands since you've been gone," Miss Blackthorne said. "I have briefed Kat on the situation. She's expecting an update shortly. I doubt she'll be happy about evacuating a hundred thousand people. She's still dealing with the fallout from the golem."

Kat Powell had helped cover up a particularly messy situation involving the unscheduled demolition of a railway viaduct. She'd somehow shifted the blame to the deteriorating structure and erased all video footage of us.

I didn't know how the woman fit into the government, or who precisely she worked for, but she could pull some pretty powerful strings and get them pulled quickly. You kind of have to if you're trying to hide the existence of an entire supernatural world from the general public.

"I'll call Devapriya now," I said.

"No," Miss Blackthorne replied. "Leave that to me. You three focus on getting to Circular Quay and helping with the evacuation. Our first priority is to minimise collateral."

I noticed she said *minimise* and not *prevent*.

"What about Freddy?" I said.

"I'll call around, see if I can get a hold of him. If the man has any integrity, he will still deliver himself to the selkies."

With a final a note of caution, Miss Blackthorne hung up, leaving the three of us in silence but for the metallic pings of rain hitting the Land Cruiser's roof.

Bree pulled up in front of our house. As I got out of the car, my mind was elsewhere, wondering whether there was any chance of stopping the selkies from attacking. Probably not, considering their new ambassador was just assassinated. He may not have been killed by the hand of the river folk, but it was under their instruction.

I was so lost in my own thoughts; I didn't see the vampire until it was right on top of me.

36

One of the things that separates wizards from other wielders of magic is our ability to channel and manipulate energy through our own effort. Witches use rituals and scribblings. Druids have to coax the spirits of the earth to lend them power. Priests recite *Hail Marys* to beg for divine intervention. Wizards, however, draw magical energy directly from The Cascade, from the very stuff of the universe around them, every atom and photon lending them its cosmic power to bend to their will.

However, all this power is worthless if you get caught off guard.

Crimson eyes glowed in the darkness as the creature tackled me, wrapping two cold hands around the back of my head. I bounced off the side of the Land Cruiser and fell to the ground with the vampire holding onto me like a blood-thirsty chimpanzee.

Now, vampires are fast, agile and have heightened senses, but they are not particularly stronger than a regular human. Unfortunately, I am markedly *less* strong than a regular human, so there was little I could do when the vampire grabbed a handful of hair and craned my head back to expose my neck. The creature's jaw opened wide, baring razor-sharp teeth.

Bree threw open the driver's side door, which smacked the vampire on the head, eliciting a harsh screech from the creature that scraped against the inside of my skull. Bree scrunched up her nose and booted the vampire in his big pale face with enough force to send him flying several feet, landing in a heap on the footpath.

She eyed the unconscious vampire as she hoisted me to my feet. "What the hell was that about?"

"Maybe Castille sent him." I cast a quick glance up and down the road. The rain made it difficult to see very far along the poorly lit street. "Do you think the vampires are still watching us?"

Oscar came around the back of Cruiser and looked up at the house. "Um, guys. I don't think they just want to observe anymore."

I followed his gaze.

Three spindly black figures crawled down from the roof, heads twisted at unnatural angles, fixing us with red-eyed glares.

"You didn't think I'd forget about you, did you?" came a honeyed voice.

Yvette approached from one of the deep shadows nearby. She'd changed her clothes and now sported a black sleeveless dress made of some kind of silky material that glistened in the rain. Otherwise, she looked the same as the last time I'd seen her – skin charred and cracking, her hair completely burnt away. She stared at me. Two blood red dots amongst a mask of melted skin.

I heard a grunt and spun to see a vampire holding Oscar from behind, his jaw hanging wide open, pointed teeth hovering over my friend's neck.

"Oscar!" Damn, they were fast. And quiet.

Bree took a step in their direction.

"Halt!" Yvette yelled. "Take another step and your wizard friend will have his throat ripped out."

Bree glared at her but complied, then looked at me.

"What do you want?" I said to Yvette.

"The same thing I told you before. To mind your own business. Stop meddling in our affairs and let us vampires get on with our lives."

"Oh, is that all?" I said. "Why didn't you just say so? Let me pack up my garlic and crucifixes and get out of your hair."

"Is that a joke?"

"What do you think?"

She frowned. "I could kill you all right now."

"Then why don't you?"

"You have proven capable of defending yourself." She gestured at her own blackened body. "Much like you, I would prefer to avoid unnecessary death. It is really up to you how this plays out."

"You sure you can take us?" I said, looking up at the house, where three vampires clung to the walls. "There's, what, five of you?"

"Five that you can see." She smiled a wicked grin, her white pointed teeth contrasting starkly against her charred skin.

I resisted the urge to peer at the shadows that filled the street and glanced at Oscar. "You doing okay, mate?"

All he could do was wince in response. I had to be careful.

"You're part of Penni's Family," I said, turning back to Yvette. "But where did these others come from?"

"All over." It was hard to tell through all the burnt skin, but she may have been trying to be seductive. "There are countless vampires who refuse to be quelled by the modern world."

"Your Father won't be happy you've gone *rogue*."

She darted forward so her face was inches from mine. "Rogue! Vasily Dragos and his whole godforsaken Family are the *rogues*! They fight against their nature every single night. Forcing themselves to eat garbage. All so they can live in a society ruled by mortals."

"You're not immortal," I reminded her. "Just old."

"Watch your tongue."

I sighed. "Look, with your Father out of the country, Penni is still in charge of Family Dragos. Needless to say, he's pissed and probably already has your family looking to round you up, along with your little gang of rebels."

"I have no family," Yvette snarled. "Not anymore."

No Family meant no rules. No rules meant blood on the streets.

"You know I can't stand by and let you guys do whatever you want." I paused, as if deep in thought. "I should really consult my wizard colleague, though." I turned to Oscar. "Hey, bud."

He cocked an eyebrow. "Hey?"

I opened my arms wide. "Close your eyes."

My skin tingled from my neck to my toes as magic rushed through my body. With an effort of will, an explosion of blistering white light burst forth, as intense as the sun. The spell required more than just creating bright light. It had to hit the right visible and invisible wavelengths to mimic the sun, otherwise I may as well be using the torch on my phone.

I'd managed to keep Yvette talking, which had allowed me ample time to figure out how to shape the spell, and even then, I hadn't been sure I could pull it off, having witnessed the spell being cast only once before. I was relieved to have more or less emulated what Jeremy did in the Ghost Tunnels. Good thing, too. I didn't have a backup plan.

The vampire at Oscar's neck reeled back with a hiss as the light seared his skin. Free of his grasp, Oscar whirled around and let loose a spell that flung the vampire through the air.

One of the vampires clinging to the house leaped on top of Bree, who apparently hadn't shielded her eyes from the big flash. Her eyes were shut tight as she swung wildly at the creature that was trying to sink its teeth into my friend's neck.

I wanted to help her, but I had pressing matters of my own to worry about.

Yvette had already recovered from my sunlight spell and pounced at me, mouth gaping. I threw up a shield, but she darted around it like a jackrabbit to get behind me, lunging at my neck. I twisted around and flicked my shield between us just in time for her to hit the translucent barrier, sending out a ripple of concentric blue circles. She bounced away and disappeared behind the Land Cruiser. I stepped back, expecting an attack, but not knowing where it might come from.

Something big tackled me to the ground. It flipped me over and tried to tear chunks out of me with rabid intensity. The vampire was a muscular bald man in a form-fitting polo top. I got a hold of his shirt collar and kept him off my neck for only a few seconds before Bree grabbed him around the waist and suplexed him into the footpath with a sickening crunch.

Remembering Yvette, I pivoted on the spot just as the vampire bounded over the Land Cruiser. I threw a quick *sneezer*, which barely slowed her down. She hit the ground and launched herself at me.

The vampire abruptly stopped short and her head jerked back, an audible "Urgk!" escaping her lips.

A *golden bracelet* bound Yvette's neck. She clawed at the air in front of me and gnashed her teeth, but Oscar's spell held her in place. He forced the vampire back up against the Land Cruiser. Still, she reached for me in frenzied desperation, her eyes burning with unrestrained fury and hunger.

"Cut it out!" I said and glanced around to confirm the other vampires were out of the fight. "You lost."

She stopped pushing against Oscar's spell and smiled. "Oh, I don't think so."

Dark figures appeared on the street, slinking out of the shadows. Ten, fifteen. I stopped counting at twenty. The vampires approached slowly, smooth and without hurry, unconcerned by the skinny wizards and the demon girl.

I glared at Yvette. "Call them off."

"No."

I stepped forward and conjured crackling blue energy in my clawed hand as I shoved it in her face. "Do it!"

Yvette craned her neck against the *golden bracelet*. "You don't want to make an enemy of us." She gestured vaguely at the vampires who had formed a loose circle around us. "We are the vampires who won't settle for picking up lifeless scraps, scavenging for the smallest creatures as if we were gutter things ourselves. We are the vampires who will return the world to the status quo, and we will not stop until we are free to do what we please, without bending to the will of humans."

"As a human, this concerns me."

"As it should. Vampires will once again sit above humans on the food chain, just as our Great Father intended."

"Pretty sure Vasily doesn't want you killing people."

"Not my father," she snarled. "The Great Father. The First Vampire and Father to all vampires."

I sensed the creatures around me. Even with my mind closed, my psychomantic abilities suppressed, I felt them. Their hate. Their hunger. They would rip us apart at a single word from Yvette. We could fight them. I could do that flash spell again, but that would only hold off the vampires for a few seconds and I didn't have the juice to do it more than a couple of times. I was tired and there were too damn many of them.

"Leave," I snarled. "Last chance."

Yvette smirked. "You are far outnumbered—"

A lance of sizzling blue energy erupted from my hand and ripped through the vampire's chest, blasting through the Land Cruiser's windows on both sides.

Yvette's bright red eyes widened, her mouth dropped open. The creatures encircling us screeched in a chorus of blood-curling wails.

"Joey!" Bree and Oscar yelled.

"Hold her there, Oscar!" I shouted back, not wanting him to drop his *golden bracelet* just yet. Vampires can live through having a hole blasted through their chest. I think.

I took my eyes off Yvette and addressed the surrounding vampires.

"Listen closely," I said, raising my voice above the unceasing rain. "Some of you may have lived here a while, probably longer than I have, but for the benefit of anyone new, Sydney is a Haven. It is protected by the Custodian, elected by the Old World. You wanna mess with this city or the people living here, you have to get through us!"

I forced energy through my left arm, and the scars blazed to life. Bright blue light ran along the wounds as magic fought to burst out of my body. Then came the agony, a searing pain that shot up and down my arm. It was a familiar sting, but that didn't make it hurt any less.

"So," I said through gritted teeth, glaring at the vampires around me. "Who wants to go first?"

The vampires shuffled uncertainly. One or two stepped back, shifting their red-eyed gaze to each other, then Yvette, then back to me. I prepped another flash spell in my chest. The first vampire to strike would cop the full blast of it. Hopefully, it would buy us the three or four seconds we'd need to get into the house. But the way the vampires were positioned, I doubted the spell would even get a quarter of them.

No one attacked.

"Who in the devil's name do you think you are, boy?" Yvette said, spitting blood as she spoke. "You're no Blackthorne. You're barely a man."

I turned and stepped close to her, the glow from my scars casting sinister shadows across her face.

"Joey..." Bree said quietly. "Don't..."

"You can't stop us," Yvette snarled. "We represent what all vampires truly desire. What we truly are. We number in the thousands." She smiled. "And we know where you live."

Goddammit.

I took a step back, raised my arm and cast a torrent of brilliant white energy at Yevette's face that made the scars on my arm feel as if they were being ripped open. I closed my eyes against the brightness of my own spell. Vampires shrieked and wailed around me.

I opened my eyes. Yvette's mouth hung wide, frozen mid-scream. Her lifeless eyes stared back at me, black and crumbling. Her scorched skin dissolved and fell apart as it was struck by the rain, washing away her features like water over ash, until there wasn't much of her left above the neck.

Oscar extinguished the *golden bracelet* and the vampire's body fell to the ground where it crumbled and the rain washed it away. I sighed deeply, took a breath, then levelled a glare at the other vampires, daring them to act.

"Get out of my city," I snarled.

The creatures hesitated, then one by one, they left, fleeing into the night. Hopefully, they kept running until they left the city. If we had time, I would have made sure of it. But we had other things to do. The vampires left us alone, and for now, that was enough.

I fell to the ground and sat against the back wheel of the Land Cruiser.

Bree rushed forward. "Joey!"

"I'm fine," I said, resting the back of my head against the vehicle. "I... just need a sec."

Good thing the vampires scattered; I had nothing left to throw at them. But that's not the reason I didn't want to get up. Nausea simmered in my gut, but I forced myself to put up with it.

Bree sat on the ground next to me. Then Oscar did the same, sitting cross-legged. They didn't speak, they just sat with me in the rain on our poorly lit street. We sat there awhile, maybe five minutes. It would have been nice to stay. Have a shower, crack a few cold ones. Maybe play a board game or something.

"We should go," Oscar said quietly.

"Yeah," I replied.

"You okay?"

"I will be."

"She was a mean bitch, Joey," Bree said. "She would have come back for us. If not tonight, then next week, next month, next year. You did what you had to."

"Then why do I feel like shit? Oscar killed a vampire yesterday, and he's fine."

"I'm not fine, Joey," Oscar said. "I spent half of last night throwing up in the toilet. The other half I spent having nightmares." He brushed his hair back. "I chalked it up as being all part of the job."

"All part of the job," I repeated quietly.

Bree put a hand on my shoulder. "Joe, we don't have to do this. I can call Miss Blackthorne. We have a good idea where the attack will happen. Hertz and Devapriya can get the right people to Circular Quay to evacuate."

"That won't work. What if Castille turns up again? Or if the selkies send a whole squadron of mages." I gave another tired sigh and pushed myself up. "We need to be there."

37

We towelled ourselves off inside, changed clothes and were back outside in three minutes. I'd thrown on my red weatherproof jacket, which wouldn't do much good if I found myself at the bottom of another river. But I was trying to be optimistic.

We jumped into the Land Cruiser and Bree gunned the engine. The wet roads had everyone driving fifteen under the speed limit, so the going was slow. Rain streamed into the vehicle as we moved, since someone had inconsiderately blown out two of the windows. At least the jacket was already being put to good use. I called Miss Blackthorne and gave her a quick rundown of what happened with the vampires.

"You need to hurry up," she said, completely bypassing the fact that I'd popped my murder cherry. "The selkies will be mobilising their warriors by now. They must be close."

"What about the evacuation?"

"Currently underway. But not as expedient as I would like. Kat doesn't want to incite mass panic."

Fair enough. Start telling a crowd of a hundred thousand people they're in danger and you risk folks getting trampled to death.

"If the police try to stop you," Miss Blackthorne continued, "just mention that you're working for me."

"What, I'm not on the VIP list?"

"No need to spread your names around if it can be helped."

"What about Freddy?"

"I haven't been able to reach Frederico. We may have to find another way to appease the selkies. I will be unreachable for the next few hours. Joseph, it is up to you to protect the people against the attack."

"Unreachable? Where are you going?"

"I have business I must attend to." She paused, then said, "One more thing. There is a low-pressure system building off the coast. If the selkies are behind that, then whatever they have planned will be big. Maybe even too big for Anjea."

"Right, thanks." I hung up.

Oscar turned in his seat. "What'd she say?"

I looked at my phone and shoved it back in my pocket. "Something about hell in a handbasket."

* * *

As we closed in on Circular Quay, we began to see groups of people walking the other way, huddled under giant umbrellas as they tried to keep their cameras and backpacks dry. It quickly became a stream of humanity, thousands of people moving slowly but persistently away from where we expected the danger to be. So many people.

A couple of blocks from Circular Quay we hit a police blockade, where people filtered around the sides heading in the direction we'd just come from. Bree stopped the Land Cruiser and started to wind down her window before remembering that I'd blasted it away while dealing with Yvette. A police officer in a bright yellow waterproof jacket jogged over to us.

He eyed the missing window but didn't question us on it. "You'll have to go back, sorry." He managed to sound both bored and authoritative at the same time. "Area's closed."

"Yeah, we know," Bree said. "We're expected."

The officer frowned. Standing out in the rain was probably not his idea of a great Monday night. He didn't need a carload of young adults talking back to him.

"Come on, don't fuck around. Turn around and go back. We're busy here."

I stuck my head forward between Bree and Oscar. "We're working with Mary Blackthorne."

The officer shrugged. "I don't know who that is."

"You better go check," Bree said. "You have orders to let us through."

He eyed us with deserved suspicion, then shook his head, muttering something about having better things to do. He turned to his colleagues at the blockade and yelled out, "Barry! Got a second?"

A squat man with a ruddy complexion came over wearing an identical hi-vis jacket. He had a thick white moustache that looked as if a hairy caterpillar had fallen asleep on his upper lip.

The man gave a curt nod to Bree, then looked at the officer who had called him over. "Everything alright here, Constable Willis?"

"You know the name Blackwell?"

"Blackthorne," Oscar said.

"Yeah, Blackthorne. You know it?"

Officer Barry stroked his bushy moustache. "Yeah, you should too. It's the name the Federal boys gave us." He peered into the car, frowning when he saw us. "What's your business, then?"

"It's classified," Bree said.

Barry's frown deepened, but if the officer was annoyed by Bree's response, he didn't show it. "Be careful on the road," he said. "Pedestrians will be coming through pretty thick."

Bree gave a sarcastic salute.

"Keep everyone moving," I said to the officers.

"That's the plan," Barry replied before stepping back and yelling at his buddies to let us through.

With one block to go to Circular Quay, we had to slow the Land Cruiser down to a crawl. People filled the footpaths and the road, walking away from the Vivid Festival. Mothers and fathers pushed strollers. Children ran around wearing glasses and necklaces made of glowsticks.

"We're going too slow," Oscar said.

Bree beeped the horn and stuck her head out the window. "Outta the way you little shits!"

"Fuck it," I said. "Leave the car. We'll go the rest of the way on foot."

We left Miss Blackthorne's Land Cruiser in the middle of the road, the crowd passing around it like water around a boulder, and jogged the rest of the way.

"Shit," I said when we got there.

There may have been thousands of people leaving Circular Quay, but there were still tens of thousands of hanging around by the water. Hunched under bus shelters, chowing down on takeaways burgers, stealing quick sips from their hidden goon bags. Far too many still walked among the exhibits, despite the rain, taking selfies with their friends and family. At least the pubs and cafés had closed and booted their patrons onto the street.

Warnings blared through the public announcement speakers.

ATTENTION. ATTENTION. THIS EVENT HAS CONCLUDED. PLEASE LEAVE THE AREA.

I felt the warnings didn't really convey the severity of the situation.

"This is a fucking mess," Bree said. "They haven't even shut the bloody lights off."

That wasn't entirely accurate. Most exhibitions that involved funky light displays or cool glowing bits had been switched off. But many of the other installations featuring mirrors, or human-powered moving parts, didn't have an off button.

Beams of light shot across the water from the Museum of Contemporary Art to project enormous moving images across the Opera House's giant white sails, illuminating the building in a medley of colours. That exhibit alone would keep crowds in the area. People could get a bit stupid when it came to taking pretty photos.

I strode up to another police officer in a big yellow jacket, who was trying in vain to get people moving while barking out directions to her colleagues.

"Why isn't everyone evacuating?" I said, almost at a yell.

Momentarily taken aback at my intensity, she looked me over with alert brown eyes. The officer was tall, with olive skin and dark hair. The wrinkles at the corners of her eyes put her in her mid-forties, and she had the bearing of someone used to being listened to. Water dripped from the hood of her jacket onto her pointed nose.

"We're getting there," she said, struggling to talk and direct officers at the same time. "We don't have much information. Train lines are down on the City Circle, but you can follow the crowd to Town Hall, or catch one of the buses on Castlereagh about half a mile down that way."

"We need to get everyone out of here now!"

Her eyes narrowed. "Sorry, who are you?"

"We work with Mary Blackthorne."

She ignored her fellow officers and the crowd for the moment to glare at me. Her gaze shifted to Oscar and Bree, then back to me. "What do you know?"

I took a moment to gather my thoughts, conscious that right now there was a fine line between coming across as informed and appearing like a lunatic. She probably had directions to listen to us, but I didn't want to see how far I could push her.

"We believe there will be an attack on Circular Quay... possibly terrorism related."

Her eyebrows shot up. "Where did you get this information?"

"I... can't say. But something's coming. We might only have minutes."

"Where specifically?" she asked, her voice tight. "The foreshore, the Opera House—"

"The wharves," Oscar said. "They won't be specifically targeting people, but—"

"But they're still in danger. Got it." The officer opened her rain jacket and thumbed the radio on her shoulder. "Attention all units, this is Superintendent Harriet Laskaris. We have a possible Code Black. I repeat a possible Code Black. Evacuation of the Circular Quay foreshore is now a priority. Move your arses, people." She looked at us over her beakish nose. "I just ordered the city's first Code Black. Should be interesting."

"Thanks," I said and turned to leave.

"Wait!" said Superintendent Harriet Laskaris. Her voice came out like a whip crack. "Where do you think you're going?"

"We need to get to the water."

"Why?"

"Trust us," I said, meeting her unwavering gaze.

She pressed her lips together and breathed out her nose. "There's a couple of counter-terrorism units scooting around in patrols boats. Try not to look too suspicious. They have orders to shoot first, ask questions later."

"Sure."

We pushed through the crowd, making our way towards the

Circular Quay waterfront. As we moved, the alarm changed its tune to something a bit more befitting of an oncoming war.

ATTENTION! ATTENTION! THIS AREA IS AT RISK OF AN IMMI-
NENT TERRORIST THREAT! THIS IS NOT A DRILL! EVACUATE
IMMEDIATELY!

The alert repeated itself at obnoxious volumes, forcing people to look up from their phones and take notice. Upon listening to the message, most hurriedly picked up their belongings and followed the crowd, which had picked up its pace.

"That's more like it," I said.

"Can't believe you just called a terrorist threat," Bree said as we walked.

"Someone needed to light a fire under their arses," I replied as I sidestepped a family dragging their uncooperative child along the street. "Hertz and Devapriya can only do so much without a whisper of evidence. Kat Powell would be the only person with the sway to get people moving but she may be more concerned with keeping the Old World under wraps than saving lives."

We reached the waterline and looked out at Sydney Harbour. The dark water churned. Roiling waves cut in every direction. Water splashed up onto the promenade, despite normally sitting a few feet beneath the walkway at its highest. Nearly all the boats had been cleared out, although I spotted a few ferries out on the water, still in the process of making a hasty retreat across the harbour. The only vessel left behind was the Parramatta River catamaran, which remained moored to one of the wharfs with thick ropes. It jumped around frenetically in the turbulent water.

I was wondering if this was part of the selkie shenanigans or just bad weather, when a wave crashed through the handrails and washed across the promenade. People too slow to heed the evacuation orders were swept off their feet by the knee-deep rush of water. Mothers and fathers picked up their children, before being knocked over by the surge themselves.

Oscar and I were thrown back several feet, coming to a painful stop at one of the massive concrete columns supporting the railway line that ran overhead. Bree had gotten a firm grip of the handrail and held onto it against the force of the wave.

Panicked screaming filled the air. There were shouts of 'tsunami.' If people weren't moving before, they were now. Another wave formed, half-submerging the wharves as it rolled forward. The catamaran bucked wildly against the ropes holding it in place.

The wave knocked Oscar and me off our feet as it crashed onto the walkway. Bree dived forward and wrapped her body around a young girl who'd been separated from her parents. Everyone else in the area, whether because they were still gathering their things or were hindered by the press of the crowd, were once again knocked off their feet as the water rushed across the promenade and onto the road.

In places where the water didn't have space to drain away, it receded back into the harbour, dragging people with it and tangling them up in the handrail at the edge of the promenade. The old metal railing had a filigree pattern, which caught people like a soup strainer, but if the waves kept hurling people against it, it was only a matter of time before the handrails were ripped out of the ground and the people dragged into the harbour.

Bree reunited the child with her very thankful parents. "Get the hell out of here!" she yelled. They nodded eagerly as the father picked up the child and took off.

Between the evacuation alerts, the freak waves and the tens of thousands of people fleeing for their lives, chaos reigned. Another wave crashed over the handrails and smashed against the invisible barriers Oscar and I had just conjured, flowing around us. I hissed out a pained breath as I struggled to hold the spell in place. It felt like holding back several semi-trailers. My scars started to itch, although I had no doubt Oscar was doing most of the heavy lifting.

Our shields bought the people behind us the precious few seconds they needed to find their feet and get away. Bree ran around helping those too old or too young to get up quickly.

"That way!" she told them. "Follow the crowd!"

The water receded and Oscar and I took deep breaths, preparing for the next one. A cast my gaze along the water's edge. Hundreds, possibly thousands, still struggled to escape the waves, not just beside the ferry wharves but all the way along the waterfront from The Rocks to the Opera House.

"These people aren't moving quick enough!" I yelled to Oscar. "We need to buy them time! If you go that way—"

"Joey!" Oscar called out. "Look!"

"Oh... fuck," Bree muttered behind me.

I couldn't have agreed more.

I watched in horrified awe as something akin to a water elemental emerged in the middle of the harbour. Only this thing stood about a hundred feet tall. Made of roiling dark water and foaming whitecaps that flowed across its surface, the creature didn't have much of a shape beyond the two thick arms that extended out from a centre mass, and had an aquamarine light that glowed deep within its body. Two blue eyes flared into existence as the immense creature surveyed the area.

38

RAIN AND DARKNESS served to obscure the massive creature, but it was pretty hard to miss. The magical energy it exuded felt like a physical weight against my brain, and I took a moment to erect a mental barrier to dull the effect.

"Joey?" Oscar said.

"There!" I yelled, pointing to a bunch of elderly people desperately clinging to benches for dear life.

"But what about—"

"Let's get them out of here first, then we'll deal with... whatever that thing is."

We started helping the old folks and had gotten most of them to their feet when the next wave hit. Oscar turned and faced the surge himself, raising his arms to create a translucent yellow wall to divert the flow around us.

"Hurry!" he shouted.

Bree and I got the rest up and moving. One man was so paralysed with fear she had to physically pry his fingers off the bench. It didn't look like the old fella's legs were ready to flee the madness either, so Bree picked him up and carried him. She glanced back at the creature in the harbour and hesitated.

"Go!" I yelled. "Get them somewhere safe. We'll deal with this thing." I hoped inspiration struck soon.

Bree turned and ran, the weight of the man she carried slowing her down not even a little. Thunder filled the air, loud enough to make my bones rattle, and the creature started moving towards the wharves. Towards us. It crossed the beam of colourful images being projected onto the sails of the Opera House and lit up in a dazzling kaleidoscope of colours that did nothing to detract from its inevitable menace.

Another wave rushed towards the promenade, twice as high as the previous ones thanks to ocean-zilla's approach. Oscar and I ran to where a thickset police officer led a small group of families through the quickly moving crowd, their strollers and toddlers making their progress slow.

The wharves disappeared under the turbulent surface as the wave rolled forward. The lone catamaran rose with the water until the ropes keeping it moored to the wharf ran out of slack, and its untethered side lifted into the air. I didn't see whether the whole thing flipped due to the wall of water that suddenly filled my vision.

Oscar and I placed ourselves in front of the families and threw our combined wills into creating the strongest defensive barriers we could conjure, which were then promptly destroyed by the wave. There's a hell of a lot of power in moving water.

The recoil from my broken spell hurt, but not as much as bouncing around on the pavement like a brick in a washing machine. It was all I could do to protect my head. Everything not bolted down was swept away. Massive planter boxes were tossed around as if they weren't one-tonne wrecking balls made of dirt and concrete.

I came to a painful stop against an overflowing garbage bin and desperately clung to it as the retreating water tried to suck me away. The front of the catamaran dropped onto the handrail, before the whole boat sunk out of view, taking a good chunk of the handrail with it.

Not everyone had something to hold on to. Men, women, and children tumbled all over the promenade, completely at the whim of the receding wave. My stomach lurched as a stroller, laying sideways in the water, rushed towards the gap in the handrails.

Inches from being washed over the edge of the promenade, the stroller gained a golden aura and froze in place, balancing on the precipice before floating gently into the air. As it floated past me, I noticed the gold bands around the handle.

It glided over to Oscar, who had braced himself against one of the Vivid exhibitions, made mostly of wood and mirrors. He reached into the stroller and brought out a crying baby, then gave me a quick nod before rushing over to the group of families who were slowly getting back to their feet.

"Somebody help!" a woman yelled. "He's fallen in!"

She stood at the gap in the handrail, pointing down into the water. If a wave came, she'd be thrown back like a cannonball. Ocean-zilla continued its approach, the projected images dancing across its surface.

I ran forward and looked over the edge. All I could see was the white hull of the catamaran disappearing into the murky depths of the harbour.

"Over here!" came a voice down to my right.

About fifty feet away, Aubrey Wan bobbed in the water, holding onto a stocky police officer, keeping his head above the surface. Thankfully, she hadn't shifted into her True Form. At this point, I wasn't entirely sure people would notice, anyway.

"Little help!" she said, as she swam backwards towards a short metal ladder leading up to the promenade. I thought about magicking them out of the water but discarded the thought immediately. I didn't have the finesse to get them up without risking broken body parts.

The woman next to me lifted her gaze to the massive creature approaching.

"You need to get somewhere safe," I said.

She turned to me slowly, eyes wide.

"Go!" I shouted in her face.

She flinched like I'd just slapped her on the cheek, then dashed back across the promenade and disappeared amongst the crowd. I ran to the ladder, where there was a gate built into the handrail. I blasted the lock and stepped down onto the slippery metal rungs, trying very hard not to lose my footing. That would be all I needed. I descended the ladder until the water lapped against my chest, then grabbed the officer by his black police vest. He mumbled something incoherent, but his body stayed limp.

"I pull, you push," I said to Aubrey.

The guy weighed somewhere in the vicinity of a small African elephant. I got three rungs up before my fingers went numb and my shoulders burned.

"Joey!" Aubrey yelled. "Another wave!"

I looked up. The rising swell blocked out the lights across the harbour and swallowed the wharves as it bore down on us.

Shit.

With no way out, I hooked one arm around the ladder, held onto the officer's vest and braced for the impact.

"Hold on!"

39

EVERYTHING WENT black as thunderous waves crashed around us. But the rush of cold water never came, never tried to wrench me from the ladder or pull me to its depths. I opened my eyes to darkness, released the air I'd been holding and took a tentative breath. Yep, definitely not underwater.

With my elbow hooked around the ladder, I conjured a *lumière*. Water rushed around us as if we were caught in a giant air bubble, and I could have sworn I saw someone swimming behind the surface.

"Let's get him up!" I yelled to Aubrey over the roar.

The protective bubble rose with us as we struggled up the ladder, then seemingly disappeared as the water receded. It took my last bit of strength to haul the police officer up onto the promenade, and I fell in a tired heap next to him.

We had mere seconds before the next wave, but I took a moment to lie on the wet pavement catching my breath, waiting for the ache in my arms to go away. Aubrey appeared above me. She had a sword at her hip – Mei's *jian* – that I supposed was intended for the hordes of selkies that were meant to invade the shoreline. I sat up and asked if she'd brought reinforcements.

She shook her head. "Mum told everyone to stay home for the night, but to be ready in case the selkies show up at our doors. I snuck out. Mum doesn't know I'm here." She looked at the stocky officer. "Is he alive?"

With a dogged grunt, I pushed myself to my knees and put an ear to the officer's mouth.

"Move away from him," someone said.

Rhoswyn strode towards me, Hamish not far behind. The selkie mage extended her hand and two water elementals splashed up onto the promenade. One of the watery creatures placed a limb over the police officer's face.

I jumped to my feet. "Oi, what are you—"

Hamish placed a strong hand on my shoulder. When I gave him a questioning frown, he inclined his head towards the officer. The elemental withdrew its arm and glided back. The police officer coughed in violent spasms, then took a big gasping breath.

I pushed past Hamish and bent down beside the officer. "You ok, mate?"

He craned his neck and half opened his eyes, before letting his head rest back on the ground. I gazed across the water at the giant creature bearing down on us, then turned my attention to the quickly thinning crowd. Most people had gotten out, but hundreds still struggled to escape the waves that continued to pummel the promenade.

I looked up at Rhoswyn. "We need to move him."

She nodded to Hamish, who deftly picked up the stocky officer and bore him on his broad shoulders in a fireman's carry.

"There are other cops down that way," I said, gesturing vaguely towards where I'd run into Superintendent Laskaris.

The selkie warrior took off at a jog.

The creature out in the water released an almighty roar, that reverberated throughout my entire body and rattled the metal handrails.

"How the bloody hell do we stop that thing?" I said.

Rhoswyn watched the creature. "I had no idea—"

"Rhoswyn!"

"It's not a thing," she said, whirling on me. "It's a Mac Lir!"

"A what?"

"Mac Lir," she repeated. "A Child of the Sea. It's an ocean god!"

The Mac Lir bellowed another roar that boomed through the air like thunder. The insane amounts of power emanating from the god assailed my mental defences, and I spared a moment to double down on my mental barriers to avoid being overwhelmed.

"You're attacking the city with a god?"

"Apparently," she said, worry etched on her face. "I knew the War Mages were preparing something big. But this... this is not normal."

"You could have given us a heads up!"

"I work for the ambassador, not the War Legions," Rhoswyn said sharply. "Does your government publicly announce their military strategies?"

Honestly, I didn't know. I don't watch the news.

"I thought it was impossible to summon a god," I said.

"It still is, as far as I know." She bit her bottom lip. "The War Mages must have sacrificed a substantial number of prisoners to enlist the aid of the Mac Lir. Had I known this was their intention, I would have killed the Encantado in his home rather than attempting to bring him to trial."

I narrowed my eyes. "Why are you helping us? Your people are attacking the city."

Rhoswyn's shoulders sagged. "You won't hear many selkies admit it, but we have grown too large. Too cold and ruthless. Such is the cost of attaining great power. Our government sits thousands of miles away, yet they call for the decimation of an entire people. They fail to remember the value of a life."

"But you've still got rules, right? You won't go after people?"

"This attack is our declaration of war, the selkie response to the murder of our ambassador – sorry, ambassadors. Our leaders will see it as fair warning to the river folk that they should leave the river and flee the waterline. After this transportation hub, the Mac Lir will immediately work its way up the river, destroying everything near the river."

"Everything?"

"Everything. Bridges, hospitals..."

"People live along the river," I yelled. "Normal people."

Rhoswyn closed her eyes and shook her head. "I know."

I grabbed the selkie mage by the shoulders and pointed out to the harbour.

"How the hell are we meant to fight that thing!"

"You can't."

A part of my brain – the small, sensible part that begs me not to touch wet paint and electric fences – sent signals to my legs to get moving, to run. Seek shelter and let everyone take care of themselves.

But I couldn't. Not when so many people were about to get the smited – smote? – by an ocean god. No, as long as there was a single person in danger here, I'd stay and fight. Regardless of how hopeless it looked.

The conflicting signals from my brain resulted in the uncontrollable shaking of my legs, and I hoped Rhoswyn couldn't hear my knees banging together.

At that moment a colossal snake made of slick mud and twisting mangrove roots burst from the water in the harbour, eyes ablaze with a deep green light. Images from the projector played off the snake's writhing body as it coiled itself around the Mac Lir, somehow grabbing a hold of the god's liquid form and pulling it away from the wharves.

That would be Anjea, Goddess of the Parramatta River, and hopefully, defender of the city. I immediately understood why there are so many stories about gods levelling mountains and carving canyons out of the earth's surface.

The two giant celestials slammed into the water, sending enormous waves shooting out in every direction. Oscar appeared by my side and together we conjured the strongest shields we could.

We needn't have bothered. With a few quick gestures, Rhoswyn directed her two elemental buddies to dive straight into the oncoming wave, diverting it harmlessly around us.

Unfortunately, once the water receded, I saw that even more of the fleeing crowd had been tossed around by the surging water. All along the promenade encircling the Quay, people lay on the ground, too tired or too injured to move.

"You doing alright?" I said to Oscar.

He levelled a weary gaze at me, water slicking his blonde tipped hair to the sides of his face. "No," he replied.

"Samesies," I said and turned to Rhoswyn. "If we can't fight the god, how do we stop it?"

"Our War Mages will be directing the actions of the Mac Lir. If we stop them, somehow break their connection to the god, the Mac Lir may lose interest in the city and retreat."

"Where would the War Mages be hiding? I can't breathe underwater."

Rhoswyn frowned at me. "Neither can selkies."

"You can't? I thought you had... gills. Or something."

"We do not."

"Then how do you—"

"Magic."

Of course.

She turned her attention back to the harbour. "The War Mages will have located themselves somewhere with a good vantage point, so that they may survey the attack."

I cast an eye over the harbour. They could be anywhere.

Bree appeared, breathless and saturated. "Joey, we're not gonna get everyone out. There's too many people and too many of these fucking waves." She looked out to the harbour. "What the are those things?"

"Anjea's fighting off an ocean god."

"Damn... Oh shit, here comes another wave!"

Rhoswyn directed her elementals into the wave again. We huddled behind the selkie mage while the surge knocked everyone else to the ground, hurling them against hard concrete walls and each other. Half the wharves had already been destroyed by the constant tsunamis. Wooden debris and broken glass filled the water. One wharf started to sink into the harbour, its structural supports obliterated.

"We'll work our way along the promenade," I said, once the water had receded. "Rhoswyn, Oscar, and I will shield the people from the waves—"

"Joey!" Bree yelled. "Look!" She pointed out to the harbour.

I struggled to see through the shroud of heavy rain, but eventually I saw it. Out on the water, past the two gods locked in combat, a ferry had flipped upside down while making its retreat.

"I will go," Rhoswyn said.

"No," I said sharply. "Stay here. Help these people." I gestured widely at the promenade, still crowded with people struggling to get away.

"Oscar, Bree. You and the selkies save who you can."

Bree's eyebrows came together, and she bit her lower lip. "What will you do?"

I turned to Aubrey. "Reckon you can drag me over to that ferry?" I didn't have a plan beyond getting out there.

The young Baiji woman looked out at the battling gods and the tumultuous seas around them. "Sure. But it won't be fun. For either of us."

Over the cacophony of crashing waves, rolling thunder and blaring alarms came two deep blasts of a foghorn. I thought it had come from the upturned ferry until I heard what sounded like a Boeing 747, followed by two more blows of the horn.

A bright red speed boat appeared through the heavy rain, cutting through the swells like a samurai sword. It was one of those jet boats that take tourists whizzing around the harbour. The vessel had two angry cartoon eyes and grinning shark teeth painted on its front. It had enough seats for twenty people, but only three were taken. Mick the Mokoi sat at the wheel, with Arthur the Immortal and Frederico the Encantado strapped in behind him.

Wind and rain blew back the Mokoi's thick black locks as he slotted the boat in between the wharves and sidled it up to the promenade. He flicked his hair out of his eyes and looked up at me with a white-toothed grin.

"Need a lift?"

40

_____

Aubrey and I scrambled into the boat, while Arthur climbed up to the promenade, claiming he'd be more help on land.

"Careful out there, Joey!" Oscar yelled.

I gave him a tired thumbs up.

"Seatbelts on," Mick said before spinning the boat around and hammering the throttle.

Then we were off. Encantado, Mokoi, Baiji and me, scooting across the harbour, while the others tried to save whoever they could on land. The acceleration on the jet boat forced me back into my seat and rain assaulted my eyes as if I was holding a shower head to my face.

Mick didn't let up on the throttle as we shot up and over the gigantic swells, making the ride feel like being in a rally car or an especially wet roller coaster. More than a few times we caught air underneath us, only to come slamming back down again, bringing manic cheers from the Mokoi.

"I know the guy who runs the Jet Boat tours," Mick yelled over the roar of the engine. "He let me borrow it for the night. It's a bloody machine, tell you what!"

I didn't reply and focused on gripping my seatbelt.

We skimmed around the fighting giants, where I realised Anjea had twisted the mud and mangrove vines into the form of an eel, not a snake. She still battled against the Mac Lir, but it seemed as though the larger ocean god had the upper hand. It seized the river goddess in two giant fists and slammed her into the water. Mick re-aligned the boat so that we rode the wave. Aubrey closed her eyes and dug her fingers into my arm.

Light from the city reflected off the upturned ferry's green hull, and the vessel's two propellers hung suspended in the air, rotating lazily. Several scattered shapes floated in the water, mostly broken seats and empty lifesaver doughnuts, but as we got closer, I could make out people, struggling to stay afloat in the raging swells.

"Mick!" I yelled. I couldn't be sure if he heard me, and I wasn't ready to undo my seatbelt just yet.

I cast a *lumière* and sent it hurtling ahead of us, bringing it to a stop above a large young man flailing exceptionally hard. Mick saw the light, then steered the boat towards it and eased back on the throttle.

"Any Mokoi on that ferry?" I asked.

"Not that one, mate. Just the normies." His smile gone, Mick watched the surface of the water with an intensity I wouldn't have picked him for. "Bloody disgraceful."

Frederico and Aubrey shifted into their True Forms and were in the water before the boat came to a complete stop. They got a hold of the big guy and pulled him over to the boat, where Mick and I dragged him up and onto one of the seats.

He wore a light blue business suit with a matching tie and had a round, cherubic face. He looked around as if wondering where he was, then recoiled when his gaze fell upon me, as if I'd suddenly popped into existence.

"You okay, mate?" I said, practically shouting at his face. "Hey! Can you hear me?"

The man regarded me drowsily through half-closed eyes.

"You were in an accident," I said. "We're going to take you some-where safe."

His gaze slipped past me to the celestial rumble nearby. His mouth hung open and his eyes widened, then without missing a beat, he pulled a phone from inside his jacket and started recording a video.

Unbelievable.

I ripped the phone from his hand and shoved it back into his jacket. He didn't resist, just stared at me with a vacant expression. I then realised how absolutely shitfaced the guy was.

"Sorry, mate. We'll get you home soon." I strapped him in and went over to help Mick pull another passenger into the boat.

We rescued seven more people floating in the water before Frederico and Aubrey said there were more inside the ferry.

"Take me with you," I said.

"You'll slow us down," replied the Encantado.

"You'll need me."

"Take my hand," Aubrey said, her inhuman face devoid of features except for big dark eyes that looked up at me. She stretched out her arm.

I hesitated less than a second before reaching out and grasping her large, webbed hand. With a firm yank, she pulled me over the edge of the boat and under the surface. I felt Frederico grab my other wrist, and the two river folk dragged me through the water at what seemed close to jet boat speeds. Seconds later, I was gasping for breath inside the upturned ferry. Orange emergency lighting filled the interior. People screamed, although I couldn't be sure whether it was because of their imminent drowning or the appearance of two alien creatures.

"Start getting them out," I said.

"Obviously," the Encantado replied. He turned to a thin, bald man next to him. "Take a breath."

The man stared wide-eyed. "Wha—"

He disappeared under the water with Frederico.

Aubrey turned to me. "There's too many. We can't save them all."

"We have to try!"

I couldn't read her expression, but she nodded and swam over to a small woman who was bleeding from the head and dragged her below the surface. Moments later, Frederico returned. He really was quick. The Encantado grabbed another passenger and took her under the water, not wasting time on exchanging words this time. I tried calming the trapped passengers but couldn't get my voice heard over their panicked shouts. I suppose from their perspective, having their fellow passengers dragged under the water by the monstrous-looking river folk might have looked like a scene from a horror movie.

They may have been terrified, but they had air and would be fine for the time being. I took a breath, ducked under the water, and pulled myself deeper to the lower level, which, since the ferry was upside down, was actually the ferry's upper level. Once there, immersed in the orange-tinted water, I forced calmness to run through me and drew in energy. Slowly, steadily collecting it in my chest.

With a nudge of willpower, I let the magic flow out of me, creating *water worms* that extended into the darkness. I sensed shapes... people... a dozen at least. Some floated near me inside the ferry, others had been thrown out of the vessel and were sinking fast. Pumping more energy into the *worms*, I reached for them. I stretched my spell as far as it could go, but the people had sunk too far, and with my magic spread so thin, their bodies passed right through my semi-solid conjurations. I tried again, pouring more magic into the spell, extending my grasp, but failed to reach them once more. When my lungs felt about to burst, I pulled myself back up to the pocket of air.

Frederico and Aubrey had been busy, and only a few passengers remained. At this rate they'd have everyone out within a few minutes, but that might be too late for the people already drowning.

I dived back in, only for a powerful hand to seize the collar of my jacket and yank me back up.

Aubrey looked at me with wide, alien eyes. "You need to see this!"

I fought for breath. "There's... more people down there—"

"Now!" she said, grabbing my wrist and dragging me through the water.

We came up on the other side of the ferry.

"Aubrey!" I gasped. "We need to—"

She placed a webbed hand over my mouth and raised a finger to her lips, although I doubted anyone would have heard us over the rain and the waves. The Baiji woman led me around the hull, dragging me through the water since my muscles had decided to call it a day.

Mick came into view, standing on the Jet Boat with his arms stretched to the sky. Two small black boats flanked him on either side, each carrying four armed men in black tactical gear. Half of them levelled their assault rifles at Mick, the other half pointed at something in the water that I eventually recognised as Frederico's head.

"Oi!" I called out, because apparently I have zero survival instincts.

I promptly found myself staring down the barrels of eight assault rifles, the flashlights on their weapons all but blinding me. Aubrey and I threw our hands in the air as you do in these kinds of situations.

"Don't fucking move!" one of the men yelled, his deep voice booming over the noise around us.

"Blackthorne! Blackthorne!" I yelled out frantically. "We work with Mary Blackthorne! Don't shoot!"

271

A few seconds of tense silence passed, during which my legs worked furiously at trying to keep my head above the water, my hands still in the air. One of the boats peeled away and approached Aubrey and me, the other stayed with Mick and Frederico.

The boat stopped beside us and one of the men lowered the muzzle of his rifle. "Easy, lads," he said. "Safeties on."

The rest of the weapons were lowered.

"Can I... put my arms down?" I panted. "I'm about... to drown."

"Get him up, fellas," the man called out. Several hands reached down and dragged me onto their boat.

By the time my eyes re-adjusted to the darkness, the other boat had pulled up alongside us. All eight men were dressed head to toe in black, with large helmets and dark cloth masks covering the lower half of their face. They regarded us with coiled apprehension, and I had no doubt those guns would come up if I did anything they perceived as a threat, so I took extra care to make no sudden movements.

One of the men pulled his mask down to his chin, revealing a short scruffy beard. He looked over at the Jet Boat, which contained Mick and all the survivors we'd picked up, then turned back to me.

"The hell is that thing?" the man said, jutting his chin towards Aubrey who was still in the water.

"My name is Aubrey," she replied coldly.

"She's a friend," I said.

Her alien appearance didn't seem to faze the man one bit. "You know Blackthorne?" he said to me.

"I do."

"Know what's going on back there?" He jerked a thumb over his shoulder where the Mac Lir was pummelling Anjea with watery fists. I wondered how much longer the river goddess could hold him back.

"Yeah," I replied. "But it'd take a while to explain."

"Care to summarise?"

"A couple of gods are having a tussle. Ocean god wants to destroy everything in spitting distance of the waterline. River goddess is trying to stop it."

"Fucking Blackthorne," the man said, shaking his head. "She could have let me know there'd be weird shit going down. Anything we can do?"

"There are still people inside the ferry," I said, quickly. "Some have been knocked around a bit. They're in a bad way. And there are people drowning in the water right now!"

He nodded. "Your name?"

"Joey Finch. Yours?"

"Dupont. Captain Dupont." He turned to the other black-clad men. "Right, lads! We got people trapped in the ferry. Let's get 'em out. Load up the worst ones onto our boats. Put the rest on the Jet Boat."

The men lay down their weapons and removed their helmets and masks, revealing a variety of beards and non-regulation army haircuts. Everyone focused on the task at hand, not wasting any time to watch the spectacle occurring in the harbour. They dived into the churning waters and set about the task of rescuing the passengers with businesslike efficiency.

"Aubrey," I said urgently. "The people sinking—"

"On it," she said, and disappeared under the water. Frederico followed her.

I went to dive back in the water after them, but Captain Dupont put a firm hand on my shoulder.

"Not you, mate. You stay here."

I tried to shrug him off, but his arm didn't budge. "She'll need my help," I said. "People are drowning."

"Finch, you can barely keep your eyes open. My boys and your... friends will grab whoever they can." He looked down at the water. "Although. Anyone who's been down there this long... probably not much use bringing them up."

Between the river folk and the soldiers, they extracted everyone in a few short minutes.

"Is that everyone?" I asked Frederico.

"Everyone worth grabbing," he replied.

I leaned over the edge of the boat. "What about the people who were sinking? You can't just leave them. They could still be—"

"They're dead, Joey," Aubrey said. "They probably drowned before we even got here. There's no one left here to save."

I wanted to dive in and search for the remaining people myself. What if Aubrey was wrong? Fatigue or not, I couldn't give up on them. I would drown pulling those people out if there was even the slightest chance they were still alive. But I knew that wouldn't help anyone.

The captain slapped a hand on my shoulder. "Let's get going, aye? Some of these people are looking pretty rough."

I clenched my jaw, blew out a frustrated breath. "Fine."

We loaded five passengers onto the black boats with the soldiers, the rest went on the Jet Boat. A collection of city workers, tourists, and young people out on the piss. Thankfully, no children. Everyone sat in silence, most of them watching the celestial clash with detached interest.

"Finch," the Captain said. "We've got cars nearby. We'll get these people to a hospital. You make sure you take the rest of them somewhere safe. The water's less rough upstream, away from... that." He jutted his chin at the gods.

"Thanks. Oh, if you see a guy covered in scars wearing a ventilator mask, don't be afraid to shoot him. He's bad news."

"Is he a wizard, too?"

The question caught me off guard. How much did these guys know?

"Yeah," I replied.

"In that case, we'll keep our distance," he said, lifting his mask back over his face. "That's beyond our remit. I'm assuming Blackthorne wouldn't have sent you unless you could handle him." He raised a finger and made a circular motion above his head. The two boats made a tight loop, then sped off in the direction of the Heads.

Frederico and Aubrey shifted back to their human forms before jumping back on the Jet Boat. The passengers were too distracted by the gods to notice them, anyway. With no spare seats, I sat on the floor up front next to Mick, feeling defeated. How many people had we missed?

Mick pointed the Jet Boat upstream before really cutting loose.

The battle between Anjea and the Mac Lir raged behind us, but it was clear how the contest would end. The ocean god had its fists around the eel's neck, the river goddess's tail thrashing weakly in the water.

We had minutes before Circular Quay was back under threat. I just hoped my friends had gotten everyone out of there.

We jetted under the Harbour Bridge and hooked a tight left around the southern abutment into Walsh Bay, where apartments, cafés and theatres sat on large piers extending out to the water. The small bay sat protected from the worst of the effects of the battle, so Mick was left to contend with the regular turbulence that comes with shitty weather.

He brought the boat in next to a wide floating platform, connected to one of the piers by a metal ramp, which led to a restaurant that overflowed with plants and fairy lights. The platform appeared to serve as an outdoor dining area, but given the weather, wasn't getting much use at the moment. Heads swivelled within the restaurant, watching our sorry-looking group as we pulled up.

"End of the ride, folks," Mick said. "Please watch your step and ensure you don't leave any of your belongings behind."

We didn't waste time tying up the boat. Frederico and Aubrey stood astride the gap, helping the more dazed passengers to the platform, but most scrambled across themselves as if they'd been adrift for days. Frederico, Aubrey and I worked together to help the big drunk guy in the blue suit across. Not an easy task, given our exhaustion and the man's inability to stand straight.

A couple of passengers who still had their wits about them had already dialled triple zero and were giving the operator their location.

Seeing they were safe and secure, I grabbed Mick's arm. "We need to go back to Circular Quay."

"Are you sure you want to get back amongst it, mate?" he asked, casting a worried eye over me. "You're not looking too hot."

"Yeah," I said, the thunderous roar of battling gods still ringing through the air. "Let's get moving."

41

I STRAPPED myself in and we zoomed back around the southern abutment into Circular Quay, carving a straight line through the waves to get amidst the chaos again. As we paralleled the section of promenade between the Harbour Bridge and the wharves, the scale of devastation hit me hard.

Hundreds of people clung desperately to lampposts, fences, anything they could get their arms around. Some lay on the ground, unmoving. Dozens more bobbed in the water, dragged into the harbour through broken gaps in the railing.

"Freddy! Aubrey!" I yelled.

Without a word of acknowledgement, the weary river folk dived from the speeding boat, working through their exhaustion to save who they could. I fought the impulse to follow them, I still had to figure out a way to stop all this, but had no idea where I would even begin to search for the War Mages.

Mick steered the boat around the gods, as the waters abruptly became calm, and the fighting stopped. I looked up and watched, through the pelting rain, as the Mac Lir lifted Anjea above its head. The river goddess barely moved.

The ocean god had won.

"Oh, shit!" I shouted. "Go, Mick! Go!"

The Mac Lir slammed Anjea into the water with an almighty splash. Mick fought to keep the boat pointing forward as the resulting tsunami sent us hurtling between the wharves towards the thick wooden supports under the promenade.

We came to an almost immediate stop several feet short of what would have been a spectacular collision. Rhoswyn stood at the edge of the promenade before us, arms outstretched, face twisted in an expression of grim determination. The boat remained stationary while the tsunami surged either side of us, crashing over the handrails and across the walkway. Moments later, the water receded as violently as it had come, and the Jet Boat dropped with it. Mick took advantage of the temporary calm and brought us next to the metal ladder then cut the engine.

Then came the screaming. Dozens more had been dragged from the walkway, and were now fighting to stay afloat in the churning water.

"Mick?" I turned to the Mokoi, and with a look, pleaded with him to help.

He hardened his jaw and removed his shirt, revealing heavy bandages around his chest where he had been struck by the Scarred Man's magic. With a quick glance up at the Mac Lir, the victorious ocean god now towering over the wharves, Mick dived into the water, setting about the task of rescuing who he could. Which likely wasn't going to be many.

I jumped onto the metal ladder and started climbing before a spout of water gathered around my legs and tossed me up onto the promenade. I landed in a heap at Rhoswyn's feet with one of her water elementals appearing next to me a moment later. She and Oscar lifted me up.

Alarms still blared over the crashing waves and heavy rain. Not just the evacuation alert, but the alarms of every shop and café rang out after having their doors and windows smashed by floating debris.

The crowds had largely vacated the area, but still about a hundred people lay on the ground near us. Unconscious, or worse. Men, women, children, the elderly, the disabled, and the several police officers who had rushed in to help. No one had been spared.

"Joey," Oscar said in ragged breaths. "We've done what we can. There's just... there's too many."

"I know, mate," I said through a clenched jaw. I turned to face the oncoming threat. We had only seconds before the god reached us.

I scanned the harbour, searching for the War Mages responsible for the Mac Lir's actions. Looking for anything that would give them away, an odd movement in the darkness, a strange light.

Nothing. Sydney Harbour is big. We could probably search an entire week and not find them.

Bree rushed to my side. "We should go, Joey," she said, placing a firm hand on my arm. Blood ran down the side of her face, but she didn't seem to notice. "We've done everything we can," she continued, "saved everyone we can. Now we've got to get out of here."

Oscar nodded. His hair wet and clinging to either side of his face. He'd lost his glasses at some point during the night's proceedings.

I looked at the people along the promenade. The people I'd failed to protect.

"No," I sighed, fighting off weariness to summon all the magic I could. "You guys go. I'll stay and fight this thing."

"Joey..." Bree said. "You know you can't."

"That's not the point," I replied, barely loud enough for anyone but me to hear.

"You're being an idiot!" Bree shouted, gripping my arm tighter and pulling me away.

I placed a hand on Bree's chest and released a small kinetic spell. She staggered back, more from shock than anything else.

"Go!" I shouted, then turned to Oscar. "You too!"

He stepped right up to me. "Bree's right," he said as I felt him gather energy. "You really are an idiot if you think we're going to leave you." He turned to face the Mac Lir as well.

Bree opened her mouth, then shook her head. "Well, there's no fucking way I'm the only one bailing." She came and stood next to me.

"Guys," I said, exasperated. "Go!"

"As if," Oscar replied.

"Yeah," said Bree. "Why do you always get to be the hero? Share the spotlight for once!"

I looked them both in the eye. Loyalty, love, family. There were no words to describe what I felt in that moment.

"I can't hold the Mac Lir back," Rhoswyn warned. "I have no control over it. I cannot protect you."

"Fine," I said. "You've already done more than anyone could have asked. Thank you. You and Hamish should find somewhere safe."

Arthur appeared. Haggard and out of breath. He put his hands on his knees and leaned forward, frowning as he regarded the three of us.

"You're staying," he said. It wasn't a question.

We all nodded.

He stood up straight and glanced along the promenade where people lay strewn about. "You guys have done enough. More than enough. Mary Blackthorne would be proud. You can leave here with the knowledge you've left it all on the field."

"We've made up our minds," I said, hearing the cold determination in my own voice.

He cast a glance along the promenade again, then stood straight, placed hands on his hips and arched his back as if stretching his body out. "Well, I can't let you kids sacrifice yourselves all on your lonesome."

"What are you doing?"

"Staying, obviously. Who knows, maybe we'll even survive this."

As he said that, something clicked. And in the space of a few seconds, a plan came together in my mind. A way to save everyone here. Well, almost everyone.

I came close to not saying anything. Almost swallowed the words before they came out. The weight of what I would ask seemed like a physical burden on my chest. My throat tightened, as if my own body didn't want to speak up.

"There is a way we can stop the Mac Lir," I said, forcing the words.

Everyone turned to me, but I returned the gaze of only one.

Rhoswyn frowned, her eyes thin slits. The selkie mage looked up at the Mac Lir, then back to me and her eyes widened in comprehension.

"No," Hamish said.

Rhoswyn lifted her chin. "Do you think it will work?"

I held her gaze. "Honestly, I don't know. But it's the best shot we have."

Hamish grabbed the selkie mage's wrist. "I said no, damn it!"

"There is no other way," she replied with calm acceptance.

"Then let me do it!"

She placed a hand on his. "No. You know it has to be me. When was the last time you prayed to our gods? Sought their guidance? My connection to the Mac Lir is deeper and far stronger than yours."

"You owe nothing to this city," Hamish said. "You owe nothing to these people." His voice was harsh and deep but held real pain.

"It's not about what is owed," she said, with a touch of melancholy. "I was willing to kill a man to prevent a war. It would be hypocritical of me if I were not willing to pay the same price."

"Hold on," Bree said. "What's going on?"

Oscar reached down and held her hand but didn't say anything.

The Mac Lir reached the end of the wharves and swung watery fists that tore through the structures like wrecking balls, sending shattered glass and twisted metal through the air. Mick was still down there somewhere, as were the people he was trying to save.

"Rhoswyn..." I said.

She nodded, turned and stepped to the edge of the promenade there the handrail had been torn out.

"Rhoswyn, wait," Hamish said, following her.

The selkie mage turned to Hamish, placed a hand on his cheek. Something passed between them. A deep affection, grown over centuries. She lifted her chin, drew her sword out of its scabbard and, with trembling hands, presented it to Hamish. Slowly, he reached out and wrapped his fingers around the grip.

Arthur approached Rhoswyn. "It's not nearly as bad as you might think. But there is always that fear, that split second before you go. Would you like me to come with you?"

She frowned. "I don't think that will be necessary."

"Oh, don't worry about me," he said. "I've done this loads of times."

"Thank you," she said, with a sad smile.

Arthur looked at me. "If this doesn't work. You guys get out of here, alright?"

"No promises," I said.

He chuckled and shook his head, then turned to Hamish, pointing to his own chest.

"The heart, please," Arthur said.

Without further ado, the selkie warrior placed one hand on Arthur's shoulder, gave the man a sharp nod, and ran the man through. Arthur's eyes widened, and a gasp escaped his lips. Hamish withdrew the sword and the Immortal Man fell to the ground, dead once more.

Hamish turned to his fellow selkie and hesitated. For the space of a few heartbeats, he didn't move, and everything seemed to go quiet. Even the destruction being wreaked by the ocean god became muted background noise.

Rhoswyn fixed the selkie warrior with her clear green eyes. "Do it."

Hamish released an anguished cry and thrust the blade through Rhoswyn's chest.

42

————

THE SELKIE MAGE gasped and fell. Hamish caught her and lowered her to the ground.

With a final gesture of her hand, Rhoswyn summoned her two water elementals. They rushed forward and collected Arthur and the selkie mage, washing them over the edge and into the dark waters below.

Hamish fell to his knees, head bowed.

We waited.

Nothing changed for several moments and the Mac Lir continued on its path of destruction, right up to the promenade where it loomed over us. Then, without warning, it stopped. As if someone had flicked a switch.

The Mac Lir went still, its giant liquid form towering over the promenade. Then, slowly, it shrunk. The rushing waters comprising its body washed away into the harbour, and the waters calmed, the raging currents replaced with the steady lapping of regular waves. The aquamarine light that once sat at the ocean god's core, sank deep, illuminating the water in an ethereal glow.

"What the hell?" Bree said, her voice sounding very small.

"You can't summon a god," I said. "But the best way to get their attention is—"

"A sacrifice," Hamish said, sitting on his heels, looking out to the harbour. "No matter how many souls our War Mages offered up. It all pales in comparison to the act of sacrificing one's own life."

"Look at the water," Oscar said.

The mystical glow had shifted to a swirling palette of blues and greens, spreading across the harbour, hugging the edges of the promenade. A ripple ran across the surface and with it came a gentle, yet powerful surge of invisible energy that pushed through all my psychic defences and brought me to my knees.

The harbour became silent. The soft waves lapping against the support piles ceased their motion. The alarms and evacuation alerts cut out. Even the people strewn about the area, quieted their sounds of pain and suffering. The soft patter of rain on the wet pavement became the only source of sound.

Suddenly, all along the promenade, from the Harbour Bridge to the Opera House, the water level lifted, like a giant wave moving in slow motion. Flashes of green and blue streaked beneath the surface as it rose high, creating a liquid wall of shimmering light.

Hamish stepped back as the wave softly curled over the edge, enfolding the promenade in a caress that lasted only a few seconds, before receding back into the harbour, silent and smooth. And once the water withdrew, I saw that all the people who had been dragged off the walkway and into the harbour were now lying upon the promenade in various states of consciousness.

"What the bloody hell was that?" Mick said groggily as he got to his feet.

As if in response, the water surged again, rising up like a platform, upon which stood an impossibly beautiful man.

And I mean *beautiful*.

I don't lean that way, but anyone – I don't care what your preference is – would have been hard pressed to come up with a better adjective. He wore only a pair of white, flowing trousers, showing off a pale body that looked like it had been sculpted from pure white marble. Muscles bulged in places I didn't know muscles existed. He had a sharp jawline and sharper cheekbones, a strong nose and full lips set into a frown, all framed by a mane of fiery red hair. His feline eyes glowed with a greenish-blue light. He stood at least nine feet tall, and the power he exuded was staggering.

I had absolutely no doubt I was looking at a god of the ocean.

In his arms, he carried Rhoswyn. It would have been easy to mistake her for being asleep, but for the patch of blood-soaked clothing above her heart. The sword had been removed from her chest and now rested alongside her body.

The Mac Lir stepped onto the promenade. "She is a brave one, this child," he said, placing Rhoswyn's body on the ground gently. The god's voice resonated deep within my skull, stirring up images of ocean depths, the quiet and the unknown.

"Thank you," Hamish said, bowing his head and avoiding eye contact. I followed suit and lowered my gaze, focusing on not letting my own senses be overwhelmed by the god's mere presence.

Another being emerged from the water, covered in dark silt and mud, and carrying Arthur's lifeless form. Anjea stepped onto the walkway and the sludgy residue fell away, revealing the dark-skinned Goddess of the Parramatta River, wrapped in a shimmering green dress and every bit as striking as the Mac Lir. Although, a wisp of weariness hung about her that she didn't have the last time I'd seen her. Getting your arse handed to you by an ocean god will do that to you.

With an equal amount of respect, she lay Arthur on the ground and turned to the ocean god.

"Fiachra mac Lir," Anjea said, her voice smooth as velvet. "You're a long way from home."

The ocean god smiled, and for a moment, I questioned which way I did indeed lean. "My home is where my children are. I apologise for my actions."

"We all do what we must," she said, giving the ocean god a severe look that only served to broaden his grin.

I stepped forward, and once again struggled to force words past my throat. "All due respect... will you now leave the city?"

The ocean god lost his smile and glared down at me. I instinctively dropped to my knees and lowered my gaze.

"I will leave," said Fiachra mac Lir. "My child has earned from me an act of mercy."

I breathed a sigh of relief. "Thank you... god... Fiachra." I chanced a look up at the ocean god and found the huge being staring down at me with what may have been a trace of amusement.

"You are a curious little one," he said.

Arthur gasped, sucking in a deep breath. He looked around, as if waking from a long sleep, and sat up.

"Thanks, Anjea."

"You are most welcome, Arthur."

Fiachra mac Lir stared at Arthur in open wonder. "Impossible!" he whispered. "I thought all the Immortals had left."

Arthur looked up at him and shrugged. "Apparently not."

A commotion erupted somewhere up the promenade as five men stormed towards us. They wore dark blue robes with elaborate silver trimming and sported lengthy grey beards and elongated ears. The men remained suspiciously dry despite the rain and weaved between the people lying on the ground as if they were stepping around piles of garbage left out overnight. Leading them at a brisk walk was Glenroch, the War Mage from our meeting with the selkies.

"Stop!" he cried. "Nobody move!" He pointed a bony finger at the ocean god. "What in Lir's name do you think you are doing?" The War Mage's face was red and sweaty, either due to his barely contained fury or the bit of powerwalking he'd just done.

Fiachra mac Lir's eyes blazed and he spoke with a thunderstorm in his voice. "Take care, mortal. Remember to whom it is you are speaking."

The selkie mages bowed in supplication, although Glenroch may have been a fraction behind the others.

"Of course, Lord Fiachra. I only wished to query why our requests have not yet been granted. The fault no doubt rests with us. Perhaps we were not clear."

"No. I understood your requests perfectly. But this little mage convinced me to change my mind."

The old War Mage's face went red again, and he hissed out a breath. "With all due respect. She is but a magus. A junior mage. Not even a member of the War Council. Surely, the orders we gave you—"

"Orders?" the ocean god repeated. He didn't need to raise his voice. There was enough power in that one word to silence the old War Mage.

"Request," Glenroch said quickly. "The *request* we made of you should take priority. For the selkie people. For the people who serve you."

"You shower me with gifts for one week and then claim to serve me? Selkies have lived long in this realm compared to its other inhabitants. You should know better." He looked down at Rhoswyn's body

285

with what may have been sadness and a touch of pride. "She has been a faithful subject. Thanking me when the seas turned in her favour, enacting my *will* whenever she had the opportunity. And in the end, she gave her very life simply to ask that I no longer do as you and your mages have asked of me. I deemed her sacrifice ample recompense for honouring the request."

"But—"

"Perhaps if you were to offer me your own lives, I would consider granting you another request."

The War Mage's eyes widened and the colour in his face drained in an instant. He looked to his bearded compatriots behind him, but they kept their heads bowed. Glenroch glanced up at the ocean god, then lowered his head. His mouth twisted into an infuriated snarl, but he said nothing.

"I suspected as much," said Fiachra mac Lir. He crouched down next to Hamish, who still knelt by Rhoswyn's body. "Take her home. Give her a proper burial."

Hamish nodded silently.

The ocean god stood and turned to the river goddess. "It was a pleasure meeting you, Anjea."

"I hope we do not meet again," the goddess replied.

"Time will tell," he said with a smile, "time will tell." Fiachra mac Lir dived into the water and disappeared in a flash of aquamarine light. The moment he left, the old War Mage whirled on Hamish.

"Traitor!" he spat. "You will pay dearly for this!"

"Take it easy, mate," I said.

"And you!" He jabbed a finger at me. "I don't know how you convinced two selkies to turn against their own kind, but I will not stand for it! This matter is between selkies and those who have wronged us. If you don't want to find yourselves dragged to the ocean floor, I suggest you keep out of our way."

"That won't be happening," I said, and with an effort of will pushed magic down my arm, illuminating the scars in blue light. The man took a half step back, staring at me with raw hatred. "The selkies are free to stay in this city," I said, "but it's going to be on our terms. That means being on your best behaviour. No picking fights with the other kids."

"You dare..." the old man snarled, rolling up his sleeves.

Oscar balled his fists, a bright golden glow coming from them. He fixed the old man with a narrow-eyed glare. "Don't," he said quietly. "We don't want to hurt you. It's best if you just leave."

Bree stretched her neck and cracked her knuckles. "I don't know, guys. I wouldn't mind blowing off a little steam."

The old man snorted. "Please. What threat could mere children pose to us?"

"Oh, you'd be surprised," Arthur said, still sitting on the ground. "They pack quite the punch. But since we have an extra friend here..." he looked up at the river goddess. "Anjea, dear. Do you have any thoughts on the people who sent the ocean god into your domain?"

"I do," she replied, her eyes blazing with emerald fire. "And they are not good thoughts."

Glenroch puffed out his chest and scowled. "So be it." He closed his eyes and began waving his arms through the air, muttering something under his breath. I felt the stirrings of magic and the sound of crashing waves as the War Mage prepared to attack.

43

GLENROCH'S SPELLCASTING came to a premature halt when Hamish seized the man's thin wrist. "Don't be a fool, old man," the warrior growled. "When's the last time you were in a fight? One that you didn't get someone else to fight for you. You start throwing spells around and you'll only get yourself killed."

Glenroch opened and closed his mouth several times before managing to form words. "This is... this is unacceptable!"

"Unacceptable or no, it's over." The burly warrior pushed the old man's arm away. "We're leaving."

Glenroch glared at Hamish, then turned his attention to me. "Where is the Encantado murderer! He still must pay for his crimes!"

"Seriously, dude?" Bree said. "Ever heard of 'quit while you're behind?'"

"No, he's right," shouted a voice behind us. We turned to see Frederico approach, leaning heavily on Aubrey for support.

"Freddy?" I said.

"The old bastard's right," he repeated, lifting his arm away from Aubrey and standing upright on his own. Barely. The man was exhausted. "I need to atone for what I've done. Otherwise, these idiots will keep coming back and kill even more people."

Anjea looked down at him, her eyes aglow. "Is this what you want, child?"

Frederico shrugged, not meeting the river goddess's gaze. "It's what needs to be done."

A wicked grin crossed the War Mage Glenroch's face, and he stepped forward. Hamish stepped in his way.

"Move aside, soldier!" the mage said. "We must apprehend him."

"The man is coming of his own free will. I will make sure he arrives in selkie custody for trial and punishment. It is my job, after all."

The old man licked his lips, obviously with plenty more to say. "He accounts for more than one death. Ambassador Calder McBrae and his escort were murdered too. Or has that fact already leaked out of your thick skull? This isn't over!"

"Last time I checked," Hamish said. "You're a member of the War Legions, not the Embassy. I will investigate what exactly happened at the meeting earlier today and deliver you a full report, as is my duty."

The War Mage's eyes flashed with anger and with nowhere to vent his seemingly limitless fury, he turned on the rest of us.

"We are done! You hear me? There will be no more relations between the selkies and the river men, or anyone else of this city. Trespassers into our domain will be treated as hostile invaders and will be dealt with swiftly and without restraint. We will no longer defend your lands from the creatures of the Trench or the ghosts of the sea, and we will not support you in your fight against the witch hunters. Do not call for our aid because you will not receive it!"

"We'll get by," I said.

He shook his head with an arrogant smirk. "That is yet to be seen."

Bree crossed her arms and rolled her eyes. "Oh, piss off, Gandalf."

The old selkie went red in the face again and started to speak, when Hamish placed a meaty hand on the man's shoulder and spun him towards the water.

"Go," the warrior barked.

Reluctantly, and with a parting glare, the old man dived into the water and disappeared beneath its murky surface, followed quickly by his fellow War Mages.

Hamish picked up Rhoswyn's body and held her tight, her hair wrapping around his fingers. "I'll talk to the surviving escort from the meeting. He'll listen to me. No one will benefit from war."

"Will Glenroch really cut all ties between us?" I asked.

"He may be an arrogant ass, but the old bastard's got clout back home. He could very well cease relations between the selkies and this city. But there's no reason you and I can't keep other channels of communication open. Unofficially, of course. It's what Ambassador Kelden would have done." He looked down at Rhoswyn with affection. "It's what *she* would have done. I have a favour to ask, though, wizard."

"Name it."

"If you come across Kelden's sword, let me know. Our blades are sacred to us."

"How do I reach you?"

"I'm sure you'll figure something out." The selkie warrior turned to Frederico. "Coming?"

The tall Encantado moved to his side.

"Oi, Freddy," I called out. "You saved a lot of people today. Thank you."

The man clenched his jaw and gave a single sharp nod.

"Don't worry," Hamish said to him. "I'll watch out for you."

With a nod to Oscar and Bree, the selkie and the Encantado stepped off the promenade and disappeared into the dark water.

Bree scratched at her arm, flashed a nervous glance at Anjea, and leaned in close to me. "I'll be back there if you need me," she whispered, before practically running along the walkway to help people to their feet.

Arthur clapped his hands together and stood up with an extravagant bow to Anjea. "Thank you, once again, my dearest Anjea."

The river goddess inclined her head a fraction in acknowledgement.

"Are you okay?" Oscar asked.

She narrowed her eyes and Oscar quickly stared at his own feet.

"Fiachra mac Lir and I were not trying to destroy each other. There would need to be serious ill will for such a thing to take place. However, he did wound me. My soul will take several days before it has fully recovered." She gazed down at Oscar. "I thank you for asking."

He gave the goddess a nervous smile.

Sirens rang out in the distance. A convoy of police, ambulance and the fire service. No doubt reporters would be hot on their tails.

A thought crossed my mind.

"Can you kill demons?" I asked. The question came out rushed before I lost the nerve to ask.

"I have destroyed hundreds of malestial beings over the millennia,"

Anjea replied. "Demons and otherwise." She turned her gaze to Bree, who was busy assisting an elderly man to his feet. "I would be happy to destroy that one should you so desire?"

"What? No, no. We... need that demon... for now. Are you familiar with a demon named Astaroth?"

The goddess's eyes blazed, and I felt the need to bow my head once more.

"The Master of Envy," she said, looming over me. "The Manipulator of Desires. What is he to you?"

I lifted my hands defensively. "We're not mates or anything. He tried to break into this realm a few months ago. Wanted to turn the city into a staging area for his demon army."

Anjea raised an eyebrow. "Tried?"

"Yeah," I replied sheepishly. "We kind of... stopped him."

The river goddess fixed me with an amused look, as if she'd just witnessed a monkey perform a new trick. Her expression quickly shifted to one of pensive seriousness. "Astaroth is an Archdemon, a Duke of Hell, and one of the most powerful beings banished to the Dark Realm. If I were to face him in open battle, I expect Astaroth would destroy me. I suggest you avoid him."

"That's been the plan so far," I said.

She turned to Arthur with a thin smile. "I would say that I hope to see you soon, my Immortal friend, but I fear you may again take it literally. So instead, I will say take care."

Arthur bowed again. "My lady."

The river goddess slinked over the edge and into the water, and I felt the easing of magical pressure against my senses.

"Is she gone?" Mick said, emerging from behind a Vivid exhibit that resembled a fifteen-foot elephant made of LEDs, which on any other night would have been flashing all the colours of the rainbow. The Mokoi winced with each step and the bandages around his chest were pink with blood.

"Anjea's gone," I said. "You're safe."

The Mokoi nodded, then turned to Aubrey. "Want a ride home?"

"Please," she said.

They jumped into the water feet first and swam to the Jet Boat which had somehow survived the night's proceedings.

"Hey, Joey!" Aubrey called out. I leaned over the edge of the promenade as the Baiji woman removed the *jian* at her hip and tossed it to me. I fumbled it awkwardly before clamping a hand around the sheath. Even with all the excitement, she hadn't needed to swing Mei's sword at anyone.

"What am I meant to do with this?"

"I don't know," she said. "But you'll get better use out of it than us. Being the defender of the city and all. Anyway, right now, I wouldn't trust my mother with anything sharp and pointy."

I examined the scabbard. Dark polished wood, with golden engravings along the sides in Chinese. I'm going to say Mandarin. I put my fingers around the grip and drew the blade out a few inches. The weapon thrummed softly in my hand and tickled my other senses.

I sheathed the sword and leaned back over the edge. "What will happen to the river folk? I don't have to worry about you guys capping each other, do I?"

Aubrey and Mick traded a look.

"As far as I'm concerned," Aubrey said, "my mum got her justice when she stabbed Frederico's dad through the chest."

"My elders may see it different," Mick said. "They'll probably want to separate the Mokoi from the other river folk for a while. A long while. But we'll all come together again, eventually." He glanced at Aubrey. "Until then, we'll try to make sure everyone behaves themselves."

I breathed a long sigh of relief. "Thanks, guys. For everything."

Arthur appeared at my side and leaned over the edge. "Give me a lift up the river, would you? This has all been very exciting, but I could do with a nice long rest at home. And I don't particularly feel like hanging around and talking to the authorities." He climbed down the ladder and stepped onto the boat before looking up at us with a wry grin. "You kids take care, alright?"

"We always do," I said.

With a flash of white teeth, Mick reversed the boat away from the demolished wharves and sped out into the harbour.

"Tell you what," Oscar said. "I could go for a drink."

I cast a gaze along the promenade. "Not yet, mate. There are a couple hundred people here we need to check on."

"All of them?" he asked.

"At least until the cops and paramedics get here. But they're probably still a couple of minutes away. I'll need to find Superintendent Laskaris and let her know the danger's passed."

Then, as if to prove again that the universe is a master in comedic timing, the Scarred Man stepped out from the shadows and attacked.

44

EVEN WITH MY mind closed and my psychic defences up, I sensed the pressures shifting around me. But just because you know something is about to hit you, it doesn't mean you possess the power or skill to do anything about it.

Castille's stream of bright red energy destroyed the rushed shield I'd conjured, deflecting just enough to strike the ground next to me and kicking up chunks of paving stones. I fell to a knee as the sharp pain of having my spell broken momentarily stunned me. Oscar stepped into my field of view and conjured his own shield as Castille sent forth another beam of scarlet energy. My friend screamed with effort, but his shield held, taking the full force of the spell head on.

I caught movement at the edge of my vision as Bree ducked behind one of the giant concrete columns that supported the overhead railway line. If Oscar and I could distract the Castille, maybe we'd have a chance.

I got to my feet and cast a glowing ball of energy that hurtled towards the Scarred Man. I called this one *Pandora's piñata*. He waved his hand in a sharp gesture, and the ball exploded long before it reached him. A flock of birds burst out of the spell – hawks, specifically – glowing the colour of a summer sky, with beaks and talons as sharp as my mind could make them. They homed in on the Venerati wizard like miniature rockets.

Castille clapped his hands together with a severe crack, creating a concussive wave that engulfed the hawks. Colour drained from my conjurations and they dissolved mid-flight, forming a black cloud accompanied by an ominous buzzing.

Only when the dark cloud shot straight back at us did I see the individual thumb-sized hornets, hundreds of them. Thousands. He had taken the magic from my spell and twisted it to fuel his own.

So not fair.

Oscar pushed his shield forward, and the hornets splattering against it like... well, like bugs on a windshield. He warped the shield as he pushed it, so it formed a half sphere curving away from him. I saw what he was attempting and created my own curved barrier that shone with a soft azure light.

Castille decided he didn't fancy being encased in a bubble with his own hornets and let his conjurations dissolve into a wispy black smoke that he drew back to his hands.

"Oscar, look out!" I yelled.

The black energy circling Castille's fists shot out, taking the form of jagged tendrils. I dived away, but I wasn't the target. The dark tendrils wrapped themselves around Oscar, binding his arms and legs together.

Enter, Bree. Stage right.

She charged forward, silent and fast. The irises had lost their colour; her eyes now two black pinpricks in discs of pure white. She wore an expression of complete and utter rage.

Castille sensed Bree coming, or maybe he'd been expecting her, because the moment she appeared, he twisted his body and raised a hand. Bree slammed into a wall of energy, jet black and completely opaque. The wall unfolded itself, like an origami video in reverse, until it fully encased Bree within a black polyhedron. Not half a second later, a series of dull thumps boomed through the air, which, knowing Bree, was her trying to literally punch her way through the containment spell.

"Oh," the Scarred Man said, eyes widening. He turned to me. "Your friend's strong. What is she? A mimic? Nephilim?"

A brief pause in the noise was followed by a sharp crash, as Bree broke through the roof of her temporary prison, landing on all fours. The black tendrils around Oscar faded, and he scrambled to his feet. Castille staggered back, blinking hard. I guess having your spell broken hurts no matter how strong you are.

Seizing the moment, I unsheathed the *jian* and sprang forward, gripping the sword with both hands. My legs pumped as I closed the distance, time seeming to slow with each step. I screamed and brought down the blade as Castille opened his eyes. In that fraction of a second, the scars throughout his body blazed to life.

He swung his arm in a wide arc that sent me flying sideways, tumbling across the pavement. The sword clattered to the ground out of arm's reach and my heart sank as I realised I'd just blown our best chance at getting out of this.

Castille's scars glowed a wicked red.

Oscar gave a wordless cry and threw both hands forward, sending forth thick streams of golden energy that weaved themselves into the shape of a charging bull. The ground shook with the animal's heavy hoofbeats. The lights dimmed as the Scarred Man gathered shadows around him, then sent forth more dark tendrils that whipped at the Oscar's conjuration. The bull continued to storm forward, so Castille sent a stream of blistering scarlet energy that shot past the animal and tagged Oscar on the shoulder.

My friend went down with a cry and the bull evaporated.

Bree leaped at Castille, who redirected his shadowy tendrils and caught her around the neck. The dark conjurations slammed her into a concrete column with a resonant crash, dislodging chunks of concrete in a cloud of grey dust.

Bree fell to the ground and lay still.

I cast *sizzle cuffs* that caught the Scarred Man around the legs. I fed the spell what little energy I had remaining to hold him in place. Spying the sword on the ground next to him, I made a move for it, getting only two steps before the black tendrils reached me, whipping around my ankles and locking my legs together. I hit the ground hard, my head bouncing off the pavement with a crack, before Castille's spell lifted me upside-down.

Half-dazed, I forced more power into the bands around Castille's legs, only for the Scarred Man to perform a sharp gesture with his hand and break my spell. Agony stabbed at the back of my eyes, like someone had just poked them with a red-hot needle.

I grunted against the pain and tried to look Castille in the eye but swinging back and forth as I hung by my legs, I couldn't even summon the raw will power to gather energy. I was too hurt, too tired, my body too spent.

Castille smiled, the glow of his scars fading as he released some of his pent-up magic. I could hear the soft whirring of machinery as he brought me closer. A new ventilator. I made a weak attempt to reach for it, but he batted my hand away.

"I haven't had a contest like that in years," he said. Despite his coarse voice, he sounded genuinely pleased. "You three are quite the surprise. Very impressive for a couple of skinny wizards and... whatever she is."

Bree lay in a heap, while Oscar writhed on the wet ground, moaning in apparent agony.

I looked up – or down – at Castille and caught his eye. "The selkies and the river folk... stopped fighting." My breaths came hard and shallow, and my skull throbbed where I'd headbutted the ground. "We... prevented the war."

He shook his head. "You think that's all I was trying to do? Of course, you would, you're still thinking small scale." I must have looked as confused as I felt, because he went on. "They're a strange people, the selkies. A strength to rival any nation on the planet, yet we hardly know anything about them besides what's scratched on the walls of old Celtic drinking halls or scrawled in ancient poems."

"You did this... to see how they'd respond?"

"Sometimes we have to poke the bear to see how sharp its claws are. But I would never have imagined they could summon an ocean god. I expected them to send half a thousand mermaids or some such." He shook his head again. "Incredible."

"You're going to attack them?"

His expression turned serious. "You still wish to protect them even after everything you have witnessed? The selkie War Mages would have killed thousands had they not been stopped. And the Mac Lir would have wreaked destruction never before seen in this city."

I tried to roll my eyes but ended up just looking at the man's black boots. "What's your point?"

Castille glared. "The Old World is a ticking time bomb. The selkies and the river men were practically begging for a reason to go to war."

I tried to laugh, but could only muster a tired sigh. "They were doing fine before you came along."

"Were they? I did little more than whisper into a man's ear. Look at the destruction that caused. The Old World isn't one big happy community. They are reckless animals willing to cause widespread death and destruction regardless of whether it affects their supernatural peers or the rest of the world. River men, selkies, vampires, witches, elves. They live only to serve their own interests, and act with sickening disregard for human life. Take Yvette, for example. She'd happily tear out your throat for the pure pleasure of it."

"She's dead," I said.

"Huh." He raised an eyebrow. "Maybe you're not such a lost cause after all." The dark tendrils lifted me up, so we were at eye level. "You can join us," he said. "You can help us fight creatures of the dark and bring order to the world. Help us bring peace."

"By destroying the Old World?"

"A means to an end," he said, academically. "Protecting our world is a hard job full of hard choices. But we take solace in knowing we are on the path of good and are creating a better, safer world. There is room for you, and your friends, within the Venerati Sanctus. We can place you on assignments that won't impinge on your delicate morals if that suits you better. Hunting vampires in the Middle East, perhaps?"

"You're fucking nuts if you think any of us would join you."

"Helena Rake didn't think so."

I frowned. "Miss Blackthorne's apprentice? The Venerati killed her."

He laughed to himself. "No, of course Blackthorne wouldn't tell you. Why would she tell you about one of her greatest failures? A source of great shame. The young child she rescued from the Venerati Sanctus, who became her ward only to run back to the witch hunters the first chance she got. The prodigal wizard."

"Bullshit."

"It's true. Helena returned to us, a fully formed master of the arcane arts. She was one of my instructors, actually. Powerful. Absolutely brutal. Last I heard, she was sorting out forest dryads on the west coast of America."

"I don't believe you," I said.

"Ask Blackthorne yourself."

"I thought you were going to kill me."

"Fortunately for you, I need you alive." He stretched out a hand to Oscar. "However, since your friends won't be joining our cause—"

Castille abruptly threw his head back and howled in agony, his body rigidly arching backwards. The black tendrils around my legs evaporated, and I dropped like a sack of weary potatoes.

I lifted my head as Jeremy winked into existence, Mei's sword grasped in two trembling hands. He still wore his cheap satin magician's outfit, soaked to the bone, his curly brown hair dripping water down his face.

The magician yelled and raised the *jian* for another strike.

Castille swept his arm up and across, creating three razor sharp tendrils that pierced Jeremy's shoulder and stomach, exploding out his back.

"You pathetic little worm!" Castille snarled.

Lying on the wet ground, I fought off the fatigue and the pain and drew in power, not enough to cast a particularly powerful spell, but enough for what I needed. As the Scarred Man turned to Jeremy, a slight breeze ruffled his coat, and it flapped open. I shot an arm forward, casting a bolt of iridescent green electricity that struck Castille square in the chest.

He swung his gaze back around and fixed me with a look of unadulterated rage. I doubted the spell hurt, but judging by the trails of smoke rising from the devices on his chest, I'd say I got in a pretty good hit.

A shimmering golden eagle rocketed in from above and smashed into the Scarred Man's side, knocking him off balance. I chanced a look behind me where Oscar stood, shoulders slumped with fatigue, his jaw set in a grimace of dogged determination. He held one wavering arm forward, the other hung limp at his side.

Castille regained his footing and saw Oscar standing, ready to fight.

"Fine," growled the scarred man.

With a rage-fuelled cry, Castille slammed his hands on the ground. My vision filled with red as a deafening boom knuckle-punched my eardrums. The wave of magical pressure overwhelmed my senses completely, shattering any vestige of psychic defences I had left.

My world went sideways, then all the lights went out.

45

THE FIRST THING I heard when I came to, was the breathing. Long and ragged, as if I was listening to a man on his deathbed. I was lying in the backseat of a car, smoky black tendrils binding my arms and legs. I tried to shout, but couldn't summon the energy to make the barest peep. Fatigue came and dragged me back into unconsciousness.

46

I AWOKE AGAIN when the vehicle came to a stop. Castille stepped out and used the black tendrils to drag me onto the street and across the road. He'd removed the machinery from his chest and taken off his mask.

Red and blue lights flashed over narrow terrace houses and twisting eucalyptus trees above. Just the lights, no sirens.

I knew this street.

I blearily noted that the front window of the police car we'd arrived in had been smashed, and a splatter of blood decorated the driver's side door, which I doubt belonged to my captor.

The tendrils whipped painfully around my neck and lifted me to my knees. If not for Castille's spell holding me up, I would have collapsed onto the road and fallen asleep for a month or so. I stared up at the Old Substation Building as the interior lights switched on.

We stood on the road, waiting in the dimness of the streetlights, the heavy silence broken only by Castille's laboured breaths.

We were out there for several minutes before the Substation's front door opened with a metallic creak. Out stepped the Venerati prisoner, Matthias Voigt, glowing red bands of energy binding the man's arms to his side, searing his clothes.

Voigt had a black cloth over his head, like he was an inmate at Guantanamo, and wore the same trousers and button-up shirt I'd seen him wearing last time, only they were dirtier and more tattered, and had accumulated several more blood stains. Many of which looked fresh.

Then out came the Master Wizard herself.

Miss Blackthorne ripped the cloth off Voigt's head. I would have gasped if I had the energy. Half the man's face was purple and swollen, like he'd gone a few rounds with a concrete golem. A trail of dried blood snaked its way down his face from a split eyebrow. Sunken eyes sat within a deathly pale face, the man looking like he'd aged twenty years in the space of a day. The Venerati commander stepped delicately down the stairs to the footpath, blinked, and looked around. A slight smile touched his lips upon seeing Castille and me.

The Scarred Man's mouth twisted into a scowl. "I see you've been taking good care of my colleague for the past months."

Miss Blackthorne stepped forward, her movements slow and stiff. "Are you okay, Joseph?"

I summoned all the energy I could muster to give a one-word response. "Peachy."

She slid her gaze over to Castille and fixed him with a flat stare cold enough to freeze the surface of the sun. He showed no reaction. But I felt it. A minute tremor in his consciousness, a sliver of apprehension.

He stood a fraction straighter. "I've come to—"

"I know why you're here," Miss Blackthorne snarled.

The Scarred Man hesitated, then forced a grin. "Of course," he said, his voice ragged and wheezy. "And it looks like you spent the last few hours giving my man the royal treatment. You are willing to make an exchange?"

"I am."

"You surprise me," Castille said with a sardonic smile. "From what I've heard, I didn't expect you to give up a Venerati prisoner so readily. I was worried for a moment that I'd need to bring all three of your little helpers to convince you."

"Mathias Voigt is of no more use to me," she said, her voice betraying no emotion. "I have learned much over the months. It was especially interesting to learn about your exploits in other cities around the country. Names, addresses. You will find that my interstate counterparts have already moved in on them."

Castille lost his smile and glared at Matthias Voigt, who smiled apologetically. "She can be very persuasive when she wants to be," he said with a shrug.

The Scarred Man sneered at Miss Blackthorne. "I could destroy you."

"No," she said. "I've seen you wield magic. You are reckless and inefficient. You rely on Wells of Power to reach levels you are unable to achieve yourself."

Castille's scars began to glow. "I've been wielding magic as long as I could walk. Learning how to fight, how to kill. Your own apprentice taught me all your tricks. You don't scare me."

Miss Blackthorne's eyes narrowed a fraction, as a cool wind blew down the street, stirring litter and fallen leaves. Branches groaned, windows rattled. A gust whipped up around the Master Wizard, a mini tornado with her at the centre. Her clothes fluttered violently, and her scarf danced in the air. She dropped her cane and spread her hands wide.

The streetlights dimmed and the night grew darker while a deep crimson light coalesced around Miss Blackthorne's profile, not from any particular spell, but from the sheer density of magical energy she was gathering. Red light burned around the Master Wizard, as if she was a beacon of scarlet-infused power, and the pressure against my consciousness was big enough to rival that of the gods. If I hadn't witnessed it myself, I would have said holding onto that much power was impossible without turning yourself into a mini nuke.

Castille shifted, as if to step back from the display, but the man caught himself and held his ground.

Miss Blackthorne fixed her gaze on the Venerati wizard, somehow looking down at the taller man. "You wouldn't be the first person to underestimate me, witch hunter." She spoke quietly, yet her voice boomed over the wind, resonating inside my head.

The Scarred Man hesitated, glaring at the Master Wizard, his lips curled back into a sneer. Eventually, the scars across his face lost their glow, and he stretched out a hand to Mathias Voigt. "Come."

Miss Blackthorne flicked her wrist and the red bands around the bespectacled old man disappeared, leaving blackened marks on his clothes, and red welts on his skin. At the same time, the black tendrils holding me fell away like ash in the wind, and I dropped to the asphalt. With trembling arms and legs, I rose to my feet and trudged towards

Miss Blackthorne. I felt unease at leaving my back exposed to the Scarred Man, but there was little to do about it.

Voigt and I passed each other, each of us moving as slow as the other. Both of us hurt, exhausted. No words were exchanged between us. But when our eye met, I knew, as sure as the sun would rise, I'd see him again. Whether it be months or years, Mathias Voigt would be back. And he'd have more than a lone wizard fighting for him.

"It is done," Castille said with a note of finality.

"Not yet," Miss Blackthorne said, the aura of scarlet light still surrounding her.

The Scarred Man tilted his head.

"Leave this city," ordered the Master Wizard, "and never return. Or there will be nothing in all the realms that will stop me from destroying you."

Castille stepped forward, but Voigt placed a bony hand on the man's arm. "Let it go, boy. We have other things to take care of. Besides," he said, turning to Miss Blackthorne with a glint in his eye, "she can't protect this city forever."

Castille threw me a vicious look and said, "Until next time."

The two members of the Venerati Sanctus walked back to the police car, and drove into the night, red and blue lights flashing down the street. The power surrounding Miss Blackthorne dissipated and the wind died down, returning the night to its sullen silence.

She picked up her cane and turned back to the house. "Let's get inside before they decide to come back." She moved up the stairs slowly. I grabbed her elbow and helped her to the door, barely able to stay on my own feet.

"Thank you, Joseph," she said once we entered the building. "I'm afraid my little display took quite a lot out of me."

"Little? I didn't think it was possible to gather that much magic. At least not without blowing yourself up." I pushed the door closed and the tension in my chest eased once I heard it click shut.

"It's possible," Miss Blackthorne said, moving to the large couch in the middle of the room and falling into it with a groan, "but it took over an hour to prepare my body and mind."

"You knew he'd come here."

"I knew he would seek to reclaim his Venerati associate, eventually.

After what happened at the meeting, I suspected he would come here tonight, so I spent much of the evening preparing for the encounter."

"And questioning the prisoner," I said.

She fixed her dark eyes on me but didn't respond.

"You tortured him," I said. The words hung in the air as long moments passed in silence.

"Yes," she said eventually.

My gut twisted and my throat went dry. I moved to the dining table where I sat on one of the wooden chairs. Could I be part of something like this? I'm all for fighting evil and monsters. I can even get on board with imprisoning them. But torture? That's not a grey area, it's just wrong.

Says the guy who killed a vampire in cold blood a few hours ago.

Miss Blackthorne limped over to the table and sat down. "Understand, Joseph, there was still information inside that man's head I needed. Because of what I did, the Venerati's plans have been disrupted significantly, not just in our city but all around the country. Hundreds, probably thousands, of lives have been saved."

"How do you know he was telling the truth?"

"He was. Mathias Voigt is a formidable man; however, he has one weakness that has been the downfall of many a tyrant. His ego. He is dedicated to his cause, and I have no doubt he would die for it, but I gave him a choice: he could die with his secrets, or he could give up his Venerati colleagues in exchange for his life. Voigt has quite a high opinion of himself and believes he is more valuable to the Venerati Sanctus, and has far more to offer, than the people he works with. So, of course, the man chose to save his own life."

"What will happen to the witch hunters he gave up?"

"That is for the respective Custodians to deal with."

I pushed my hair back, still wet after spending the entire night running around in the rain and swimming in the harbour. There is only so much a waterproof jacket can do. I rubbed my eyes and wondered absently what the time was.

"Tea?" Miss Blackthorne asked, pushing a large mug towards me, while holding her own in another hand.

I grabbed the mug in both hands, letting it warm my fingers before taking a sip. I still didn't know how she conjured her seemingly unlimited supply of hot tea. A question for another time.

"I failed tonight," I said, staring into the steaming liquid.

"Oscar called me," she replied softly. "Twenty minutes before you and the Scarred Man arrived. I do not see how you failed."

"Frederico is gone, taken by the selkies. I couldn't save him. And who knows how many people drowned tonight?"

Miss Blackthorne's dark eyes bore into me. "Joseph, it is easy to dwell on what could have been, but you are one man. You cannot hope to save everyone, and you shouldn't expect to."

"The river folk are divided," I said, staring at my tea. "Mick and Aubrey will do what they can to stop the Mokoi and Baiji from killing each other. But nothing changes the fact that the Encantado Chief killed Mei's daughter. And to top it off, Rhoswyn's dead. One of the only bloody selkies who actually gave a damn about anyone else, and she's gone." I shook my head. "What's the point in protecting these guys if they're going around killing each other, anyway?"

"The point is the fight," Miss Blackthorne said. "We fight to protect who we can. You helped save the lives of thousands of people tonight, Joseph. Old World and the mundane. That is no small thing. Now, if the river folk really want to start a civil war amongst themselves, there's little we can do to stop them. But I'll be damned if we don't try."

"How long do you think until they're back?" I said. "The Venerati Sanctus?"

Miss Blackthorne sipped her tea. "In all honesty, I would be surprised if they leave the city in the first place. If you're asking when they will next act... we'll have to wait and see."

"Castille said he was testing the selkies, seeing how they respond."

"It's what they do, the witch hunters. Whether it be the Old World, governments or multi-national organisations. They research, gather intelligence, and find weaknesses to exploit. They may not use the information on the selkies for hundreds of years, but it adds to their ever-growing bank of knowledge on the Old World."

"That man, Voigt. He's dangerous, isn't he?"

"Of course," Miss Blackthorne said. "He's a witch hunter." I sensed there were volumes she wasn't telling me, but her steely eyed gaze wasn't offering any hints.

I rolled the mug between the palms of my hands. "Are you sure you made the right choice? Trading him for me? Do you think the number of lives I save will be greater than the number of lives he'll destroy?"

Miss Blackthorne placed her mug down, and her expression lost a bit of its edge. "I would have traded a hundred witch hunters for you. In this line of work, there are choices we must make, impossibly difficult choices that will weigh on our souls until our last breath, regardless of which road we take. Taking you back from the clutches of the Venerati wizard was not one of those decisions. I am not a complete monster."

I nodded and dropped my gaze.

"Listen to me," she said, leaning forward, her voice low. "I will never abandon you, Oscar or Bree. Ever. You are my apprentices."

I saw the earnestness in her face, in her posture, but more importantly, I felt it. It shone bright as one of the truest things she's ever told me.

"What about Helena?" I said tentatively. "You told me the Venerati Sanctus killed her. But it turns out she's alive and well."

"I said she fell to the Venerati and that they do not let their people simply walk away. I didn't say they killed her."

"You also didn't mention that she kills for the Venerati, that she trains wizards for them. Wizards like Castille."

Miss Blackthorne's mood darkened.

"Helena Rake spent her childhood being brainwashed by the witch hunters. Throughout the entire time I trained her, not a day passed where she didn't feel the compulsion to return to the Venerati and serve their cause. I tried to give her a new life, but I failed. In the end she returned to her captors and is now one of their greatest weapons against the Old World."

There was bitterness and sadness in Miss Blackthorne's voice, and when she looked at me, her gaze was cold as ice.

"Now, Joseph, I will say this once and once only. Never speak of Helena Rake again."

We stared at each other without speaking for what must have been a full minute.

With a sigh, I raised my tea. "Cheers."

47

OSCAR AND BREE arrived at the Substation with sunrise still a couple of hours away. They found me asleep on Miss Blackthorne's couch, wrapped in a thick blanket. Dead to the world, and happy to stay that way.

"Hey, Joey," Oscar said quietly. "Let's go."

I tried to open my eyes, but they were glued shut. I just needed another ten minutes' sleep. My plans were thwarted when Bree grabbed my shoulders and shook me like a piggy bank.

"Get up, lazy arse. We're going home."

I groaned and sat up, giving both of them a bleary-eyed stare. Their hair looked freshly dried, and they wore matching blue T-shirts with NSW POLICE across the front.

"Nice shirts."

"A gift from Devapriya," Bree said. "She and Hertz rocked up with half the fucking state's police force. They'll be there a while."

"How's your shoulder?" I asked Oscar.

He pulled down the neckline of his shirt to show a large square bandage where Castille's spell had struck.

"Not as bad as it looks," he assured me. "The skin's a little burned and the muscles are a bit stiff, but otherwise, I'm fine. It felt like I was dying at the time, though. Like my insides were on fire. But I think his spell was meant for incapacitation. It died away when he left."

"Jeremy?"

"Alive," Bree said. "Barely. It was touch and go for a while, but he was the first one the paramedics took to the hospital. He's already been stitched up, apparently."

I gave a sleepy nod. "Castille was about to kill both of you when Jeremy stepped in using his vanishing trick. Turns out he's braver than I thought he was."

"Really?" Bree said. "He was whining like a baby when the ambulance took him away."

"Well, we owe him."

"I called," Oscar said. "As soon as Castille took you away, I called Miss Blackthorne. She said he would bring you here. How did she know? How did she get you back?"

I couldn't tell them about Mathias Voigt, the Venerati commander whom Miss Blackthorne had locked up, because then I'd have to tell them where she'd been keeping him all this time. I couldn't burden my friends with the knowledge that our teacher had her own prison in the basement, that she tortured her captives for information. I knew, and wished I didn't.

"She let him go," I said. "In return for handing me over, she allowed him to leave the city on the condition he didn't return."

"What a pussy," Bree said with a smug grin.

Oscar hesitated, and for a moment, I thought he might question me further. "I'm glad you're alright, Joey," he said, but I could tell from his expression that he knew I wasn't revealing everything.

Sorry, mate. It's for your own good. Trust me.

"So, I guess tonight will be splashed all over YouTube by lunchtime," Bree said.

Oscar went to push his glasses back, only to realise he'd lost them. "Maybe not," he said. "Miss Blackthorne's government contact should be able to stop that happening."

"Unfortunately," Miss Blackthorne said, coming out of the library, "pulling all the photographs and video recordings from each person's mobile device may be beyond her ability. Katherine Powell has a great many strings she can pull, but even she has her limits. Let us hope the disorder, the dark and the rain did enough to obscure people's perception of what truly transpired."

"Two gods had a punch up in the middle of Sydney Harbour," Bree said. "It'd be pretty hard to play that up as a fancy light show."

"You'd be surprised," Miss Blackthorne replied.

With not a small amount of effort, I hoisted myself to my feet. The right side of my face throbbed and felt swollen when I put a hand to it. My clothes clung to my skin uncomfortably, and I had a sudden desire to take a really, really long shower.

"Let's call an Uber," I said with a yawn.

"No," Miss Blackthorne said. "Take the Land Cruiser. I won't be driving anywhere tonight." She hobbled over to the door and held it open for us. "Go straight home. You all need time to recover, so I suggest you get a good night's sleep and—"

The Master Wizard stopped mid-sentence when she looked outside, and turned back to us, her frown deep.

"Can one of you please explain what happened to my car windows?"

* * *

AFTER PROMISING to get the windows replaced, Bree drove us home through dark streets still slick with rain, and parked in front of our house.

I got out of the Land Cruiser and stepped onto something soft and wet. A black dress lay under my foot. The dress Yvette had been wearing when I killed her. There was no sign of the vampire's corpse, having turned to ash and washed away with the rain. I froze.

"Joey?" Oscar said, appearing at my side. He looked down and understood. "Let's get inside."

"She was bad, right?" I asked.

"Pure evil," Oscar said.

"And a total bitch," Bree chipped in.

I gave them a weak smile. "You guys ever wonder whether we're doing the right thing? Making the right choices?"

"All the time," Oscar said, putting a hand on my shoulder. "We'll make mistakes. We're human. We just need to try and do good where we can. No one can ask anything more from us."

I looked up at my lanky friend. "Thanks, mate."

"Fuck's sake, you two," Bree said with a roll of her eyes. "Get a room."

"How are you feeling?" I said. "You took a pretty big hit from Castille."

She bent her neck from side to side, eliciting several snaps and pops. "I'll survive. Wiljara came in pretty handy again, didn't he?" She rapped her knuckles on the side of her head and looked up. "Nice work demon boy. Keep that up and maybe I'll just let you stay."

Oscar and I shared a meaningful glance. Neither of us wanted to mention that the demon only had six-and-a-half years left in Bree's head before it made the jump to mine. We'd deal with that problem when we came to it.

"Let's get inside," I said with a yawn. "I need sleep."

"Or..." Oscar said, "we could pull an all-nighter."

"You're kidding," I said, deadpan. "It's three in the morning."

"We've got plenty of beers," Oscar said, a wicked grin on his lips.

"And there's leftover pizza in the fridge!" Bree said.

My stomach grumbled. I couldn't remember the last time I'd eaten something.

"We could watch a movie!" Oscar suggested.

"Ooh, let's do Lord of the Rings! I haven't watched *Fellowship* in ages."

I stared at Bree. "You want to watch a movie where the wizard dies?"

She shrugged. "He gets better."

I threw up my hands. "Fine. Fuck it. Let's do it."

Oscar and Bree cheered and practically ran to the front door. I followed at my own pace, and despite my weariness and the many exhausted hours ahead of me, I still felt a smile touch my lips.

EPILOGUE

"Where are they?" Bree said. "It's about to start."

"They'll be back soon," Oscar assured her, casting his gaze over the crowd behind us.

I cupped my hands and blew a warm breath into them. We sat on small plastic seats amongst a sea of red and green, the rugby field before us lit up bright by the stadium lights. The mob grew more raucous with each passing minute, drunken chants booming from boisterous pockets like battle cries preceding a fight.

As far as seats went, you'd be hard pressed to find better for a rugby match. Front row, smack bang on the halfway line. We could practically see the beads of sweat on the stocky sports reporter as he yelled into the camera, hyping up the game to the viewers at home.

It was to be a big match, apparently. The Sydney Roosters against the South Sydney Rabbitohs. The oldest rivalry in the league. Tonight's winner would go on to play in the Grand Final next week. Of course, all of this information was spoon-fed to us minutes ago, since none of us watched much sport.

I nudged Oscar. "How are you holding up, mate?"

He'd broken things off with Georgie Boy the week before.

Oscar shrugged. "Better than I expected. I suppose I always knew it wouldn't last. Not when I was hiding half my life from him."

"Plenty more where that came from," I said cheerily. "Maybe we can find you a nice wizarding lad. Or a strapping young merman."

He shook his head with a smile. "Joey..."

I rubbed a hand over my chin. "Perhaps a centaur. Are they real? I bet they have massive—"

"Joey!"

"Rugby," Bree said abruptly.

We both turned to her. "What?"

"I should play rugby. I'd be unstoppable."

"I'm sure there are plenty of women's teams around," I said.

"The uni has a women's team," Oscar added. "They're pretty good, by all accounts."

"Nah, fuck that. I want to take on these guys."

"Would you even be allowed to play in this league?"

Bree crossed her arms. "If I can't, they're sexist."

"It wouldn't really be fair," Oscar said. "Given where your strength comes from."

"I'd be more worried about the exposure," I said. I glanced around, then lowered my voice. "The Venerati Sanctus knows who we are. They even know where we live. I don't want to do anything that'll bring them down on us prematurely."

"Ha!" Bree laughed. "Let them come. If two gods can get away with fighting in the middle of Sydney-friggin'-Harbour, I don't see why I can't tackle a few meatheads for a bit of cash."

She had a point.

It had been two weeks since the battle at Circular Quay, and a lot less footage emerged of the incident than I'd expected. Plenty of photos circulated of the mini tidal waves and the long procession of evacuees, but very little of what had actually transpired out on the water. Some videos of the celestial scuffle made it onto YouTube, but most of them were shaky and out of focus, the camera phones barely able to make sense of the spectacle through the rain and low light.

Funnily enough, the clearest footage came from the young drunk bloke we'd pulled out of the water, which prompted people to commend the City of Sydney on presenting such an amazing display of light and sound. However, there were still some commenters who noted that the previous year's Vivid Festival had more to offer.

News reports had focused on the activation of the terrorism alert system, then shifted to the freak weather before inevitably moving onto the casualties.

Five of them.

Five people had died. An elderly couple and a young man who had been washed into the harbour by the barrage of waves. Two of the deaths were passengers on the capsized ferry. They'd found their bodies two days after the madness. In all likelihood they would have drowned before we'd arrived with the jet boat, but that didn't make it any easier to swallow.

Five deaths.

When you compare it to the thousands of lives it could have been, it's a commendable outcome. But not if you were there. Not if you were the one swimming in pitch black water, trying to pull them out. Not if you were the one who didn't save them.

Thankfully, Jeremy had survived his injuries and Hertz agreed to fill in some legal forms certifying the magician's robustness of character, which would apparently go a long way in helping the former criminal get more one-on-one time with his daughter.

"Geez," Oscar said. "I think he bought half the shop."

I turned to see Stefan gliding towards us, the vampire slipping past the people seated in our row with feline grace. He cradled what must have been a dozen hotdogs in his arms. His light grey trousers, crisp white shirt, and leather suspenders were at odds with the rest of the crowd. Behind him, Arthur followed at a much more natural pace as he balanced our drinks, apologising to each person whose knees he bumped.

"Hungry?" I said as Stefan passed me one of the hotdogs.

He cast a quick eye over the crowd. "It has been a long while since I have put myself around this many people. The energy, the smell..." The vampire shook his head as if to clear it and gave me a thin-lipped smile. "Better I keep my mouth busy."

"Unbelievable seats, aren't they?" Arthur said, a giant grin hanging between his ears. He passed us our plastic cups of liquid gold.

"I wanted to get us a private box," Stefan said apologetically. "But this was the best we could do on such short notice."

Arthur waved the comment away. "You want to be amongst the rabble for this kind of thing. You've got to feel the energy of the crowd. It's the only way to watch it. Was the same way with the gladiators."

"You used to watch gladiator fights?" I asked.

"Watch them? Lad, I was *in* them. A truly horrible experience at the time undoubtedly. But there's something to be said about several thousand people screaming your name."

"Thanks again for the tickets, Stefan," Oscar said. "You really didn't have to."

Bree slapped Oscar on the arm. "What are you talking about, dude? We're heroes. It's about time Blackthorne let someone shower us with gifts."

Stefan smiled as he removed the hotdog from one of the buns, ate half of it, grimaced, then shoved the rest in his mouth. "No matter the transgression, we vampires never take pleasure in hunting one of our own. You did Penni a great favour by ridding us of Yvette. Of course, he can never openly admit that. Penni can't be seen to condone wizards killing vampires willy-nilly."

"Of course," I said with a smirk. "Now you just have to worry if the *rogue* vampires will attempt a comeback."

"It is more a question of *when*," Stefan replied, then flashed an insolent grin. "But that's a worry for another day."

"Here we go," Arthur said, standing up. "Let's go, Rabbits!"

The crowd erupted as both teams took to the field. We joined in on the hollering and cheering, getting carried away in the excitement of it all.

And in that moment, I was happy. Despite the growing responsibilities being placed on my shoulders and the very hard lessons that had been thrust upon me. I had food, I had beer, and I had friends on either side – Immortal and vampire included. Feeling content, I turned my attention to the game, and watched the Rabbitohs get thrashed.

ENJOYED THE BOOK?

Firstly, thank you for reading! Writing novels has been a dream of mine for a long time and simply by reading this book, you have helped that dream become a reality.

As a new writer, I appreciate any little bit of help you can offer. If you could spend a minute or two to leave an honest review on Amazon that would be bloody amazing. Reviews of my book help to bring them to the attention of other readers and provides me some much needed encouragement to help me get the next book out.

Thank you so much!

GET 2 FREE SHORT STORIES!

Building a relationship with my readers is one of the most exciting things I look forward to as a writer. If you sign up to the mailing list I will occasionally send out newsletters with details on upcoming releases, writing progress and general stuff about what it's like living in Sydney, Australia.

I'll also send you an e-book copy of:
MATTERS OF STATE – a Mary Blackthorne novella set before the Joey Finch series
NIGHT STALK - a Joey Finch short story set after the events of *THE STOLEN WIZARD*

You can sign up for free on my website at www.peterjwoodsauthor.com

ALSO BY PETER J. WOODS

THE JOEY FINCH SERIES

The Stolen Wizard

The River Men

SHORT STORIES & NOVELLAS

Matters of State

Night Shift

ACKNOWLEDGMENTS

I would like to acknowledge the Eora Nation, the traditional custodians of the Land now known as Sydney and pay my respects to the Elders both past and present. This book contains references to the First Nations people of Australia, their beliefs and their traditions, and while every effort has gone into being as respectful as possible, I am human and therefore likely to bugger things up every now and then. If there's anything glaringly inaccurate or offensive, please let me know.

ABOUT THE AUTHOR

Peter J. Woods is the author of the Joey Finch urban fantasy series. He lives in Sydney, Australia and spends his spare time watching fantasy and sci-fi films, swimming in the ocean and resisting the urge to overdose on coffee and desserts. He thinks all those 'About the Author' sections sound a bit silly, because they are always written in third person, even though we all know it's the author who writes them.

If you'd like to say a quick hello, or send through any feedback, you can connect with Peter via his website, email, or social media.

Website: peterjwoodsauthor.com
Email: peter@peterjwoodsauthor.com